"VRIDAR HUNTER could no more
have lived without women than
without air. Morbidly sensitive, and to be
for many years to come, incurably erotic,
he saw women as the core of life. . . .
They drew him irresistibly. They were
the gravity of his being; he was water,
seeking its level. And no more could he
remain on the heights . . . than water
could resist seeking the sea."

In this moving novel of young Vridar Hunter's
search for love, Vardis Fisher displays a rare in-
sight into the tremulous and frustrated soul of
youth. With *Passions Spin the Plot* he demon-
strated beyond a doubt that he had become one
of America's major novelists.

This book is the second in a series of four inde-
pendent novels about Vridar Hunter, of which
the first, *In Tragic Life*, was also reprinted as a
Cardinal edition. Both titles were published orig-
inally by The Caxton Printers, Ltd. and Doubleday & Company, Inc.

Other books about Vridar Hunter

BY VARDIS FISHER

———————

*IN TRAGIC LIFE

WE ARE BETRAYED

NO VILLAIN NEED BE

*Published in a CARDINAL edition

CARDINAL EDITION

PASSIONS SPIN THE PLOT

by

Vardis Fisher

POCKET BOOKS, INC., NEW YORK, N. Y.

This Cardinal edition includes every word contained in the original, higher-priced edition. It is printed from brand-new plates made from completely reset, clear, easy-to-read type

Passions Spin the Plot

Doubleday edition published January, 1934
1st printing .... January, 1934

Caxton Publishers edition published 1934

British edition: Boriswood, Ltd., London, 1935

CARDINAL edition published December, 1952
1st printing .... October, 1952

To My Brother

'Tis morning: but no morning can restore
What we have forfeited. I see no sin:
The wrong is mixed. In tragic life, God wot
No villain need be! Passions spin the plot:
We are betrayed by what is false within.

GEORGE MEREDITH

PART ONE

... For I remember when I first entered this college as a student, with my heart out of me at the wonder of it; and how I sat in awe before my instructors; and how my hunger for honest and fearless leadership was greater than my hunger for bread. A few students come here with the credulity that I had and they find, not wisdom and courage, but meanness and envy and feuds. There's more than one kind of murder, and the worst kind, in my opinion, is to be found in our universities. . . . I may be fired before another year is out. But what of it? Better men than I have been kicked out and greater men than I have starved for it. I won't be a Judas with my students. I won't be a hypocrite to get promotions here. I won't yield an inch beyond what I think is courageous and right. Of course I'll be as tactful as I can and of course I'll not make a fetish of principle. But please stop writing to me as if you regard me as a fool seeking martyrdom. . . .

I

‧

VRIDAR felt sick and lost. Pressing his face to a pane, he strove to look back; but Rigby was far behind him now and his parents were far behind. They would be going homeward in a lumber wagon, turning from lane to lane, entering the hills and the east. And the train under him, with roar and shriek and desolate song of its rails, was bearing him out of his homeland to a far strange place. To the right of him, houses sped by; barns and coops, gardens and ditches and posts; and to the left of him was a backbone of mountain, hauntingly blue and remote, yet very close to his heart, like the mountains of his own home. He felt hot grief in his eyes. In his stomach was the awful convulsed nausea of homesickness, and homesickness was a hard bitter pain in his throat.

He bowed his head low and wiped his eyes and he tried to blow his nose without giving the sound of tears. At his side was Stanley Trout, his high school classmate, his college mate and roommate now. Stan was very tall and slender and had dark curly hair. He was a strange fellow. He was going to be a great engineer.

Vridar put a hand to his brow and looked between his fingers at Stan; and he saw that Stan was very calm and aloof; and he felt a little better. He strove mightily to feel old and world-weary, as if riding trains, as if going to far and unfamiliar places, had long been a part of him. But when, in the landscape to the right, he saw a house vaguely like his own, a patch of brush, marshland, or a creek that recalled to him childhood scenes, then the nausea swarmed in his vitals and all his blood waited in his heart. And he bowed to his arms, shaking with grief.

When the train reached Pocatello, sixty miles down the line,

3

Vridar raised his head and looked at Stan. On Stan's lap was a college catalog and some sheets of paper black with algebra. Stan looked as serene and intellectual as a schoolbook picture of Shakespere. He chewed a pencil and meditated on the curricula or he glanced outside or he shut his eyes upon a profound thought. Vridar was amazed by Stan's calm and he stared at him, the tears in his eyes bright against a luminous envy; or he looked out at this mean ugly city, hating its barren gray mountains to the east, its arid hills to the west; and he sank again into a sharp intense dread, into revulsion that was almost frantic, as the train moved again upon its pilgrimage into the unknown.

The first of his clan he had been to graduate from high school; the first he would be to enter college; and there was a thought, somewhere in the sick ache of his being, that these achievements ought to make him proud. These ought to give him strength. But in this moment, with life rolling over the miles, with life taking from all things the fever of haste and the color of the friendless, he would have sacrificed his ambition, his career, to have been in the haunted lonely bowl of his home. He would have been a farmer, unclean and untaught, turning furrows and milking cows. . . .

"Stan," he said.

"Yes," said Stan, a bit sharply.

"I wondered, aren't you a bit homesick?"

"Homesick!" Stan appraised him with incredulous eyes. "No. Are you?"

"A little bit, I guess. I—I feel queer."

Stan's gaze was unpitying and hard.

"You look like you been bawlun," he said.

"I haven't."

"You sure look like it."

Vridar retired into silence and loathed himself. Here was he, a young man of nineteen—older than many when they married, older than some who were fathers—; and yet his mind was sick with memory, his heart was sick with doubt. He tried to shake off his fear, his loneliness; he strove to feel aggressive and bold. Rising from his seat, he went down the aisle, having observed that others did so; and at the far end he turned clumsily about, looking for a drink. Unable to release the water, and feeling upon him a hundred curious eyes, amused or derisive, he flushed and stared about him, as if seeking something, but seeking nothing at all. Shame burned hot in his face. He could feel the cold limp indecision of his legs, of his tongue, of his eyes. And with a gasp, half of panic and half of rage, he fell to an empty seat and hunched forward so that none could see.

For an hour he did not move, and during that hour he fought against being drawn into the dark. The desolation of his high school years was with him again, and was going with him, the only familiar thing in a world that was strange. His mind was full of train rhythm, of mad song and of hiss and shriek; and under these was a great void, awful in its quiet. Knowing that he must do something, he stirred and fetched his thoughts out of their depth. He looked himself over and noted that his mail-order suit smelled of wool; and from a lapel, he drew a long black hair like that from a horse's mane. This suit, he remembered, had been guaranteed all-wool: he would have to write to his mother about the horse hair in it. . . . His shoes, which at first had seemed wondrous things, were pug-toed and ugly in comparison with many around him. And his shirt cuffs, showing pompously below his coat sleeves, were adorned with huge vulgar studs; and with dark misgiving, he pushed them up and out of sight. And then with a gasp of alarm he thought of his money.

He dug into a pocket and alarm closed upon him like a sheath of frost as he reached down into emptiness. But the money was there. His fingers shut round it like steel and he drew it forth. Hiding it within his coat, he thumbed the notes: ten of them, fifty dollars in all: a part of his parents' savings in twenty years. He rolled the bills into a wad and grasped them and looked round to see that none had fallen; and he counted them again and still again. He pushed the wad down into a deep pocket. He drew his hand out carefully, lest the money follow; and he looked round him again and searched the seat and the outside of his pocket; whereupon, still unconvinced, he slipped a hand down and fingered the roll and drew his hand carefully out. Then he stuffed a handkerchief into the pocket on top of the money and let his breath out in a great sigh.

Two hundred dollars, his father had said, would be enough. It was an enormous sum. It would take eight hundred dollars to put Vridar through college, eight hundred for Mertyl, and a like sum for Diana. Twenty-four hundred dollars. Vridar deliberated this staggering fortune, trying to see its limits. It would buy a herd of cattle as big as a hill; or enough Antelope land to graze ten thousand sheep; or half the empty lots in Rigby. And of this granary of gold, his parents had saved only a fourth in twenty years of toil. . . .

He was passing now through barren country, unrolled in a plateau of gray to the Utah line. There was a girl behind him whom he wanted to look at again; but he dared not turn to the aisles of faces. She reminded him of Neloa and she had looked at him. He drew from his pocket a letter. It was so nearly wornout that it lay in his palm like a handful of flakes. And now, as in a thousand previous whiles, he put the flakes together and read:

Dear ——:- I was sure surprised to get your card. I am up in paradise now. I guess you know about Amos Hufford being married. I was to his wedding dance and had a swell time. We have a dance up here every Friday night and have lots of fun but I guess you don't care about anything up here. Don't be so long writing next time. Well, I guess you will be tired reading this nonsense so will ring off. Goodnight and sweet dreams from

NELOA.

xxoo

all for you

He valued this letter above all things but the reading of it always filled him with grief. The number of kisses, he reflected, was most generous; and the blank in the salutation indicated, to be sure, that he was privileged to write in any word of his choice; but her going to dances was another matter. She was only fifteen. He had not seen her in two years; not, indeed, since that night when, abject and worshipful, he had followed her like a dog into the theater. But he had written to her and in roundabout ways he had declared his love; and at last he had admonished and rebuked her, declaring that she must stay away from dances until she was twenty-one. She did not write after that. . . .

He bent low over the fragments and kissed them and laid them away. Feeling more at ease now, he wanted to go to Stan and talk with him. He yanked at his tie, he covertly wiped dust from his shoes, and with a match he dug at his nails. How, he wondered, did the back of his head look to all those searching eyes; because a hundred persons, he had no doubt, were watching him. They knew his mother had cut his hair. They knew he was embarrassed and trying to seem at ease. They knew, of course, that he was a mountain-lad, a hill-country plowboy, who had spent twenty years fenced by a river and a wall of stone. They could tell by looking at him that he had never been on a train before, that he had never been far from home, and that he was scared to death.

He had noted that men left this car, from time to time, and entered the car ahead. He did not know they went to the smoking-car. They were worldly folk, he supposed, bent on seeing what they could see; for they wore their courage jauntily and they did things that would have made him sick to think of. They blew their noses in blasts of thunder or they thrust feet upon the cushion ahead or they marched back and forth, wholly unconcerned with staring eyes. Their gall was offensive and superb.

While meditating on such bold browbeating of life, Vridar saw a man in overalls and rundown shoes enter the car; and he reflected that where such a man went, he, too, could go, and he stood up, quaking a little, and prepared for adventure. But when he came to the first door and tried in vain to open it, he gave way to panic. He cast about for a hiding-place but could see none. If it had been possible, he would have jumped off the train. And then, out of desperation, came the thought that he could pretend; and he looked through the glass of the door as if searching for someone, and he shrugged, as though bored or impatient; and with his very best worldliness he returned to his lone seat. Thereafter, with furtive interest, he watched men open the door, hoping to discover its secret; and when sure he could open it without fumbling, he rose and went forth. But first he peered through, as if still seeking; and then, with a sudden start, intended to convince onlookers that his quest was genuine, he swung the door wide and passed through the next door and into the smoking-car. There were many empty seats here and he chose one and sat down, feeling that he had acquitted himself quite well. Those who had watched him would not think him such a zany after all: for nobody, surely, who was riding a train for the first time, would thus walk boldly from coach to coach.

Only men, he observed, were in this car and they were all smoking. Vridar had never smoked, save one disastrous attempt with filched cigars, but he wished now that he had a cigarette. There was magnificence in the gesture of a young snob who sat ahead. He knocked his ashes with an imperious finger and stared with obvious and withering disdain at the country round him. While studying this man, and noting with vast envy each detail of his dress, Vridar came to himself with a start; because across from him a huge-bellied fellow was appraising him with cold blue eyes. Fetching himself together, Vridar acted a part; he reached into his pockets, as if for cigarettes; he patted himself and seemed annoyed; and he looked back into the other coach, suggesting to the blue eyes that he had left his smokes there.

"Here," said the man, and offered cigarettes.

Vridar took one and flushed a deep red. "Thanks. I—I guess I've lost mine." He searched vainly for a match and the man struck and held a light. Vridar's first draw ended in a violent snort. Coughing racked him and tears swam to his eyes. A swift desperate glance told him that the man was smiling.

"I guess you ain't much used to smoking," the man said.

"No sir," Vridar said.

"It's a bad habit," the man said. "If it made me choke like that I wouldn't smoke."

"I guess I got some in my—in my—in my stomach, I guess. But these are pretty strong, aren't they?" And Vridar stared at the cigarette, pretending to read its name. In a little while the man asked:

"Where you off to?"

"College," Vridar said, and pride set him on a dizzy height.

The cold blue eyes gave him a long stare.

"What college?"

"Wasatch College. It's in Salt Lake."

The man was silent for a long moment. Vridar puffed at his cigarette and tried to make it seem that he was inhaling. He would hold the smoke in his mouth and breathe down through his nose, and then, in a long thin stream, he would blow the smoke out.

"What you intend to be?" asked the man.

"A teacher. A high school principal."

"That don't pay much. A big corporation lawyer, that's the thing."

Vridar wondered what it was. He said he would think it over and perhaps he would be one. "I thought some of being that," he said, lying in the way that fear and shame had taught him. "That or an electrical engineer. There's money in that," he said, and was startled by his impudence.

At this moment, Stanley Trout pushed the door open and came in. He saw Vridar smoking a cigarette and he was too amazed to speak. He drew his small mouth until it looked like the mouth of a fish and his small eyes darkened. And because Stan was a fanatic on diet and exercise and health, Vridar enjoyed his consternation.

"I'm talking with this gentleman," Vridar said, "about being a corporation lawyer."

Stanley looked at the gentleman and then swung and disappeared.

"Is that your friend?" asked the man.

"Yes sir. He's going to college, too. He's awful religious and doesn't believe in smoking. He won't even eat pepper."

"The hell he won't. What religion he belong to?"

"Mormon."

The man grimaced and stretched out lazily to the seat ahead. "That explains him. He'll go to heaven and I guess it will serve him right."

A few minutes later the train stopped in the lovely little hamlet of Brigham. Most of the passengers got off and stood in warm sunlight and Vridar returned to his seat with Stan. Having talked with a man of the world and having smoked without disaster, he felt quite friendly toward himself. He wanted to leave the train and sun himself as others were doing but he was afraid of being left behind. Stan was bent low over the college catalog.

"This is Brigham," Vridar said.

"Tell me something I don't know."

"There's a lot you don't know!" Vridar said hotly. "A little algebra, that's about all."

"That so? Well, you don't even know algebra."

"Oh, don't I! Well listen: we'll see who goes farthest in school. That'll tell, I guess."

"And I suppose," Stan said, "your parents know you smoke."

"I don't smoke. I don't smoke any more than you eat pepper."

"Pepper! Never mind about me not eating pepper. If you'd eat what you should you wouldn't be such a scrawny runt."

"Oh!" Vridar cried, as if struck. "You tall shitepoke, you! Pepper——"

"Talk to yourself, I'm busy."

"I'll tell you what I'll bet. I'll bet you——"

"Leave me alone."

Passengers now entered and Stan pored over the catalog and Vridar looked out the window, again feeling desolate and lost. Stan Trout, after all, was to be his roommate, a sort of anchor: the only friendly thing in a city that was big and friendless, the only strength and the only light. He did not want to quarrel with him. He wanted to be a brother to him. But under Vridar's physical cowardice and misgivings lay his pride, remorseless and unwavering; and it made him a stranger among men, it made nearly all men strangers to him; and it was so now and it was to be so for many years to come.

And he bowed upon his arms to hide his grief. Not for kingdoms would he have told Stan of his loneliness, of his sick fright, of his need for a friend. Rather than do this, he would suffer his way into madness or he would kill himself; and he felt again, with increasing intensity, the strange wildness that haunted his youth and that still lay within him, close to his heart, dark and deep in his mind. It was something to fight alone, to conquer alone, or it was something to go down under, with none to know how he went down. . . .

Dusk was falling now and he saw so many things—groves of trees, reaches of gray land, far mountains in blue and mist —that recalled to him the hills of home and that piled in memory all the stricken hours of his life. But he must be strong now. He had embarked on a great journey and with him went the trust of his parents, working like slaves to set him on a high clean place. He would have to be a man now. . . . But as lights spread over the valley, as so much sped by that was strange and apart from him, he shook with violent grief. He was so horribly afraid that he wanted to leap out and to roll in the black night to his death; and so be done forever with the pitiable play of trying to be what he was not. And when the train poured with the sound of rolling boulders into the city and drew up before a great station of light, Vridar grasped his bags and stood up, shaking uncontrollably. He would have to be a man now, he said, but he could no longer hear his own voice. Its small haunted meaning was lost. And into this mighty eddy of a train's journey, he went with his head down, with his eyes blind; and he hunted through the crowds and the station and came to a broad brilliant street and stood upon the shore of a new world.

II

•

AFTER walking the streets for two days, seeking a room
that would be given in exchange for firing a furnace or doing other chores, Vridar and Stan found themselves in a vile
den in the dark underground basement in the home of Professor Jeremiah Stokes Yupp. Their room was sixteen feet by
six. Its only window was one small pane so dirty with coal
dust that it gave almost no light. The south wall was the
furnace itself and a darkness that led to a pile of coal. Their
furniture was an old shabby bed, two broken chairs, a table,
one gas-plate, and a handful of dishes in a cupboard. This
cupboard was a packing-box spiked to the east wall.

For this dismal room, the uncleanest that Vridar was ever
to see, they were to fire the furnace, carry the ashes out, and
sweep the autumn leaves from the lawn. Though unaccustomed to a modern house or to luxury of any kind, Vridar was
sickened by this underground cell. It would not have been
so bad, he reflected, if the furnace had been shut away; but
standing, as it did, almost within the room itself, it filled the
cell with intolerable heat and it covered everything with
ashes and smoke.

In Yupp's house, Vridar afterward learned, there were
thirty-two rooms, most of them large enough for only a bed,
a chair, and a gas-plate. The professor and his family in-
habited the first floor: it smelled of old furniture, of dust-
filled rugs and of age. Above him were three floors, with the
once spacious rooms partitioned off into stuffy little dens;
and above the fourth floor was the garret, itself containing
four rooms, each with a wan little sky-window, each with a
ceiling that would not allow a man to stand up. Each floor
in the rear had a deep porch; and Yupp, in overalls and un-

aided, had made four rooms on each porch, building the
three additional walls of rough lumber and battening this
with strips from grocers' boxes; and all these overgrown
birdcages he also rented to students. His house when seen
from the rear looked as if a drunken carpenter had nailed to
it, from the ground to the roof, an outlandish assortment of
hencoops.

The professor himself was a lean spinsterish fellow with a
face like that of a coyote. His chin and mouth were weak,
his forehead narrow, as if a part of his face had melted and
run into his huge nose. He had handsome gray hair, but
this, Vridar learned, was a wig; for in classroom one day, an
impudent wind, finding the sash open, leapt and took Yupp's
hair off, and his head was as bright and bare as a skull. And
Vridar learned, too, that Professor Yupp, an old man now,
was being slowly retired by the contempt and derision of his
colleagues.

"You will please be saving of coal," he said to Vridar and
Stan. And he moved about, gesturing alertly like a bird. In
overalls and denim jacket and canvas gloves, he showed them
how to stoke, how to remove ashes, how to regulate the water
and heat. Vridar observed that Yupp never gave him a direct
glance, a steady frank look. His eyes darted thither and yon,
as if spying out enemies, as if afraid of what they might see.

In contrast with his new home, the college campus was a
glorious thing. It had evergreens—spruce and fir—and magnificent buildings and a library that took his breath away.
While looking at reference books, he saw students busy at
the card catalog; and later he ventured over to see what they
had been doing. As he turned the cards and read titles, he
became drunk with excitement; and he made notes of those
volumes which he must soon read; and within two weeks, he
had seven hundred and ninety-eight books on his required
list. He decided that, like Coleridge, he would read the library
from end to end; and for several days he wondered which
end to begin at.

But he had no time now. His courses kept him busy and
day by day opened wide avenues of which he had dreamed.

The kingdom of learning was a lordly, a precious, an unutterable thing. He knelt to it in awe and dedicated himself to the world of books.

His professor of sociology was Fred Orange Bogan, as queer a person as he had ever seen. His more insolent students called him the monkey and the name was apt. Bogan was an old man and very lean and small. His face was almost entirely hidden by a stubble of beard and out of this stubble spread a curious nose, flattened in the arch and gaping in the nostrils. His eyes were small and close together and full of simian alertness, and above them were bushy brows and under them was beard. And when Bogan walked, he moved like an ape, as if unaccustomed to going on two legs: with his small shoulders hunched up and his head thrust forward, and with his eyes, all pupil and darkness, constantly shifting as those of a monkey do.

But Bogan's mind was as young and alert as his eyes. In his very large class, some students slept and snored, some made love or yawned, and others kicked about as if ill-treated; and Vridar, who sat well to the front, saw that Bogan's eyes missed nothing of what was done. Now and then his stubble would crack into a faint smile and his eyes would sparkle with sudden bright malice. His throat would rumble for a moment and then in a slow drawl would come his dry wit.

"Mr. Young," Bogan would say, and he would pause on a mirthless chuckle, "don't you think Sumner would say that a parlor is a better place than a classroom for making love?" Or to a young man shuddering under his snores:

"Mr. Homney. Will someone please wake Mr. Homney up?" And after Mr. Homney had sat up, looking wildly sleepy: "Mr. Homney, after this would you mind taking your afternoon nap in the ladies' rest room?" Or again, to a young man with a leg cocked over the arm of his chair and with a bored gaze fixed upon the world outside:

"Mr. Ivins, what does Bachofen in *Das Mutterrecht* have to say about the origin of family life? . . . Mr. Ivins."

A student prodded Ivins and he swung around.

"What?" he asked. "Was you speakun to me?"

"I made an attempt," said Bogan, and resumed his lecture.

None of the students ever guffawed over these dry witticisms. There was something so ominously quiet, so gently sinister, about them that nobody dared laugh. Nevertheless, Vridar liked this strange shabby little man. He sat in reverence before the wealth of his learning, his dry anecdote, the whimsical patience of his way.

And for his professor of history, too, he had the most ardent respect. William Purdue Johns had a handsome kingly head, bushed over with hair like bronze. Of all members of the faculty, he looked most like a thoroughbred: a splendid animal, stately, yet charming, approachable but proud. His place, both by temperament and training, was in the academic world.

Of Professor Yupp, Vridar was not so sure. Yupp digressed, again and again, into a tirade on cats. He hated cats because they killed birds, and birds of all things he loved most. When he spoke of this slaughter, his sallow cheeks would burn like pink fire and his eyes would look strangled and wild. His voice would choke and hiss and climb to a furious screech and then expire in a wail of anguished reproach. And Vridar while staring at the man would want to say:

"Yes, cats eat birds but birds eat worms. Eat or get eaten is the law of life. So what are you howling about? And besides, you rave about cats, and the tenants on your attic floor are freezing to death!"

Vridar distrusted Yupp, because Vridar, too, was a fanatic. He was still a socialist and a crusader. He still invoked God's wrath on injustice and millionaires, white-slavers and snobs. . . .

The course to which he gave his enthusiasm and his heart was composition. The writing of themes, which most students found detestable, was the only ecstasy in his life: he wrote and revised, tore up and wrote again, and needed only a typewriter to make his destiny complete.

His instructor of English, Hartley Wiggerton Arnold, was his favorite of all. This dark man, whose ways hinted of dynamite, had a twisted sardonic mouth, eyes in which his thoughts

burned like black fire, and a precision of words and idiom
that filled Vridar with joy. Arnold always paced back and
forth when lecturing: his hands behind him, his mind reaching out into all fields of knowledge, his sentences dropping,
trimmed and burning, like aphorisms of flame. Vridar worshiped him.

Before all his professors, as a matter of fact, he sat in most
humble awe; marveling endlessly on their knowledge and their
nimble familiarity with the far strange realms and their power
and poise. He dared not believe, he had only a faint hope,
that he would ever be their equal: for they were the princes
of learning and he was only a lad from the distant hills.

He sat in absolute awe. But years of loneliness, of self-
searching, had given to him, even at this early age, a pre-
ternatural accuracy in reaching human motive, in looking behind subterfuge and disguise; because in all these he had
found himself guilty, he knew their deviousness and their
ways. But when he saw in his professors, now and then, what
seemed to be small tricks of dodging, pompous philandering
with honesty and truth, his heart discredited what his mind
saw. His heart was wholly credulous, not of all humankind
but of these lords of wisdom. He did not believe that they
could be guilty of envy and malice. He trusted them and
loved them and gave them his soul. And it took bitter years
to force upon him the appalling truth of university life, the
venom and cowardice of its household. . . .

At the end of his third week, he was sitting with Stan on
the campus. He was overflowing with what he had seen and
heard. His heart was so full of wordless things—the enchant-
ment of learning and the glory of those who taught—that his
eyes were wet with tears.

"Stan," he said.

"Yes," said Stan.

"Isn't it wonderful! Being in college, I mean."

"I guess so," Stan said.

Vridar deliberated for a long moment.

"Do you think—we'll ever know as much as these professors?"

"I don't see why not," Stan said.

"I never will," Vridar said. "If I studied a thousand years I never would."

"You sound silly," said Stan. He looked at Vridar. "You bawlun again!"

Vridar's inner softening of tears hardened to bitter rage.

"You're stuck-up!" he cried. "What do you know? Nothing! You can read and write and do a few equations! That's all. You'n——"

"Oh, leave me alone!" cried Stan. "Beat it."

Vridar rose and went away. He wished someone would listen, someone would sympathize, while he poured out his soul. He had been losing himself and his fear in books. The empire of knowledge was so broad and various, the kingdom of beauty so sweet and clean; and he was such a nobody, such a guilty terrified nobody, that it made his heart sick to think of it all. It made his heart break to realize how little he knew, how much was to be known. If he had someone to talk to, someone to sense with him, in its tremulous wide immensity, the incredible wonder of life! But he had no one—no one but his books. And with wet eyes he climbed to the library and buried himself in *Jude the Obscure*.

III

STANLEY TROUT was a strange young man. He was opinionated, violent of temper, and imperial in his scorn. He had read everything he could find on dieting and health and exercise; his god was Bernarr McFadden; and his bible was the physical culture magazines. And for anyone with habits or values different from his own, he had haughty contempt.

Every night at ten he went to bed and every morning at

six he got up. If he found his sleep disturbed, he would rise and take soda or he would massage himself or he would take a walk. His principal desire during these weeks was to increase the size and strength of his neck. Promptly at nine-thirty he would erect himself on his head, with his long legs thrust to the ceiling; and he would move his shoulders back and forth or from side to side, until his eyes bulged and his face was dark with blood. For ten minutes he would grunt and distort himself. Then he would lie on the bed, with his body bridged from skull to heels, and give his long slender neck further punishment; and his veins would swell as if to burst. He took abdominal exercises, too, or he would rest on his heels and alternately rise and sit, or he would bridge himself on his palms and toes and move his body up and down.

At first Vridar approved all these doings and became a student. He, too, wished to have a thick neck, legs and arms like those of old gladiators, and muscle on his belly like steel plate. He stood on his head so long that he ruptured a blood vessel in his neck; but he persisted, and after a while he could hold the position for half an hour, and his neck got so large that he could hardly button his shirts. And Stan watched him with pleasure and gave advice.

"You don't eat right," he said. "You shouldn't eat meat. You should eat just fruit and raw vegetables."

Stanley ate all his food uncooked. He never used the gas-plate. He would fetch home carrots and turnips, radishes and lettuce, apples and raisins and coconuts; and these he would eat, skin and all. For breakfast he ate a cereal called grape nuts; for lunch he had a glass of buttermilk, a handful of raisins, and an apple; and for supper he would eat turnips and carrots and a pint of milk.

For many days Vridar ate as Stanley ate. He ate grape nuts until the stuff made him sick to look at. He devoured all kinds of raw things and still felt starved and he hungered for a chunk of meat and a slice of bread. Stanley's diet was inexpensive, but it was calculated, so far as Vridar could tell, to starve a person to death. Nevertheless, though as frail and lean as a crane, Stanley looked healthy and he never took physics or caught colds.

One day Vridar slipped to their room and got busy frying a piece of steak. The smell of it made him ravenous, made him feel as if his blood and bone were alloyed with carrots and apples. But while he was eating it, in desperate haste, lest he be caught, Stan entered the room. He sniffed the air like a vice-sleuth and strode over and saw the meat.

"You eating flesh!" he cried.

"Yes," said Vridar through a mouthful.

Stan seized the dripping meat and threw it into the furnace. Vridar turned upon him, shaking with rage.

"You got your nerve!" he roared. "You know that cost me ten cents?"

"I'll give you the ten cents," Stan said.

"Oh, you will! To hell with you!" Vridar stared round him, choking on meat and fury. "Listen you! You eat what you please, don't you! And it's none of your damn business what I eat!"

Stanley's small eyes shone with crusading zeal.

"All right," he said, "kill yourself. Eat meat and get yourself constipated. You'll die of constipation. You know constipation is what's wrong with people?"

"Oh, you don't say! Well, I'd as soon die of that as of carrots. And it's my business how I die, isn't it?"

For six days—Vridar counted them—neither spoke to the other. Stan's manner was Olympian in its calm. He took his exercises and ate his raw food; he stoked the furnace on alternate days; he read his magazines and then hid them and he kept his peace. And Vridar became more and more annoyed. He was afraid of the silence and he hated the slow patient measurement of vengeance. But Stanley disliked him and had no wish to talk to him and this quiet association pleased him best. It drove Vridar back into his old desolate loneliness and he resolved to force matters to a crisis.

Stanley's gymnastics, he decided, chiefly in self-defense, were a lot of silly twaddle; and at last he said so. He was tired of going to bed always at ten and getting up at six. He was tired of having a gawky youth usurp the bed for a head-stand. All this he declared in a furious voice and then waited a moment and then resumed.

"I can't stand your crazy monkeyshines any longer! You might be another Sandow or Strongfort or whatever you call him but you're only a carrot-eater to me! I'm sick of having the light turned off while I'm reading! You think I'm a babe? . . . Do you hear me?"

He waited for answer but Stan ignored him. Stan was reading his latest copy of *Phsyical Culture*.

"I'm talking to you!" Vridar howled. "Has all your raw food made you deaf?"

"I heard you," Stan said calmly. "But as usual you didn't say anything worth listening to."

"Oh I didn't, didn't I? You long gandershank of a turnip-eater! And what have you ever said to astound the world? . . . You reader of silly love-stories! You *Saturday Evening Post* fanatic! A great college student you are, reading about weight-lifters and circus freaks. . . ."

"You'll be sick again," Stan said quietly. "Anger fills your blood full of poisons."

This cool rebuke made Vridar sputter with wrath. He glared for a moment at Stan's magazine and then smote it and knocked it fluttering to the opposite wall.

"If you're looking for trouble," he roared, "you can find it! Stand up and I'll give you the massage of your life!"

Stan walked quietly over and got his magazine. He sat again, but his eyes, when he glanced at Vridar, were black with spite.

"This room," Vridar went on, mixing his words with gur-gles of rage, "isn't big enough for both of us! You'n stay or get out, take your choice!"

"I been intending to leave," Stan said. "I can't live with such an idiot as you."

"Idiot yourself, you coconut chewer! You crazy stander-on-your-head!"

"That'll do," said Stan. "I said I'd leave."

Deeply ashamed now, feeling that he had been unspeakably

mean, Vridar did not know what to say or do. He wanted to forgive and be forgiven and to be friends again. But he knew that Stan disliked him and that there was nothing to be done.

"All right," he said, "you'd better move tonight."

"No, I won't move tonight."

And forthwith Stan went over and stood on his head. He lay down and massaged himself and grunted. He looked at his tongue and his teeth and with a thermometer he took his temperature.

When Vridar returned in the next evening, Stanley was gone. Two weeks later he left the college and Vridar never saw him again. He heard years later that Stan was an osteopath in a small town.

Alone with himself now, Vridar was both frightened and pleased. He was his own boss. He could eat what he wanted and go to bed when he got ready and dream over a book all night if he wanted to. He could wander downtown and stare at the lovely girls, and when he came home, nobody would ask where he had been. But he felt, on the other hand, an awful loneliness in this small dirty cell. There remained in it the personality of another, as if a dear friend had died. In all its homely details he could see a curly-haired youth and he could hear a deep quiet voice. The place became haunted and he became afraid of it. And so he spent little time here, save to tend the furnace and to eat his meals and sleep.

It was terror, with him now as it had been with him in high school, that led him to seek a friend. He wanted a woman to whom he could talk. But he was afraid of women and he was driven to the company of men. And in November he first spoke to a young man who was to be a vital factor in shaping his life.

A. M. McClintock—he swore by all the angels that he had no first name—was twenty-one, an orphan, and a sophomore. He was a handsome youth with a strong face and with perfect teeth. His eyes were of a strange metallic gray and all that the man was or had been was recorded in his eyes. They were stealthy eyes, now bright with insolence and devilment, now calculating and hard.

For six weeks Vridar had sat by him in the classroom. He asked for Vridar's paper during an examination and Vridar gave it to him and with unblushing candor, McClintock copied it, word for word. This brought upon both the suspicion of Professor Yupp. He stared at them later with the enraged eyes of a fox and tapped the papers and spoke wildly of cheating.

"He won't expel us," McClintock said. "We're his tenants."

McClintock lived in an attic room on the top floor. Learning that Vridar was below, he came down often to visit or to parade his new clothes or to talk of his latest girl. Vridar distrusted him but he liked him. He liked his arrogant swagger and his brash way with women and life and his boasting and greed. And he liked him, too, because he knew that McClintock respected his studiousness and knowledge. Besides all this, they were both social nobodies among the college aristocracy. And still further, Vridar himself aspired now, in moments of despair, as in former whiles when he watched Jed Bridwell, to a life of careless wickedness. He wanted to disport himself in cock-a-hoopish insolence.

He called McClintock Forenoon and the name stuck.

"You got a-go with girls," Forenoon told him. "I got an old one you'n take."

Vridar toyed with the notion. What, he asked, was she like.

"Dark, this one. She loves with her arms and legs all the same time. She'll kiss the breath right out of your throat."

Vridar's blood raced. He looked at Forenoon and hated him for his intimacies with women.

"Or I got a blond. Anything you want. White, yellow, short, tall, fat, slim, hot, cold. Just say what you want."

In every third or fourth evening, Forenoon would come to tell of another conquest. He spoke of so many that Vridar thought he lied. He told him he lied.

"All right, I'll show you. Just walk down the street and I'll show you. I'll knock your eyes out."

After days of envious brooding, after nights of wild fancy

and dream, Vridar consented to walk. They went down State Street and entered a drugstore.

"It's the blond," Forenoon said. "The purple skirt."

Vridar stared at this girl. She was very lovely, though he told himself she was not; and she was obviously infatuated with Forenoon, but this Vridar denied also. She came up, smiling and dimpling. Round the end of the counter, she gave Forenoon her hand and he squeezed it and she giggled. She did not look at Vridar at all. And he despised her and thought her very silly. Nevertheless, when he left the drugstore, he turned and looked back and he saw her staring after Forenoon with her eyes full of light.

They went to three other shops and Forenoon wooed three other girls, all of them very lovely and sweet to look at. Then at a window he stopped.

"I can't go in there," he said. "I got that girl in trouble." He withdrew beyond the window. "The dark one at this end."

Vridar looked at the dark girl inside. She, too, was lovely, and while staring at her, Vridar deliberated this young rake, getting innocence into trouble, and fury boiled within him. Beyond his fury, though, lay a warm amorous hunger, a sense of denial and loss. Not for anything, he assured himself, would he betray a girl or stoop to such lust. And men who did ought to be locked up. They ought to be caponized or shot.

"You're a fine one!" he said, turning away. "Isn't there any manhood in you?"

"What's the matter now?" asked Forenoon.

"Seducing innocent girls. My God!"

Forenoon was not amazed. He had heard Vridar talk this way before. He shrugged.

"If I didn't," he said philosophically, "some other bird would. I'd rather it'd be me than the other guy."

"That would be his sin, not yours."

"Sin! I don't know what you mean by sin. The girls want it, don't they? I give them what they want."

Vridar's thought went back to Turner, his high school teacher, who told him there is no sin; and now, as then, the statement seemed meaningless, yet strangely full of light.

"They don't really want it," he declared, feeling strong and ancient. "They just don't know what they do."

"The hell they don't. When I get done with them they know. And they like it."

"Rot!" Vridar cried. "You're a hell of a citizen!"

"They like it," Forenoon said again. "They chase me to death."

Vridar dwelt, for a moment, on this horrible picture of a scoundrel pursued by innocence. He groaned and blew his nose.

"You're a fool," Forenoon went on. "Get you some girls before the other guy gets them. Ten to one you'll marry a girl someone has seduced. Most men do."

"Oh, you think so! Watch me!"

"Would serve you right," Forenoon said. "You pure guys rave around and get left. Then you marry some jane who could tell a lot. And you think you got something."

"Oh, yes?"

"I'll get you some. You just as well start sowun your oats."

But he would have to spend a little money. Forenoon himself allotted five dollars to each girl: if she did not surrender when he had spent that much, he gave her up. Five dollars would take her to three shows, buy her two boxes of candy and one bunch of flowers. That was generally enough to do the trick.

"If she isn't throwing her arms round you by that time, you just as well get on another track. I've had bad luck with only two."

On the next Saturday evening, McClintock came down, attired in his smartest outfit. He brought some clothes for Vridar. To tell the truth, he said, no man could get a girl with such outlandish clothes as Vridar wore. A girl looked at clothes before she looked at the man. If the man wore barnyard shoes and a necktie like a piece of ribbon and a self-laundered collar, he might as well stay home and read a book.

And these descriptions, Vridar realized, were appallingly apt. His ties were cheap silly things. His cap—he had no hat—

cost seventy-nine cents and was a shapeless rag. His shirts
and collars and all his other clothing he laundered himself.
And his suit still smelled of wool and looked like the stuff
out of which saddle-blankets are made.

But Forenoon had sleek pointed shoes and gay shirts and
ties and three tailored suits. He looked like a prince when he
got himself ready for the chase. His hair was oiled, his nails
neatly trimmed and polished, his face scrupulously shaved.
And his hat—an excellent one which he had stolen—he wore
at a cocky angle.

"Put on these clothes," he said, "and we'll step out."

Vridar protested. He said he had lessons to do. He said he
was not feeling well. He said he didn't care much about girls
and would be bored to death in their company. But he yielded
at last.

The suit, looking as if it had been made for him, set him
off in lordly style. He wore Forenoon's silk socks, a pair of his
thoroughbred shoes, one of his shirts and one of his broad
flowing ties. He submitted to having his nails cleaned, his thin
beard shaved, and his hair slicked back and oiled and perfumed. And when he entered the street, he felt as meticulously
curried as an earl.

Tonight, Forenoon said, they would pick up some girls. He
wanted a new one. This proposal made Vridar shiver. Rather
than accost a strange woman, he would have fought wildcats
or gone to war. And to change the subject, he said:

"I been thinking of enlisting. Let's go to war."

He had been thinking of nothing of the sort. The war rag-
ing in Europe he had thought of, but only as a pacifist who
condemned. Not yet, Forenoon said, would he go to war.
There were three girls whom he wanted to seduce first, one
of whom had made a donkey of him. He thought he had her
pinned down the other night but she got scared and ran
away. And he added:

"How the shoes fit? . . . Say, good God, you got your hat
on backward!" He grasped Vridar's hat—Forenoon's hat, really—and turned it about. Vridar had not known that the bow
ought to be on the left side. "And your collar," said Forenoon,

appraising him. "Didn't you ever wear clothes before?" He adjusted Vridar's collar and tie and picked two hairs from his lapels. "Little things like that," he said, "makes a girl stick her nose up. It's clothes makes the man."

"I never thought much about clothes," Vridar said, feeling very meek. "I guess I never had any to think about."

"Watch yourself," Forenoon said. "Just a hat on backward has spoiled a lot of seductions. Girls don't mind going to bed with a guy but they want him to look right."

Near State Street they saw two girls coming toward them. Forenoon stared at them with critical interest and said they looked all right.

"Get ready now. Have some nice things to say."

But Vridar's mind was wordless confusion. He strove desperately to think of polite phrases, little engaging nothings, but all he could think of was hello and how do you do. And as the girls drew nearer, he fell into wild panic, with his heart shaking him like blows.

"Get up here!" Forenoon whispered.

Vridar made a stupendous effort but still lagged behind. He heard Forenoon talking to the girls. He heard him say, "Hello, sweethearts, you going my way? . . . Sure it is. Couldn't you tell I was walking backward? I was on my way to your house all the time." And then: "Damn, what gorgeous dresses! Who told you those dresses matched your hair and eyes? . . . Don't kid me! Don't kid your uncle, my dear, don't kid your uncle. . . ."

One of the girls was twittering in a choked way, and the other, a little more dignified, smiled. Clearly, though, they both liked Forenoon and his nonsense.

With a lordly gesture, Forenoon swung to Vridar.

"Here, I want you to meet my friend, Mr. Keith Foxhall." (The Foxhalls were one of Salt Lake City's most snobbish families.) "He's the most brilliant student in college," Forenoon went on. "Me, I flunk everything. But Keith, just open his mouth and you'll see a book. . . . Keith, I want you to meet two darn lovely girls."

Vridar's face was as red as the flame in his tie. Forenoon

took one of the girls by an arm and turned down the street. Vridar stumbled along with the other girl, feeling unspeakably awkward and silly. The girl ahead looked round at her friend and winked. The girl with Vridar made a droll face and shrugged. And Vridar knew that both girls preferred McClintock and he wondered how he could excuse himself and slink away.

Forenoon was talking to his girl. He was fingering her scarf and gently caressing her arm and knocking at her leg with his knee. Glancing swiftly at the girl by him, Vridar saw that she looked stiff and annoyed. He ought to talk. He ought to flatter her and make little amorous gestures but he did not know how. He said:

"You live in Salt Lake?"

The girl's shrill laugh was almost a whinny.

"Do I live in Salt Lake? Madge, you hear that? He wants know do I live in Salt Lake."

Madge looked around and giggled.

"No," she said, "she lives in China. She's just visitun."

Blood dyed Vridar from his necktie to his hair. He hated this girl and wished he could humiliate her.

"They both live in China," Forenoon said. "They're Chinese. Can't you see their eyes are slanted down to their nose?"

Both girls laughed at this. The one with Vridar kicked playfully at Forenoon and he yelped and capered as if struck. He turned and walked backward and the girl with him said:

"Turn round here! You're my escort."

Vridar made another heroic attempt.

"Are you a college student?" he asked of the girl by his side. He intended to be gently ironic. The girl clapped a hand to her mouth and shrieked.

"Madge, listen! Now he says am I a college student!"

"Sure," said Madge. "The college hard knocks and big bumps. Two more kicks and she'll graduate."

Well, Vridar decided, there was no use talking to this creature. She was annoyed with him and she was stupid and he wished she would fall and flatten her face. But he trudged along, self-conscious and wretched, yet aware of all that was said, of every little thing that was done. When they came to Main Street, the girl boldly left him and walked with her friend. For a little way Vridar trailed abjectly and then he dodged. He vanished into the foyer of a hotel and passed through to a barber shop and then emerged and headed home. He walked rapidly as if beset by devils. What, he asked furiously, did he care about girls! They were a giggling and stupid and deadly lot and they could all be seduced for all that he cared.

But he thought, nevertheless, of Neloa Doole, that lovely dark lass whom he had idolized for nine years. She was of a different sort: no amorous twittering there, no daft interest in clothes and feeble wit, no school-girlish infatuation with philanderers like A. M. She was as chaste as a June morning and as unapproachable as the philosophy of Kant. He would write to her.

And he got to his room, still thinking of Neloa's mane of Indian hair and of her colorful mouth and of the sad tragic silence of her way. He felt a little faithless: for he thought of Neloa as a shy maid lost in a big room, repulsing all wooers, yearning for him. He wrote a burning letter of loneliness and love. He poured into it all his indignities and heartache. He said he would be very studious, giving his time only to books and to the stern discipline of thought; and when the Antelope Hills were again golden, he would come to her. "Dear darling girl, wait for me," he wrote, "for I'm coming back! I'll send you a poem soon that will tell you what I feel. It will be intense and tremulous and far-reaching, like the wing of a bird. I love you, Neloa, I love you! . . ."

He read the letter and wept. Then he remembered that Neloa went to the Antelope dances and waltzed with such scoundrels as Dave Wolf and Alvin Kress; and he hated her, too, and wept afresh. He tore the letter into an assortment of triangles, becoming absorbed in the doing of this and mutilating, with increasing pleasure, all the words of promise and endearment. Then he banked the furnace and went to bed.

IV

‖‖‖

•

BUT IN spite of himself, he could not put girls out of his mind. He was still thinking of them when Forenoon strode in.

"Where the hell," he cried, "did you sneak off to?"

"I went home."

"Looks like it! What'd you beat it for?"

"I didn't like that girl. She didn't like me. Why should I fool around with her?"

Forenoon dropped to a chair and gave him a leering appraisal.

"You can't expect a girl to like you all at once. You got a-make her like you. They're fussy, girls are."

"To hell with girls," Vridar said.

"You watch me, brother. I'll be in bed with Madge in a week."

"I don't care."

"And with Verla, too. That's the other one."

"All right! I tell you I don't care. Sleep with the whole damn world if you want to."

"You're a fool," McClintock said. "What you gettun out of life? You need some decent clothes. Steal some."

"I'm not interested in girls."

"Bellyache! You're not a steer, are you?"

"Oh, shut up and get out!"

"I'll tell you. I'll fetch a girl right to your room."

"No you won't!" Vridar cried. He was alarmed. He stared at Forenoon, wishing he had never seen him. "Mind your own business," he said.

Forenoon rose and got his things. He said he would fetch a girl to his room and Vridar could stay with her all night.

"You're just bashful," he said. "Soon's you get over that you'll have your arms full." He deliberated a moment. "You got a-sow your wild oats or you'll never be happy when you get married. That's what men tell me."

"I don't care what men tell you."

"When I get a girl," Forenoon said at the door, "I'll let you know. I'll get a hot one. You won't have no trouble."

"Beat it!" Vridar howled. Forenoon vanished and Vridar heard him gloating down the hallway.

For days Vridar strove not to think about girls. He wanted more than he wanted food and air to be with them and to share their youth and love. His hunger was like an intense burning pleasure that fed on pain. He even thought now and then of abducting a girl and dragging her into his dark room and ravishing her. This notion he found despicable, but it lay, large and warm and watchful, among the unused impulses of his heart.

On the right of him in sociology sat a very lovely girl named Delia Farns. She was attracted to Vridar and Vridar knew it: in one glance from a girl, he could read most unerringly her favor or her scorn. Delia was small and fair, with hazel eyes and an austere manner. She was one of the few brilliant students in the class. She was not stricken speechless, as Vridar was, when spoken to by the instructor, but she had, nevertheless, the kind of timid aloofness that he adored. But he never spoke to her. He gave her now and then a swift scared glance or he peered between fingers at her shapely legs; and his senses swam in dark ecstasy when her arm touched his.

In his English class was a sprightly lass named Lottie Ulster. She, too, was interested in Vridar: more boldly than Delia, because she often looked at him and smiled, or sometimes spoke. Lottie was small and dark and very pretty, save for a mustache. Vridar stared with a sinking heart at the black hair on her lip. When he looked at her vivacious black eyes or at her lovely throat, he felt shaken and undone; but when he looked at her mustache, he felt appalled.

Nevertheless, goaded day after day by self-scorn and encouraged by glances steadily more challenging, he resolved to take Lottie to a show. When class was done, he would slip out and wait in the hall, hoping she would be the last to emerge; but she always came in a group and smiled at him and left him witless; and he would march out to the campus, feeling very absurd. For nine days he waited for her in the hall.

One day he saw her alone on a campus bench. There was snow, the weather was cold, but she did not seem to mind. Perhaps, he thought, she had come here purposely, believing he would find her and speak. He hid behind a snow-covered bush and stared at her. He went off a little way and examined his emotions and his courage and returned. For almost half an hour he watched her. From time to time she would look up, as if expecting someone; and at last, when she seemed about to leave, he prodded himself and went forth, pretending not to see her at all. He would walk close to her but he would be in deep thought, with his gaze on the earth. If she called to him, then he would show surprise. If she did not, then he would pass on and forget about her.

But she called. He gave a violent start—much too violent, he realized—and turned and looked at her.

"You taking a stroll?" she asked.

"I—I guess so," he said.

"I wish you'd tell me," she said, "what a gerund is."

"A gerund?" He went over to the bench. Well, at least he could speak of gerunds. "Why, it's a verbal noun. It's derived from a verb but used as a noun."

"Oh, is that it?" she said. And he knew she was not thinking of gerunds. She was one of Arnold's most capable students and she knew all about gerunds.

"I guess it isn't always easy to tell a gerund," he said, staring at her book. "Running is good exercise. Now the word running is a gerund."

"Oh," she said. Her black eyes were fixed on him, intent and searching. "I've heard you're the best student in class."

"Me!" he cried. He blushed and looked away. "I've never heard that. Someone has been making a joke."

"I think you are," she said.

"Thanks," Vridar said.

He looked at a spruce bowered with snow. He stepped a little to one side and glanced anxiously down a walk, as if he had heard sounds of murder there. And then he felt very silly.

"I been wondering," he said, "If you—I mean—" He looked at her. She was dimpled, smiling, waiting. He liked the warm friendliness of her eyes. "Would you go to a show with me?"

"Of course," she said. "When?"

"When?" he said, his mind running empty. "Oh, any time."

"Tonight?"

"Why, sure—I guess."

She wrote on a slip of paper. She handed the paper to him and on it he saw an address and a telephone number.

"In case you can't come," she said, "you'n call me up."

He liked that. It was very thoughtful of her. It offered a way out if his courage failed him.

But at eight o'clock he stood trembling at her door and rang the bell. The bell sounded very loud in the house and he wondered if he gave it too much of a yank. A moment later he was ushered into an enormous room. It looked kingly in its ceiling and costly in its rugs. Lottie came out draped in folds of red and gave him her hand and said she was very glad he had come.

"I am glad, too," Vridar said, and then felt too preposterous for words.

Of this evening, he afterward remembered vividly only one thing. They went to a show and they walked up and down a street and they rode on a car. But all these became very blurred and unreal. While riding on the car homeward, there was only one thought in his mind: a dilemma, tremendous and dark. Should he be the first to leave the car or should she precede him? He did not know. He agonized over this awful matter and he would have given anything to have known. Lottie talked to him and her words were gay and witty, and in a gesture of goodwill she pressed his arm; but he had mind only for this one monstrous predicament. Perhaps, he reasoned, he could tell by her manner what he was expected to do; and when they came to her stop, he preceded her down the aisle and then stepped aside, as if waiting for her. She looked up at him. She seemed a little surprised. And Vridar did not move, convinced, in this moment, that Lottie should go first. Women, it seemed to him, always went ahead of men, and if this was an exception, it was a horribly stupid one.

After her swift glance at his face, Lottie stepped lightly down and off and Vridar followed. He knew at once that he had blundered. Her manner was different now. Save only for a cool goodnight, she did not speak again, and he turned away, sweating with shame. He went like a whipped thing to his room. And for two days he missed his classes, not daring to face Lottie's scorn; and when he did venture in, she did not look at him. She never spoke to him again.

This unhappy experiment with women and love convinced Vridar that he ought to leave both alone. He buried himself in his books. Women, he assured himself, were not worth a man's time, and love was the nonsense of earth. And for the niceties of convention, which had always annoyed him, he now cultivated a stupendous scorn.

But McClintock for some obscure reason was determined to have Vridar share his own amorous adventures. He came down often; he told, with leering relish, all the little details of his affairs; and he urged Vridar to a party or to a dance. When he spoke of girls, telling how they loved, how they kissed and what they said, Vridar choked with envy; but he affected not to care. He would try to look wearied and sleepy. But his mind was alive with pictures and his blood was like fire.

One evening Forenoon told of Ardeth Young. He had seduced her the week before, right on the sofa of her living-room; but he was sick of her now. She wanted to marry him. She wept and implored and threatened to jump off a high building. She said she would go to the president of the college and tell him all about it.

"I want you to handle her for me," Forenoon said. "You

go with her. Get her mind off of me. . . . God damn her, I don't
want a-marry the fool!"

"I go with her!" Vridar said. "You got your lousy nerve.
You think I want your castoff mistresses?"

"As a friend," Forenoon said. "Do it as a friend. I'd do that
much for you."

"To hell with you. If you get in crazy scrapes you'n get out.
If you go around seducing every girl you meet, that's your
business, not mine."

"Listen, I'll pay your expenses. You take her to shows. Buy
her some flowers and stuff. I'll pay for it all."

"No. Marry her. That would serve you right."

"Marry her! I'll bust her damn neck. . . . Listen, Vreed,
she's a swell kid. You won't have no trouble with her. I showed
her the ropes and she knows her stuff."

"Oh, thanks! But I'm not interested."

"A hell of a friend you are. You think I'd treat you this
way?"

"I don't care what you think. If you get in trouble, you'n
get out of it."

"All right! All right, but wait till you get your old foot in
it! Then don't come bellyachun to me."

"Wait till I do. Just wait till I do." He stared at Forenoon
and thought of his doings. "This city will be full of your kids.
You'll soon see them on every corner."

"Horse manure! Every man worth his salt has a lot of kids
he's never seen." He mused a while and added: "You know
Bertha Owen? I guess you don't. Well, she's married now. Married the guy she was engaged to when I met her. She has a
kid but it's my kid. Her old man thinks it's his kid. . . .
Listen, Vreed. None of us know our own dad. It's a cockeyed
fact. You'd be surprised how many girls pan kids off on another guy."

"I'm not interested!" Vridar cried angrily. "A lot of girls
are pure and they're the only ones I care about!" And he
thought of Neloa Doole.

For an hour after McClintock had gone, he thought of her.
It was pleasant to know that she was chaste and sweet, proud

and dignified. Forenoon would never get anywhere with her. She would slap his lewd face and send him back to Cedar City.

On an evening a week later, McClintock dashed into the room, agog with excitement. He found Vridar in bed. He shouted down at him that he had great news.

"Get up!" he howled. "Listen to this: I got a girl for you! I got a swell skirt and she's right here, almost under your nose!"

"Stop that shouting."

"Listen." Forenoon glanced round him, his manner stealthy. He now whispered. "Listen. She's up in my room."

"Up in your room!"

"Here, for God sake, don't shout like that. She's up in my room, now, this minute. I locked her in. Listen. I'll sleep with her tonight and you'n sleep with her tomorrow night."

Vridar trembled, though he could never have told why. He left the bed and drew his trousers on and then looked at Forenoon. Forenoon's eyes were greedy and cunning. Still whispering, he said he found her on the streets, starved and penniless; he fed her and brought her to his room. And there she was, already undressed and put to bed.

"Tomorrow," he said, "I'll fetch her some stuff to eat. I'll keep her locked in. I'll give you the key tomorrow. I'll sleep here."

To all this Vridar said nothing. He was too amazed to speak. And reading his silence as consent, Forenoon said not to forget and slipped out and away. Vridar heard him climbing the uncarpeted stairs. He lay on his bed, thinking of the matter: now Forenoon was with her, in bed with her, drawing her to him in close embrace. Vridar groaned and sat up. He hurled a pillow at the wall and then paced the room, wondering what he should do. He thought of this girl as a poor forlorn waif, abducted and locked up; ravished and made a prisoner of; and he deliberated rescuing her, as heroes used to do in old books. McClintock he thought of as a villain with a black heart. Here was life, indeed: as melodramatic, as darkly plotted, as any. Here was the old triangle: the villain and the hero and the maiden who implored help.

In a score of ways he planned a rescue. He saw himself pitching McClintock like a sack of barley through a window and carrying a weeping and very lovely girl in his arms. He saw himself soaked in glory, with his name on the front pages and his heroism burning in the editorials. But with another groan he sank to the bed and knew that he would do nothing at all.

As a matter of truth, he wanted to see this girl and be alone with her. He would not, he dared not, be intimate with her, but he liked to play with the notion and to luxuriate in his fancies of what an embrace would be like. He kicked his trousers off and went to bed and was tormented all night in his dreams. On the next morning he got up, still thinking of this girl. On his way to the campus, he looked up at Forenoon's window, trying to realize that she was there. And in his classes he heard nothing, saw nothing; for his mind was busy, trying to catch and clarify what had happened last night. And as the day waned and night drew on, he began to shake, not knowing what he would do or what he wished to do.

Early in the evening, Forenoon came in, not excited now but jaded and spent. He looked as if he had not slept at all. He said he had not. It had been a wild and tumultuous night, he said. The girl was a little scrawny, but she could love a half-dozen men blind.

"I feel," he said, "like I'd been kicked through a knothole. Tomorrow that's how you'll feel."

"You think so?" asked Vridar, and he fetched a long sigh. His voice, he realized, had been strangely hopeful. Well, he would pretend that he was going to sleep with the girl. He would have to pretend that or McClintock's scorn would wither him.

"Here's the key," Forenoon said. "Don't make a big racket going up the stairs." He lay down and stretched out and yawned. "You just as well go now. I want a-sleep."

Vridar stood up and his knees shook. He went to the door.

"In the morning," Forenoon said, "leave the door unlocked so she'n sneak out. . . . Well, run along. This is where you get burnt up."

Vridar passed into the hall and found the street. He stood here, his thoughts running wild races, and wondered again what he should do. He crossed the street and looked at the window but the window told no tale. Still, there seemed to be a light behind the shade. He came back and stood in wretched indecision. Three girls passed him, amorously a-twitter, like adolescents in springtime. Vridar stared after them until they passed from sight. Then he climbed the stairs.

Half-way up he paused and considered again. It was while he was standing here, undecided on advance or retreat, that he thought of Neloa Doole. Memory of her was like a burst of light. He would keep himself pure for Neloa because she was pure. She was not another Tess and he would not be another Angel, violating the bridal.night with confession of old wrong.

He climbed again. He came to a small unclean stairway that wound upward in a corkscrew like those in a tower. This he followed and came to a low-ceilinged room, used as a kitchen by the attic tenants; and ahead of him was McClintock's door. He went softly to it and listened. There was no sound within but a spray of light came through a crack. For a little while he stood here, trying to control his shaking legs and his wild heart. Then he gently inserted the key and turned the lock. He stepped in swiftly and closed the door.

The girl was sitting on the bed and she was looking at him with large dark eyes. He saw at once that she was very thin and pale: a tiny creature with a pinched face, and with big eyes that were like black ink filmed with oil. She had her shoes and stockings off, her dress loose at her breast, her hair down.

"Hello!" Vridar said in a preposterous whisper.

The girl did not speak. She looked at him with something cruel and flickering in her eyes. Vridar went over and fixed her with a solemn pious stare. There was nothing amorous in him now. He was feeling a great pity for the girl; thinking of her as a virgin two days ago, and now a forlorn thing, ravished and undone. He drew an enormous sigh and spoke again.

"Why are you here?" Her answer to this was a hysterical giggle. "Tell me," he said.

"Why am I here! Good God, where should I be?"

"This," said Vridar sternly, "is no place for a woman. Where is your home?"

"My home! The streets."

"You mean you have no home? Where is your mother?"

"My mother! Christ, how should I know!"

Vridar sat on the bed and studied her. She was a little too enigmatic. There was something hard in her tone, as if she had long been kicked about, homeless and unloved. Perhaps her parents had deserted her. Perhaps she had fought a brave fight, keeping her virtue and her pride until hunger drove her here. And while he was summarizing her thus and detesting McClintock, the girl moved close to him and fell into his arms. He thought she was sick and faint; and he held her and looked at her pitiful face, and he felt luxurious with compassion and strength.

"Why don't you go back home?" he asked gently.

"Back home. Listen, kid, the world is my home. It's all I have. It's plenty."

"Yes, I know. But you need a mother's care. How old are you?"

"Old enough to know my way around." She reached up and caressed his cheek. "Where's your beard?"

This allusion to his thin beard annoyed Vridar. He scowled at her.

"Never mind my beard. I came here to talk of serious matters."

"Yes, dearie, like a whore's dream. I know what you come for."

"It's a lie! I'm not that kind of a man."

"Oh. What kind are you?"

"Well, I'm not like the skunk who stayed with you last night."

"He's not a skunk, darling. He give me lots of nice things to eat. He give me a new pair of stockings."

More and more this girl baffled Vridar. Her casual use of endearments, her profane tongue, her hand on his thigh: what did all these mean? He thought perhaps she was desperate. She was sick and abandoned and did not care. What she needed was a good lecture.

"Now listen," he said. "You stay here tonight. In the morning you're going back home. You belong there. Tell your mother you've sinned and she'll forgive you and you can start all over again. . . . Promise you will."

Her hand still stroked his cheek. Her other hand was between his thighs and he took it away.

"Honey," she said; and she seemed almost to purr. All her movements were feline.

"Stop that! Promise me you'll go home." He shook her a little.

"Don't do that!" she cried. "I hate cavemen."

"Never mind cavemen. Promise me."

"You mean I should go to church?"

"Sure. You should make a new start in life. It's no big crime to sin if you're sorry and start all over again."

"Listen, brother, where'd you get that line?"

"What do you mean line?"

"Darling, I want some ice cream."

"No! Be serious now. You——"

"You up here to sleep with me?"

"I should say not!"

"You are. Your friend said you would. Well, I guess you'n get me some ice cream. What you expect for nothing?"

Vridar pushed her away and stood up. His patience was almost gone.

"I'm here to help you!" he cried, scowling fiercely. "But I can't help you if you won't help yourself. Not even the Lord can do that."

"The Lord, my hinder! You got a cigarette?"

"I don't smoke."

The girl looked at him curiously. Was he really here to help

her, she asked. Vridar swore that he was. And now he saw in
her a sudden swift change. She began to weep. She threw herself on the bed and sobbed wildly, as if overcome by remorse;
and this was precisely what Vridar had hoped for. Now he was
all gentleness and compassion. He sat on the bed and clasped
one of her hands and he said comforting things. He said noble
enduring things, such as he had read in the Bible and elsewhere. But the more he reassured, the more frantic became
her grief; until she was kicking out with naked legs and pulling
her hair.

"This won't do!" Vridar cried. "Straighten up! Life hasn't
licked you yet. Where's your backbone? Sit up and let's talk
it out."

And with amazing alacrity, the girl sat up, her eyes running water, her hair in a ragged tangle. She moved over to
him, shuddering, pitiful; she lay again in his arms and pressed
his hands.

"What shall I do?" she asked. Her voice, he thought, was
astonishingly clear.

"Go home," Vridar said. "Get out of this big wicked city."

"But I can't. I'm broke. I'm flat on my rump."

Vridar considered this.

"Where is your home?"

"Butte."

He considered again.

"How much is the fare to Butte?"

"About fifteen dollars."

"Fifteen dollars! I can't give you that much."

"Then how'n I get home?"

"You'n write your folks."

"They ain't got any money, kid. I'm broke now. What can
I live on?"

"Well," said Vridar, torn by inner conflict, "I—well, I won't
let you starve. How—how much would you need?"

"Fifteen dollars."

"I tell you," he cried, "I can't give you that much!"

"Ten dollars."

"I can't give you ten, either."

"Five."

"All right, I'n give you five."

She sat up. She tossed her hair back and looked at him.

"All right, kid, give me the five."

"I don't have it with me," he said. He dug into all his pockets, not to find money but to convince her that he had none. "I'll give it to you in the morning."

"You're just like all men," she said, her eyes narrowing. "I thought you was different but you ain't."

"I am," he said stoutly. "I mean it. I'll give it to you."

"Where?"

"Well—on the drugstore corner. Just below. Just a few rods below here."

"What time?"

"Oh, eight o'clock."

"Honest, kid? I can't go home without you help me."

"I'll help you." He stood up and looked at her. "And now," he said, "you need rest. Go to sleep and try to forget. Life will be different soon." And he said goodnight and left her sitting on the bed. At the door he looked back and saw her large dark eyes watching him and her thin mouth drawn into a bloodless line.

Again on the street, he strove to clear his wits. He knew little of women and nothing of harlots, but he had an unhappy conviction, nevertheless, that this girl was what the world called a whore. He would help her, just the same. A good deed bore fruit to the doer; credulity was paid in harvest by God.

Resolved not to seek his own room and there face McClintock's scorn, he walked the streets all night. When morning came he entered his cell. He shouted, and Forenoon awoke on a snore and rubbed his eyes.

"Hello," he said. He looked sleepily at Vridar. "Have a wild time?"

"Sure," Vridar said. "Don't I show it?"

"God yes. You look like you'd been boiled with carrots. . . . Well, how you feel?"

"I feel all right. A little sleepy, that's all."

Forenoon yawned and reached for his socks. From time to time he looked at Vridar and gave him a faint grin.

"Don't say I never done you no favors. Now you got started we'n have some fun. . . . How was she? all right?"

"Sure, she was all right."

"I ain't so sure," Forenoon said. "I think she give me a dose."

Vridar did not know what this meant.

Unobtrusively he slipped out and took five dollars to the girl. She was waiting for him. She looked at the money and thrust it into a ragged glove.

"Now remember," Vridar said, "you're to go home. Just as soon as you get a ticket."

"All right, kid. Well, goodbye and be good to women."

"I will," Vridar said. He watched her go down the street. She looked very frail and homeless and he felt a great pity.

A few days later, Forenoon burst in, howling with rage. That lousy slut up in his room had given him a pretty one. It would take half his money for a cure.

"You get a dose?" he asked.

"No," Vridar said.

"You lucky bastard! That's the third time I been caught!"

He stormed outside, cursing women. They would pay for this, he said. They would pay and pay and pay.

Vridar sank to the bed, his face in his hands. For two long hours he did not stir.

V

FEELING like a simpleton and vowing that no woman would ever trick him again, Vridar set about recovering his loss. With five dollars he could have bought a pair of shoes and a hat; or he could have had a decayed tooth crowned; or he could have equipped himself with a dictionary and a thesaurus. Over and over, tormented by his stupidity, he counted the things that five dollars would buy.

During the holidays he got a clerkship in one of the big stores. He was among the groceries. There were seventeen clerks here and he was determined to be the best of the lot. When not serving a customer, he memorized prices or learned where merchandise was stored or observed the ways of the old clerks, copying from each what seemed to him wise.

But his work here after two days was not pleasant. The customers exhausted his patience and he wanted to boot them into the street. On his third day he was hailed by an enormous woman with a sour face.

"Here, boy," she said, and he hated her for calling him boy.

"Yes, madam. Can I be of service to you?"

"You'n take my money, I guess. That's what you're here for, ain't it?"

"I'm here to serve you," he said politely.

"Serve me!" she snorted. "You're here to grab my money. Don't call it other names." She moved like a barge from place to place and Vridar followed her. "Here, boy, where's your lettuce?"

"This way, madam."

She went to a crate of lettuce and pawed with both hands. "Ten cents a head."

"Ten cents! It ain't worth five cents a ton. Where's your potatoes?"

"This way, please."

"You don't have to say please. If I want a-buy, I'll buy. You can't coax me. . . . How much are they?"

"Three cents a pound or a dollar a bushel."

"Bushel! Who said I wanted a bushel? . . . Three cents a pound, you said."

"Yes, madam."

"Or four pounds for a dime."

"No, madam. Three cents a pound unless you take a bushel."

"I told you I didn't want a bushel. And don't call me madam." She looked at him. "How long you been here? You a new clerk?"

"Yes."

"I thought so. Where's Maggie? She always waits on me."

Vridar looked about him. "I guess she's still out to lunch."

"Well, let's see your loose coffee."

"This way, please."

"Don't say please to me! I know what I want."

"All right, this way."

She went over and stared into a barrel of coffee. She took a handful and smelled of it.

"How much a pound?"

"Thirty-three cents."

"Give me a pound. And don't weigh the sack."

Vridar got a bag and scooped coffee into it and set the bag on the scales.

"That ain't a pound," she said.

Little by little, Vridar added more. When the hand on the dial stood at sixteen ounces he stopped.

"More," she said. "You're weighun the sack."

He added a little more. He knew now that the manager of the department was watching him.

"More," said the woman.

"That's a pound. It's more than a pound."

"Boy, don't you think I'n see? I'm not buyun your paper sacks."

At the end of his patience, Vridar took the bag off and began to wrap it. The woman was abusive and the manager came over and spoke to her.

"He's tryun to cheat me," she said. "When I pay for a pound I want a pound."

"It's a pound," Vridar said.

The manager took the bag and weighed it.

"It's seventeen ounces," he said. He opened the bag and poured some out.

"I won't pay for your paper!" the woman cried. "Where's Maggie Simms?"

The manager said she was out to lunch but would return

soon. The woman said she would wait and she went to a bench and sat down. She folded enormous arms across an enormous bosom and glared at Vridar.

Vridar knew what the trouble was. After two days here, he had learned that several of the clerks were cheats. Maggie Simms was one of them. When Maggie's friends came in, they bought a few bulky things like vegetables and breakfast foods; and into the bags, Maggie slipped small costly articles: canned chicken and olives and vanilla, relishes and jams. At least four other clerks did likewise. He knew but he said nothing; and the fact that he knew and said nothing led, a year later, to one of the most dangerous episodes of his life.

Aside from this giving to relatives and friends, there was another matter. The clerks were on a competitive basis. If Vridar's sales averaged fifty dollars a day, the manager had said, he would be kept as a Saturday clerk throughout the year. Vridar thought this was fair enough.

But he soon learned that many women came here, expecting more than they paid for, and that some of the clerks gave them more, thereby making of them steady customers. Vridar gave to each buyer what he paid for and in consequence many of them never came to him a second time. Only by working swiftly, by being alert, did he keep his sales up; and for his alertness he got the dislike of clerks who had been here a long while. The manager liked him, nevertheless. When he dismissed him he expressed regret. He did it, he said, to keep harmony in the department. And Vridar wanted to shout, "Your clerks are cheaters! You're awfully dumb or you'd know it!" But he held his tongue. For telling tales, Jed Bridwell had half-killed him. He would never tell again.

He earned fifteen dollars and stored it away. If he earned ten dollars, he had promised himself a pair of shoes and a hat; but he thought of his mother whose shoes had always been ugly and wornout, and of his father, whose overalls and shirts were patched. He resolved to earn twenty dollars before buying anything for himself.

To find another job, he went to Annie G. Foote, the dean of women. Aunt Annie, she was called; and the more impudent students, when speaking of her, said Aunt Annie gee! She was a huge woman with a face to match her well-padded frame. She was elderly and a spinster and a tradition.

When Vridar entered her office, she was busy giving loud and imperious advice to a professor. She said he was not eating the right food and he was not exercising enough. While she talked, Vridar sized her up.

She had a tight mouth, hair twisted into a knot, and large powerful hands. She would weigh, he imagined, about two hundred and forty pounds. Never before had he seen so much womanhood in one dress. But it was her eyes that fixed his interest. They were small and gray and full of light and it was the light in them that baffled him. It was a ravenous light, strangely alert, strangely greedy and flickering. They were the eyes of a full passionate woman, still curious about sex, almost morbidly concerned with its doings; yet lost among duties, bound to the cold exile of a deanship.

After the abashed professor had got his hat and slunk out, Annie Foote swung in her chair and looked at Vridar.

"Well, young man, what can I do for you?"

"Why," he said, "I—I wondered if maybe you could help me find some work."

"Supporting yourself?" Her manner of speaking, hard and clipped and deep-bosomed, was almost offensive. Her questions came like blows. "A freshman?" "Living alone?" "Sit down."

He sat down and she stared at him.

"Where you from?"

"Idaho. Antelope, Idaho."

"Never heard of it. Parents living?"

"Yes maam."

"Farmers?"

"Yes maam."

"Poor?"

"Yes maam, quite poor."

For a little while her strange eyes studied him.

"Where you living now?"

"Professor Yupp's."

"In one of those dry goods boxes?"

"No, in the basement. I tend the furnace."

Under her breathing, her bosom moved up and down like a great pillow. One big hand on her desk toyed with an inkstand.

"Cook your own food?"

"Yes maam."

"What you eat?"

"Oh," he said, flushing a little, "cereals and fruits and vegetables."

"Uncooked?"

"Some of them, yes."

"You don't eat enough. You're too pale and skinny. Sleep with your window open?"

"Well, no, it won't open."

Her grunt was a grunt of scorn. Professor Yupp's basement, she said, wasn't fit for hogs.

"Eat more. Get lots of fresh air when you sleep. If your window won't open, sleep outside. Drink lots of water?"

"I—I don't know. I guess I do."

"Drink lots of it. Exercise every day?"

"Just walking."

"Go to the gym. Well, soon as spring breaks I want my back yard dug up. That'll be good for you, out in the air. Meanwhile, I'll see what I'n find."

Vridar stood up, thinking the interview closed.

"Sit down," she said. He sat down. "Now remember, eat more. Get fresh air and exercise. You're too puny and pale for anything."

"Yes maam," he said.

"You smoke?"

"No maam."

"That's good. Come in tomorrow." She turned to her desk, dismissing him, and he almost tiptoed outside.

When March came, he spaded in Annie Foote's back yard. Birds sang round him and the earth was rich with growth. He felt an awful homesickness for the river and mountains of An-

telope and for all its wild flowers and blue mist and loneliness. Thinking of his homeplace, he knelt to the odorous earth
and breathed of it and then looked with wet eyes to the far-
away valley and the open roads.

Late in one afternoon, Annie came out to watch him toil.
She said he was working too fast. She said he looked as white
and scrawny as he did two months ago. Had he been drinking plenty of water and sleeping in fresh air?

"Yes maam," he said.

It was while standing here that he got his first, his only clear,
vision of the woman's soul. She had some chickens, and a
rooster started in pursuit of a hen. He overtook the hen and
mounted her, and Vridar, a little embarrassed, looked at Annie Foote. What he saw in her face and eyes, he could never
have found words for; but its meaning was clear to him, as
clear as if he had seen it in print. Never before had he seen
and never afterward was he to see such a morbid fixed interest,
such girlish adolescent wondering, such starvation and loss, in
a woman's eyes. His heart went out to her in great sympathy.
He understood her now: her imperious manner and all her
strange ways; and he loved her.

He was still looking at her, amazed by what he saw, when
she noted his stare. A wave of blood went up her throat.

"Get busy!" she cried. "That's no way to stare at a person!"
And she turned and entered the house.

Vridar earned four dollars spading her yard. He had nineteen dollars of his own now but he bought nothing for himself.
On the contrary, in his wish to save, he went to extremes of
labor and denial. He still laundered his clothes and cooked his
bread. From where he lived, it was two miles to the shopping
center, but he always walked.

He bought only on Saturday night so he could return after
dark and not be seen. If he saw students coming or anyone
who looked like students he would pull his cap down to hide
his face. He would even take a roundabout way home.

One of these journeys he never forgot. He had his arms full.
He had a bag of flour and another of sugar, and some canned
goods and vegetables and fruits. He thought he could carry

all these but after he had gone three blocks he had misgivings and after he had gone a mile he was exhausted and white. Sitting on a curb, with no house close by, he wondered what he should do.

At one side was a huge billboard on a vacant lot. He went behind this and dug a hole and buried his sugar and flour. The rest he carried uphill and to his room, and early in the next morning, when few were astir, he returned for what he had left. It was in this way that he saved a nickel, not for himself, but for his parents, in whose lives a nickel meant an hour of toil.

It was in this way and in other ways similar that he saved sixty-five dollars of the two hundred which his father gave him. And in later years, when he heard young men say they would have gone to college if they had had a chance, if they had had the money, Vridar would snort with scorn. Yes, they would have gone; but only if their meals were cooked, their room cared for; only if they had money for fraternity dues and girls and clothes.

"But not as I went! You wouldn't break your precious back carrying groceries two miles up a mountain to save a nickel! You wouldn't wear hideout shoes and a rag of a cap and one shapeless suit! You wouldn't live in a smoky den and stoke a dirty furnace and fight loneliness and heartache! . . . If you had a chance? A chance, hell! If you had wanted to go you would have made your chance!"

VI

VRIDAR had not expected to find snobs in college. He had expected to find a body of students, humble and studious, without pretense or arrogance or scorn. He had thought they would all be lovers of books.

And he strove for a long while to believe that college was what he had imagined it would be. He tried to keep his faith and his dream. He resisted the truth of what he saw and fought stubbornly against it. But the evidence of his folly was overwhelming and little by little, in spite of all he could do, it filled him with dismay. Week after week, month after month, he saw more clearly that Wasatch College was a noisy melodrama, a grotesque assortment of postures, a stupendous farce. Its disregard of truth appalled him. Its fawning obeisance to wealth and politics made him sick.

Because its students, save only a handful, were not interested in books at all. They were interested in its social world: its fraternities and sororities, ranging in snobbish exclusiveness from its three nationals to a score of locals; in its clubs, which established the prominence of the choicest aristocrats; in its Junior Prom., a stiffly formal extravagance afforded only by a few; and in dances and athletics and love-making. They were interested in making donkeys of their professors and a casual compulsion of their studies. And after watching them for an hour, Vridar would turn away, trembling with disgust.

The social leaders he could tell at a glance. He knew them by their smart clothes, but most of all by their yawning boredom in the classroom and their deference to instructors. They were brawling adolescents in the halls. They gathered near the bookstore in the main building and the men cut capers and guffawed and the girls in one moment looked haughty and in the next they giggled and squeaked. The noise and milling here was deafening. Often Vridar listened to what was said; and he heard so many obscene things, especially about the dean of women, that he marveled at such lewdness right under the President's nose. He wondered if humankind was as vulgar at it seemed to be.

And always, no matter where he went, he was conscious of derisive eyes. He would look about, curious to know if he was the shabbiest person in the College; and he decided that he was. Others were out of style, others wore cheap clothes. Others went timidly about, as he did, overcome by the splendor and the scorn. But none seemed to launder their own collars or to look so homespun and out of place.

In a class, while intent on what his instructor was saying, he would become aware of searching eyes. He would turn to meet them and he would find one of the aristocrats looking him over. Then he would sweat with shame and his mind would be a void. Perhaps it was his long hair which needed trimming or his self-laundered collar stained from the iron or his ridiculous tie. Often on the campus, students would turn to look at him, and they would speak to one another or they would giggle or shrug. And he would burn with fury, with dark and awful hatred for his race. He would remember, but with little comfort, what a critic said of Dickens: "He disliked a certain look on the face of a man when he looks down on another man. And that look on that face is the only thing in the world that we have really to fight between here and the fires of Hell." While pondering this statement, he would wonder where democracy had fled to, and why in a college, of all places, it was not a splendor and a light.

For there was no democracy here. Even the lowliest class—the bookworms, the sons and daughters of the soil—aspired, it seemed to him, to social distinction. McClintock said they did. When this young man spoke of fraternities and of the other social life denied him he got into a furious sweat. He cursed the school and his humble birth.

"If you have the money," he said, "you belong. If you don't, your brains ain't worth a cent."

"Nonsense!" Vridar cried. "You know what Ruskin says?"

"Ruskin who?"

"He says self-complacency is the mark of a second-rate intellect."

"Broomsticks! Who's Ruskin, a professor of education or something? Anyway, if you've got the money you don't have to worry about the brains."

"I'd rather have the brains," Vridar said.

"I wouldn't. You take my brains and give me your money. We'll see who's happiest."

"I haven't much money," Vridar said dryly, "but it's enough, I guess, to buy your brains."

"Listen, Vreed. Next year I'll be in the Poison Skull. See if I'm not."

The Poison Skull was the College's most exclusive male club. Only juniors were eligible. They were chosen by the Albatross and Padlock, the senior members of the Poison Skull. In each year the initiates clowned about the campus and then disported in the auditorium. In this spring Vridar watched them.

They appeared on the campus in garb chosen by the Albatross and Padlock: one of them as an Indian with feathers in his hair and red paint on his naked arms and legs; another as an old woman with a broom; and a third as Bushman, carrying a half-dozen cowbells. A fourth was dressed as a young girl and was rumored to be a very amorous virgin. A fifth was an escaped jailbird, attired in outlandish pajamas. The sixth was an idiot and went about jibbering or pursuing girls or thieving from the bookstore. And the seventh, a huge fellow, was grotesquely padded, with two pillows on his chest, and represented the dean of women.

Into the history class one morning came the Bushman, his bells in terrific dispute. The class shouted approval but Professor Johns had only contempt for such antics. He flew into a rage and ordered the Bushman outside; and in indignant sympathy, the amorous virgin and the dean of women rose and left the class. The students whooped with glee.

During this week, as a matter of fact, the campus was turned into an orgy of nonsense. Classes were deserted and students in hordes followed the clowns. During the noon hour they gathered in the main corridor and mounted in turn to a large box; and they told jests so vile that Vridar's ears burned. Many of these jests were obscene thrusts at spinsters and some of them were directed at the dean of women herself. And the students roared with applause. A professor ventured, now and then, to hear what was said and then slunk away.

But all these indecencies were nothing when compared with the show in the auditorium. After the Bushman had given a vulgar dance, and after the amorous virgin performed so lewdly that the assembled students dared not applaud, the one affecting idiocy made preposterous attempts to rape the dean of women. Later in burlesque shows, in New York and elsewhere, Vridar saw nothing more boldly vulgar than this scene. It was so vile that the few instructors who had come and many of the students left the hall.

So this, Vridar reflected, was higher education when it relaxed. For this his parents had hoarded and for this he had fought his way through school. He had expected an austere studiousness and he had found filth that would choke a vulture. He had expected quiet and he had found an orgy of riot. For often in the classroom, the instructor had to pause, had to wait, on account of honking horns and racing motors on the driveway outside. And in the library, study was impossible; for this was a rendezvous of social groups and lovemakers and clowns.

And besides all this, Vridar learned (chiefly from Forenoon) that cheating was as common as vulgarity. One fraternity house had a room devoted exclusively to old compositions, term papers, and the solutions of problems in science. In Vridar's own class, he was told, Arnold had read and praised compositions which were ten years old. . . . Yes, this was college. It was for this that he had cooked his own meals and lived alone with Mertyl and suffered madness and loss. And again and again, when thinking of it, he would feel the old desolation closing in, the old nightmares of horror; and he would go for a long walk and he would reason with himself until he was less afraid.

Nevertheless, but for another matter, he could have reconciled himself to all this. It was the faculty, after all, and not the students, on which he had set his faith. If he had found them noble and generous, without envy and malice and subterfuge, he would have been satisfied; he would have had an anchor then and a goal. He would not have minded what his clothes were like or that he was looked upon with derision. But little by little, no matter how stubbornly he resisted, some of his teachers, even if only indistinctly, he came to see as they were. Annie G. Foote, in spite of all her absurd ways, he admired and loved; and he never lost his respect for Arnold and Bogan. But most of his teachers were not guides; they were not philosophers and friends. On the contrary, he perceived more and more clearly, they were self-appointed detectives whose mission was to track down cheats or they were intellectual frauds for whom the truth was an impure and a dangerous thing.

During his second semester, he entered a course in literature under James McFarlane Bush. Bush compelled his class to memorize long sections of *Paradise Lost* and of other turgid poems; and during examinations, he moved up and down the aisles, going as stealthily as a cat. If he caught a student cheating, his glee was huge. He would reprimand and exhort and then order the student to leave the room. And again he would prowl about, an educator who was a small sleuth, a leader of the young who gloated over misdeeds.

Yes, this was college; and when April came, Vridar was sick of it. He cast about for something else, something big and splendid, to which he could give his heart. Religion and democracy and education: these seemed to be arid fields where circuses deployed. Was there nothing else? Was there nowhere in life an honest and undefeatable strength to which he could anchor his terrified will, and so fight more surely and serenely against the bitter memories of his life? He read wolfishly in books but he found none. And while he searched for a new faith, there came to the campus a famous novelist, Mr. Harold Bell Wright. Mr. Wright spoke to Arnold's class; and Vridar, shaken by excitement, went eagerly to the room and took a front seat.

The novelist gave what Vridar thought was a splendid speech. His dark eyes shone with the great and beautiful purpose of his mind. Thrusting a hand at the floor, he said, "Some choose to write down here, of the mean and the common; but I [and his hand shot to the ceiling] choose to write of the things up there!" Vridar knew he meant the stars, of course: the lovely and enduring quests of life. And Vridar left the room convinced that he had found a new and shining track.

Here was a man whom he could esteem. Here was a famous man who was what every man should be.

He went to the library, hoping to find Mr. Wright's novels there. And most of them were there. He had searched vainly in a former time for the works of Turgenev and Meredith and Flaubert; but this he now forgave, and he thought with pride of the library, his library in his school, that stacked its shelves with the thoughts of great men. He chose a novel and began to read.

At first he thought the book was all right. He read greedily but the farther he read, the more he was filled with doubt; until at last he shut the book and strove to think. There was something wrong here. There was something terribly empty and silly about these pages but he could not tell what it was. He opened the book and read again. He came to this:

> He was really a fine looking young man with the appearance of being exceptionally well-bred and well-kept. Indeed the most casual of observers would not have hesitated to pronounce him a thoroughbred and a good individual of the best type that the race has produced.
> "——Barbara," he cried, "don't you *know* that I love you? . . . Your desert has taught me many things, dear, but nothing so great as this—that I want you and that nothing else matters. I want you for my wife."

These words and other words like them awoke in Vridar a sense of pain. He felt strangely choked and betrayed. He could not have told why. But somehow, the book had taken a common experience, a sweet and lovely experience, and had made it indecent and silly. The man was a sawdust creature, that was all. He was a shop-window dummy and words came out of him as they might out of a phonograph and there was no meaning in the words. And the desert, vast and terrible in its beauty: could it teach no greater lesson than that!

He returned the book to the desk and went home. He sat on his bed, remembering the novelist's earnest face and his ringing words. And he felt now as he had felt during his high school years, that life was shifting sand under his feet and a great desolation to the end of his road; and that no matter how bravely he fought, alone and unheeded in his small bitter world, he would break in some desperate hour and be forever lost.

VII

WHEN April flowered and the city became a garden of green on the mountainside, Vridar took long walks, lonely and meditative walks, and strove to see his place in life. To be a high school principal was not his dream now. He wanted a more dignified, a more austere, profession than that, and he cared little what it would pay in dollars if it paid a great deal in self-respect. He thought of authorship, a field in which a man could build magnificently beyond the reach of death, but he doubted his intensity and power. The sweetness and light of surfaces he had no interest in and the dark depths of being he did not understand. Again and again he thought of medicine, because doctors, it seemed to him, were among the noblest of ministers; and one day he went to a big room in a building that smelled of acids and ether. He was sickened by what he found there.

A student of anatomy spread a rubberized cloth on a dead Negro and then sat on the Negro and ate his lunch. In a big vat, Vridar saw another dead man, and he shuddered at the sight. This was called the Chamber of the Stiffs. The whole room reeked of death and alcohol.

And while these students ate their lunch, Vridar heard them make jest of this Negro, and of this other man, a murderer who had been convicted and shot.

"Hear this guy!" said the student perched on the Negro. "He let off a hell of a squawk."

"Maybe he isn't dead," declared another. "Whack him on his casa innominata."

"He's rumbling," said the perched student. "His Haversian canals. The bloke is full of air."

Another student came over and pulled the cloth back from the head. "He was sure a big bastard. What knocked him over?"

"Diabetes mellitus. And boy, he had it plenty. It took a ton of it to kill him."

"I'd like to cut him up. I've always wanted to carve a nigger. Now me, I've just got a dame what died of ovarian tumor."

"You're lucky," said a fourth, who was sitting on a vat, eating a sandwich. "You would get a woman."

"A dead woman. What can a guy do with a dead woman?"

"Some do plenty. Ever hear of necrophilia?"

"No, I'm not a learned man. I've just heard of liver fluke. . . . Well, what is it?"

"Never mind. It'd be dangerous to tell a guy like you."

Vridar, meanwhile, was moving about the room, pretending he was only mildly curious. He envied these lusty youths who could make a jest of the horrible. He felt an awful nausea in his stomach and he returned to the door and waited there, ready to flee.

"Over in that jar," said one, addressing Vridar, "is what you looked like twenty years ago. It has a tail."

They all glanced at Vridar and another student spoke.

"Sure, we all had tails."

"You looked like a rabbit."

"Like a fish first. Then like a rabbit. Then like a monkey."

"You still look like a monkey."

"He was born too soon."

"Say, this nigger is squawking again. When I move he lets off a big sigh."

"Get off of him, you fool. You're right on his stomach. You're killing him."

"That's all right. He ought to be killed."

"He'll stand up in a minute and knock you over backwards. He used to be a prize-fighter."

"The hell he did. Well, if he acts up with me I'll shove him back into the vat." And the one sitting on the Negro drew an apple from his pocket, wiped it on his shirt sleeve, and began to eat.

Knowing that he would vomit soon, Vridar went into clean air. No, he could never be a doctor. He could never cut up the dead and the living. Not without pain could he wring the neck of a chicken; he would swoon away if he ever laid open the belly of a man.

And he thought of law, too, but the students of law on this campus were so aggressive and self-assured, so emotionally calm and shrewd, that he gave up all notions of law. Only teaching was left to him. In some college or university he would be a great and wise leader. He would not dodge the truth or maneuver for advancement or heap into the hours the dull tautology of his notebooks.

For days he brooded on this vision, and then, almost frenzied with high purpose, he dedicated to it his life. He would teach with courage and honesty; and this resolve became, second only to one that stood far ahead of him, the mightiest of his years. If he could have foreseen the bewildering struggle into which it would lead him, he would have chosen, it may be, another plan; but he did not foresee, and having decided the matter he felt a great relief, as if a splendid road lay before him.

On every Sunday now he would climb to the northern peaks and sit here a long while, looking over mountains and valleys toward his own home. The buttercups were out now. Blue-birds and finches, warblers and meadowlarks, were in every bush and tree. The hills of Antelope were turning green and upon these hills, by the looped and dusty highway, lived Neloa Doole. When he went home in June he would pass very close to her house. She was sixteen now. He had not seen her for two years but he knew she would be tall and queenly, with long hair like a mantle upon her back.

He thought he should write to her and he phrased a letter on his journey down. But he did not send it. He had written a hundred letters and had posted none of them. He hoped she was not going to dances and riding about, as many Antelope girls did, with drunken men. He wished she would go to school, because his wife, like himself, would have to be a lover of books.

A week later, there came from his sister Diana a short letter. It said:

> Dear Vreed, everything is about the same on the ranch. It looks like an early spring. Father is getting out wood and mother is cleaning her coops. There isn't any news.
>
> I guess you're still interested in Neloa Doole. I don't like to be a tattletale but I think you ought to know some things. She's running around with Dave Wolf. You know what Dave is. He'll have Neloa in trouble if she doesn't look out. I've heard it said she is pretty wild. I only know what I hear and I just write this in case you'd like to know.
>
> Your loving sister,
> DIANA.

Vridar read the letter and began to shake. He read it a dozen times, and the implications, it seemed to him, became more horrible with each new reading. He knew Dave Wolf: a lewd sandy man deserted by his wife and given to all sorts of devilment. He could not believe that Neloa was going with him. Still, here was Diana's letter and Diana would never lie. She was only fourteen but she was a serious little body and she kept a searching eye to her brother's welfare.

Vridar took the letter with him and walked for hours. From time to time he would pause to read again and thereupon would go swiftly, his thoughts in a storm. He had never known until now how intensely, how inexorably, he loved Neloa, or with what earnestness he had chosen her as his wife. That her running about was wholly innocent, he never doubted. She was only having a little fun. Nevertheless, it was very undignified of her, very stupid of her, to be seen with Dave.

Returning to his room, he wrote a letter to Neloa, and then

another and another, until he had nine of them: striving, with each new effort, to say with tact and firmness what he had to say. The letters, it seemed to him, became more feeble and childish with each new attempt. He read them, with his doubt multiplying its anguish. He went out and walked again and came back and wrote. And at last he chose this one:

Dear Friend: I have been told that you are going with Dave Wolf. That is your business, of course, and not mine; but I think you should know that he has already contaminated young girls and that he has no decent interest in you. You are young and thoughtless and I hope you will think the matter over and see that I am right.

Love as ever,
VRIDAR.

The word contaminated he had recently acquired. His use of it was a pompous gesture, calculated to impress upon her his adventure into more lordly fields. Aside from this, his letter was an earnest appeal, almost a prayer, straight from his heart.

After he had posted the letter, he again walked, striving to put down his jealousy and forget his grief. If Dave seduced her, Vridar resolved to kill him. He would toss a gun to him, in the manner of strong men everywhere, and they would blaze away until one of them dropped. He knew, of course, that he would do nothing of the kind. Just the same, it was good to think of doing it and to gaze in fancy at the man, sprawled and still.

Of his former ideals, he had only one that had not been laid upon by the rigors of disillusion. He still believed that Neloa was sweet and pure. And she was his. She had belonged to him, she had been the loveliest glory in his dreams, ever since that morning, nine years ago, when he saw her in the road. Faith in God, faith in college, this he could lose and the loss of it he could endure; but to lose faith in Neloa, this would lie beyond his strength.

I'm silly, he reasoned. I'm upset over nothing at all. She has gone to a dance with him and has been thoughtless, but she is still all right. And he drew a long breath. Neloa was too inscrutable, too proud, to give herself to any but the man she loved. She had a mother who would admonish and guard her. She had an alert father who would protect his own.

But back in his room the doubt returned. He paced the floor in utter wretchedness and wondered what he should do. . . . He would write to Diana, that was it: asking her to be very explicit, to declare in plain words exactly what she knew. How did she know Neloa was going with Dave? Who had seen her with him, and when, and where? Was it not all a lot of rumor? Who told these stories and to whom and why?

Four days later an answer came. It said:

> Dear Brother, your letter sounds like you don't think I told the truth. Have I ever lied to you? Everyone in Antelope knows she's going with Dave. She's been teaching the Nevel kids this winter and Dave was up there for three days and just him and Neloa was there with the kids alone. I know this is true because father was out there and saw them.
>
> Of course I'm not saying Neloa has done any wrong. I don't think she has. I just wrote to tell you because I thought you would like to know. If you don't care about it I won't mention it again.
>
> DIANA.

If he didn't care about it! Upon one clause—*I don't think she has*—Vridar fixed his burning eyes. He stared at it until he could see only a black line in a mist. Well, Neloa was all right. She was playing with very thin ice but she was all right. And with terrible impatience, he waited for a letter from her.

Two weeks passed and none came. Goaded and desperate, he sent another warning, a little sharper of tone. And he waited again. With no interest in school now, with no interest in anything save this one dilemma, he moved about like a dazed person occupied by one thought. He deliberated leaving school and going home. He thought, indeed, of innumerable things to do, all of them very childish, all of them frenzied and mad. He lost his appetite for food and he was so distracted that he could not sleep. After the postman had come, bearing nothing for him, he would walk through the city and over the hills; or he would go to the post office, intending to ask, "Are you sure there is not a letter here for me?" and then turn away, furious with self-loathing; or he would stand by dance-halls and listen to the music until stricken with tears.

And in an hour when he had abandoned all hope a letter came. It was only a short note in girlish scrawl. In all his years afterward, it stood in memory as sharp and clear as flying geese in a vague sky. This is what it said:

> Antelope, Idaho
> May 14, 1916
>   Dear Friend:- If you don't like my gait (gate) don't swing on it.
>   NELOA DOOLE.

PART TWO

Vridar listened patiently and meditated on the hunger and loss in Telv's eyes. And then he said:

You're the sort of fool I used to be. Tons of sentimental mush have been written about the country girl. The Maud Mullers, raking the new-mown hay! Wordsworth's highland maidens! And on the covers of magazines, all the innocent-eyed creatures, standing by sheaves of corn or with their tresses flying in a wind or with a lot of lilies in their arms!

You're cynical, said Telv.

Cynical? All right. But I no longer have Anglo-Saxon notions about women. I've out-grown the cult of the virgin. I don't get into a monastic fever about chastity. Chastity, Telv, is the silliest vice among the virtues and you should have learned that. . . . Do you know why men demand chastity?

Keep it to yourself! I'm sick of hearing all life explained in terms of emotional leprosy!

You're sick, Telv: that's it. . . . Well, find you a virgin. But don't go to the country for her. Go to bedlam. A lot of them are there.

Telv got his hat and went to the door but he came back. He looked at Vridar.

Where's your gin? he said. I want another drink.

I

·

SUMMER was warm and full on Antelope now. The lower hills flanking the hamlet of Poplar were a gray desolation, but they were always so, being little save sand dunes and coyote nests. Rising above them in the east was a rolling prairie of green draped in shimmering haze, and beyond was a great arc of mountain, sculptured in purple and black. Over in the northeast where the bowl of his home lay with the river flung like an arm around it, Vridar could see clouds like white floating islands. Beneath those clouds was awful quiet.

When he came to Antelope Creek he paid the mail carrier with whom he had ridden and set his bags by the roadside. Across the six miles between him and his home he would have to walk. But he was in no hurry and he went off into a cove with his bags and sat in thought. He was curious to know how he felt, now that he was so close to that spot where he had spent the bitter summers of childhood and youth. Would its power seize him as in former returns and shake him with the old dread, or had the last nine months almost set him free?

And for another reason, too, he sat here. Not far away he could see the log shack where Neloa lived. He wanted to see her and not be seen and to discover if his love for her was only a fancy. She was nowhere in sight. He stared at the place, thinking of her as walking in that yard, down that road; sleeping under that dirt roof or sitting in that swing: striving with each of these pictures to make it seem real that she lived there. After a little while he became aware of his furious heart and he knew that he loved her and this was all that he wished to know.

He left the cove and climbed a hill and came to another glen not far from her house. Her father was in the yard, the furtive Indian-looking Tim Doole, and her mother, a large gaunt woman with tragic eyes. Then he saw her brothers and sisters and he lay on his belly and watched. They were all running about and shouting, trying to get a beast into a corral. Vridar was sick with misgivings now. Neloa was not there, else she, too, would have been in sight. She was off somewhere with Dave. For two hours he waited, hoping for a vision of her. Then he rose to his feet, hating her and hating himself, and turned homeward with his bags. And as he trudged through sagebrush and across wheat fields, he became certain of one thing: if Neloa was to be his wife—and he could imagine himself with no other girl—he would have to act at once. If he did not, she would marry another, and he would be cast into bachelorhood. He would have to meet her and declare his love and ask her promise, and then he could see to it that she behaved herself.

But where to meet her, and how and when, was another matter. If he knew how to dance, his problem would be simple. If he had a team and buggy, he could take her for a drive, but his father had no buggy and no team that he could use. And Vridar was afraid to call at her home. . . . He devised a plan, and though it seemed to him very childish it was all he could think of. He would give a party in his mother's home. Neloa would be invited and others, and if she came, he would go into the woods with her and tell his love. That, he reflected, would be a lovely, a most romantic, way.

Having settled the matter, he went swiftly, eager to reach his home. He wanted to learn if its old power endured. And as the upper benchland came in sight, Black Canyon and Burns, the river and the Bridwell place, he knew that it did, for the old fear was heaped upon his heart. If he had spent all his life in a hospital, and then had gone into fresh air and returned, the smell of ether and medicines and sickness could not have been more vividly real than this power, impalpable and odorless, that claimed him now. Though a thing apart from sight and smell, these, nevertheless, were the mask behind which it lived. It was not the river but it was inseparable from the river's sound. Out of yellow sunlight, out of song and foliage and the smell of flowers, it came to him and built its prison; until he walked at last as a man entering the solitary, as a man weary of hiding, returning to his cell. And he realized that this power which had always been his nightmare would have to be broken, if he was ever to be a free man, by an effort more tremendous than he now had strength for. Nine months away from it had been nothing at all. Years of absence, he imagined, would lead him to triumph; but in this he erred. And nothing more amazed him, in later years, than the way in which he conquered this awful possession of his soul.

As he walked now he felt more and more oppressed, borne down, defeated. He fought against the power, knowing that his struggle was useless. Fetching a quick breath, he would shrug, trying to shake it off; and for a moment, indeed, he would. He sang songs and thought of his college books, and he made of his mind a map of far countries, strange shores: striving to grasp and hold that detachment which alone could be his strength. But this force was like a body of water: he could strike out and so, for an instant, achieve a vision of freedom; but the water would close in, patient and inescapable.

In the mountain southwest of his home lay a wedge-shaped canyon, as if a section had been cut and lifted out; and on the brink of it he sat for a long while. He looked down into his homeland, staring at each strangely familiar thing. The old house stood deserted now and a new house of lodge poles stood among trees. He saw his mother enter a dugout coop and then appear and go to the stable. He saw his father down in the marshland, digging cress out of a slough. But it was at the river and the Bridwell place, the islands and the steaming springs and the upper wilderness of aspen and serviceberry, that he gazed most earnestly. It was the old dooryard where, crazed with fear, he had awaited his mother's return; and the high bank where Hankie and Jewel had played husband and wife; and the field where Jed had thrown him down and stuffed his throat with earth: at these and a thousand others, each a landmark in his pilgrimage of terror.

Whether he loved his home more than he hated, or hated more than he loved, he could not tell. It made him shudder

but it also made him weep. It filled him with dread but with
poignant yearnings also, because it was so dignified in its loneliness, and in its unpitying estrangement so much was lovely
and soft. He had suffered here almost beyond endurance, but
so many hours had been alive with flower-smell and bird-song,
with taste of wild rose petal and chokeberry and gilia,
with visions of blue mist and golden dawn: all these lying in
gentle beauty beyond the pain. The earth he loved and the
pine trees and the fields of clover and the meadows of straw-
berry blossom and dandelion; but superimposed upon all
these, like one photographic negative upon another, was the
weird pattern of delirium and blood and death. He looked
into memory at these and saw flowers beyond. He felt again
the terrible silence but within it was the fluting of larks. He
touched the yellow insanity of the sun and felt under it the
warm deep peace of earth. And so the picture shaped itself
and stood in memory, with friendliness in the brooding desolation, with ruthless violence in the loveliness and quiet.

He rose and took his bags and started down. And it seemed
to him now, as formerly, that his journey fell into prison, down
from the hills and the sky. A moment ago, he could look a
hundred miles into the west, but now the picture closed like a
shutter, until nothing was visible save his home and its river
and walls. He looked up at the roof of sky, feeling terrified
and lost. There was nothing to fear in this canyon but he went
headlong, glancing back, from time to time, to see if anything
pursued. And when he reached the house, he was white with
exhaustion and drenched with sweat.

He saw his brother first. Mertyl during the past year had
been a senior in high school. In Mertyl's letters Vridar had
sensed a change. For Mertyl had been president of his class
and had assumed a leading rôle in the school's drama and had
edited the yearbook. No longer a slave, credulous and humble,
he now looked at his brother with dubious eyes.

"Hello," Vridar said. "Where's mater and dad?"

"Outside, I guess."

For a long moment the brothers looked at each other. This
young man, Vridar realized, was a stranger to him and had

always been so. For seventeen years they had lived side by side, later sharing the same bed, cooking their own meals when away to school, and suffering in school a common derision; but they were strangers now.

Vridar left the house and went to the barn. On the way he met his father and grasped his powerful hand.

"Hello," he said.

"Hello," said his father.

"Where's mater?"

"She was here a minute ago. She's around somewheres."

Vridar found her sitting by a bush. She sprang up and came to him and he folded her in his arms. He kissed her hair and her tired face and then held her off to see.

"How's mater?" he said.

"Oh, I'm all right. How's my son?"

"All right, I guess."

They went to the house, neither speaking, and Vridar felt ill at ease. His mother, too, was a stranger and had been since his birth.

When they entered the house, Diana came from a bedroom. She ran over to Vridar and kissed him and then drew back.

"How's my old sis?" he asked.

"Your old sis is all right."

Vridar sat down and he knew that the whole family was watching him. Mertyl smiled a little, his eyes shrewd and appraising; and the others, too, searched him for change. He writhed under the scrutiny and turned in his chair.

"Glad to be home?" his mother asked.

"Yes, I guess so."

"You guess so! Ain't you sure?"

"Well, sure I am."

"How you like college?" Diana asked.

"Oh, it's all right, I guess."

"You don't sound like you care very much."

He looked at his parents and he saw in their eyes what he had seen there before: pride in education and knowledge, pride in their daughter and sons. He had always returned from school disappointed in what he had found. It had been so in Annis, in Rigby, and it was so now. But knowing how proud they were and how they had slaved to send him away, he had never told them the truth and had always pretended that schooling was a glorious thing. Reading their doubts now, he said:

"Sure, college is a grand thing. Everyone ought to go."

That was better. The doubt left their eyes.

"What you learnun about?" asked his father.

"Oh, English and economics and sociology. . . . Nature study."

Joe and Prudence looked at each other. Their glance said, "That is very fine, indeed." They looked at him.

"Mertyl," Prudence said, "has been a leader this year." She looked at Mertyl who had always stood in his brother's shadow.

"Yes, he wrote me about it."

There was a long silence. It was the silence of strangers who were growing more strange. For the homecoming of her sons, Vridar saw that his mother had cleaned and repapered the house; and of a photograph of him and Mertyl, she had had an enlargement made. It showed two young men, lean and pale of face, very earnest in their mouth and eyes. They looked as if they had never smiled or had an amusing thought. An awful seriousness filled the picture from top to bottom and from side to side.

"You like it?" Prudence asked.

They all looked at the photograph.

"I guess it's all right," Vridar said. "They look terribly serious."

"They are serious. You'n see they have big serious thoughts."

In his face and in the face of Mertyl, Vridar saw an earnest credulity, a weird zeal, that annoyed him. He was not what he had been a year ago. No, indeed: he was a world-weary skeptic now.

He said he guessed he would go out and see how things looked and he left the house. Towser was an old dog now with a lot of gray in his hair. King, second in favor of all beasts here, was graying also and looked shaggy and forlorn.

He was the most intelligent horse Vridar had ever known. Formerly, when at the sawmill, he would escape and come to the river; but he would not plunge in blindly as other horses did. He would choose his landing and then go up the river, looking across, from time to time, as if to judge the speed of the water, the distance to the far side. Other horses got lodged under a high bank or pitched into whirlpools or bashed against rocks. But King was too foxy for that.

Vridar stroked his heavy mane, much too thick and long for so small a horse. He was a grotesque fellow, being very handsome in his head and neck and very ugly elsewhere. And he was cynical, too. While Vridar stroked him, King looked about for a halter, suspicious of such kindness; and after a moment he walked away and then looked back.

While standing here, Vridar saw a coyote in the meadowland. He went to the house and Joe grasped his rifle, and the father and sons and dog were off to the chase. Joe sat where he could overlook a wide clearing and Vridar and Mertyl with the dog entered the jungle. Towser picked up the scent and was off. In a few moments he entered the clearing at full speed, and Joe, who was three hundred yards from him, fired one shot. Vridar and Mertyl came out and found Towser dead, with a bullet almost in the center of his forehead. They stared in consternation at the dog, "My God!" Vridar cried. Joe came over, thinking he had shot the coyote.

"Good God!" he said.

They all loved this dog but it was Vridar who loved him most. Years ago, terrified and weeping, he had gone for the cows and it was Towser who had gone with him; and in many an hour it was Towser, more than anything else, that had kept him from going mad. It was Towser who had been the friendliest thing in his life. And now he was dead.

Vridar gathered the dog in his arms and carried him to the house. Prudence reproached Joe but he needed no reproach. His grief, too, was deep. They all looked at the dog and they were all silent. Vridar felt tears on his cheeks and he went away for a little while; and then he got a spade and dug a grave. He put Towser into a box and lowered him into the

grave and he let the sod fall gently; and he and Mertyl sat by
the mound and looked at sunset, burning the sky.

"I feel like I'd lost my best friend," Vridar said.

"Yes," said Mertyl.

For a long while they did not speak again and in silence
they went to the house. Supper was eaten and in silence the
family went to bed. Vridar could hear the river and a great
wind in the trees, the terrible haunting sounds of his childhood; and he saw in memory one hour and another on the
wild desolate hills when he had run, sobbing with terror, and
Towser had run at his side. He left his bed and went to the
grave. He remained here all night.

II

·

A S THE days passed, golden and lazy, he tried to lose himself in work. He tried to be cheerful and now and then he
jested or attempted to laugh. His mother said to him:

"It sounds funny, son, to hear you laugh. Let's hear you
laugh again."

"Why? Didn't you ever hear me laugh before?"

"Not much. I don't seem to remember any time."

"I can't remember, either. I guess I never did."

And she said, too, that something was preying on his mind.
What it was, she could not tell. He went around like one in a
trance and she wanted to know what bothered him.

"Nonsense!" he cried. "Nothing bothers me."

"I know, son. You can't fool me that way." He looked at her,
wondering how much she knew. "Why don't you tell me? You
used to tell me everything."

"I never told you very much. Anyway, I've got to stand on
my own legs." She said he would always be her baby, her lit-

tle man, as he used to be. This annoyed him. He frowned at her, remembering his dark years.

"Tell mother. I want to know." She came over and put arms to his neck. She said he was her sweetheart and would always be and this statement filled him with rage.

"Don't!" he said, and he pushed her away.

"I know," she said. "It's Neloa. Son, are you really in love with her?"

"I don't know." He flushed and went to the door.

"Then you should go and see her. I don't like to say this but she's gettun a bit wild."

"That's all gossip! Why do you listen to gossip!"

"Well, mebbe it is, mebbe it isn't. If there's smoke, there's fire."

"You don't like her. That's the trouble with you."

"Why, son! For shame. I've always liked her. But she's very young and I don't think her father watches her."

He paced the room, wishing he could invoke God's wrath on gossip. In spite of her curt note, she was still sweet and pure and he would thresh anyone who said she was not.

"I been a-thinkun," his mother went on, "you could have her here. A dance or a party or something. If I ask her I think she'd come."

"Would you? Ask her here, I mean?"

"I guess it would be all right."

"When?"

"I could ask some others, too. You could find out then if you loved her. . . . Why son, you're shakun all over!"

"I'm not!" he said, and bolted outside.

And so the stage was set, the plot laid; and Vridar, unable to eat or sleep, built all his life to the meeting. The party was to be on the Fourth of July. Diana went out to the Antelope Hills, riding a wild mustang called Fury; and she invited a dozen young persons, including Neloa, and rode home. During her absence, Vridar was unable to think at all. He prowled about as if crazed; he went up the dugroad, hoping to meet his sister; he lost himself in a leafy shelter and sat there for an hour, trying to quiet his heart. He could not believe that Neloa would come. In his life, there could be no such wonder as that. Neloa here, in his home—or with him alone in some solitary fragrant place? Impossible! She would not come. She would write another impudent note and that would be the end of his dream. "If he wants to see me, tell him where I live." That would be all.

When he heard Diana coming, he leapt from the shelter and ran to meet her. She came up, her horse prancing madly, and Vridar circled round her, his whole being listening for her words. But she only grinned and said nothing at all.

"Is she coming?" he cried.

"No, she won't come."

He drooped. He felt as if all life had been knocked out of him. His face was so woebegone and his body so limp and ridiculous that Diana laughed.

"You lied!" he shouted, and ran stiff with new hope. "She is coming, isn't she?"

"Mebbe."

"Why mebbe?"

"If she'n get away."

"Di, how did she act? Tell me! For God sake!"

"Oh, she just smiled and said she'd like to come."

"Who—who did you say invited her?"

"You. I said you wanted her to come."

"Honest? And what did she say?"

"I told you, darn it. She said mebbe."

"Di, what else did she say?"

"Oh, I can't remember everything was said. We talked quite a while."

"Did she mention me?"

"I don't remember she did."

"What else did you talk about? Tell me. Di, please!"

"Oh yes, she asked had you got back from college."

"And what did you tell her?"

"I told her you had, of course." Diana stared at him and then laughed merrily. "What you shakun for?"

"I'm not!" He looked down at his pitiable legs. "Di, what did you tell her?"

"Why, I told her you got home when you did and you liked college all right and you was dyun to see her."

"You did! And what did she say?"

"Oh, she said she guessed you'd live."

"You liar! . . . Is that all she asked about me?"

"All I'n remember."

"And is she coming the night before and stay all night?"

"Mebbe."

He approached his sister but the horse veered wildly and stood on its hind legs.

"Tell me," Vridar said, imploring her across the distance, "you think she'll come?"

"I guess. If she don't get sick or anything."

Vridar's sigh was long and full. "Thanks," he said, and he went off alone with the delirious joy of his heart. Everything around him seemed tender and sweet and good. There was no darkness now, no fear. There was only rapture that wanted to spill out of him and bubble and purl like a brook; only a fluttering ecstasy, full of music and light. It swam in him like wine and poured its floods through his thought, heaped its unendurable splendor around his heart. He wanted to shout and sing; to run in the bewildering white light of this wonder, ravishing this one certainty, breathing it, drinking it, crying its name.

He went over the hills, frisking and capering and spending his joy in wild fierce nonsense, and anyone seeing his transports would have thought him mad. He embraced trees or climbed them and tumbled down. He scaled a ledge of stone and went shouting like a lunatic after a hawk; leapt over bushes and fell and then gurgled with pure delight. But there was no outlet for the tides that shook him. He was wound up and he struck about him and howled, stood on his head, turned somersaults, or loped on hands and knees and barked. Gesturing at the sky, he addressed to it a burning rhapsody of love and promise, letting out of him all the bitter loneliness of his years. . . .

After an hour his mood changed suddenly as if a light had been turned off and he walked in darkness like an old man. He was convinced now that she would never come. She would be sick or her mother would be sick or someone in the family would die. And he reproached himself now for having been a wild fool. He sat down in horrible disappointment and wondered what he should do.

When he came in to supper, he looked so haggard that his mother was alarmed. Mertyl and Diana stared at him.

"Son, what's the matter? Where you been?"

"Oh, out and around."

"What has upset you?"

"I'm not upset!" he shouted. "What's the matter you people, anyway?"

"Son!"

"Don't son me! Let me alone, will you!"

"He's just in love," Diana said.

Vridar did not eat. He entered a tiny bedroom and crawled into bed. He could hear the family in the kitchen, talking of him; and a little later his mother entered and sat on the bed. She took one of his hands and stroked his hair back.

"Son, what is it? You've acted so queer ever since you come home. . . . Tell mother."

"There isn't anything to tell! Why do you keep saying there is?"

"Because I know. Son, do you really love Neloa?"

"Oh, I don't know! Don't ask such silly questions!"

"You love her a lot, don't you?"

"I hope not."

"She'll be here soon. So what is troublun you?"

"She won't come!" Vridar cried, and choked with self-pity.

"Of course she'll come. Diana said she seemed very glad."

"She has no way to come."

Prudence studied his face. Again she stroked his hair.

"Well, Diana can go and fetch her. Does that make you feel better?"

"Nothing can make me feel better," he said, speaking as if

he had lived a thousand years. "But I'm all right. I'm just sick of life."

"I don't like to see you this way. It makes me unhappy to see you unhappy."

He looked up at her tired patient face. He sat up and kissed her cheek.

"I'm all right. The ranch just makes me blue, that's all."

"I know, son. Well, you won't come here many more times." Her eyes filled with tears.

"Now," he said, "who's worrying?"

"No, I'm all right. I just think of this place without you children. I'll never be able to stand it. . . . Well, have a good sleep now. I know she'll come."

She kissed him and patted his hands and left the room. He thought of her for a long while: her devotion and slavery and her dreams. "I'm a hell of a son!" he thought. "I'm too selfish to live. I ought to be dead. . . ."

He spent three days and nights of intolerable waiting. He slept little and ate little and he felt very silly and futile. Diana was amused, Mertyl was amused and scornful, and his parents were full of doubt. Though common peasants of earth, they were very proud and they had hoped he would marry a college girl. They liked Neloa and her family, but the Doole clan was a thriftless and nomadic lot, indelibly marked with Sioux Indian and with no more interest in education than they had in the Baffin Islands. Neloa was all right, his mother said. She was a sweet and lovely girl. But would he be happy in marriage with a girl who had been only through the eighth grade?

"You must think about such things."

"If she's my wife," said Vridar, "she'll go to school."

"Well, that would be all right. I've heard she likes school."

And Prudence told Joe that Neloa would go to school and Joe's stare became less dubious. If she went to school, she would be an all right daughter-in-law; but he didn't want his sons to marry ignorant nobodies.

This talk of marriage bewildered Vridar. He was interested

in love, and marriage, for the present at least, had nothing to do with it.

"I'm not planning to marry," he said, scowling at his mother. "I'm only a kid yet." And he glanced at Mertyl, in whose eyes of late he had seen only cool derision. He saw only derision now. "Love and marriage," he said, "are only fiddlesticks. Bosh on them." And he shrugged and looked at Mertyl again. Mertyl's derision had spread into a thin smile.

Diana saddled two horses and said she was going to get her woman. "I'll fetch her," she said, "if I have to rope her."

Vridar began to tremble and he found a chair and sat down. It was very absurd, as even he could see, for his family to act as if Neloa must be brought here, dead or alive. For three days now, Diana had been jesting of what she would do. "If she says she won't come, I'll hog-tie her and drag her here." And again: "Vreed, cheer up. I'll herd her over here just like she was a wild cow. I'll fetch her, don't you fret."

And here Vridar sat on his heels—preposterous Romeo, shivering clown!—watching his sister prepare to fetch the bride. He was the one to go. It was very silly to send Diana, as if he were afraid, or as if he were an Asiatic lord, recruiting for his harem. And he rose and left the house, detesting himself.

Diana mounted Fury and grasped the lead-rope of another beast. She smiled and waved goodbye. "Cheer up, brother. In three hours she'll be here, lookun at you." He watched her go up the dugway and over the mountain and into the sky. And then, throbbing with excitement, he went off and hid.

While in hiding, he dramatized his meeting with Neloa, giving to her a blushing coyness and to himself a princely air. He would be superbly cool and dignified. When he spoke to her, his voice would be firm and quiet, his English perfect; and she would be a little appalled by his magnificence.

But he knew he would be nothing of the sort and he came out of hiding like a scared thing and began to walk. He climbed the mountain, reproaching himself as he went: thinking with scorn of his limp and irresolute manhood, of the birdlike fluttering within. He was a great fellow, indeed! "I'm all right," he said. "What do I care? If she doesn't like me, what the hell do I care! . . . Will, when looking well won't move her, looking ill prevail? . . . I'm all right." But he was not all right. The more he reasoned with himself, striving for poise, the more he shook and gurgled, as if full of deadly ills. Talking to himself was of no use and walking did no good. And excitement gave to his voice an adolescent squeak that was too silly to think of.

He stood at the top of the dugway and looked west. As punishment for his want of strong manhood, he hoped she would not come, that he would never see her again. That would serve him right. No woman should ever look at him, save to laugh, or ever speak to him, save to ask why he shook. They should say, "You must have a fever. Look, will you? how he shakes around. Isn't he silly!" They should say, "Here, boy. You'd better take a physic. You'll fall to pieces in a minute. . . . " Yes, that was all he deserved.

And while he stood in the road, torturing himself with ridicule, his heart leapt to his throat and caught there. Not far down the road came two riders, Diana and Neloa, and with a gasp he fled. He went down the road like a hare and then left the road and went pellmell, jumping over bushes and trying to get lost. Under a bank he came to a stop, wheezing like a foundered nag; he mopped his brow and fanned himself. She was coming! . . . Her glance would say, "Well, you invited me. Why do you sit there and shake all over?" Ah, Lord! And what would he do? He would writhe in his chair and hesitate.

Going quietly down through trees, he came to the grove east of the house. He stopped again, wondering what he should do. It would be best, it seemed to him, to pretend that he had work: to get a spade and set posts, as if he had forgotten Neloa was coming, or did not care. And he went to the house and got a shovel and came out to a fence and set to work. He dug a hole and set a post. He spaded at another hole but he could wait no longer; and he knew that he would sneak up guiltily like a spy to see what Neloa was like.

Round the trees he went, quietly as a fox, and came to the woodpile and hid in a bush. In a few moments the girls came to a halt within forty feet of him. Diana was talking but Vridar had no ears for what she said. His eyes, his whole being, was fixed on this tall lovely girl, with hair falling to her waist in dark splendor, with the light of a thousand mornings in her eyes. She was such a vision that he held his breath and this moment was one of the supreme and wordless moments of his life. With all his senses he devoured her. He saw her dark voluptuous beauty, heard her rich throaty laugh; felt her warm deep-bosomed womanhood; and in fancy touched her and trembled at the touch.

Then the girls went to the house and Vridar stole back to his work. He grasped the shovel and dug furiously, as if he had acres of labor to do; and his body was drunk and his senses swam in memory. He saw her again on the day when she first entered his life; and on the evening when she stood at his side in the school's contest, with her hair spilling round her; and on that winter night in Rigby when, after the show, she stood by the gate and looked at him. His whole life, it seemed, had been full of her, as, indeed, it had. . . .

"Vreed!"

For ten years he had loved her. He had loved others, too, but not with such earnest passion, not clear to the bottom of his soul. Helen he had loved, Norma he had loved. But Neloa he had worshiped. . . .

"Vreed! Hey, where are you?"

He turned and listened. For several minutes, he realized now, someone had been calling his name.

"What you want?" he asked.

Diana came through the trees.

"What you up to? Why don't you come in?"

"Come in! Hell, I'm working, can't you see?"

"I got a surprise for you."

"Never mind. I'm busy." He pretended that she spoke in riddles. He scowled at her and shrugged and the shrug ran through him like a shiver. "Can't you see I'm busy!"

"Listen, you big egg! Neloa is here."

"Oh, is she?" he said.

"Why don't you come in?"

"So she came after all, did she?"

"I made her come. She howled all the way up here."

He went over to his sister and looked at her. He could pretend no longer.

"Di, did she want to come or not?"

"Sure. She was crazy to come."

"Don't be smart!" he howled. "Tell me the truth."

"That's the truth. But she'll go back if you don't show up." She grasped his arm. "Come on."

He shook her hand off and retreated.

"Go on in. I'll come soon. Say I got to finish some work."

"Oh, your work can wait!"

"Di, don't be a fool. Please. I'll come in a minute."

Diana left him and went to the house. Vridar resolved to stay here until at ease, but the more he fought for control, the more he shook. In despair with himself, he grasped a barbed wire and jerked it and the barbs cut a furrow down one palm. He looked at the blood and he felt quieter now. Now he would have an excuse. He would enter the house, seeking iodine, and if he saw Neloa, he would affect surprise.

He went to the house and lingered at the door. He looked round him for a place to hide if he heard anyone coming. And then, after another long moment, he pushed the door open and stepped inside.

His mother came to the door and saw his bleeding hand.

"What you done?" she asked.

"Oh, cut myself a little. Where's the iodine?"

She searched for iodine and he searched, too, and from the living-room door, Diana rebuked him with a scowl. Prudence found iodine and poured it into the wound and while Vridar distorted his face with agony she bandaged his hand. He liked the pain: it was a small punishment for his cowardice. He wished he had cut his hand off.

To postpone his entrance into the living-room, he found fault with the bandage, asked his mother to use stouter cord, and in one way and another delayed the meeting. But at last, with his mother impatient and with Diana mocking from the doorway, he could pretend no longer. He had to enter now. But first he got a drink and brushed his hair a little. Crossing the room, he got his hat from the floor and hung it on a spike and then stepped outside to brush dust from his shoes. He came in, with his mother and sister watching him, and drank again, feeling more and more absurd, and suddenly, desperate and goaded, he swung and faced them and stalked in.

III

·

W ITHOUT looking at Neloa he crossed the room to the north wall and sat close to a chiffonier, hidden from Neloa's sight. His mother and the girls talked. He stared at the floor and answered questions in a word or a phrase. The sound of Neloa's voice, bringing to him, as it did, memories of other times and of a few priceless hours with her, made him shake, and to hide his emotion he moved back and forth or from side to side in his chair. His mother's eyes watched him closely: eyes full of compassionate amusement; and Diana mocked him outright.

She wanted to know if the cat had his tongue. She wanted to know if he was scared or if he was trying to act worldly.

"He's talked about you for weeks," she said, with that awful want of tact common to sisters. "Now he's dumb as a egg. Lordy, he hasn't slept a wink for four nights!"

"Yeah?" said Vridar, glaring at her.

And very suddenly he started and almost left his seat. Across the room from him was a large wall-mirror and when he glanced at it, for the first time since coming here, he saw Neloa watching him. "My God!" he thought, and was horrified. He had thought himself securely hidden and she had been watching him all the while! What had he done? What queer distortions of face, what agonized postures of body, had she seen? He felt a terrible rage. It had been mean and silly of her to spy on him.

But when he glanced again at the mirrored face, all the rage left him. She was smiling at him and her smile was friendly and warm. It was a little curious, a little amused, but it was all right. . . . He looked again and their eyes met and he blushed and turned away. Thereafter, from time to time, he glanced at her, and her gaze was always fixed on him. It was searching but not critical.

"Move out here," Prudence said. "Mebbe Neloa would like to see what you look like."

He scowled at his mother and then remembered that Neloa could see his scowl; whereupon, seizing his chair and wrenching it, he moved out into full view, feeling horribly exposed. Anyway, she could not see him in the mirror now. While affecting to examine his chair, he glanced at her, and he saw that she was still smiling, that her gaze was still very intent. He sat in utter wretchedness for a few minutes and then excused himself and bolted outside.

He did chores until after dark and when he came in he was thankful for pale lamplight. Sitting back to the wall and listening with all his being, he glanced at Neloa from time to time, giving her swift guilty appraisals; or he stared boldly when she turned her back. She was taller than he had thought she would be. She was more than five feet and a half but very graceful and queenly. Her body, his mother had said, was perfect; and he fed on her loveliness, wondering if this was so. Her bare arms seemed perfect, and her hands, too.

Once when she sat, her skirt was drawn above her knees; and Vridar glanced at her legs, not as an amorous lover but as a pious guardian who disapproved. He would teach her to keep her dress down. And once when she stooped, he saw the womanly fullness of her breasts; and this carelessness, too, he severely condemned. His own sister had been taught to stand with her heels together and not to sit with her legs crossed; to wear her clothes firmly, so they would reveal nothing; and not to bend over like a man but to sit gracefully when she recovered anything from the floor. Neloa's teaching, he reflected, had not been of much account; but he would take care of that. She was still young—only sixteen—and he could instruct her in the manners of a lady.

He went with Mertyl to bed and the girls slept in the living-room. While they undressed, he could hear them gurgle with nonsense, and once he heard Diana shriek, her voice running high and wild. At all this he scowled, wishing both would show more dignity and sense. He felt vaguely, but not as a clear admission, that shrieking girls were amorous girls, and the thought displeased him. He refused to think of any girl as amorous, preferring to believe that her mind dwelt above sex, aloof if not unaware. Nor was his own response in any way amorous. His love was so pure as to be almost impotent; and when at last he fell asleep, the most that his dreams dared, and all that they wished, was to be alone with her.

When he awoke the next morning he heard Neloa talking, and there came to him again the incredible wonder of her being here. He dressed and crawled through his window and went to chores. He came awkwardly to breakfast, content to be silent, to be speechless in his happiness. During the forenoon the family sat and talked, waiting for other guests, but none came. Then Prudence took Vridar aside.

Did he want to take a walk with Neloa, to be alone with her for a little while? Did he! Ah, Lord!

"I been thinkun," she said. "It would be nice to go across the river. You could walk up to the old millsite."

He left the house, his heart pounding like mad. What a golden mother she was! What a miracle it would be to walk with Neloa up the canyon, through huckleberry gardens and under the pines! Not far up was an old millwheel and a millstream: as in that song which spoke of these and first meetings and village queens. To walk with Neloa there, alone, with so much loveliness around, would be heartbreaking.

But first, of course, he would have to ask her to go. He could not ask her with the family present: there would be

Diana's giggle and Mertyl's scorn. He would have to be a clever rascal, plotting the matter to suit himself.

He went outside and prowled about, now looking up the road, as if he saw amazing things there; or now inspecting one thing and another, as if they needed mending; or now moving off swiftly, as if bent on an important errand. Then Neloa and Diana came out and went to the barn, lingered there a moment, and came back; and Vridar knew they were out here for him to speak. Prudence had spoken to Diana and Diana had entered the plot. But Vridar would rather have died. His heart was half out of him and his thoughts were like leaves in a wind. But he approached them, nevertheless, his face terribly earnest; and he said something, though he could never remember what. He maneuvered until he stood by Diana and then jabbed her ribs with an elbow. She cried and looked amazed.

"What's the idea?" she said.

Well, that sort of thing would never do. Diana knew all about horses but she didn't know much about love. . . . He strove to speak. He glanced at Neloa again and again and made an attempt; and then choked and burned and looked away. She was smiling at him. Her eyes were bright and mischievous, as if she found him a most engaging riddle. He tried again.

"I—I been wondering if you'd—would you like to take a walk?"

"I guess so," she said. "Where?"

"Oh," he said, looking desperately round him at all the canyons and peaks. "Anywhere. . . . We—I guess we could take a boatride."

"All right," she said.

"Sure," said Diana, "let's all take a boatride."

Vridar glared at her. A worse idiot, it seemed to him, he had never seen. . . . But the matter was settled: Diana said they would all take a boatride, and she ran off to find Mertyl, leaving Vridar and Neloa alone. Red with confusion now, and unable to speak, he stared earnestly at far mountains and heard the ridiculous pounding of his heart. Neloa's gaze was steady.

"You like college?" she asked.

"Oh, I guess it was all right."

He knew that she was still smiling and that her eyes were amused. Great God, he wished Diana would come!

"When does college start this fall?"

"September, I guess. I—I don't know exactly."

"Will you go this year?"

"Yes, sure. I guess so."

Then they were silent and Neloa still watched him and Vridar saw nothing at all. He was thinking of her curt note about her gate and his swinging on it. He could hear his heavy breathing and was annoyed. But remembering the note gave to him, though he could never have told why, a little ease, a little boldness and a little scorn. He swung and stared at her, and his gaze, for a moment, was so hard and searching that she looked surprised.

Diana now came, fetching Mertyl, who looked sardonic and bored. They all turned up the lane. At first Neloa walked with Diana, but Diana in her blunt way took care of that.

"Get back there!" she said, and pushed Neloa toward Vridar. "Mert, come up here. You're my feller today."

Mertyl walked ahead with his sister and Vridar and Neloa walked behind. Diana overflowed with gay nonsense and tactless quips but the others seldom spoke. Vridar kicked at the dust, feeling more and more ridiculous; or he glanced up at the sky, wondering if it might rain; or he stared at meadows of hay, noting their depth, trying to think of them. If a bird hopped out, he would turn to look at it, as though he had never seen it before: but in every instance it was only a robin or a chickadee. And all the while he was trying to seem at ease and casual, as if walking with a girl bored him a little.

They came to the boat and stopped. He bailed water out, glad for this brief refuge. It was Diana's notion, clearly enough, that they were all going across and have a look at the old millstream. Vridar watched her and when she looked at him he winked mysteriously.

"What you winkun at me for?" she asked.

When the boat was ready, Vridar set the oars and leapt out. Neloa stepped from the bank to the boat and her skirt was drawn up, showing part of one thigh. It was a lovely thigh but a most indecent exposure and Vridar was ashamed of her. Beyond any question, she would need a lot of teaching. . . . Then Diana moved to enter but Mertyl grasped her arm.

"You're staying here," he said.

"Like heck," said Diana, looking at him. "What you mean?"

"Beat it," Mertyl said to Vridar, and he held Diana's arm.

Vridar grasped the oars and shot the boat into deep water. Neloa sat facing him now. Her smile was inscrutable, a dimpling warmth on the surface of her thoughts; and her eyes were inscrutable, too. Vridar glanced at her and bent to the oars. A skillful hand with a boat, he was determined to amaze her with his deftness and strength; but he realized, after a moment, that she was not interested in his rowing. He abandoned his titanic efforts to pull the boat in two and luxuriated in a mild rage. There were girls, he reflected, who would have been astounded by his might.

When they reached the far bank, he anchored the boat and looked across. Mertyl and Diana were sitting like Indians on a stone. Neloa left the boat and he turned with her into a forest and in a few moments they were lost.

Of all times in Vridar's life, none surpassed in pure romantic glamour the two hours that he spent here. They were cloudless and infinite and perfect. He and Neloa walked on an old road and they said little, but no happiness before, none that came after, was deeper than this. It was enough, it was almost too much, to have her so near to him, and alone. Now and then, when a branch lay on their path, he lifted it aside; now and then he glanced at her lovely face; but in all else he only moved in a dream and marveled at the wonder of this hour. He never took her arm, never touched her, save by chance; and when her arm did touch him, or when, as once, she slipped and put a hand to his shoulder, the rapture that flooded him darkened his eyes. It surged through him in tides of blood and rolled in a surf of glory over his heart. While alone in these hours, he did not kiss her or have a conscious wish to do so. Out of the hunger of flesh, he distilled a spiritual ecstasy, and this, for the present at least, was enough.

When they came to the old mill, he knelt at the stream and drank and then washed his hands and she drank from his cupped palms. When her lips touched his hands, something went through him that was like flame. They sat on a grassy bank and heard the low murmuring of the stream, and they breathed the fragrance of bearberry and wild currants and fir; or they gazed up at the dark blankets of evergreen; or they looked at each other and smiled as children do.

Vridar felt more at ease now. His joy, intense and throbbing within, broke on a great sigh and he laughed. Neloa laughed, too, and he glanced at her and laughed again. Their laugh, he recognized, was a mutual recognition of his shyness, of his desperate wooing in Annis, and of a thousand other matters in which he had been too silly for words. He felt as if a darkness had been lifted away.

"Wonder if we should go back."

"I guess so," she said.

"I don't want to," he said. He faltered and the darkness closed round. He caught himself in retreat and he made himself say what had been on his tongue. "I want to stay here with you—just to be with you."

Her only answer was a smile. To such a confession, it seemed to him, a smile was not enough. He had offered his heart and she must have known that.

"We'n stay a little longer," she said.

Ah, that was better. She must love him if she wanted to stay. He looked at her and his stare was very devoted and realizing this he blushed. He grasped a stick and whipped at his legs.

"Someone ought to kick me," he said, and his laugh was strange.

"Why?"

"Oh, I'm such a queer guy." He rather liked calling himself a queer guy. He wanted to be inscrutable, too: a riddle that none could read. "I guess you think I'm funny, don't you?"

"A little bit," she said.

He stared at a dark mountain flank. He thought of an adventure in the last summer and spoke of it. Last summer, he said, he had killed a bear without hitting it, but he had never understood how. Perhaps he shot over its head and stunned it. Anyway, it rolled off a ledge and broke its neck. . . . He looked at her and he saw that she was not interested in his tale.

"What makes you think I'm funny?" he asked.

"Oh, I don't know. You just are."

"I hope you like funny people."

She looked at him and her smile was faint and baffling.

"I like you," she said.

They turned down the canyon, walking slowly; and the half-mile to Vridar was only a hundred yards. On their way down, not a word was said. He felt that they shared a common mood and that their way lay together through life. She was a little shy, of course; she was not used to being alone with men; and he liked her shyness and silence. . . . When they reached the river, Mertyl bawled at them.

"Hurry up! You been gone hours!"

They entered the boat and crossed, and when they came to the far bank, Mertyl rebuked again. Sitting here, he said, had been no fun. And that, Vridar reflected, was a great way for a brother to talk.

"I'm sorry," he said.

On their way down the lane, none of them spoke. Mertyl scowled ahead of him, and Diana walked very soberly, as if her day had been spoilt. Prudence left the house and came to Vridar. How, she asked, was Neloa going home? Did he not want to hike out and borrow his uncle's buggy and drive her to Antelope?

At such a prospect of heaven, he began to shake. He told his mother to watch Neloa and see to it that Diana did not run off with her. In feverish haste he ran to the barn and harnessed a team and then went up the mountain and over the hills.

"For why you want it?" Dock said. His eyes were large and cunning. "You takun a girl out?"

"Sure."

"Who? That Doole girl?"

"Maybe. What if I am?"

"All right," he said. His grin was big and round and lewd. "You'n take it. But none of your monkeyshines now. A lot of girls has learned things in them-there buggies."

Vridar dashed home with the ramshackle buggy lurching from side to side. He saw Neloa at the woodpile. He came up at a gallop, with the wheels squealing like a herd of pigs, with the boards of the seat clattering; and when he swung the team, the buggy spun round on two wheels. He fancied himself a wild and devilish fellow and he liked the consternation on his mother's face.

"Whoa!" he shouted, and sprang down from his chariot. But now all the boldness left him. He walked round the team, pretending that collars needed adjusting, that the neckyoke was broken, that a bridle was too large. When he could no longer fumble here, making a clown of himself, he came in sight and tried to speak. A horse snorted and this gave him another excuse. "Hey you!" he said, shouting like a schoolboy; and he was busy again, doing nothing at all.

"Son," his mother said, "Neloa is ready to go home."

"Just a minute!" he said, annoyed. He yanked at the belly-band and set it up a hole. Then Neloa came to the buggy and he moved to assist her but she sprang lightly up without his aid.

"You must come and see us again," Prudence said.

"Thanks. You should come and see us."

"We'll try to. But we're awful busy these days."

"Better hang on," Diana said. Neloa laughed.

"I will," she said.

These aspersions at the buggy made Vridar furious. He looked darkly at his sister and jerked at the reins. And then they were off. The buggy rattled and shook, and the wheels, turning on axles worn thin, wabbled drunkenly from side to side. He was so shamed by the vulgar squealing and the wired doubletree and patched tongue, the rickety seat and the lopsided dashboard, that he looked straight ahead of him for a long while and did not speak. They climbed the dugway and came to the benchland; they went down a dusty gray road, with the horses trotting now; and he looked to the north or the south, wondering of what he should talk. It was quite dark now and stars were out and the night was fragrant and warm. Once when the wheels on Neloa's side fell into a deep rut, she threw an arm to his neck, and ecstasy poured through him like wine. An impulse came up from his wild heart and found words, bold incredible words, which he had never dreamed he could utter.

"It's all right to keep your arm there," he said.

Her laugh was low and pleased.

"All right," she said; and she laid her arm across his shoulders, her hand almost to his cheek.

Rapture filled him and shook him and mist gathered to his eyes. For a half-mile they journeyed in this way, neither speaking a word. When the buggy lurched, her hand touched his cheek; and after a while, obeying another impulse, he pressed his cheek to her hand. Then he looked at her and he saw that her eyes were full of bright tenderness. Feeling bolder, he drew the horses to a walk; and he wished they could ride all night, forever and ever, with her arm against him. This was heaven, deeper and fuller than his dreams of it, and more than he deserved. A sweet vibrant ache lay in his breast and throat and rose in tears to his eyes. He had never been so happy before. He was never to be so utterly happy again.

Seeing ahead of him the Doole farm, he was driven to do something in an effort to hold this hour and make it eternal. If he let her go now, perhaps he would never see her again. He could never let her go, now. He loved her with all his strength and faith and hope; with her, life was a garden, beautiful and clean; without her it was desolation and he was lost. No, he must love her and worship her and care for her. And this, he told himself, was no spontaneous love, no passion of the hour: it reached back into his childhood, having its mighty roots there; it had grown into him, in the way that branches reach to a tree's heart, and it had given to him all the foliage and springtime that he had known.

But he doubted that she loved him and pride would not let him confess his own love. Yet he must speak. This blinding intensity, built out of his years, and so awful in its earnestness and power, was surging through him like his own blood. He looked off into darkness and strove to be calm. The whole world around him was a mist of softness, for his eyes were wet. And when at last he spoke, his voice was so strange, so broken, that he did not recognize it as his voice. He said:

"Neloa, if you loved a man, would you let him kiss you?"

"Yes," she said.

He gazed ahead of him, blinking his eyes fiercely to shed their tears. He moved as if tortured and spoke again.

"May I kiss you?"

Her answer, as before, was a low vibrant yes. But he did not kiss her at once. He thought of his questions, her answers, doubting that either had been spoken, wondering if he dreamed. Then he stopped the team. He turned to her, trembling in all his body, and drew her to his arms. She came willingly with a little sigh and her hair fell in glory round his face. He kissed her soft mouth and then pressed his cheek to her cheek.

After a few moments he released her and spoke to the team. A full moon rose now and everything was very clear and he could see far down the road. He clasped one of her hands and they rode to a corner and made a turn. And he spoke again.

"Neloa, do you love me?"

"Yes."

He could not believe this. Turning to her, he looked at her eyes, trying to read there the falseness or truth. They were dark luminous eyes with something in their depth that made him tremble. He looked away, his heart caught in his throat.

"Will you marry me?"

"Yes."

This he doubted also. Surely so much of heaven was not meant for him. He dreamed that she was here with her arm round him: this girl whom he worshiped, for whom he would have died. It was all a trance and he would awaken soon. He would find himself in bed after a night of dreams and life would be what it had always been. He pressed her hand and looked at her, trying to make the hour seem real.

"Are you sure? Neloa, be sure."

"Am I sure of what?"

"That you love me."

"I am sure."

"But it can't be!" he cried. "You've seen me only a few times. You've never thought of me."

"Oh, haven't I! How do you know that?"

"I know you haven't. . . . Have you?"

"Yes."

"No. Neloa, be serious, please. If you don't love me, send me away now! Tell me to go and I'll go!"

"I don't want you to go."

"How much do you love me?"

"Lots."

"As much as I love you?"

"Yes."

"You don't. You never will. You never could. . . . Tell me this: how long have you—loved me?"

"Oh, a long time."

"In Annis?"

"I guess so."

"When we went to the show in Rigby, did you love me then?"

"Yes."

"When will you marry me?" he asked, still tortured by doubt.

"When do you want me to?"

"Tonight. Will you marry me tonight?"

"Yes."

In a frenzy of joy, he drew her to him and kissed her again. Then they came to Neloa's home and Vridar stopped at the gate. He helped her down and then hitched his team to the fence, and they stood here by the gate for a long while. He held her to him, but not firmly, not with her legs touching his; and he searched her face, still goaded by a fear that he dreamed.

"Neloa, if you love me, please say it again."

"I love you," she said.

"But you—you're not impulsive like me. You don't—" He finished with a sigh. For a little while he studied her face. She was a very lovely girl, he thought. Her eyes were like a darkness of luminous velvet. Her hair was a black wonder hanging to her waist. Her teeth were the most perfect he had ever seen. "I wish," he said, and stopped. He trembled and shrugged. "Neloa, I wish I could tell you how I have loved you for years and years. But you wouldn't believe it. Nobody would. . . . And how much I love you now. You'll never know. You'll die without ever knowing. Tears came to his eyes and he looked at her through tears. "I—I worship you, Neloa! My God!"

He turned away and tried to shake his grief off but it surged up out of his dark years and he was overcome. Going to a post, he sat there and bowed to his knees. In a few moments Neloa came over and sat by him and put an arm round his neck. He kissed her hand.

"I'm silly!" he cried. "I hate myself! But you don't know! God, you don't know! . . . I have loved you so much!"

When his grief was spent, he rose and she came to him and they stood as before. He saw that there had been no tears in her eyes.

"We'll be married," he said. "We'll be happy. That is all I ask. . . . It's more than I'm worth."

She squeezed his hand. He drew her closer and kissed her lips and her eyes and her hair. The time was past midnight and she said she would have to go now.

"Stay a little longer!" he implored her. And he added, "When'll I see you again?"

"When you want to."

"No. I want to see you all the time. I'd rather die than leave you now." He thought of the work at home. "Next Sunday," he said. "I don't want to come to the house. Meet me on the road."

"All right," she said.

"Neloa, at one o'clock. You won't be late?"

"No, I won't be late."

"Just above the bridge."

"All right."

She turned away, smiling at him, and went toward the house. He felt sudden awful despair. It was as if she had gone and he would never see her again. He leapt the fence and ran after her.

"Neloa!"

"Yes?" she said, turning. He came up to her and he was trembling so that he could hardly stand. He looked at her, again searching her face and her eyes.

"Oh, Neloa, I hate to let you go!"

But he saw that she wanted to go. Instead of being resentful, as was his proud suspicious way, he thought her quite sensible, himself very silly, and he said goodnight and went back to his team. He watched her and when she came to the house she turned and waved to him. Then she entered and the door was closed and he was alone. He waited for a little while, hoping she would come out; and if she had returned, eager to see him, he would have been delirious with joy. But she did not come and Vridar sprang to the buggy and drove away. He drove through a wide gleaming night. His heart ached so that it choked him and now and again he stood up to get his breath. It felt as if a hand had reached into him and now lay within.

And while he rode home, there came to him in a sudden flash, as if lightning had filled his years ahead, a premonition that was terrible and dark. It could have been no more sharp and real if someone had spoken. But in an instant it was gone, and nothing remained but the deep fragrant night, full of memory and dream.

IV

•

FROM this July day until September 6, Vridar's life, save for two small incidents, was perfect. It was a cloudless interlude, an idyl of glory, of a kind he had never known and was never to know again. When he looked back upon it, from a later time, he saw it as a handful of golden days. He saw it as a cloud, bright and soft and nebulous, hanging between a darkness out of which it rose and another darkness into which it passed.

After reaching home on this first night, he lay awake until morning, passing in shining review the wonders of the last hours. A little after dawn, he heard Joe speaking to him.

"Time to get up. Fellers who go to dances have to pay the fiddler."

Mertyl awoke and stared at him. In his father's words as well as in Mertyl's dubious stare, Vridar perceived a touch of malice. The one envied him, having left all ecstasy behind; the other thought him foolish and held women in contempt. His mother, too, after he had dressed and entered the kitchen, regarded him with eyes that were a little caustic. Why, Vridar wondered, was love a subject, not only here but elsewhere, of ironic jest.

They all wanted to know why he had got home so late and what he had done. At the breakfast table they thrust at him, now with a veiled hint, now with a question; and he grinned at them and tried to seem at ease.

"I guess he's in love," Diana said. "It didn't take him long."

"In love!" said Prudence. "He's been in love a long time. . . . How long you been in love with Neloa, son?"

Vridar blushed and looked sheepish.

"I don't know," he said.

Joe's eyes were bright with unspoken banter. Mertyl looked at him with undisguised scorn. And on the next day, when Vridar announced in a voice that betrayed him and ran into a high falsetto, that he was engaged, the family regarded him with amazement. This, said Joe, was faster than young men worked in his day. Ordinarily they went with a girl several times before popping the question; and he stared hard at Vridar, as if wondering what kind of son he had.

"He sure didn't waste no time," Diana said. "The big stiff! He went round here like he was scared silly and the minute he got alone—" And she stared at Vridar with sisterly misgivings.

"Just as well get it over with," Vridar said. He ventured a strong manly laugh and failed. He blushed and turned in his chair and then, with sudden interest, was intent on his hands.

"Well," Diana asked, "did she say yes?"

"If she didn't, I wouldn't be engaged, would I?"

"And you always said you'd never marry young!"

"Well, I'm not married! I won't be for a long while."

"He's just trying her out," Mertyl said; and this was his only comment.

When alone with Vridar, Prudence drew near and studied his face.

"You know, son, mother wants you to be happy. Neloa is a nice girl. I like her. . . . But when you're married, you're married a long time."

"I love her," he said, scowling at the floor.

"You're pretty young. . . . Well, mother just wants her son to be happy. She's a sweet girl but I ain't sure she's the wife for you."

"Why not!" he cried in a voice so loud that it startled him.

"Well, I just don't feel she is. Mebbe I'm wrong. . . . Son, I'd be awful sure."

While pitching hay he thought of these admonitions. What kind of girl, he asked of the sky, did they want him to marry. And what was it their business, anyhow! Why were mothers always suspicious of their daughters-in-law, and why did they suppose they knew best what their sons should do? To hell with mothers and their snooping! He was a man now and he would choose his own wife and hell and high water could not stop him. And as a gesture of his manhood, he heaved mightily with the pitch fork and snapped its handle in two.

But he knew his blustering was very silly. His parents loved him and had slaved for him and wished only to guide him to a happy life. Just the same, their doubting that he loved Neloa: could anything be stupider than that! Do I love Neloa? he asked himself; and all his blood surged upward in a great affirmative. It was the one hot and tremendous certainty of his life.

Yes, he loved her, and he never asked himself this question again. Even in a later time, when his world was split open, his heart almost torn out of him, he never asked this question; because no matter what he did, no matter what he said—and he came to say and do most incredible things—there always stood within him, from end to end of his being, his love for this girl.

And during these days, while waiting for Sunday, he could think only of this proud queenly person who was his. His fixation was so extreme, his absent-mindedness often so ridiculous, that he was laughed at, jibed and made fun of; but he merely grinned and said nothing, because out of passion so overwhelming, there was nothing to be said. Neloa was his consciousness and his dream. He dwelt on the touch of her arm and the smell of her hair and the sound of her voice. He relived his hours with her, telling them over and over; until she was life and the only meaning and everything else was dark. Now and again he doubted that she had been here; and he decided to fetch some token home, a lock of her hair or a statement of love in her own handwriting, to convince himself that his happiness was real.

When Sunday morning came he rose at daybreak. He saddled his pony and was ready to go when he remembered that their meeting was for one o'clock; and he groaned at his stupidity and hated himself for a fool. If he had said eight o'clock, they could have spent the day together, and part of the night, too: seventeen hours in all, for he counted them, one by one. And now their hours would be only twelve. He deliberated going at once: he would dash up madly to the house and summon her and they would go away. But he could never do that. He went to the house and stared at the clock and he hated it. He was infuriated by its round face and by the smug preciseness of everything it did. For fifteen years he had hated clocks.

His mother came out, brushing her hair. She looked at his doleful face and laughed.

"Why son, what's the matter? Why you up at daylight?"

He looked at her and blew his nose, twisting it so savagely that he felt a stabbing pain.

"I don't know," he said.

"When you to meet her?"

"One o'clock."

"And it's only five-thirty now!" She smiled at his woe and came over and kissed his cheek. "Love is an awful thing, ain't it? I don't know, son, if it brings more sorrow or joy."

He left the house and went to the river. He sat on its bank and watched its silver acres rolling to the sea. His mood was a strange one: intense in its longing, tragically sad: a need to weep, to pray, somewhere far down in his joy; a mist of pain, a bright searching loneliness of soul. It seemed so queer that his eyes should be wet now. In a little while he would see her and walk with her through the golden hours; and yet his need, the great ache of his being, seemed to go out and beyond. It was a terrible hunger that made him reach to what he had never heard of, to build his dreams on what he could never find: as if Neloa were only a stepping-stone to the light. . . .

When he returned, the family was eating but Vridar did not eat. He watched them with his heart bursting. Only music, only the sadness of violins, was an answer to this pain in his heart.

"You better eat," Joe said, his gray eyes twinkling. "I never fell so deep in love I couldn't eat."

Vridar's grin was sick and tortured. All eyes turned to him: curious or sympathetic or amused.

"If you don't eat," Mertyl said, "you'll have rumblings in your stomach. You can't make love with all that noise."

"No," Joe said, "you can't make love on a empty stumick."

"In a few hours," resumed Mertyl, "a steak will taste better'n a kiss." This statement so amused Diana that she choked on a biscuit and left the room. She came in, coughing and giggling, and suddenly her laugh pitched into a shrill wail and died.

"When I fall in love," she said, "I'll sure eat. I'll get so fat and big he can't hug me."

Vridar looked at her plump body, already womanly in its fullness.

"You won't have to eat much more," he said.

"Better eat a bowl of mush," said Joe. "Mush is what you need to make love."

All this jesting Vridar thought in poor taste. It seemed to be the way of persons—of most persons, at least, whom he knew—to make a silly monkey of love. It was the glory of earth; but not for his father's people, the Hunters, the O'Rourkes, the McGards: for them it was a lewd adventure that begat babies and consternation. And he remembered all the obscene clowning during his school days in Annis.

He went outside and walked. His love would be strained of all impurity and would flow in soft light. Such wooing as he had often seen—prancing like a stallion and biting and whinnying or climbing naked to a stump and roaring in amorous thunder, in the manner either of Dock Hunter or Borg Swensen—would never be his. And how anyone could make of love nothing but vulgar postures of mating was one of the dark riddles of life. It ought to be soft and tremulous and clean. For a man and a woman, it ought to be what song was to a bird, sunrise to the morning. . . . Yes, for him and for Neloa, love would be like that. It would be the fragrance of their common mood and the light of what they said.

He got his pony and mounted. The time was still early but he could linger on the way. After going up the dugroad, though, he did not linger, but gave rein to the pony and went like the wind. The sky was a glorious blue pasture and the mountains were banked to it in purple mist. Larks sang in cove and dell and fields of wheat dimpled under the breeze.

Upon coming to Antelope Creek he rode westward and stopped a half-mile from Neloa's home. He looked at the sun but it was still journeying across a mellow forenoon. Going up on a hill, he peered over at the Doole buildings, waiting a long while for Neloa to appear; and when she did not, he returned to the highway and took a road into the south. He went for two miles and came to a jungle of aspen, and here he sat for a few minutes, looking over the Antelope Hills. Black Canyon was a great secret of forest and mist, and upon northern peaks, clouds were piled like hills of wool, with a warm pink fireplace in their lower bank. Far into the east, he could see Swan Valley, like a darkness lost under blue veils.

Around him were flowers, many of them nameless to him; but he found harebells and geraniums and gilias, and he thrust a few gilias into his lapel. It seemed to him now that the sun had passed its zenith. He rode back to the highway and galloped west.

After rounding a curve he stopped, overwhelmed by insupportable joy. He dismounted and led his horse; and in a few moments, he saw Neloa far down the road, coming slowly toward him. His heart now shook him so that he could see the flowers tremble under its beat. This meeting was to be another picture, etched indelibly in memory, and to remain until death as one of the most vivid things of his life.

He walked down the road leading the pony and she came toward him, looking very queenly, yet very girlish, too. He saw that she wore a simple pink dress and that her hair fell over it in dark wealth. He saw that she was smiling and that her eyes were full of light. This he saw, this he never forgot, though everything around him was phantomland. And as into a mist, as through a strange dream, they came together with the earth and the sky gathering into the moment. Nothing in his life had ever been more unreal than this meeting. Everything was impalpable blue wonder, and in this wonder he said hello and she answered, but it seemed to him that neither spoke. She came into his trembling arms, but this also was very unreal. He kissed her and he remembered afterward that they both laughed.

Then they turned and walked down the road. They left the road and came to a narrow lane and they came to a brink, and they looked down over mountainous blue at a river of light. They had walked a mile and neither had spoken. It seemed to him there was nothing to be said. The silence was perfect and the day was shimmering glory; and they were alone. Now and again he glanced at her, still doubting that she was with him. There was a lustrous splendor in her eyes, the heart of springtime in her cheeks. Her mood was his mood, deep and wordless; her thoughts were his. So it seemed to him: and he was afraid of such happiness: it was too profound and complete.

Leading to the river was a dugway and they took its path. They crossed bottomland and came to the river and then Vridar tethered his pony and they sat on the bank. They both looked into a swirling eddy that lay under their feet. Then Vridar looked at Neloa and reached out and touched her hand.

"I thought the days would never go," he said. "They seemed years."

"Yes," she said.

Into her dark eyes now, as in later whiles, came something that baffled him. As nearly as he could ever put the thing into words it was this: a brightness of love, of hunger, and beyond these, a single question fixed in loneliness: one dark solitary fear, against which, as against a backdrop, her soul stood in silhouette. She looked at him and he saw this strangeness written in her eyes, and then her lashes fell. He was troubled a little by what he saw but he was too happy to ponder what it meant.

"Neloa, you love me still?"

"Yes."

"Come here."

He drew her to him across his lap, with her hair falling over him and over the earth. She looked up at him and then closed her eyes. He looked at her mouth and wanted to kiss it and did not dare.

"You happy now?"

"Yes."

"I could sit like this forever. Until I died."

She smiled and glanced up at him and her lashes fell again. She talked very little, he reflected; most of her answers were only yes. But he did not like girls who talked. Born to silence and always afraid of it, yet he loved its worth, sensing in it the far-reaching and the eternal. And for a long while now he did not speak again. He gazed down at her, thinking of her loveliness and trying to convince himself that this hour was real. He looked at her body, at her lovely bare arms, at the fullness of her breasts; but there was nothing amorous in his gaze. Her lying against him stirred no passion: tenderness only, a wish to cherish and protect, a prayer for so much that was his. Her breathing was slow and deep but he could tell by her face that she was not so serene as she seemed. Lifting her a little, he bowed his face to her hair.

"Neloa, remember the first time I saw you? On the butte in Annis?"

"Yes."

"That was long ago. How long?"

"Oh, seven years—eight years."

"Ten years and ninety-eight days today."

"Have you counted all the days?"

"A thousand times. . . . And I followed you to school. Or did you know that?"

"Yes, I knew."

"And how I watched you all day long. But you didn't know that."

"No."

"And remember when I walked home with you? I tried to, I mean."

"Yes, I remember."

"I was awfully silly. But I loved you so much, even then."

She stirred in his arms and clasped one of his hands. This response shook him: it was the first of its kind today.

"And the school contest? We stood in the front of the room and you had your hair down like this."

"Yes. I missed erysipelas. I can spell it now."

"And then you went outside and wept."

"I was silly, too."

"I wanted to kiss you then. . . . And remember the show in Rigby?"

"Yes, I remember."

"You were awful," he said. "You ran off and left me."

"I was just a little girl. I was a kid then."

"You're still a little girl. You're only sixteen."

"I'm a pretty big little girl. I feel big as a house."

"Would you like to be smaller?"

"I don't want to be a mountain. I get bigger and bigger."

"You're just right," he said. "I wouldn't want to change you a bit."

Again they were silent for a long while. Very stealthily, Vridar drew from his pocket a pair of small scissors and severed a lock of her hair. He stored the lock away and returned the scissors and drew a deep breath. Raising his head now, he watched the surge and foam below him or he worshiped her face, and each bewildered glance at her fetched another sigh. It was ridiculous to think that Neloa loved him, and yet it was so. He had kissed her only once today. He wanted to kiss her again: not with passion, but only to make certain that he could, that it was his right to do so. Drawing a handful of hair to his lips, he kissed it; and then he took her free hand and kissed it and pressed it to his cheek.

"You know what?" he said, with a strange self-pitying laugh.

"No. What?"

"I want to kiss you."

She looked up at him, her eyes wide and bright.

"Why don't you?" she said.

"I—I guess I'm afraid."

He hoped she would draw him down and kiss him, acting on a wild impulse; but she did not. Spontaneity was not her way. She only smiled a little and studied his face. He flushed and turned from her.

"That isn't fair!" he cried.

"You'n kiss me if you want to," she said.

He looked at her and the blood was hot in his cheeks.

"If I want to! I don't want to unless—" He frowned at her, feeling very wretched. His vanity rose from its dark depths and overwhelmed him with self-pity. "I don't think you want me to," he said.

One of her most charming mannerisms was a scowl full of humor and light. She scowled at him now and tried to shake him; she rebuked him with eyes mocking and intent.

"I don't," he said stubbornly, and felt himself sinking into a bog. He was spoiling the hour and the fault was his. He wanted to say he had been a fool but out of desperation, vanity rose again in a moment of triumph. "I just judge by the way you act."

"How do I act?"

"Like you don't want me to!" he cried dismally. He sat up and stared at an eddy of foam. Again she shook him a little.

"Kiss me."

"I don't want to."

That was a horrible lie but it made him feel better. Well, if he had to, he could go alone through life, solitary and misunderstood. He could be a desolate titan, overlooking the peaks. . . . But these impossibilities gave him no comfort. They darkened the sky and made him shiver.

Neloa now sat up and tossed her long hair back. She studied his face; and then, like one who despairs of winning, she strove to draw him to her. He resisted and wished himself dead. Why did he always have to be a stupendous fool! Still, he was not going to ask for every kiss, fall to his knees and implore, make a beggar of his love. He had pride: where were her eyes that she did not see it!

"Vridar," she said, and it was the first time he had ever heard her speak his name.

"What?" he said. He looked at her. She was staring at him

as if he were an insoluble riddle. It helped a little to know that he baffled her.

"Why won't you kiss me?"

"Why should I?" And with his heart threshing wildly, he added: "If you don't want me to, why should I?"

"Who said I didn't want you to?"

"I did."

Again she studied him. Her eyes were neither cold nor hurt: they were only baffled. And Vridar, feeling now that she would never break down his will, never reach through his absurd mask and heal the hour, fell into bitter words.

"You don't love as I love! I'm an idiot, a plain fool! I worship you, I've worshiped you for years, but I wish I didn't! I wish to God I had some sense!" He was so vehement now that his words, his stinging unkindness, poured out of him in a great breath. He got to his feet and looked down at her and spoke again. "What do you know of love like mine? What will you ever know? I would die for you, I would cut my heart out for you, now! anytime! Everything about you, your clothes, the dust on your shoes, means more to me than life! And what do you care! And what do you care! I ought to hate you! In God's name I wish I could! Oh, I wish I could!"

He stopped, white and exhausted; and Neloa now rose, a little pale and shaken, and looked at him. With the right word, the quick warm impulse, she could have broken him to tears and to wild penitent devotion; but she did not understand him—his passionate idealism, his loneliness, his violence. Unimpulsive herself, she could only stand bewildered, looking at his tortured face, feeling the awful destroying power of his scorn. He started for the river, half-determined to throw himself in. Then he swung and faced her.

"You mean life to me," he said, his eyes dark and burning, his lips white. "All of life, that is what you mean. When I said I'd die for you, I meant it. When I said I worship you, I meant it. But if you don't love me I don't want you. I'd rather you'd leave me now. I'd rather——"

He broke off, amazed. Her eyes were wet. He saw mist in

them first and then tears that gathered to her lashes and fell. She looked at him through her tears.

"I do love you," she said.

"Neloa! Oh, Neloa!" And now, unable longer to control the flood, he dropped to earth and let his desolate grief find its peace. For several minutes the anguish poured out of him, unendurable, blind. It was the grief of one whose years were still lost in terror and loneliness, whose mind still lived in an awful dark exile of its own.

"Vridar," she said: but she did not try to quiet his grief. She did not touch him. She waited until he was spent. Then she sat by him in quiet humility, and he sat up, loathing himself. After a few moments he looked at her. If he had seen in her face the smallest hint of scorn, of amusement or of doubt, he would have left her here and walked out of her life. But he saw none of these. Her eyes were sad and questioning. With a cry he threw himself to her lap and put his arms round her and shook again.

V

AND SO these weeks passed, each with its six days of intolerable waiting, each flowering in glory at its end. Had it not been for his father, Vridar would have gone oftener, riding out in any evening when his heart was full; but Joe held him to the discipline of work. Once in seven days, he said, was often enough to see any woman. When he courted, he had gone only on Sunday, spending the other days in the fields. A lot of men wasted themselves in love.

When Sunday came, Vridar was up at daylight and without breakfast he was off, meeting Neloa at sunrise. They would spend nearly eighteen hours together; and when midnight fell, he would gallop home to face another eternity of waiting. Always they went over the hills to the river and spent the hours there. And these Sundays—there were nine of them—were all perfect save one.

In the calm morning of this day, while night was still a faint fog in cove and glade, they were going down Antelope Creek. They left the road and turned into a river-lane and climbed a hill; and upon looking back they saw a man filling his tank from the creek. He was a farmer and he was hauling water to his beasts. Who he was, Vridar did not know nor did he care. But when he looked at Neloa, he saw that her eyes were curiously alive; and with unerring penetration, born of loneliness and self-searching, he read in her eyes, in something strangely shadowed there, a warm alert interest in this man. His world darkened, as if the sun of his happiness had passed into a cloud. He grasped her shoulders and looked at her eyes but what he had seen there was gone. And then she amazed him by saying:

"I know who he is."

"Who who is?" asked Vridar, beginning to feel lost. She inclined her head to the distant man. He looked at her and at the man, at one and then at the other, and he wondered what her words meant. And the man was now looking at them.

"Well, who is he?"

"Francis Henderson."

"Oh, you don't say! Well, who's Francis Henderson?"

"He lives over there," she said, and she looked at a distant farm.

The man now waved to Neloa and she returned his greeting and jealousy rose in Vridar in a vomit of rage. It choked him and for a few moments left him speechless. He stared at Neloa, sick with doubt. And perceiving now that he was furious, she changed suddenly, in the manner of a playing child that is rebuked. Something strange entered her eyes and the smile left her mouth.

"Let's go on," she said.

"No," Vridar said. He was determined to settle this matter now. "How long you known him?"

"Oh, about a year."

"You been out with him?" His face was so morbidly earnest that she shrank and looked scared.

"Yes," she said.

"How many times?"

"Only once."

"Only once. When was that?"

"Oh—" She sighed. "About two months ago."

"How long before—before you came up to our place?"

"Oh, about two weeks." She was annoyed. Her voice trembled now and there was dark resentment in her eyes.

"Do you love him?"

"Don't be silly!" she said, and her eyes for a moment were like fire.

Vridar had never seen this Neloa before. He was touching depths that he had suspected but had never found. He drew a long breath, feeling that he was silly beyond all doubt. She had gone with him once, she had waved to him in greeting; but these, surely, were no matters to get furious about. He took her arm and they walked again. She was pensive and sullen now: if he pressed her arm, she gave no response; and he wished deeply that he had not been such a fool.

"I'm sorry," he said. He looked round, trying to meet her eyes. There was an angry dying flush in her cheeks. There was something hard and glittering in her stare. "Neloa, I'm sorry. It's just because I love you so."

"You were mean," she said.

"All right, anything. But let's not spoil our Sunday. . . . Neloa, please!"

She did not sigh or in any way betray her thought. Her face was still brooding and dark. He stopped and drew her resisting to his arms and she put her hands up and strove to push him away.

"Neloa, please! I'm awful sorry, honest. Please don't spoil our day!" She looked at him and he did not like what he saw in her eyes. He had seen it in her father's eyes. He had never discovered what it meant. "Neloa!" he cried, becoming frantic.

"What?" she asked, and looked far away.

"Neloa, don't you love me now?" She hesitated a long while. "Neloa! Don't you?"

"I guess so," she said.

"Then please don't act like this! Darling, please! . . . Neloa, please smile."

"No!"

"Yes. Please!"

"I said no."

He drew her to him again and she did not resist now. He kissed her lips and eyes. "Smile!" he said. "I'll kiss you until you smile." She looked at him and very slowly she smiled. The darkness left her eyes and there came in its stead a whimsical humor that he loved. "Now we're all right," he said. "Neloa, aren't we?"

But not for hours did he recover the lyric sweetness of their former days. Something troubled her. Her gayness, never bright or spontaneous, touched her but lightly now, and her eyes, again and again, were shadowed and still. But he reposed in her, largely because his need was so great, the simplicity and the trust that were the heart of his life.

And another incident, also trifling, it seemed to him on reflection, occurred a few days later. With one exception, he saw her only on the Sundays of these weeks. But on the Mormon holiday, the twenty-fourth of July, he mounted his pony and rode forth, telling himself with enormous glee that he would surprise her.

When he came within sight of her home he stopped. He saw Neloa in the yard, and she saw him, too, it seemed, because at once she dodged round a building and entered the house. He rode down the lane and through the gate. After greeting her parents, who stood in the yard and looked at him, as they always did, rather curiously, he threw the reins over a post and went to the door.

"Is Neloa inside?" he asked.

"Yes," said Tim Doole.

He pushed the door open and strode in.

Neloa was lying on a bed. She seemed to be asleep but he

knew she was not. Nevertheless, when he spoke to her she did not answer and when he went over and sat on the bed she did not move.

"Neloa," he said, "you're not asleep."

She affected to wake and to be astonished. She stared at him and blinked her eyes; and her acting was so silly and artless that he didn't know whether to be furious or to laugh.

"When did you come?" she asked; and she rubbed at wide-awake eyes.

"When did I come! You saw me coming. Why do you act this way?"

"I guess I was asleep," she said.

"You weren't. You were out in the yard and you ran in here to pretend. . . . Neloa, why did you do it?"

"Do what?"

"Pretend this way."

And now she affected anger. She rose from the bed and went to a mirror and brushed her hair. He followed her.

"Neloa, why?" She tried to look at him with scorn but her eyes were guilty.

"What makes you think I wasn't asleep?"

"I know it. So why did you lie?"

"I didn't."

"Listen, have you ever lied to me before?"

"I've never lied to you."

"Except today."

"No, not today. I *was* asleep."

"That's a lie! If you're going to lie to me—Well, suit yourself." He got his hat and moved toward the door. She came toward him, swift and wild. She grasped his arm and tried to drag him away from the door and he allowed her to. But when he faced her, she did not speak. She merely looked at him, her eyes guilty and anxious. "I don't want you," he said. "I don't lie. I don't want a liar."

She laughed, and her laugh was strange and low, tremulous and dark. She strove to draw him to the bed and he scowled at her and refused to budge.

"Did you lie or didn't you?"

Her lips trembled now and she went over and sat down. He stood in wretched doubt, staring at her. If she would only talk instead of sinking into this awful silence!

"Neloa, tell me why you did it." He waited but she did not speak. He turned to the door again and she was after him, frantic in her haste. He grasped her chin and forced her gaze to his. "Why?" he said.

"Oh—I wanted to see what you would do!" Her tone was full of vexation and grief.

And now Vridar felt, as in the former matter, that it was he who had been silly. She had only been playing, had wanted to see what he would do; and he had threshed about in fury, trying to make a mountain of this molehill. He took her hand and led her outside and down the road.

But save for these two incidents, his ten days with her were as flawless as light. Time and again, it is true, overcome by doubt, by loneliness, he would fly into a rage and rebuke her; he would declare that she was only playing with him; and he would get himself into such a rage of panic and despair that he would have to throw himself to the earth and weep. But these explosions of temper only heaped sweetness upon the hours that came after. Then he would lie in her lap or take her to his arms, and his peace, in contrast with his madness, would be deep beyond words. Then he would know beyond all question that his love for her was utter and that life without her would be worse than death.

And not always did he maneuver the day into a tantrum. Often they gathered wild flowers, breathing of the gentian and gilia and fireweed, of aster and golden rod, of mimulus and cinquefoil and rose. Or he would put a yellow rose in her dark hair or he would press rose petals to her lips and then to his. Or they would sit by the river, laying their hands in its coolness and watching the trout. And often they climbed to pine trees and gathered gum and chewed it and breathed the smell of ripe chokeberries and of evergreen. In all these doings, there was so much tenderness and peace that he would marvel at life, having suddenly found it so clean and good.

Nor at any time during these days with her did Vridar hunger for her body or feel any hint of passion, even when she lay in his arms. The purity of his love, its unalloyed soulfulness of power and thought, was so very extreme that it came to be for him, in a later time, the most incredible circumstance of his life. Not even when he kissed her did he have a conscious wish to do more. Because for him she was like the flowers and the sky, like the evenings and the mornings, and he could no more have proposed intimacy, or have wished it, than he could have taken his own life. His desire was to protect her and to worship her. She was his god and his hours with her were his testaments and his prayer.

VI

•

THE FLAVOR of his love is to be found most amazingly in an experience that fell in August. It happened in this way. Neloa said she had to go to Idaho Falls to nurse a relative, and if Vridar wanted to see her on the following Sunday, he would have to see her there. He said he would. He rode down with the mail carrier and met her in the railway station, two hours after dark.

She smiled and came toward him but he did not take her in his arms here. Too many persons stood around and there was too much light. Without speaking, save as his trembling body spoke or his eyes, he led her to a street and they walked into town. He was troubled by the thought that she would leave him soon and he would have to spend the night alone, and as they turned from street to street, he wondered how he could keep her with him. He was willing to sit on a park bench all night but he could not ask her to do that. The night was warm, and he wanted to go into the country and sit somewhere under trees; but this, too, he imagined she would think a foolish

thing to do. Besides the bench or the country, there was nothing but a hotel.

"Neloa, when do you have to go? . . . I mean where you're
staying."

"About midnight, I guess."

They passed a drugstore and he peered in.

"It's ten now. That's only two hours."

"Mebbe I can stay till one."

"That's only three hours. . . . Neloa, why can't you stay with
me all night?" She looked at him in astonishment. He pressed
her arm. "Why not? It wouldn't be wrong, would it? We
could go to a hotel."

She did not answer. He thought she was horrified by such
a notion and he pleaded for it, urging its right. They were betrothed, he said. They were in love and they would be married and it was their own business what they did. They could
get two rooms. He had enough money for two rooms. They
could sleep alone, but he would be near her, even though a
wall lay between.

"Will you? I can't let you go in three hours. I won't. . . .
Neloa, say you will."

"I don't know."

"Why don't you know?"

"I should go back, I guess. My aunt is quite sick."

"But you would go to bed. Wouldn't you? What difference
would it make?"

"I don't know."

She drew away from him and went to a window. She
looked at dresses, spread in piles of color under a light. Vridar
was annoyed. How could she look at these, when another matter, so vast and important, weighed on their souls!

"That's a pretty dress," she said. "Isn't it?"

"I guess so," he said; and he scowled at an overflowing mass
of pink taffeta. They went down the street and Neloa stopped
at other windows, and Vridar wondered how she could spend
their precious hours in such utter silliness. He felt resentful
and wished he hadn't come.

"Will you?" he said.

"What?" she said, gazing at a velvet skirt.

"You know what. Will you?"

"I don't know."

"Neloa, please!"

They walked again. He saw in her eyes a bright hunger for lovely things. At a jeweler's window she stared earnestly at brooches and rings, bracelets and necklaces and watches, lavallières and beads. She said she wanted a lavallière and he said he would buy her one when he could. Then he took her arm and led her away. But she turned as a child does, looking at every bright thing in the street. It seemed to him that she was attracted by glittering and noise and gypsy gewgaws. Desperately he led her into a drugstore and to a booth. He gave her the menu and he could see her eyes brighten as she read.

"What do you want?" he asked.

She chose ice cream, dressed with marshmallow and pecans —a dish, it seemed to him, that looked terribly expensive—; and he chose a plain soda, having noted its low price. Whether he would now have money for two rooms and for his journey home, he did not know; and his worries multiplied as he watched her eat. She was excited tonight, not by him, he realized, but by the life around her; and she looked very lovely, with her eyes shining and with so much color in her cheeks.

"You haven't answered," he said. "Neloa, will you?"

"Mebbe," she said. Her eyes for a moment were very dark and wide.

"Say yes."

"Yes."

He forgave everything now: her window-shopping, her interest in jewels, which he found barbaric and detestable, and her misuse of their hours. That she would spend a night with him, in spite of her shyness and innocence, was overwhelming proof of her love. She trusted him and put herself in his care and that was enough.

On their way out, he fell behind and glanced at the bill. Until this moment he had loftily ignored it, as if bills did not matter; and when he saw that it was only thirty cents, he felt more at ease. He smiled at the cashier and said good evening as if he were a worldly fellow who knew his way about.

The time now was eleven and he hunted the streets, seeking an unpretentious hotel. Most of them had magnificent lobbies. Their guests, stretched out in lordly chairs, looked snobbish and bored. He would have to find a small hotel, rather dark and shabby, and he pretended that it would be best to do so. In the larger hotels, he said to Neloa, they might be recognized.

"I know one," she said. "I stayed in it once."

"Where?"

She led him to another street and he found himself staring at a building that was very gloomy and still. He hesitated, wondering if the rooms were clean; and then, summoning all his courage, he took her arm and opened a door. They climbed a dark stairway and came to a small desk, feebly lighted, and he read a sign which asked him to push the button at his right. His heart was beating terribly now. His hand shook when he pressed the button and he felt guilty and lost.

From a dark corridor on the right came a huge woman. Her face, it seemed to him, was lewd and adulterous; her voice was sharp.

"Well?" she said, and looked at Vridar.

"Do you—have any rooms? Vacant rooms? . . . I—want two."

"Two!" she said, and looked at Neloa.

"You see," he went on, "I—well, we're not married, you see. We're engaged, I mean." Her stare was incredulous and he hastened to explain. "You see she's down here nursing and I— I—well, I came down to see her. I live on Antelope. . . . We just want a-be close together. . . . If you have two rooms—" He broke off. The woman's shrewd eyes were looking clear through him.

"I got only one room," she said.

"Only one!" Vridar cried. His heart sank. "You sure you got only one?" The woman was now staring at Neloa.

"You'n have it."

"But we're not married!" Vridar cried.

Her smile was faint and sardonic. She looked at him and he felt chilled.

"It will be a dollar and a half for two."

Vridar turned to Neloa, wondering what she thought of this. Her eyes were bright and her face was a little flushed. And then it occurred to him that they could take the room and Neloa could sleep and he would sit up all night.

"We'll take it," he said.

"Sign here," the woman said.

Vridar signed his name and Neloa's name and his hand shook so that his own writing was strange to him. The woman got a key and led the way into a black corridor. She unlocked a door and ushered them into a room that smelled of old bedding and dust. She turned a light on and looked at Vridar a moment and went over and drew the shade. Then she went out and softly closed the door.

Vridar did not turn to Neloa at once. He was too astounded by his boldness and too afraid that he was unwise. What did she think of him, fetching her alone to a room and asking her to spend the night with him! He walked about the room, pretending to examine this and that but really fighting against a sense of shame. For several minutes he did not look at her. And when he did, he was surprised to see how happy she looked and he was glad he had brought her here. They would spend the night together, and if there was greater happiness on earth, he could not imagine what it was like.

"Neloa, you're not mad at me?"

"No."

He took her in his arms and kissed her and then they both sat on the bed. She laid her head to his shoulder and he put an arm round her waist. For several minutes they sat this way.

"I guess she thought we were up to mischief. She acted like it." Neloa did not answer. Vridar wished she would talk a little more and not keep so much of herself deeply hidden. He went over to the one dirty window and peered behind the shade and into the street. And he was aware now for the first time that the woman had drawn this shade and looked at him with cunning eyes. Well, she was a fool. She thought that if a man took a woman to a room he was bent on sin, and in this matter she had much to learn yet. She thought he had lied to her, the stupid old fool! What she did not know about life would take a long time to tell; and he drew a great sigh and felt proud of himself.

He came back and sat on the bed. Neloa seemed flushed and excited but he did not blame her, so incredible was the thing he had done. He would be very gentle with her and she would feel more at ease in a little while.

"Neloa, you don't love me any less, do you?"

"No," she said, and she gave him a strange dark look.

He framed her face in his hands and forced her gaze to meet his. He could not read the meanings in her eyes. Very rarely had he been able to. So much was there now, so much had always been there, written in the soft and inscrutable depth.

"Are you sleepy?"

"No, just a little."

"Would you like a drink?"

"Yes."

He went over to the dirty washbowl and found a dirty glass. This he scoured and then filled with water. He brought it to her and she thanked him and swallowed a little, and he reflected that she was not thirsty at all. He wondered what else he could do to make her feel at ease. Turning the cover back, he examined the bed: the mattress was old and unclean and rotten, the springs sagged. The covering was unclean, too. He hoped there were no bedbugs or lice.

Neloa was very quiet with her gaze fixed on the wall. He sat by her and took her hands. What should he talk of now?

"Do you want to lie down?"

She glanced at him and then at the bed. He folded the pillows and lay against them and drew her to his arms. She could sleep like this, he said. He would lie awake and look at her and see to it that she was warm; and he laughed a little, thinking how absurdly happy he was.

Neloa gave no answer to this. She was deeply silent and he could not imagine of what she was thinking. Out in the hall he could hear a woman's protests and a man's angry voice and he went over to lock the door. But there was no key, no latch. He stood a chair on its heels and propped the door and came back. The man was loud and abusive and the woman cried as if in pain; and then steps went down the hall and the building was silent. Vridar looked at Neloa to see what she made of this.

"Sounds like a quarrel, doesn't it?"

"Yes."

He turned the light off and the room was very dark. Telling Neloa she had better sleep now, he drew covers back and she kicked her shoes off. She lay on the bed and he put a quilt over her; and then, after taking only his shoes off, he lay at her side and put an arm round her. But he lay without cover, feeling that it would be indecent, even with clothes on, to enter the bed with her. He asked if she was warm and she said she was. After a little while, he became aware that his arm was lying against her breast. He moved it down to her waist.

She lay on her back and he lay on his side, with his arm round her over the quilt, with his face in her hair. Her hair was clean and fragrant and he loved the smell of it. He kissed her hair and he wanted to kiss her mouth but he did not. Perhaps she was too sleepy for kissing now.

"Are you all right?" he asked.

"Yes," she said.

"You happy?"

"Yes."

He felt very tender and protective, as if they were lost in an alien world and she was his to defend. She would sleep but he would not. All night he would lie awake, thinking of her, trying to realize that she was here. When they were married he would lie with her in every night and smell of her hair. They would be very happy then. Life for him had always been so terrible in its pain and loneliness and now it was so clean and sweet. It made him weep to think of it.

In a little while she slept. She turned to her side away from him and he moved his face close to her, but not his body, and he thought of how innocent she was and how she trusted him.

Well, it would always be like this. Their life together would be a soft glory, a warm splendor of light, across the years. And he sighed again, for his heart was very full.

He became sleepy after a while but he did not sleep. His hours with her, so few in each week, must all be given to realization and thought. If he were to sleep, he might as well be in China, he might as well not have come. No: he would lie here and listen to her breathing and tell himself over and over how much he loved her and how happy he would be. And this he did, shaping his dream until morning came. Again and again he kissed her hair, piled round his cheeks, and he gathered it and covered his face with it; or he rose to look at her sleeping face; or he patted her arm and kissed it as, in years gone by, he had kissed the Bible. And he despised himself a little because his eyes were wet.

And when morning came, Neloa still slept, and Vridar lay by her, worshipful and awake.

VII

•

BUT THIS interlude in Vridar's life came to a sudden end. It had been a fragrant morning and a calm noon, overhung by a golden sun; and on the Wednesday evening after his night in Idaho Falls, the sun dropped into darkness and he was again lost. At three o'clock of this day, everything seemed perfect; and at ten o'clock, he had suffered the most terrible disillusionment of his life. As strange as lightning in a clear sky came its first intimations, and then, flash by flash, it heaped its blinding truth upon his world; and he went home like a crazed man, with something in his heart that was always to be there.

Unable to wait for Sunday, he had ridden out and had gone with Neloa upon the hills. Leaving the dugway they went down over a bluff and into heavy timber and here for a long while they sat under a huge pine. And it was here that Vridar did a childish, a most ridiculous, thing.

Credulous, yet suspicious, and with jealousy that could become insane, he had never convinced himself of Neloa's love. Not that he had any reason for doubt. She went with no other man and she was always happy to see him and she yielded to the shaping power of his will. It was something which he felt in her: in her eyes at all times, often in her voice, sometimes in her way. And at last, unwilling to live forever in doubt, he decided to test her love.

Because he was proud and lonely of temper and because he gave to chastity a value which it could never possess, he resolved to lie to her about his love-life. And under this tree after much hesitation he spoke.

"Neloa, I have something to tell you. It's an awful confession and I guess you won't love me any more. But we can't get married with any secrets between us. . . . Can we?"

"No," she said.

"It happened last winter," he said, staring at his hands. "I was pretty wild, I guess. . . . Well, anyway I ran around with a girl. She fell in love with me. She said she did. She wanted to marry me. We went to shows and dances. . . . Well, I was with her a lot." He glanced at Neloa. She was looking at him with something dark and unfathomable in her eyes. He toyed with a stick, both because he wished to seem ill at ease and because he was; and then, during the remainder of his tale, he watched her steadily, trying to read the effect of his words.

"Well, there isn't much to say. We—I—the truth is I was intimate with her." He saw Neloa catch her breath a little. He saw a strangeness in her eyes. It was like pain but it was more than pain. "Well," he went on, determined to make this a real test, "she, the girl, I mean—well, she's going to have a child. It's my child." Now he saw her eyes darken and then become bright and wet, and tears gathered to her lashes and fell. Her mouth trembled a little. But she did not speak; she only looked at him, as if hurt beyond the power of cure. And he wanted to cry that he had lied and that he loved only her, and so take the pain out of her eyes; but he must be very sure.

"Neloa, will you marry me?"

For another long moment she looked at him and then her eyes were blinded and she broke to the earth and wept. More than all else in life, Vridar wished to comfort her; but he sat apart and listened to her grief. After a little while she looked at him again.

"Neloa, will you?" She gave no answer. She looked away from him and tears rolled down her cheeks. "I love you, Neloa. I did not love this other girl. I don't want to marry her. . . . And I know I've sinned. If you tell me to go, I'll not blame you for that. . . . Neloa, shall I go?"

Again she looked at him. He rose to his feet and started away and as he did so she made a choked sound and bowed to earth. He went a little way up the mountain and looked back at her. For several minutes he stood here but she did not look up.

"Neloa, shall I go?"

She did not look up. He could tell that she was shaking with grief. Going a little farther, he turned again.

"Neloa, I am going now!"

He went through trees, glancing back from time to time, but she did not raise her head. He was out of sight and he was convinced that she intended to let him go when he heard her voice ringing in his name. He waited and she came frantically toward him but when she saw him she stopped. He went down the mountain and faced her.

"Neloa, shall I go?"

She gazed at him and her eyes were dark and strange. She was trembling, and never, he reflected, had he seen her so deeply moved. But she did not speak.

"Shall I?"

He went up and touched her arms. With a palm to her chin he forced her eyes to meet his and for several moments he looked into their wet darkness. They told him nothing that he wanted to know.

"Neloa, shall I?" She drew a deep breath.

"No," she said.

With a cry of gladness, Vridar took her in his arms and

kissed the tears from her eyes. He led her back to the tree and sat there with her lying against him.

"Neloa," he said, "I have another confession."

With a gasp she fought away from him and sat up. He struggled with her and drew her to him.

"It was all a lie," he said. "What I told you was all a lie. I swear to God it was. You're the only girl I ever went with, except once to a show. You're the only girl I ever really loved."

He thought she would be overwhelmed by relief but she was not. As a matter of fact, her behavior now completely baffled him. She moved away from him as if his touch annoyed her and she stared into distance for a long while. Vridar searched her face and strove to understand. And at last she said:

"Mebbe I should confess, too."

"You!" he cried. He grasped her arm and drew her to him. "What could you confess? That you danced with Dave Wolf? You confess!" he said; and the idea was so preposterous that he laughed. "Neloa, you don't have to test me. I love you. I was only testing you, that's why I lied."

She gave no answer to this. She still gazed at the far mountain and there was something sad and wistful in her gaze. Vridar kissed her and helped her to rise and they went down the mountain and to the river. He was sorry, he said, for his lie. He had been very silly. And he hugged her to him and kissed her with such rapturous devotion that color drenched her cheeks.

Three hours later he saw initials carved upon the pale green of an aspen. They had been put there by men, he supposed, and he thought nothing of them. But in the next moment Neloa amazed him.

"Look up there," she said.

He looked up and he saw on the tree ten feet above his head these letters:

H.K.
N.D.

"Whose are those?" he demanded and stared at her. "N.D., that's yours." She was smiling up at the letters as if very glad to see them there. Vridar looked at her face and a horrible doubt paralyzed him. "H.K.," he said, "H.K. Who is H.K.?"

"Harvey Kress."

"Kress!" His heart sank. His thoughts went back to his school days in Poplar and to Alvin Kress, the tawny lad who had wooed Helen and whom he had threshed. "Is he Alvin's brother?"

"No, his cousin."

Certain for a moment that he was going to faint, Vridar went to a fallen tree and sat down. What was the meaning of this? And why did Neloa smile so happily when she looked at the carving and when she spoke of this man? My God! he thought; and he stared at her, a jealous rage filling him. She came over and stood before him. The smile had left her face now. She looked frightened and helpless.

"You mean," he said, "you were down here with him?" She did not answer. In her eyes was that baffling strangeness which had always been there. "Were you?" he shouted.

"Yes."

"When?"

"Oh, last spring a year ago. Last summer it was."

"A year ago! Did you spend the whole day here?"

"Yes."

"When you were fifteen!"

He strove to think of this. She had been here with Harvey Kress and had spent a whole day with him and they had wandered about here like lovers and he had climbed that tree and linked her name with his. And what did all that mean? What had they said, what had they done?

Vridar stood up and the world was swimming and dark. Laying rough hands on her arms, he swung her to face him. He searched her eyes but their lustrous velvet told him nothing at all. When he spoke again, his voice was hoarse and choked and his hands shook on her arms.

"Did—did he ever kiss you?" And now there came into her eyes something which he understood. It was cold annoyance, a kind of sly contempt, mixed with bewilderment and fright. It made him shake with fury. His fingers sank into her flesh until she cried with pain but he was remorseless now. "Did he?"

"Yes."

As if struck a blow he released her and sat down. He strove to understand this simple fact: that she had been kissed—kissed by another man—but the meaning eluded him and went off into darkness and became an inexplicable thing. For how could it be so! She was so guileless and so young: how could it be! . . . She had been down here, he told himself, sitting with his head bowed to his hands; she had wandered here with another, even as she had done with him; and they had kissed and laughed. He shut his eyes tight and breathed through his mouth, breathing like one in fever; he shuddered and then was still for a long while. . . . How could it be so? It seemed so silly to tell him that!

When he stood up he looked haggard and beaten. Without looking at Neloa, he stumbled through brush to a path and found the road. Neloa followed him, keeping many yards behind at first, but narrowing the distance, little by little, until she walked at his side. He did not look at her. He stared ahead of him up the mountain and in the anguished darkness of his mind he recalled details that had baffled him: her saying that she knew Francis Henderson and the light in her eyes when she waved to him; and the deep guiltiness of her stare; and her curt note about her gate and his not swinging on it. And as he walked, the doubt within him grew and took hold of his heart and laid its waste through his being. He began to feel weak and sick. He began to feel the terrible strangeness of his high school years and awful fancies drew his mind to thoughts of death and murder, and to a black exile of loneliness worse than these.

Again and again he strove to think of what she had told him. A kiss itself meant nothing, or very little, but it did no good to tell himself this. It would take more than a kiss to explain all that leapt into meaning now. And of what she could tell him, his certainty became so appalling that he sat by the road, his head sunk, and tried to steel himself for what must come. For almost an hour he sat here and Neloa stood in the road and waited. Not once did he look at her. Not once did she speak. Darkness came and he rose and walked again and very silently she walked at his side. And he went as one drugged. He stumbled as if unable to see the road, as indeed he was; and once he fell and lay for a long while without realizing that he had fallen. For his body moved as if it had been severed from his mind, and his mind was an intense and isolated darkness of its own.

For two miles they walked and neither spoke. Then he came to her home gate and crawled through and she followed him and he went up the road and entered the barn. He became aware now that he was sweating and with a trembling hand he wiped his brow. Going over to the manger he leaned into it, thinking he would vomit, but he only retched and then felt deathly sick. But it was sickness in his blood, not in his stomach; and it possessed him from head to feet. Here by the manger he stood for quite a while.

He then bowed his head to the pony and tried to weep, feeling that he must get this awful desolation out of him or go mad. But there were no tears in him now. His anguish was too deep and dark and his heart seemed to have been dropped into it out of reach and it seemed to be eating his mind away. He knew only vaguely that Neloa was standing by the door. He tried to realize why she was there and to think of her, but doing so was like probing into a wound and he recoiled, drawing away from her and into the dark.

For half an hour he did not move. And then, out of utter despair, came a sudden bright hope. Perhaps she had been innocent, save only in her kissing and in her rambling with men. He could forgive that, he could take her to his heart and let his grief out; for his need for her was greater than his pride. And he went over and laid hands on her arms. He turned her so that moonlight fell on her face and for long moments he stared at her; but what he saw in her eyes and round her mouth left him no hope. His fingers tightened on her arms and he spoke.

"Have you ever lied to me?"

"No."

"But you never told me."

"You never asked."

"I never asked!" Great God, no: his trust had been absolute. "Tell me now."

"What?"

"Everything."

She looked away and he saw the secrets in her eyes. Her eyes, indeed, seemed to be only a black record of untold things. His heart sank. It went down into him like lead.

"Tell me."

"What?"

"Everything! And don't keep saying what!" In her eyes now he saw fright.

"I don't know what you want me to tell."

"You're a liar! Be quick!"

"You mean about Harvey?"

"Yes—about Harvey."

For several minutes she would not speak. When he clutched her arms she looked annoyed and said he was hurting her. She strove to release his hands. This infuriated him and he shook her so savagely that she gasped.

"Stop it!" she cried.

"Yes, I'll stop it!" His voice rang with hatred now. "I'll kill you in a minute! All these weeks you've deceived me, lied to me, made a fool of me! I've worshiped you and good God, look! . . . Hurry up!"

Her gaze was set on the far dark hills. In her faint smile there was contempt for him. He shook her again.

"Don't!"

"I'll give you a minute! If you don't speak I'll kill you dead!"

"Well," she said, "it happened last summer."

"What happened last summer!"

"This you want me to tell."

"Go on!"

"I went to the valley with daddy, and Harvey, he went too. We went to Idaho Falls. . . ."

"Go on!"

"Well, that night daddy got two rooms, one for me and one for him and Harvey."

"Yes?" Vridar said, staring at the strange light in her eyes. "All right, go on!"

"You'n guess the rest," she said.

"I'n guess the rest! No!" he roared, his voice choked with fury and grief. "I won't guess!"

"Don't, you're hurting me."

"Go on, I said!" She shrugged.

"Well, when daddy got the rooms, Harvey took the key to my room. He said he would give it to me later. . . . You'n guess what happened."

"I won't guess! Tell it!"

She glanced at him and her glance was scornful. She shrugged again.

"Well, Harvey came to my room. . . . I don't see," she cried, and there was sudden fire in her voice, "why I got to tell any more! I guess you'n use your imagination."

"Oh, my imagination! Yes, yes, indeed. Did he stay all night with you?"

"No."

"How long?"

"Oh, about an hour."

"And what was your idiot of a dad doing?" She did not speak. "Some father you have! Jesus Christ, some father! He takes his fifteen-year-old daughter to the Falls— Isn't that the Kress who went on a mission?"

"Yes."

"—and turns her over to a Mormon missionary son-of-a-bitch!" Vridar's heart was now so wild that he could feel blood surge in his throat. He went over and leaned against the pony and within him everything was a horrible confusion of hatred and pain. He knew that he would break soon, that he could not endure this without some awful violence; but not until he was through with her, not until he had heard every word. But there stood above his desolation a bright ruthless cunning and a thought of murder. He went back and faced her again. He grasped her and swung her to the light and she cried with pain and struck him. He grinned faintly and his grin was remorseless and diabolic.

"How many times?"

"Let me go!" she cried, and her eyes were like black venom.

His fingers sank into her flesh and he broke her to her knees and then lifted her to her feet; and he saw terror in her eyes.

"How many times with him?"

"Two."

"Where was the other?"

"Down by the river."

"Where we were today?"

"Yes."

"And—did you stay in the hotel where we stayed?"

"Yes."

He released her, staggered by this blow. She had been intimate with this man, perhaps in a spot where he had sat with her, worshiping her; and she had led him to the very hotel in which she had been seduced. In this hotel he had lain with her, only ten days ago, perhaps in the same room, on the same bed; and he—simple fool that he was!—had never thought of intimacy, had wished only to cherish her and to be with her alone.

He stood by the pony and shook with humiliation and self-loathing. He went back to her, his face white and awful to look at; and his voice, without pity for himself now, was implacable and hard.

"Is that all?"

"All what?"

"Neloa, don't fool with me. You understand?" His words were so gentle, and so terribly ominous in their gentleness, that she shrank back, horrified. She moved as if to flee but he seized her and dragged her back. He broke her to her knees and then slammed her to the wall. He helped her to stand and then forced her eyes to meet his, and when she saw his eyes and the faint grin round his mouth, she cried as if struck and fought to get away. But he held her with one unpitying grasp on her wrist.

"Please don't!"

"All right, tell the rest. Who else you been intimate with?" He grinned. "I should say whom else, shouldn't I?"

"Please let me go!"

"Who else?"

"No one."

"You lie."

"I don't lie!"

"You do lie. . . . Neloa, don't you think you'd better hurry?"

"Oh, please!"

He deliberated and studied her face.

"You believe in God?"

"Yes!"

"All right, go get a Bible."

"I won't!"

"Neloa, you'd better hurry."

With fearful eyes she looked at him. She backed away from him and then turned and went to the house. And while Vridar waited, he seemed to be very calm: he looked round him and saw a pitchfork in one corner and an old hame suspended from a nail; and he wondered which of these he would use to kill her. He seemed very calm; but under his calm, he knew very well, was a mad strangled violence, a wild unreason, that waited and beat through him and that would wait only a little while. He could feel now, as he had felt in former years, the dark and throbbing might of it. It lay against his control like floods against a dam.

Then he heard Neloa coming. She entered the stable and laid a book in his hands and he held it in moonlight to be sure of what it was. He told her to place both hands on the Bible and she did. He told her to repeat these words:

"I swear to tell the whole truth and nothing but the truth, and if I don't, I ask God to send me to everlasting hell." She hesitated. "Hurry up, say them."

"I—I swear to tell the truth——"

"The whole truth."

"I swear to tell the whole truth and if I don't——"

"—the whole truth and nothing but the truth."

"—and nothing but the truth——"

"Start over."

"I swear to tell the whole truth, and nothing but the truth, and if I don't, I—I——"

"I ask God to send me to everlasting hell."

"—I ask God to send me to everlasting hell." Her voice shook and her hands trembled on the Bible.

"And now," said Vridar, "keep your hands there and remember how awful it will be to tell a lie on the Bible. . . . What other man you been intimate with?"

She looked far away and caught her breath.

"Answer."

"Dave Wolf."

He would have been no more amazed if she had thrust a knife into his heart. With the blackness storming his mind, he turned away. He went to the pony and leaned against him, thinking he would faint; and he clutched its mane to support himself. A violent retching shook him and came up his throat and he wiped bitter froth from his lips. He stumbled back and looked at her. In the voice of a man past all hope he said:

"Go on." She stood clasping the Bible and stared at him. "Go on," he said.

"You—you mean tell about him?"

"Yes. Go on."

"It was up at Nevel's. I was teaching his kids."

"When?"

"Last winter."

"Go on."

"I was alone with him and the Nevel kids. Mr. and Mrs. Nevel, they went to the valley."

"How long were they gone?"

"Two days."

"Well, go on."

"That's all."

"How many times with him?"

"Two."

"Remember where your hands are."

"Only two, so help me God!"

Vridar stared at her face, trying to understand. All this was so much to understand, to believe.

"Any more?"

"Yes."

He started as if struck.

"Great God, you mean there are more than two!"

"Yes."

He put a hand to his brow, unable to see, barely able to stand.

"Who?" he said at last.

"Francis Henderson."

"What! The man you waved at down on the creek?"

"Yes."

"When? . . . When!" he yelled, his voice becoming insane.

"About two—two weeks before I went up to—your place."

This was another blow but he was past all feeling now. Two weeks before she walked with him in Black Canyon, before she promised to be his wife, she had lain with a man. That was what she said. It was very hard to understand it, to see any meaning in it.

"Where?" he asked.

"On the bed."

"Oh, bed. . . . What bed?"

"Just outside our house."

He thought of this bed against the north wall. He felt a strange impulse to go out and look at it now.

"How many times with him?"

"One."

"How many times you go with him?"

"Just once."

"You mean—you mean—" But why try to think about it! It was all a part of the darkness now. "Who else?"

"That's all."

"Oh, that's all. You're sixteen and that's all. It—it seems to be enough."

He moved away from the barn but without its support he reeled and had to grasp a log. Again and again he passed a hand over his brow, his mind fumbling and lost, his mind trying to plot his death and hers. A little while ago, it seemed to him, he had thought of a way. He tried to stand alone but he fell in a heap; and he sat up and supported himself by spreading his legs and putting arms to his knees.

"Sit down," he said.

She sat down and laid the Bible in her lap. He strove to study her face but his eyes were full of agony and mist and he could not see.

"Do you—love any of these men?"

"No."

"Did they want to marry you?"

"Only Dave."

"Didn't that missionary bastard want to?"

"He never asked me."

"Would you have married him?"

"I don't know."

"Would you!"

"Mebbe then. But not now."

He sat with elbows to his knees, hands to his hair, still trying to understand. The deep quiet within him was more terrible now. It was the same loneliness, the same dread, that had terrorized his childhood, his youth. For several minutes he neither moved nor spoke, nor did Neloa, and he could hear only his breathing in the profound silence. He was fighting against the power that held him but he knew it was useless to fight. He would have to break into some kind of frenzy and let it out.

And suddenly he felt an impulse to laugh. The first sound he made was strange and choked; and then he sprang to his feet and roared. It was violent laughter, empty and desolate. It was furious and wild. He walked round the barn, pouring the frenzy out of him. Then he stopped and the emotion surged up and was dammed in his throat and held there. He threw his arms out, threshing at the air as if strangled; and with a horrible cry he hurled himself to her lap. He moved away from her and back and again away, trying to release his torture, trying to purge himself with an overwhelming flood of grief or rage. It was grief that saved him. Bowing to her lap, he let it out of him in a convulsion of sound and tears. It beat within him and rose in great gasping sobs and it shook him until he was blind.

And out of his grief, as if it had been there all the while, came a wan hope. It was a prayer that she had lied to him, as only a few hours ago he had lied to her. "Make it all a lie!" he whispered to God. "Oh, please make it all a lie!" He sat up and looked at her but he could not see. He reached and found her hands and kissed them. He pressed her hands to his cheeks and to his mouth.

"Neloa, it's not the truth! Darling, say it's not the truth!"

"It is the truth," she said.

"No!" He grasped her shoulders and for a moment he intended to choke her. "It isn't, I tell you! It isn't!" He was frantic now. He wanted to kill her and he looked round for a club but he could see nothing at all. Screaming at her, he said, "Tell me it isn't!"

Struggling free of him, she stood up. He rose, shaking, and faced her, his eyes trying to read what her eyes said. In a voice that was desperate, crazed, he implored her to say she had lied. "Please say it! Great God, please!"

"I can't," she said, backing away from him.

Her voice trembled now. He dashed an arm to his brow and stared wildly round him and he saw the Bible in her hands. He grasped it and told her to place her hands on it and when she hesitated he roared at her with such ungovernable fury that she obeyed.

"Swear everything you told me is true!" he shouted.

"I swear everything I told you is true."

For several moments he stared at her. The furious hope died within him and again there was only desolation and dread. He led the pony out and sprang to its back and the pony leapt ahead at full speed. Neloa ran after him, crying his name. He glanced back and saw her stumble and fall. Giving the horse rein, he went wildly through the night, seeing nothing around him but shadow, hearing nothing but galloping feet. When he came to the long dugway he galloped down it and when he drew up at the house, the pony was white with lather and foam.

VIII

<hr>

•

H E TURNED the horse free and went running to the house. There was a light in the kitchen, and when he burst in, he found his parents there as if they awaited him. Prudence sprang up with a cry and even Joe rose to his feet and both of them stared at this son who looked like a wild man. They asked what had happened but Vridar only strode round the room, knocking chairs over, acting like a person entirel out of his wits. He sat down and clutched his face and t. en paced as before; and again sat down. Prudence talked to him but he did not understand what she said. She strove to stop him in his frantic strides but he pushed her away and he looked at her as if he did not see her at all. Joe then became alarmed and tried to force his son to a chair.

"Don't!" Vridar shouted. "Leave me alone!"

They left him to his pacing until he was exhausted, until he fell to a chair and began to weep. He shook and moaned, or he would start up, his woe roaring in great sobs, or he would walk round and round the room, fighting the air, striving to calm himself. And when he was quieter at last, though still violently shaken, he told the bitter story of this night. It poured out of him in sobbing, inarticulate words; he hurled it from him in frenzied gestures; and when it was all told, he broke down and wept again. His parents were amazed and for a long while they did not speak. Then Prudence tried to comfort him but he spurned her gentleness; because he was deeply ashamed now and he wished he had not told.

He bolted outside and went to the grave of Towser. His mother came out but he roared at her and said he wanted to be alone. She went up the path and he bowed to the grave and shook. All night he sat here, now goaded to new frenzy, now trying to believe that the confessions had been a dream. When daylight came he walked. He climbed the mountain and went among trees; he stared at the river, obsessed by a wish to kill himself, and so be done forever with humiliation and grief. Pride told him to renounce Neloa, to spurn her, to forget her. But within him there was a voice stronger than pride, a love stronger than death, a morbid vanity that would see no defeat; and the more he agonized over the matter, the more convinced he was that he could never spurn her. She had taken hold of his life as nothing else had done. Rather than live without her, he would have chosen death.

But his pride, too, was inexorable, and for hours love and pride fought within him, until he was driven beyond his endurance, until he cursed himself and his birth. If he went with Neloa, how could he forget! He could never forget how calmly she had told him, how unconcerned she had seemed to be; nor how abject he had been in his pleading; nor how stupid he had been during these many weeks. And perhaps he could never humble and chasten her or make her understand how much of self-esteem his being with her must cost him. And if he went without her, what could life be for him save emptiness and loss!

He climbed the mountain and came down and climbed again, trying to wear himself out. He wanted to see her and talk with her: to learn if she had also wept in agony of soul; to learn if her dream had been his dream. "To hell with her!" he shouted. She had given herself easily. She was little better than a whore. Why did he love her and why had he been deceived! "To hell with her!" he said.

But this cry was so traitorous to his heart, and his need of her, his wish to see her, was so overwhelming, that he came down the mountain and went to Diana. She looked at him in amazement.

"I want you to go to Antelope," he said, speaking desperately. "Promise you will." Diana promised and Vridar resumed. "I want you to take a letter to her. Right now. Will you?"

"I guess so."

"I'll write it. You get your horse."

He entered the house and again he felt an awful humiliation and wished he had not told. Ignoring his mother, who looked as if she had not slept, he went to a bedroom and sat at a desk. He wrote this letter to Neloa.

Dear Neloa:

Even if I tried, I could not tell you how deeply I am hurt. I'll never be the same person again. All night I've told myself that I should spurn you and I think I should. But I can't. In spite of the awful things you have done, I love you and I'll always love you, I can see now.

I want to know how you feel. Last night you did not seem ashamed of what you had done. I cannot love you and I will not marry you unless you. __ _ret is deep and lasting. You will have to change your ways and go to school and be the kind of wife I want. You will have to understand what you have done to me and how utterly I believed in you, and you will have to restore that confidence which you have lost. If you will do these things and if you want to do them with all your heart and soul, Diana will fetch your letter. If you don't want to do them, I will never see you again.

VRIDAR.

Diana took the letter and rode away and Vridar followed her to the benchland to wait there. Three months ago, he had filed homestead claim to some land here and had built a shack on it and he now went to this shack. Standing in the doorway, he watched Diana vanish over western hills. It would take her an hour to go, an hour to return, and possibly she would be there an hour: three hours to wait, three eternities, and with nothing to do. He sat on a log and at once stood up and looked westward and then sat again. After a little, he began to walk but he did not go far. He walked into the east but he kept looking backward to the west. He listened for the sound of a pony's feet.

Going two hundred yards away, he returned, and again

went and again returned, completing this aimless journey a
score of times. Within the log hut he sat on a pile of straw
but at once he came out, feeling stifled with a roof over his
head. Now he went down the road where Diana had gone and
he stared over the western hills. He came back and strove to
think, tried to understand what he should do, but it was impossible to think. His whole being was fixed on the homeward
gallop of Diana. If he imagined hoof beats, he would start
westward, running down the road; whereupon, seeing nothing, despising his weakness, he would return to the shack and
walk aimlessly or he would look at the sun, trying to tell the
hour. What would Neloa write to him? What would Neloa
write to him! This was the one, the only, question in his mind.
Would Diana find her weeping her heart out and would she
write to him her loneliness and her grief?

Going again on the hills he circled and came back; and
again he went. And in this manner he spent a desolate and un-
forgettable day. Diana, it seemed, had been gone years, and
he knew she had been gone many hours. The sun was only an
hour high now. He took the road westward, breaking from
time to time into a run; and almost unaware of what he did,
he covered half the distance to Neloa's home. He stared down
a long gray lane but there was no moving thing to be seen.
He sat by the road and waited and the sun sank and the hills
were blue with dusk. Detesting himself for being here, he
started home; but again and again he sat by the road and
waited. He hated Diana and he hated Neloa and he loathed
himself. Stars were out when he came to the shack. He waited
here perhaps a minute, though it seemed an hour, and took the
westward road again; and on a far hill he saw the streak of
white in the pony's face. He ran to meet Diana with his heart
intense and smothered in every breath. Looking up to her
face, his eyes asked a question, and Diana, with grave pity,
looked down at him.

"Where's the letter? Great God, give it to me!"

"She didn't send any."

"She didn't send any! You mean—you mean she didn't send
any?"

"Yes."

"Di, don't fool with me! Give me the letter!"

"There isn't no letter. I asked if she was going to write and she said 'no.'"

Vridar stared at her and felt horribly sick. Diana got down and sat on the high bank of the road. Vridar still looked at her.

"Set down," Diana said. "I'll tell you about it." Vridar turned and sat, reaching under him for the bank, because not for a moment did he take his gaze from Diana's face. "Well, first I give her your letter. She took it and read it and then she tucked it in her dress. I watched her face and it didn't seem like she cared much what you wrote."

"What—what did she say?"

"Not very much. We went in the house and she helped get dinner. I wouldn't say she seemed very bothered or upset or ashamed. While we was there, Dave Wolf came in——"

"What!" Vridar shouted. "Dave Wolf!"

"What you shoutun for?"

"Dave Wolf," Vridar said, and bowed to his knees. "Go on."

"Well, he stayed for dinner and talked some and that's about all. I had to wait till he went before I could see her alone."

"And was—how did she act with him?"

"Oh, about like she would with any man. They talked and she smiled at him and he smiled at her. They set together when we had dinner."

Vridar stood up in a black world. Only last night she had sent him home crazed and today she sat at dinner with a man with whom she had lain six months ago. It was impossible to understand that.

"Di, what else?"

"Well, when Dave left I got Neloa alone and said you wanted her to stay with me in Rigby and go to high school. She said she would. I said we'd go down day after tomorrow and to be ready and she said she would. I guess that's all."

"And—and—she didn't send any letter?"

"No. I asked did she want to and she said no."

"Did she say anything about—last night?"

"No."

"And—and you say she acted happy?"

"Well, I wouldn't say she was heart-broken or anything. She smiled and talked. She acted like she always did. . . . She et a big dinner."

Vridar turned away. He took the road and Diana followed, leading the horse, and on their way to the house nothing was said. Without eating supper—he had not eaten since breakfast of the day before—he went to bed and lay in silence. Again pride and love fought. Mertyl came in and Vridar saw him undressing in the gloom. He wanted to talk with Mertyl and ask his advice, but toward Neloa and toward Vridar's love for her, Mertyl had shown a strange hostility. He did not seem to like her. And he rarely spoke to Vridar and the gulf between the brothers was wider and darker than before.

Mertyl turned to the wall and was soon asleep. Vridar lay in silence, tortured and enraged, his mind turning over pictures of Neloa with Harvey, with Francis, with Dave: seeing her embraced by one and by another, seeing the man's mouth on her mouth, hearing the man's words; until at last he dressed and went outside, feeling murderous. He walked about, plotting the murder of four and of himself; thinking with dark savage pleasure of their cries for mercy; and wondering where he could find Harvey Kress.

In the kitchen a while later he wrote a scathing letter, born out of hurt pride and hurt vanity, out of loneliness and defeat. It said:

Dear Miss Doole:

It must seem to you, as it seems to me, that I have been an awful simpleton. You have had a lot of fun with me, but you have taught me much, dear lady, that is worth any price. I shall never be a fool again.

I don't like your gate and I will no longer swing on it. After you are older, you will realize that what you did is the sort of thing that women are usually paid for. In any case, I am ambitious and proud and it would be ridiculous, as even you must see, for me to marry a woman like you.

There are women in this world who are not the common property of every man. They do not devote themselves entirely to seduction. And as for you, marry Dave Wolf and live with him in an Antelope shack and have a bunch of kids. Grow old and tragic like your mother and then count your loss. I shall go on. The woman I marry will hate evil as I hate it and will love honesty and truth as I do. But all this, of course, you have no power to understand.

And flatter yourself, if you want to, with this: I have not eaten or slept for two days, and to you, who ate with such relish a few hours ago, I must seem the last word in stupidity. I am. But years ago I fought a worse fight than this one and still kept my feet and I'll keep my feet again.

Let Dave swing on your gate, lady. It's a fine gate!
VRIDAR HUNTER.

He read this letter and then sat and stared at it and then fed it to the lamp. He could no more have sent it to Neloa than he could have cut off his hands. And he knew it. And it was this bitter knowledge that sent him to bed despising himself, heaping scorn upon himself, until he sank abject under the withering derision of his pride.

On the next day he resumed the struggle. He little realized that this decision, so difficult to make, was to be the most important of his life. It seemed to be only a choice between love and pride but it was infinitely more than that. If pride had won. . . . But love won. He told his mother that Neloa was going to Rigby, there to live with Diana and go to school. The decision was made. The second great crisis of his life had been passed.

And Vridar went again to college but he was not the credulous youth who had gone the year before. Hating credulity, and hating above all himself and what he had been, he cut free of his old anchors; and his life for three years became reckless and wild. Betrayed by home-training, made a fool of by devotion to mother and God, he plotted his life toward moral disintegration and the ways of the social outcast. And only his love for his parents, only his loyalty to them, saved him from utter ruin.

PART THREE

Mac's grin was full of derision and spite.

You're ambitious, he said. Well, so was Caesar. Caesar wanted to conquer the world and you want to get into Who's Who. . . . Now tell me why in the hell you want to write an honest book.

Vridar looked with amused eyes at this gaunt sardonic student of Machiavelli.

You couldn't understand. You'd distress me by your effort.

Listen, Hunter, don't try to be subtle. You're about as subtle as a Rotarian eating beans. Mac turned to Ferd who, drunk and theatrical, was intoning an old ballad. See your friend here, he said. See the mighty rhonchus of rhetoric! He's going to write an honest book! Mac stared at Vridar, affecting amazement, and then helped himself to another glass of punch. Why, he asked, are you going to be silly? Why should anyone write an honest book?

Vridar sipped his gin and looked at Mac.

Because every other kind has been written, he said.

I

•

AGAIN Vridar lived in the basement den and stoked the furnace and again A. M. McClintock lived in the attic above. As in the year before, Vridar cooked his own meals, laundered his own clothes, and lived in all respects as frugally as he could; and Mertyl lived with him. He enrolled as a sophomore in the school of arts; he devoted himself for three weeks to his studies; he planned for himself a quiet and meditative life. But the plot of his life was now beyond his control.

If Neloa, too, had devoted herself to study and had written to him of love and penitence, urging him to forgive and forget, he most likely would have been sober and industrious in this year. He would have forgiven, even though he could never forget; he would have lost himself in his love of books and scholarship. But Neloa's letters were not penitent, except when he rebuked her savagely; and books for her were not and never could be what they were for him.

During this while Vridar kept a journal and he set within it all his vanity and bravado, all his bewilderment and doubt. It records how for two months he pleaded or spurned, humbled himself and then threatened, hoped and despaired; and it records, too, the unwise rôle of Diana, because it was she who spied on Neloa and wrote to Vridar her warnings and advice.

September 15—Tonight Neloa and I spent an hour together before train time. Sweethearts we part, and perhaps strangers we shall meet. She promises a letter every week, no matter if I write or not: will she keep that promise? Her test has started. My fight has begun!

145

September 18—Today Mertyl had his eyes operated on. The operation was terrible but he did not flinch. He will be blindfolded for two weeks.

September 22—A week has passed and no letter yet! But what the hell do I care? I do, I do. Mertyl is bearing up splendidly. What courage and patience he has!

September 23—Eight days and no letter. . . . Worked in the department store today. There are some nice girls here. I think I'll cut loose. Other men sow their wild oats. Am I to be a simple fool all my life, mortgaged body and soul to an adolescent love-affair?

September 25—Got two letters today. Neloa's was a nice spray of ice. There seems to be no humility in her, no shame, no pride. I was a fool two weeks ago and I put my pride under my feet but I'll never do it again. Wrote a long letter to Diana. She will keep her eyes open and let me know what is going on.

This is the "spray of ice" which Neloa sent:

Sweetheart:—Well, I am in school and I guess I like it all right. The weather here is awful today. It is cold and windy and I am shivering while I write this. Diana and I get along fine. We both cook and keep the house clean and we usually walk to school together. I have been looking for a letter from you.

Well, I don't want to bore you so will ring off for this time.

As ever,
NELOA.

Vridar remembered now that in her other letters to him, written in former years, she had always closed with the statement that she would ring off. It annoyed him. He thought it wanted dignity. It was girlish and silly. And he reflected on the kind of letter Elizabeth Barrett wrote to Robert Browning. Neloa's letter he decided to burn, but after reading it until he knew it by heart, he kissed it again and again and stored it away.

September 29—Watched the football squad last night. Am taking boxing lessons with anyone I can find. Went over and looked at a matinee dance. How presumably civilized people can so contort themselves, so indulge in lascivious embrace, and call it clean is beyond me. I think all dancing ought to be suppressed.

September 30—Worked again as a clerk. Some of the girls here seem to fancy me but I can't believe it. Haven't decided whether to study or to run wild. Which? It depends on her.

October 1—Shall I write to her? I don't know. I'm journeying like a leaf in a wind.

October 3—Well, got a letter from her. I wrote her to get someone else to swing on her gate. I should have written her that long ago.

This is the letter he received from Neloa:

Dear Boy, I don't know why you haven't written. I guess you don't care any more and I should worry. We have some snow here today and the weather is very cold. I think my English teacher is a cross old hen. She makes me write themes and I hate themes. Well, I will ring off for this time.

As ever,
NELOA.

And this is Vridar's answer:

Dear Girl, if you feel the way your letter suggests, you are wasting stamps. When I left you in Rigby you said I could put your love to any test I could think of; and now, because you haven't received a letter, you write as if you don't give a damn. Is that your idea of love? Does it all mean to you no more than that? If so, please address your letters to another name.

VRIDAR.

October 6—Got a letter from her today. It's all right. But she will have to learn humility or to hell with her. . . . Strong men, I imagine, never fall in love. Such nonsense is for simpletons like me.

October 9—Well, her letters like Wilson's Mexican negotiations leave me no wiser. She evades. Am going to enlist or head for South America. . . . Last night a man here named Gudler said I tried to sneak into bed with his wife. It was Forenoon. The woman screamed and has been hysterical all day. . . . And I think the fool ought to be slept with if she feels so insecure. There's something funny about it. Is a really virtuous woman ever hysterical? I'll know some day.

October 12—Letter from her: sweet, earnest. Will send her a ring now. . . . I have a rented typewriter and am in heaven. I want to write a novel but don't think I know enough.

October 21—No letter this week. So I made a date with a girl in the store. The playboy of Antelope: no care, no disillusionment. I'd give the world if I could be a reckless spender and a gay dog.

October 22—Well, the joke is on me. The playboy sits at home and it begins to seem to him that he's a worm and womankind is a robin. The girl ditched me. I'll be a scholar and some lovely thing in fiction will be my wife. Elizabeth Bennett. Portia. The Wife of Bath!

October 31—Letter from Diana says Neloa is flirting with other men. My God!

November 1—Why am I taking dancing? 1) To acquire self-poise; 2) to learn more about women; 3) for social intercourse; 4) for manners. I think the last two are piddle. Nor do I understand why any man should want to learn about women. . . . But on with the one-step!

November 9—Wilson won. Thank God, for I had no time for Hughes and his whiskers. . . . Talked today with a Miss Graves, author, feminist, educator. Asked if she thought it possible to combine the emotional and academic. Said she did. Fine. That's what I want.

November 11—Am learning the Canter Hesitation Waltz, the most side-splitting assortment of advance and retreat and St. Vitus ever devised to work up a person's lusts.

Most people don't know why they dance. I'm convinced of that. And a lot don't know why they marry! I didn't know a few months back.

December 1—Diana says Neloa is also writing to several men. I was so God-damned mad I went for a long walk and then sat down and wrote her—as if I had not already written her the same thing a hundred times!

This is what Vridar wrote:

Dear Neloa: When I left you in September, you said I could trust you henceforth in all things. We were to have no secrets, tell no lies. Now I learn you are interested in other men. You are writing to other men. Are deceit and lying a hopeless part of you? Will you never be honest or have any wish to be? I expect an answer at once and no damned fooling about it, for I'm awfully sick of being a fool and loving where loving is silly. I fancy, though, there may be cures for love.

If you don't want to write, send the ring and I'll know we're through.

VRIDAR.

And to this letter Neloa answered:

Dear Vridar, you seem willing to believe your sister instead of me. I'm not flirting with anyone. It's true I've answered some letters from old friends. They're just friendly letters and I didn't bother you about them. You can see them if you want to. It's all for you to decide. If you say to send the ring, I will, and the poem you sent with it. You say you can't love a liar. Well, I can't love a man who believes his sister instead of me.

NELOA.

Vridar read this letter and was furious. But he did not send for the ring; he did not write. In agony of doubt again, he walked a long while, trying to see his way out. And he was still in doubt, still enraged and tortured, when two unexpected events entered his life. They plotted his life for him and he followed where they led.

II

•

THE FIRST of these was the dastardly way in which he changed lodgings. McClintock was a sly and undisciplined youth who thieved and whored with equal relish and who had a most unscrupulous sense of fun. For Vridar only of all the persons around him did he have either affection or loyalty, and for many weeks he had been trying to persuade him and Mertyl to share rooms with him elsewhere. He was sick of his cold dark room in the attic. He despised the avarice of his landlord. And one afternoon he told Vridar he had found two rooms that were well-furnished and well-heated and low of rent.

But Vridar demurred. He liked Forenoon but he knew it would be unwise to live with him. And there was Mertyl, still a very pious lad who voiced sharp disapproval of Forenoon's ways. "He's no good," Mertyl said. "He's headed for the dogs." Nevertheless, after deliberating for hours, and in spite of his best judgment, Vridar told McClintock to engage a truck.

"We'll leave in the night," Forenoon said. "I owe a month's rent. We got a-sneak out."

Vridar considered this. He owed no rent because he stoked a furnace for his underground den. And he went to Professor Yupp and said he was leaving, but he said nothing of McClintock's going, for this, it seemed to him, was none of his business. Then he and Mertyl packed their things and waited for the truck. It was to come at midnight.

An hour before midnight Forenoon came stealthily down with his bags and whispered that Yupp was asleep. Vridar brought his things to the sidewalk and for a little while the three young men waited here. And then Forenoon, with the pretext of going to a lavatory, sneaked back into the house and did a most malicious thing.

After a few minutes he returned and he began to laugh, unable to restrain his glee. He clapped hands to his mouth and sputtered and choked; he reeled down the sidewalk, bellowing like mad. And Vridar, watching him, became suspicious; but he affected a most obtuse unconcern. He laid his plans and confided in Mertyl, and Mertyl decoyed Forenoon to the corner drugstore. Then Vridar dashed to his room and what he found there amazed him.

McClintock had utterly demolished the chair and the table, the dishes and the light. All these were scattered in ruins. And he had jumped on the iron bed and distorted it into rainbows; he had kicked holes in the springs; and with the aid of a knife, he had made of the mattress a pile of cotton and rag. He had jerked the curtain down and torn it into shreds, he had riddled the window shade, and he had smashed the box-cupboard from the wall. The room looked as if it had been struck by a cyclone.

Filled with wonder and rage, Vridar stared at all these broken things; and then, with only vengeance in his mind, he went quietly up the stairway and entered McClintock's room. Working swiftly, and yet as softly as he could, he destroyed all the dishes and stabbed all the pots. The rickety chair and table he knocked apart and the more fragile pieces he broke across his knee. By jumping on the bed, or by wrenching its frame with his hands, he made it look as scarred and twisted as if it had come through a fire. He demolished the shade and curtain, and with a knife, he riddled the ugly faded paper on the walls. Pausing then to see what else he could do, he saw the shabby linoleum and this he tore into shreds. Then he went down the stairway and to the sidewalk.

Forenoon and Mertyl were still in the drugstore but in a few moments they came up the street. Forenoon giggled and then burst into devilish joy, and Vridar stared at him as if amazed. Forenoon walked round and round Vridar, looking at him with bright malicious eyes, howling with glee.

"Shut up," Vridar said.

Forenoon sobered a little. But his joy exploded in sudden snorts and he went to the corner and out of sight and there he howled again. Vridar looked at Mertyl and winked. "He broke everything in our room. I slipped up and returned the favor."

The truck now came and the baggage was loaded. They rode to Second East and unloaded their stuff and entered their new home. The two rooms were small and shabby but they were clean. The man who owned them was a Jew and had a grocery out front, and Forenoon said he would steal all their food from this store. Then he strode about like a showman, leading Vridar to the bath, a small ugly place on a hall, and to the beds. Forenoon chose one and sat on it. He stooped to unlace his shoes and fell to the floor, roaring like a demon, his hands threshing the air. Vridar began to laugh, too, and in a few moments his roaring disputed with McClintock's and shook the room. Someone knocked on the door.

"Come in!" Forenoon cried. A Jew in pajamas thrust his head around.

"What's all the racket for?"

"Beat it!" Forenoon said.

"I can't have any noise after ten o'clock. It's past midnight."

"Take your mug away," said Forenoon, "or I'll throw a shoe at it."

The face vanished and the door was closed. In a few minutes there was another rap and the Jew entered with a policeman.

"What's the trouble here?" asked the policeman.

"Nothing much," said Vridar. "We were laughing and he told us to be still." The policeman glared around him.

"No more racket," he said, "or I'll run you in."

Forenoon was looking rather sheepish now. After the two men were gone he told of what he would do. He would steal the Jew blind and seduce his daughter; and if he didn't like that, he would knock his chin into his cerebellum. Then he undressed and crawled into bed, chuckling all the while; and during the night from time to time he awoke and guffawed, and Vridar, awakened, howled with him. And when morning came, Forenoon was bursting with the secret.

"You must be a fool," he said, grinning at Vridar. "Are all the people in Antelope simple as you?"

"People in Antelope know more than they tell."

"Listen, you know what I been howlun about?"

"Of course I know."

"Like hell. You'll blow a slat out when I tell you."

"You're the one who'll blow a slat out."

McClintock pondered this. He became suspicious. "Why?" he said.

"Listen, Forenoon, fools are grown down in Cedar City where you came from. My room looked pretty bad, didn't it? Well, it looked like a palace in comparison with yours."

"You mean you went up and busted my room!"

"Busted it! I didn't leave anything as big as your thumb."

Forenoon scowled. He came over to Vridar, his gestures menacing, and Vridar faced him, his hands clenched.

"I wouldn't start anything," Vridar said.

"That was a dirty trick!"

"Sure it was. But you started it."

Forenoon turned away and sat down. In a few moments he was roaring again. What, he asked, would Yupp do. He would have a convulsion and bite himself. And Forenoon lay on the floor and howled until he was spent and white. Then he rose and said he was going out to the store. He wanted to see what the Jew's daughter was like, or perhaps he would steal a pound of butter or a can of jam.

In a few moments he returned with a can of peas.

"I couldn't see any butter," he said.

They now had breakfast but Mertyl would eat none of the peas. Vridar ate of them and said they were damned good. He was beginning to feel like a scoundrel, and he was a bit alarmed but he was also pleased. The Jew's daughter, Forenoon said, was a swell thing to look at. He would have her in bed in a week.

"Get me one, too," Vridar said, and wondered if he meant it.

"Sure. You know Peg Winters? You'n have her."

"All right. Fetch her around."

They walked to the campus and on their way they came face to face with Professor Yupp. He stopped and looked at them. His small eyes were full of pain, his mouth twitched. Never had he known, he said, that there were such young men in the world. Never would he have believed it. And he asked:

"What would your parents say?"

"I don't have none," Forenoon said. "When they saw me they gave up."

Yupp looked at him and then at Vridar. His eyes filled with tears and Vridar felt horribly ashamed. He stared at the earth and did not speak.

"It would have been bad enough," Yupp went on, "out of common street hoodlums. But that college students—I can hardly believe it yet."

He turned down the walk and Vridar and Mertyl and Forenoon went to the campus. "To hell with the old skinflint," Forenoon said. "He froze me to death all last year. I wish I'd kicked his house down."

But Vridar, though he despised Yupp's greed, felt only shame for what he had done. He slipped away after a while and went to Yupp's home. He knocked on the door and Yupp came and stared at him.

"I want to explain," Vridar said. "What I did was cowardly and I know it. But McClintock slipped in and smashed my room and I was furious and I smashed his. I am very sorry. I want to apologize and to pay for what I broke."

Yupp looked at him for quite a while.

"All right," he said. "I'll send you a statement of the cost." And very coldly he bowed to Vridar and closed the door.

For this mean escapade, Vridar never forgave himself. He always looked back upon it with shame.

The other event reached farther into **his** life. It led him to a most perilous and foolhardy undertaking and could easily have brought him to disaster. It started in the grocery where he was a Saturday clerk.

Some of the clerks who had been here a long while were thieves and Vridar knew they were thieves. His suspicions had been aroused by small and casual doings, and he had watched them, and he had learned what they stole and how. One of them was a man and this man slipped small and costly articles into his pockets when he went to lunch and again when he left at night. Another was a large sour woman named Maggie Simms. Her relatives and friends would come in and buy bulky articles and into the bags Maggie slyly put many things that were never paid for. Three other women also thieved in this way but they were all trusted clerks. And Vridar wondered why the manager of this department was so stupid and why he did not see what was so clearly to be seen.

On a Saturday late in November Vridar's sales broke a record. This record, which had stood for four years, was held by Maggie, and now she openly detested him. He saw her talking about him to other clerks and then to the manager; and the manager came to him, after a while, and drew him aside. He wanted to know how things were going and Vridar said they were going all right.

"May I see your book?"

He took Vridar's sales-book and studied the records. He returned it to him and went over to the cashier and talked with her for a long time. And during this evening, Vridar knew that he was being closely watched. He resented this spying but his record was clean and he had nothing to fear.

On the next Saturday he was watched again. From time to time the manager would go to the cashier's window and study the sales-slips there. The cashier was a lovely girl and Vridar liked her and thought she liked him. When next he gave her money he lingered by her window and spoke.

"Why am I being watched?" he asked in a low voice.

"I wouldn't stand there," she said.

He looked at her gratefully and moved away. Thereafter she watched him, too, but only with sympathy, he supposed.

Just before closing time the manager came to him. He was cool and officious. Mr. Drake, he said, wanted to see Vridar in his office. Archibald Drake was president of the store.

"All right," Vridar said; and he went at once to Drake's office.

"Sit down," said Drake.

"You want to see me?" Vridar asked.

"Yes." For several moments Drake studied him. "You needn't come next Saturday. We don't need you."

"Don't need me! You mean—I'm fired?"

"I mean we'll not need you any more."

"But why?"

"I do not care to discuss the matter. You may go now."

Vridar stood up. He felt insulted and he was furious. When he spoke again his voice shook.

"I'm being dismissed. I've a right to know why. Hasn't my work been all right?"

For several long moments Drake stared at him. His eyes were searching and without pity.

"I do not care to discuss the matter. You may go."

"I won't. If you don't tell me you'll have to throw me out!"

"Well, if you insist. We have reason to believe that you are dishonest. Is that clear enough?"

"That I'm—I'm dishonest! Who told you that?"

"I have no more to say."

The man now took a paper and began to read. Vridar looked at the paper and shook.

"I haven't been!" he cried, speaking to the face behind the paper. "I swear to God!" There was no answer. The paper was turned and the man read on another page. "You do have clerks who are cheats!" Vridar went on furiously. "Why don't you fire them!" The paper fell and the man looked at him.

"Will you go now?" he asked quietly.

"Yes! But first listen to this: anyone who says I cheated

is a liar, a dirty lowdown liar! And that goes for all of you!"

Then Vridar swung and left the room. He was so blind with fury that he could barely find his way down the stairs. He went to the cloakroom, his mind busy with vengeance; and while he stood here, taking off his apron and jacket, his glance fell on a stack of sales-books. Without knowing why, he thrust one of these books into an inside pocket. Then he put on his cap and climbed the stairs and found the street.

He went home convulsed with rage and trying to plot vengeance for this insult. Entering his rooms, he sat on a bed and tried to think. How could he avenge himself! How could he outwit this wealthy snob who had called him a thief and whose only evidence had been spiteful gossip! . . . During his life, it was true, he had stolen a few things; but what lad had not? He had filched candy and cigars, he had staggered home under a case of beer, but only because others had done so. He had stolen in bravado then. And now, after having been honest. . . . He rose, choking, and paced the room and he was still pacing when Forenoon and Mertyl came. Roaring in anger and self-pity, he told them what had been done.

"I'll get even! I'll outwit that insolent snob! I'll do it if it costs me my life!"

Forenoon liked this outburst. A petty thief himself, who laid hands on what he could take, he had urged Vridar to steal with him, suggesting that they might become Robin Hoods. And besides this, he could now smell a profit.

"Make him feed us," McClintock said. "That would be a swell vengeance."

Vridar hadn't thought of that. He seized the idea and pondered it. One plan and another stood like dark silhouettes in his mind, and each he examined, probing the possibilities and the dangers. And at last he said:

"He'll feed us. I've decided that."

He walked the streets for hours and he evolved a plan that was as cunning as it was dangerous. Archibald Drake, he announced, would pay for his insult with groceries.

"He called me a thief. All right, I'll be a thief."

"What—whu-whu-whu-what's the plan?" asked McClintock, so excited that he stuttered.

But Vridar would not explain. For two days he deliberated, weighing risks, searching the unforeseen: exulting as he wrought his pattern of details.

"Realize," he said to McClintock, "we run a big risk. If we get caught, it's ten years for us. . . . That's all right for you. You don't have any parents."

"Thank God. They're a big nuisance."

"If you lose your head——"

"Lose my head! Who the Christ you talkun to?"

"You blunder things. When you swipe a can of peas, you shake around for an hour. . . . And if you blunder things, I'll blow your head off."

"Here! You tryun to bluff me?"

"I mean it. So if you haven't the guts, say so."

And very carefully, step by step, Vridar outlined the plan. Then he stared at McClintock for a long moment.

"You," he said, "will get the oranges. You'll fetch me the sales-slip. I'll write the order and you'll get it and the oranges into the box. . . . Is that much clear?"

Forenoon shivered. He looked at Vridar and grinned.

"But how'll I get it in the box?"

"I told you, damn it! Cut a hole in one overcoat pocket. Reach your finger through the hole and carry the oranges under your coat. You'll be standing by the box and someone will push you and you'll drop the oranges——"

"Who'll push me?" McClintock was trembling now. "And what if I get caught?"

"Keep a cool head."

"Is that all I have to do?"

"That's all. I'll take care of the rest of it. . . . All you do is get that package into the box."

"My God, that's enough!"

Vridar looked at him pityingly. McClintock was a thief but he had the courage only of a petty slinking thief and sometimes he hadn't that.

McClintock rose, shaking in all his limbs, and went outside. Vridar turned to Mertyl.

"You don't have to be in on this."

"You'll be caught," Mertyl said.

"Not if Forenoon does his part."

"I wouldn't try it," Mertyl said.

"Oh, the hell you wouldn't! You think that son-of-a-bitch can call me a thief and get away with it? . . . And what do I care about life or jail or death? They're all the same to me now."

"What would mater think?"

"She won't know. I've got the nerve, so don't fret. Everything will be all right."

McClintock came in and stared at Vridar.

"Your plan sounds fishy," he said. "I won't do it unless you do it first."

"You coward."

"Coward, hell! It's fishy, I tell you!"

"Will you do it if I show you how?"

"Sure—if it works."

"All right," Vridar said, "I'll show you how."

III

•

DURING this night Vridar tossed in dream, his mind reaching for the crafty stratagem; and on the next morning, after pondering the matter again, he knew he would have to be a forger also. This thought terrified him a little but after a while he liked it and was not afraid at all. In the imitation of handwriting he possessed remarkable skill, having spent, during his high school years, many hours over the signatures of poets. He had copied their names because he envied them and wanted to be like them and because in their handwriting he read their character. And besides all this, he little cared now what he did. His world was in chaos like a sky of storm and he felt the lightning and the death and was unafraid.

"Forgery, too!" Forenoon cried.

"Yes."

"You can't do it!"

"I can."

And Vridar copied Forenoon's signature until that young man, bewildered and amazed, couldn't tell the one from the other. In great excitement he went to the store and got a bag of oranges and Vridar sat by a window and studied the sales-slip. It was a woman's writing, small and precise, and it would be difficult to copy.

"Why the hell," he asked, "didn't you get a man clerk?"

"God, I never thought about that."

"Damn it, I'm no wizard. Go back and get a man clerk."

And while Forenoon was gone, Vridar went to a drug-store and called the grocery. He asked the price of one thing and another and he wrote them down with painstaking care. He came to his room and Forenoon gave him another slip and for a long while he copied the writing; and Forenoon stood by, protesting, advising, and ready to flee.

"Here!" he yelled. "I don't want my name on the damn thing!"

"Shut up."

Forenoon looked at the order.

"That's a hell of a bunch of food to go to jail for. Get some fancy stuff."

"No. We're playing safe."

McClintock said the order looked fishy. He held it to the light and turned it over and over.

"It won't work," he said. "My God, I tell you it's fishy!"

Vridar took the order and looked at it. He was trembling a little. The crucial moment had come.

"I'll take it," he said. "Get yourself ready for jail."

"I'm going to beat it," McClintock said. "Good God, I tell you it's fishy! Mert, look at this!"

Mertyl came over and looked at the order.

"I wouldn't try it," he said to Vridar.

"Bosh!" Vridar cried. "What do I care about jails!"

In a pocket of McClintock's overcoat he cut a hole and then put the coat on and reached down through the hole with a finger and thumb and grasped the bag. He felt a little unnerved but when he looked at McClintock's white face he shrugged.

"A hell of a crook you are!" he said.

He entered the store and could barely move through the crowd. He was shoved about and in a little while came to the box, and by the box he stood tiptoe, as if looking for someone; and a moment later, when a woman pushed against him, he pretended to lose his balance and almost fall, and in this moment he dropped the bag of oranges into the box. He scowled at the woman as if annoyed and he moved away, still gazing about as if searching; and he came to the door and the street. He wanted to run now. But he stood on the corner and looked at faces around him. He moved slowly down the street. When he heard a bird sing, he stopped to listen, as if in no hurry at all.

Back in his room, he affected to be at ease but a tremendous excitement shook him. McClintock dropped to a chair and mopped his brow.

"We're goners!" McClintock said. He stared at Vridar. His face was like chalk. "Good God, let's beat it! What you want a-sit around here for?"

Vridar crossed the room to get a drink. He looked at his hands and saw that they trembled. He shrugged.

"For Christ sake!" McClintock howled. "Let's go! Are you crazy? In an hour we'll all be in jail!"

"That's all right," Vridar said. "A lot of good men are in jails."

McClintock mopped his brow again. Sweat was running down his face now and his small greedy eyes were bright with terror. At every unexpected noise he leapt up as if kicked. He went to a window and peered out or he stood by the door and listened. He lowered his voice to a whisper.

"We're goners! We're goners sure as Christ!"

Vridar took a book and tried to read or from time to time he looked at McClintock. Forenoon's cowardice amazed him.

"Stop your damned fussing!" he cried. "Get hold of yourself."

"I'm going!" McClintock said.

Feverishly he began to pack his things. He jerked a bag open and was piling clothes into it when a knock sounded on the door. For a long moment no one spoke. McClintock rose to his feet and looked at Vridar and shook. And then, in a last desperate effort to escape, he vanished under a bed.

"Come in!" Vridar called.

The door was opened and a man entered carrying a box. "Groceries for McClintock."

"Set them on the floor," Vridar said quietly. He went over and looked into the box. He checked the groceries against the bill and said everything was all right. The man went out with the box and Vridar went over and shut the door. From under the bed, McClintock thrust a white face.

"Is he gone?"

Vridar burned the sales-slip and destroyed the ashes. McClintock came out and looked at the stuff on the floor. He lifted one article and another, his eyes shining with greedy interest.

"We just as well a-had a lot more stuff," he said.

From December until early spring Vridar maneuvered with care and cunning and his groceries cost him only a few cents in each week. To the constant urgings of McClintock he yielded, little by little, until at last he ordered only the best of everything: the choicest fruits and pickles and jams, shrimp and boneless chicken, imported cheese, nuts and stuffed olives, and the finest of sifted peas.

"We need better lodgings," McClintock said one day. "We need a swell joint."

And now, as formerly, he urged Vridar to larger orders,

so that they would have stuff to sell. They could buy it in case lots and sell it at a discount.

"As a fool," Vridar said, "you haven't any competitors."

"You call me a fool!" McClintock roared. "Listen, I'll lay your eyes right out on your cheeks!"

"I can imagine that."

"I'll beat your daylights out one these-here days. You realize that?"

"Go ahead."

Vridar looked at McClintock's muscular frame. He was a powerful young man and he was quick; but twice before Vridar had called his bluff and McClintock had swaggered and cursed and gone out like a match. And now he said:

"Well, let's eat. I'm hungry as a dog."

And during these weeks, Mertyl protested again and again. "Not that I care about jail," he said loyally. "If you go, I'll go with you. But it isn't right."

"Right, hell!" Vridar cried. "Organized society is organized theft. Some steal openly; some exploit the humble and the weak; and others filch in the name of charity and God. One thief gets punished and another gets his name written on a bronze tablet. . . . What the hell do you mean by right!"

"Just the same," Mertyl retorted impatiently, "you don't have to steal because others do. Besides, all thieves get caught."

"Yes? If they did, the only persons out of jails would be dead ones."

"And there's dad and mater," Mertyl went on. "What would they think?"

"I've thought of that," Vridar said; and he said no more.

He thought of it often. He blustered and cursed; he said he was sick of the world, of humanity, of life; he said a jail terrified him no more than a piece of cotton on the end of a string. And then he would remember his parents, their devotion and trust, and he would feel sick and lost. He would walk to the mountains and climb them and look northward and his eyes would fill with tears; and he would return to his room, wishing he could die. "Little I care," he said to Mertyl, "what happens to me"; and in this he was sincere. But he cared what happened to his parents; and week after week he fought the bitter fight, drawn in one hour to desperate plotting, to vengeance and hatred, to the ways of the outcast; and drawn in the next to a sense of the beautiful and the good. . . .

And on a day in April, the second of these forces conquered and he announced that he would thieve no more. He was sick of it, he said. He sat on a chair and hid his face in his hands. And McClintock implored him not to be a fool; begged him to write one more order; threatened him with ruin if he did not. The threat stirred Vridar to fury.

"You'll do what?" he asked, rising to his feet. "Listen, McClintock, do you want to be killed as dead as a doorknob? I'm through with stealing. You understand me? And take a tip from me and keep your God-damned mouth shut!"

"Yeah? You're going to heaven, I guess. You're going to wear wings."

"Just remember, that's all. I've been a thief. All right. Just open that mug of yours and I'll be a murderer, too." He advanced, his hands clenched, and McClintock stepped back. "It would be a public service to kill a man like you, McClintock," he went on, grinning, "you understand me? You understand I'd as soon bump you off as look at you?"

Forenoon stared at him for a long moment. He crossed the room and got a drink.

And Vridar thieved no more. But this was in April; and before April came, he had been guilty of another theft and he had been busy with other kinds of devilment. The story now reverts to a record of these.

IV

•

McCLINTOCK was a malicious and destructive person. Emotionally immature, undisciplined and unmoral, and with fierce resentment against his humble origins, he vented his spite in nihilism. His glee in smashing furniture or in enraging landlords was fiendish; and he seemed never so happy as when pursued by one whom he had outwitted. Before a week had passed here, he had broken all the lights and demolished the mirror in the bathroom and twisted keys off in several doors along the hallway. And when he could find nothing to destroy, he tricked Vridar.

One day he locked Vridar in the bathroom and left him there, impotent and furious, for hours; and a week later, when the rascal was asleep on his belly, Vridar bound McClintock's hands behind him with cord and roped him to a doorknob. He leapt off the bed cursing and made such a racket that the Jew came and told them to get out.

They went to a hotel and engaged a large corner room. Now, McClintock said, a maid would clean their room; and that, he declared, winking lewdly at Mertyl, was not all she would do. And at once he prowled through the building, looking for the maids.

But they were in this hotel only eight days. Under their corner was a drugstore, and the druggist had piled upon a long glass case an enormous assortment of lotions and perfumes. . . . McClintock liked this drugstore. While buying a pencil or a package of gum, he would steal dyes and laxative tablets and garden seed, and a lot of other things for which he had no use. On one day he stole a gross of paper napkins and on the next he came guiltily in with a syringe under his coat.

Often in this winter, he and Vridar wrestled, sometimes in the school's gymnasium, sometimes in their room. Or sometimes they boxed, using a set of gloves that McClintock had stolen. And nearly always in these bouts, Vridar triumphed, often drawing blood from his opponent; and Forenoon became spiteful or insolent. He taunted Vridar about women and about his Antelope heritage.

"Are you a maphrodyte?" he asked one day. Vridar tried to ignore him but Forenoon would not be ignored. "Don't you ever dream about women? . . . Hey, are you a capon? or don't you know what a capon is?"

Vridar did not. He wondered about it and read a book.

"Vreed, you ever kissed a girl yet? . . . Honest to God, have you?"

"Sure I have."

"She must a-been a homely bitch. She must a-lived on Antelope." He stared at Vridar and added: "You know how many girls I've slept with? I got ˜ecord every one. I intend to publish it some day." He rummaged among his things and found the record. "Listen, now. . . . Well, here's Mary Smith. Sounds like a fake name but there's lots of Mary Smiths in the world. This was a relative of the great and original Joseph. . . . Now listen. I spent three dollars and ten cents on Mary. . . . God damn! She ain't the first one. . . . Here, I'll tell about the first one."

Vridar turned pages of a book and pretended to read but he was all ears.

"The first was Susan Dalton. . . . That was when I was fourteen. She was fourteen. I didn't spend no money on her and it's been so long I've forgot what she looked like. . . . Well, the next was Kate Olson. I was sixteen and Kate cost me only a dollar. I took her to two shows and bought her one ice-cream cone. . . . And I don't remember what she looked like, either. . . . Say, when I publish this book, I should ought to have photographs of them, shouldn't I? . . .

"Well, the next is Mabel Turner. A fat blond. I did it to Mabel on her back porch and once was enough. God, she was sure fat! . . . The next was Ophelia Summers. That was here in Salt Lake. She cost me four dollars and sixty cents. It says here I bought her some sweet peas and two boxes cherry-covered chocolates. I got them on sale. . . . Well, the next was Janice Hunter. Vreed, you got any relatives here? I'll bet Janice was your cousin or something. . . . Vreed, you got a sister? . . . Hey, you capon, you got a sister?"

"Go to hell."

"Tell me: you got a sister?"

"Yes. Now shut up."

"Wish she was here. Bet I could do it to her in a week."

Vridar laid his book aside. He looked at McClintock.

"Leave my sister out of it."

"Go on. I'd even sleep with your mother."

Vridar stood up, feeling hot.

"Listen, Forenoon, talk all you damn please about women but leave my mother and sister out of it. You understand?"

"Say, big boy, draw in your horns. Draw in your horns! I'd even seduce that girl from the sticks. What was her name? . . . Neloa something. I'm sailing up some day to give her the works."

With a yell of fury, Vridar leapt to McClintock's throat and they struggled and rolled to the floor. They fought like tigers and the room shook. They were on their feet and went reeling to a bed, with Vridar seeking Forenoon's throat and with Forenoon fighting desperately to escape from the mad hands. Then Vridar whipped under McClintock and pitched him over his head and the two of them came down like bags of sand. There was a terrific crash in the drugstore below. Sobered at once, they dived into a closet and locked the door after them. In a little while a knock sounded and Vridar heard two men come in. They walked about the room and talked excitedly, and McClintock, meanwhile, doubled over, with hands clapped to his mouth, trying to restrain his glee.

The two men left and Vridar and McClintock came out; and an hour later they went down to the drugstore. It looked as if a bull had been loose there. Broken glass was scattered over the floor and counters, and into the street poured the heavy sick fragrance of lotions. Two men and a girl were still busy with brooms.

In this evening, the hotel-keeper presented them with a bill for a hundred and seventeen dollars and twenty cents. They would have to pay it, he said, or suffer arrest.

"All right," McClintock said, and took the bill. As soon as the man had gone, he touched a match to it. "It's move again," he said. "I'll get a sleigh and find some rooms."

Two hours past midnight they took their luggage quietly down a back stairway, leaving no clues behind them, and hauled it to rooms on Seventh East Street. . . .

"The only thing I hate," Forenoon said, "is leaving that girl. I had her dizzy. You notice how she smiled at me when she cleaned our room?"

For six weeks they lived on the second floor of an old house. Their landlady was a tall bleak spinster who never smiled. But she was patient and for a long while they played the devil here without drawing from her more than a soft rebuke. Once they wrestled and shook the ceiling below, and she climbed the stairs and rapped and said gently they would have to stop. Two pieces, she said, had fallen from her chandelier. And once when Vridar shoved McClintock through a window and that astonished young man crashed to a porch roof and then bounded off, demolishing some lattice-work, Vridar was reproved so politely that he went at once and repaired all the damage. But they became steadily more violent, nevertheless, and in their sixth week here their devilment reached a crisis.

There was talk of war and there was talk of prohibiting alcoholic drinks, and this gossip, particularly of the latter, aroused Vridar's interest. He had never drunk anything but beer. But he knew the fragrant smell of whiskey, having sniffed, in time of childhood, some of Charley Bridwell's empty bottles. And when he read in a local paper a dull sermon against alcohol, declaring that it caused all catastrophes, from idiocy to pauperism, he resolved to taste the stuff. It would be a pity to die and not know what whiskey was like.

"Let's get a bottle," he said.

"Get it," Forenoon said. "I'll pay half."

Vridar entered a saloon and was spellbound. He saw thousands of bottles, each with its own lovely color, its regal stamps and seal. This room was a deep and beautiful wonder on the edge of life. It was a glorious eddy on the wide dark stream, full of odor and witchcraft; and he rebuked himself for never having come here before.

"What you want?" a man asked.

"I don't know. Just let me look a while."

He gazed at bottles and breathed the smell of beer and watched men come in and drink. Foam was like milk-froth on their beards. One man drew hair into his mouth and licked the foam off; and they all drank with such relish, and seemed released to such good fellowship, that Vridar made a resolve: if he ever found himself in Europe, he would drink of everything he could find.

With a quart of Bourbon he went home. When a little way up the street he tore a part of the wrapping from the bottle and read the label again. And he carried it softly as if it were a babe in his arms.

"What you get?" asked McClintock.

"Bourbon," Vridar said, speaking as if he knew all about whiskies.

They opened the bottle and smelled of its contents. Vridar breathed of the rich fragrance until his senses swam. Then they began to drink. They offered the bottle to Mertyl but he spurned it and went outside. In a little while he returned.

An hour later both Vridar and Forenoon were drunk. Vridar did not know he was drunk. He knew only that he was besieged by all sorts of weird and ridiculous impulses. He wanted to laugh and then he wanted to cry. He wanted to write to Neloa and he thought of her with a vast and hungry tenderness; but in the next moment he wanted to fight or sing or stand on his head and grimace. And it was very strange, he reflected, that he should be in such a predicament as this: feeling by turns so elated or so wretched; now lusting for battle, now overcome by an enormous love for humankind. The room danced and Mertyl sat in a blur and Forenoon moved about like a phantom. The whiskey shot through and through him like an ecstasy of flame. His thoughts came and went in flashes of chaos or in tenuous wraiths of fire or in a sudden black bewilderment that shut away the light. He wanted to fly, to enter some soft voluptuous eternity, and to move round and round there in the loveliness of a waltz.

He stood up and the whole world spun in darkness and seemed to be a faint and melodious song. He sat again and shook his head and strove to see. After a while he smote himself and kicked out, trying to clear his senses; and he began to talk.

"What's matter with me?" he asked. He giggled and broke into a high shrill laugh. This astonished him and for a time he was silent. "Say, I feel queer!"

"You look queer," someone said. It was Forenoon speaking but he could not see Forenoon. . . . Yes, he could see Forenoon. He was over by a window and he was doing something there. "What you up to? . . . Hey, McClintock, you fool. You awful fool!"

"Fool yourself. Big dumb fool yourself."

"What you doing there? McClintock, answer me."

"Shut up."

Hanging to the eaves were enormous icicles and Forenoon leaned out and grasped one, a tapering cylinder of ice weighing a hundred pounds. He broke it off and dragged it inside. He clutched it in his arms as he would a bag of grain and staggered round the room with it.

"What'll I do with this?" he said.

He went in circles round and round the room. Mertyl rose and supported him and Mertyl told him to throw the ice out but Forenoon said he wanted to do something with it. Water from the ice now ran down him and filled his clothes.

"What'll I do with this!" he howled.

"Kill yourself with it," Vridar said. He liked this notion. He rose and staggered about with McClintock; and again he said: "Kill yourself with it."

Forenoon stumbled across the room and entered the hallway. For a moment he stood by the baluster and looked down and then with all his might he heaved the chunk of ice to the floor below. It fell with the sound of crashing glass. Forenoon giggled with glee and Vridar went out and they both giggled and looked down at the pile of ice. The landlady came out. She gasped with amazement and stared up at them and Vridar thought her face looked very silly.

"What does this mean?" she asked.

Forenoon leaned on Vridar's shoulder and choked with happiness, and Vridar, pushed off balance, nearly went headlong after the ice. The woman came up the stairs. She faced them and Vridar could tell that she was very angry but he did not care.

"Who done that?" asked the woman.

"He did!" Forenoon said; and he shoved Vridar and Vridar sprawled in a heap. When he looked up, the woman was gazing down at him.

"I didn't," he said. "He did. That fool did."

"Why ain't you a young girl?" McClintock said. He looked round with a drunken leer. "I'll bet you was some ladybug once."

"You clean that mess up!" the woman cried. "I'd be ashamed! I'd go off and hide your faces!"

"A face like mine?"

"Yes," said Vridar, still piled up by the wall, "a face like yours. Hide your face, McClintock. For shame! Where's your manners, you lubber? . . . Shame-shame, double-shame——"

The woman was growing hysterical.

"You clean that up!" she wailed. "I'll have you arrested!"

"He'll clean it up," Vridar assured her. He felt very happy and bold. He grinned happily at the woman. "He's a gentleman, he'll clean it up. McClintock, clean that mess up! McClintock!"

"Go to hell! I'm going to puke." He leaned over the railing and the woman seized him and dragged him back.

"You nasty drunkard!" she shouted. "Get out of my house!"

"Let me be!" McClintock said.

"You let him be," Vridar said. "He's my friend. . . . Miss What's-your-name, you let him alone."

"God, I'm sick!" Forenoon groaned. "I'm sick as a dog."

"He's sick," said Vridar. "He's sick as a dog. . . . Well, go on and die, you dog. You dirty nasty drunken dog, you! . . . McClintock!"

"What you want?"

"Go on and die. A nice disgrace you are. Dropping ice in nice ladies' houses. You ought to die, McClintock."

The landlady had entered their room and was talking with Mertyl. Forenoon doubled over and groaned. He was dying, he said. In a minute he would vomit all over the city. He would blow whiskey clear to the Mormon temple. Vridar came over on hands and knees.

"Get to the bathroom," he said, and he yanked at Forenoon's legs. "Hey, for God sake, don't puke here! Down there, see the bathroom. . . . Forenoon, can't you see?"

Vridar drew himself up and put an arm round Forenoon and tried to lead him away. He broke Forenoon's clutch on the railing and then they both reeled and pitched headlong. The woman came out like a hornet. She was crying wildly and threatening arrest and police and disgrace and all these threats came with vague gentle insistence into Vridar's mind. He rose to his hands and knees and looked up at her.

"I'll clean it," he assured her. "Please don't talk that way. We're gentlemen. We're gentlemen and we'll clean it up."

He moved on all fours to the head of the stairway. He strove to go down the stairs on hands and knees but his arms folded under him and he rolled and fetched up at the bottom with a yell and a crash. For a moment he threshed about him as if fighting enemies. Then he looked up and he saw, as if far away, the face of the woman and the face of Mertyl.

"I'll clean it up," he said. "Just give me time." Moving about like an animal with four legs, he got a chunk of ice and crawled over to the door. "See," he said, "I'm cleaning it up. I'm a gentleman and I'll clean it up." And while laboring, still on hands and knees, he poured a stream of assurances and declarations at the floor above. "You look down here and you'll see I'm cleaning it up. Watch me. I always do what I say. . . . I'm a gentleman. I drank some whiskey, that's what's wrong with me. . . . I never did before. . . . Well, I'll pay all the damage. You just give me a bill and I'll pay all the damage. . . . If you want your lawn cleaned I'll do that. I'll cut your wood or milk your cow. I'll do anything. Ask my brother if I won't do anything. Mert! Hey, Mert! You tell her I'm a gentleman. Tell her I'm all right. Tell her I just got—well."

He sat on the floor and looked up, trying to see the woman. He saw a face but he could not tell whether it was her face or Mertyl's. Laying an arm across his breast and then gathering ice and banking it against him along the arm, he spoke to the face.

"Up there, you listening? . . . Well, I got my heart busted, that's all. That," he said, glancing up, "is what's wrong with me. I loved a girl. She lied to me and I don't care much now. Send me to jail, I don't care. Shoot me, I don't care." He moved over to the door and tossed the ice out. He came back and piled other fragments against his arm. "Go on and have me arrested! You think I care? God damn, no. Do what you want to. I'm headed for the dogs. A woman lied to me and I'm headed for the dogs. Lots of men go to the dogs on account of women. Did you know that?" He looked up through a fog. "Did you know that? . . . Well, maybe you didn't." He slid over and threw the armful to the porch. He came back and stacked the chips again. "You know what I intend to do? Enlist and be shot. Go to war and be shot. Then I won't worry any more. I'll get blown up. That'll be the end of me. . . . Well, that'll sure be the end of me."

He threw another armful out. When all the pieces were gathered, he took his handkerchief and mopped the floor. He would crawl to the porch and wring his handkerchief dry and then return and soak it. Everything was so blurred that he could barely tell water from shadow. After the floor was wiped dry, he crawled up the stairway and into his room. The woman was sitting on his bed, weeping and blowing her nose. He sat on the floor and stared at her.

"Don't cry," he said. "I cleaned it all up. I'll pay all the damage. . . . You'n have me arrested if you want to. I don't care. Put me in jail if that'll make you happy. Just do what you like."

He looked at her with sober interest. He wondered why she wept now. And after a few minutes he wanted to comfort her. His eyes became full of mist and he felt a great tenderness and pity for everything. He loved the whole big sad world and this woman and McClintock and Neloa, and he felt borne down by loneliness and tears.

"Don't cry," he said. He drew himself to the bed and patted her arm. "Please don't cry. Everything is all right now."

V

•

AFTER the woman left the room, Vridar sat for a long while, feeling depressed and sick and McClintock lay on the bed and groaned. He said he was dying and Vridar said he hoped he died. Mertyl read a book and from time to time Vridar glanced at him. My brother, he thought, thinks I've disgraced him. A woman deceived me and now I'm drunk as a fool and I'm sick as a fool, too. I've disgraced my parents and myself and I'm sick and the world would be better off if I were dead. . . .

McClintock rolled off to the floor and sat up. He looked at Vridar and whinnied with shrill glee.

"So your heart's busted," he said. "Now who done that to your poor little heart? That Antelope hick?"

"Shut up," Vridar said.

"She busted your heart, did she? She lied to you, did she? My God, how my heart busts for you!"

"Shut up, I said!"

"You're through with women now, I guess. You won't love

nevermore. Oh, never, nevermore!" He giggled and his giggles ran into hiccoughs. Loping over to the window, he leaned out as if to vomit; he heaved and moaned and then came back and lay on the floor. "Once," he said, "I puked right out of a window. I puked right on a swell guy. He had a cane. He humped straight up and yelled and long as I could see him he was humpun and yellun. . . . Well, so you're going to the dogs. You're through with girls, I guess."

"Hell no," said Vridar. "I'm just starting."

"Let's step some out tonight."

"It's all right with me."

"I mean some wild ones. Some that kiss like tannic acid."

"Any kind suits me."

"Let's have some more drink."

"Sure, let's stay drunk."

Mertyl looked at Vridar, his face obscurely cynical. Forenoon got the whiskey and drank and then Vridar drank. Vridar wiped his mouth and said he would die a drunkard.

"Some of my mother's people drank themselves to death." He considered this. "A lot of poets did. James Thomson B. V., he did."

"James Thomson, B. V. D.," McClintock said and snickered. "Well, slick up. Comb your hair. Why don't you ever comb your hair?"

Forenoon went to a closet and laid out two suits. He said Vridar could wear one of them, as well as a pair of his shoes and one of his hats. Then he got tonic and powder and rouge and told Vridar to put on some dog.

"No wonder girls lie to you," he said. "It would be awful to tell you the truth."

"Doll me up," Vridar said.

McClintock poured tonic on Vridar's hair and then saturated the hair with perfumed oil. He combed the hair and it shone like polished metal. He got his razor and scraped the down off Vridar's face and massaged his face with powders and scented water. With a pencil he darkened Vridar's brows.

"You look a little better," he said. "You're a homely bastard but mebbe you'n get a girl now."

"I'n get lots of girls."

"I mean good-lookun girls. The kind I get."

Vridar put on one of Forenoon's suits and a pair of his shoes. He manicured his nails and rubbed on his hands something that smelled of heliotrope. He liked to smell of his hands now. Then he drew on a shirt and Forenoon adorned him with a gay tie, putting into it a knot two inches long. Long slender knots, he said, were the style now.

"Maybe they're phallic," Vridar said.

"They're what the girls want. You got a-give a girl what she wants."

When he was fully dressed, Vridar strode about the room, appraising himself. He stared in a mirror at his polished and scented head.

"You're all right," Forenoon declared. "One sniff of you and they'll faint in your arms."

"Hope so," Vridar said.

"You better drink some more. You need some nerve. . . . And slick your shoes up."

In a cupboard on the hallway, Vridar found some stove polish and rubbed it on his shoes. They were blackened but they did not shine. He eyed them with misgivings and looked at McClintock.

"That won't do!" Forenoon cried. "No girl likes a guy if his shoes ain't slick."

He got another pair and told Vridar to put them on. Vridar looked at the shoes and considered. All of McClintock's shoes had been stolen: three pairs from the college gymnasium and two pairs from stores.

"I guess I'll wear mine," he said.

"Good God, you can't get a girl with Sears Roebuck shoes on!"

McClintock poured shaving-lotion into a peanut butter jar and then filled the bottle with whiskey. He drank and Vridar drank and they entered the street. Forenoon began to sing and Vridar pitied him. Though no songster himself, he could feel his way through a simple melody; and he reflected now, while staring with approval at his well-pressed trousers, that if there was to be any singing tonight, he would have to do it. He thought of one song and another and wondered which he would sing first. And while he walked westward, toward a sea of yellow sky, he hummed in his breath and fancied himself as a very stunning knight.

"What kind a girl you want? You like blonds?"

"Any kind."

"What does this Antelope hick look like?"

"Shut up about her!" Vridar yelled; and he swung angrily and pushed McClintock off the sidewalk. "Just never mind her!"

"Hey, stop shoving me around! I'll knock holes through you. I'm a tough son-of-a-bitch when I'm half-cocked."

"So am I!"

"Well, just don't be so fresh with me. I'll smack your ears off."

"Then shut up about her."

"To hell with her! The sagebrush hick!"

"Shut up, I said!" With a clenched hand Vridar pushed McClintock backward and squared off. McClintock's eyes shone with whiskey and spite. He approached Vridar as if to strike; and then stopped and looked at him; and then grinned.

"When I lick you," he said, "it won't be over no Antelope chippy."

These words stung Vridar like a whip. He howled with rage and stripped his coat off.

"You take that back!"

"Go to hell. And listen, if this is how you feel, go back and take my duds off."

"Your duds! My God, you stole them."

"You never stole nothing, I guess. Listen, we got a-be friends. I could send you to jail for life. You know that?"

"Try it!"

"We got a-be friends. We got a-be friends for life." McClintock went into deep shadow and drank and Vridar went over and drank with him.

"Well," Forenoon asked, "are we friends or enemies?"

"Just as you like."

"We're friends. Here, shake hands." They clasped hands. "Now," Forenoon said, "we're friends. We're two crooks and we're friends."

They returned to the sidewalk. Vridar staggered a little and hoped he was drunk. He looked up at the sky and thought of the enormous dark world: of all its taverns and love-making, its carousals and feasts and brawls; and of its men and women—how many thousands in this moment he could not imagine—in voluptuous embrace, with their souls melting lip to lip and with their blood pouring like fire. And it seemed to him in this moment that life, and all the wonder of life, was only a carnival of dance and love, and that books were strange things hidden in closets, and that birth and death were two clowns in eternal joust. He hungered now, as he had hungered in Rigby, for dancing and a woman's arms, a woman's smell and touch and eyes; and he remembered dances of which he had read—boutade and saraband, jig and schottische and Highland fling, cakewalk and bolero, mazurka and riga-doon minuet—; and the world seemed full of music and passion and dancing feet. . . .

Forenoon said they were going to visit the Bateman sisters: Molly and Joan. He had seduced Joan but he hadn't seduced Molly yet. Joan wanted to marry him. Molly was plump and golden and full of the devil.

"She'll make you boil like a Stanley steamer," he said.

"What's her name?"

"You fool, I told you her name!"

"Oh yes, you told me her name."

"They're twins. They're twenty-two. Never fool around with girls under eighteen. If you do the law will take your pants off."

"I guess," said Vridar, thinking of the waltz.

"Good God all-Friday!" McClintock cried.

"Now what's the matter?"

"I know some more sisters. Dark and hot. They'll pile on you soon as you get in the door."

Vridar began to shake. He wished he had not come.

"I prefer Molly," he said. He asked for the bottle and drank and for a little while he kept swallowing like a choked dog. He looked far into the gray north where the Antelope hills lay.

"Verna," McClintock was saying, "will warm you up. You won't have to do a thing but jest set and let her work on you. That girl, if she was buried in ice she'd drown in ten minutes. She's that hot. . . . Well, you want her?"

"I want Molly!" Vridar howled. "You heard me, didn't you?"

They walked down State Street and from time to time they went into an alley and drank. Vridar said he was drunk now.

"I'm drunk as a fiddler," he said. "God, I'm drunk as a—a—fiddler." McClintock said he was drunk, too.

When they came to Ninth South, Forenoon pointed to a great barn and said he danced there. He met Gertrude Grant there and slept with her on his third night out.

"You should see me one-step," he said. "I'm the one-step-punest fool in Zion."

Vridar wanted to ask about Gertrude: what was she like, how did she kiss, and had she wept. Lorry Kale, that lewd sallow youth in Rigby, had said all his girls wept. . . . Vridar looked at McClintock, trying to realize that this young man had been intimate with women: with girls as lovely and clean as flowers, with girls as eager and passionate as life; and he hated him. He choked with bitterness and grief.

"I want a drink!" he cried.

"It's all gone."

"I want a drink!" He turned furiously and pushed Forenoon off the walk. "Damn you, I want a drink!"

"What's the matter you! You crazy?"

"I tell you I want a drink!"

"Shut up that bellerun! You fool, there isn't any drink."

"All right, I won't go." He paused, sulking in self-pity.

"Come on. Molly has some drink."

"But I want a drink now. I want a-get dead drunk."

"You act crazy to me. Come on."

They went up Ninth and stopped before a house. It was

a shabby illbred huddle of old masonry and Vridar felt better. In defiance, in an effort to seem what he was not, he kicked savagely at shrubs by the path; and he kicked the steps when he reached them and then boldly kicked the door. But when Forenoon pushed a button, and when, a few moments later, a girl approached from within, Vridar began to shake.

"Gosh, I'm cold," he said.

"Shut up," said Forenoon. "Show some breeding."

The door was opened and in the wan light Vridar saw a young girl. She was alluringly half-dressed, as if awaiting a lover. Hair fell in a cluster of ringlets to her breast.

"Hello, Molly."

"Hello," said Molly. "Come in."

Forenoon strode in and Vridar slunk after him. He found himself in a huge vulgar room with sofas and cushions everywhere and with calendars and magazine covers on the walls. With a lordly gesture, Forenoon drew his gloves off and gave them and his hat to Molly.

"Miss Bateman," he said, bowing low, "may I present Mr. James. Mr. Vancouver James."

"How are you?" asked Molly, and she gave to Vridar a small soft hand.

"Where's Joan?" asked Forenoon.

Joan was dressing. She would be out in a minute; and if they would excuse her, Molly said, she would dress, too. As soon as she vanished, Forenoon turned to Vridar and leered.

"Your name is Vancouver—what did I say?"

"You said James."

"James. And mine is Jack Welland. Don't forget."

"You mean——?"

"Listen, simpleton, you heard me. You lived all your life in Antelope?" Vridar moved toward him, murderous, shaking with rage. "Set down!" Forenoon grasped Vridar's shoulders. "We're friends for life. Crooks and friends, ain't that it? Now play your part. . . . You're a swell actor. You'n knock their eyes out."

Vridar felt better. He liked to be called a swell actor. He

'glanced at the crease in his trousers and tried to seem inscrutable and world-weary; but he said:

"I need a drink."

"Listen," said Forenoon, whispering now. "Act bored. Always act bored around women. They like it. Seem like women was no mystery to you." He looked at Vridar and added: "Yawn once in a while, like you'd been up late. Be well-bred but act like you'd been to Europe. . . . And call me Jack."

McClintock now walked about the room, looking at magazines and books or whistling softly or humming a love-song. He was enviably at ease, Vridar thought: a worldly chap, a prince of pilgrimage, waiting for his mistress. And Vridar strove to look bored and a little impatient; and he, too, strolled from this to that, now turning a page, or now staring vacantly as if his thoughts were in Belfast or San Isidro. But he was volcanic ash within. His emotions burned to cinder under the reproachful scrutiny of his mind and he felt white and washed-out. He felt as alive with excitement, yet as aimless and futile, as autumn leaves in a wind. There was something horribly anemic in the surge of his blood: as if it had been filtered through fear and had lost its color and heat. . . .

From a room came girlish warbling and giggles, throaty laughter, and the sound of water boiling round a bowl. Then Joan came out. And Forenoon, Vridar perceived instantly, affected not to see her. He thumbed a book and whistled softly.

"Mac," Vridar said. McClintock turned slowly and looked at him.

"Did you say Jack?"

Vridar flushed and looked silly. All the self-control left him. He could feel it leaving, as if siphoned, and he sank weakly to a chair.

"Oh, hello," said Forenoon, speaking to Joan. Slowly, a little wearily, he took her hand and led her across the room. "Miss Bateman, allow me to present Mr. James. Vancouver James, a grandson of Jesse James, the famous outlaw."

Vridar staggered to his feet, sweating under this new shame. He bowed as if pushed from behind; he came up, his face red and agonized; and then he pawed for a handkerchief and buried his face in a violent sneeze. He could hear Forenoon talking but he did not understand. All life, all meaning, was sucked into his humiliation, his blind furious effort to seem at ease. And he could think only of this: that he had burned like fire when introduced to a girl and then had snorted wildly. Keeping the handkerchief to his face, and having no power to look at Joan or McClintock, he turned aside, pretending for the moment to be undone. He placed a hand to his breast and coughed gently. He strove to cough when he had no need, reflecting, in bewildered fashion, that he might somehow excuse the sneeze, or at least make it seem reasonable, if he could lead her to suppose that it had been only a sort of cough, politely restrained too long. Because of the two, it seemed to him, coughing was more respectable.

When at last he glanced up, he saw Forenoon watching him. Joan was nowhere in sight.

"I told her," Forenoon said, "I put pepper in your handkerchief. She thinks it was a joke. I told her to fetch you a drink."

"Thanks. Did she—did she——?"

"I said you was a dead shot with a gun. Women like dead shots. And now for Christ sake straighten up!"

"I—I need a drink," he said.

He wanted the fire and courage of whiskey. Moving round the room, with McClintock's eyes on him, he tried to realize fully what he was doing and where he was. He ached to sit by Molly and feel her warmth but the thought terrified him. And he began to tremble and he glanced again and again at the door, wishing he could sneak out.

"I got a-have a drink."

"I thought you was a good actor," Forenoon said.

Vridar shrugged and went over to a couch and sat down. Above all else, he wanted to be a good actor: an inscrutable person, affronting the world. He wanted to be stared at with annoyed baffled eyes. And now he stretched his legs out and yawned.

"Listen, Welland. When do I get a drink? Isn't there any drink in this dull stupid house?"

"That's better. Yawn like that every once in a while."

The girls entered the room. Joan bore glasses on a tray and came first to Vridar.

"Will you have a drink?" she asked. She smiled at him but Vridar thought her smile was a little pitying.

"Thanks," he said.

Joan went to Forenoon and he rose and bowed and took a glass. "I thank you," he said. "This is very kind of you." And he bowed again.

Vridar, closely observing, was appalled. He had sat as if roped to his couch; and McClintock, with his manners glittering, had accepted the favor with a smile, two bows, and a pretty speech. And Vridar was furious, too. In social decorum he smelled the superficial and the insincere: manners, it seemed to him, were fraud and perjury and humbug. They ambushed the soul and dressed it up in monocle and spats.

"How's it taste?" Forenoon asked.

"Oh, all right."

"Is it strong enough?" asked Joan, smiling again.

"Yes, it's all right."

"He'n drink a barrel of booze," McClintock said, "and walk a tight-rope. . . ."

Holding his glass and hand to conceal his face, with a finger against his nose, Vridar stared at Molly. Half-buried in a fluffy dress, she looked very soft and womanly, with a bright crimson in her lips and cheeks. Vridar imagined the color was of rouge but it did not look like rouge. . . . And then his earnest stare fell downward to her breast and to her hips and to her ankles. She was very alluring. He tried to realize how it would feel to have her in his arms: all her supple flesh against him and all her ringlets showering in his face. . . . He sighed and looked up, and when he saw that Molly was gazing at him, he started and almost dropped his glass. Burning in a flush, he drank his cocktail and looked round him for a place to set his glass. Molly came over, her whole face like a smile.

"You have some more?"

Vridar looked up at her and her eyes held him speechless.

His heart raced so wildly that he could feel a throbbing pulse in his neck.

"Give him some more," McClintock said.

And now, still holding Molly's gaze, Vridar saw the smile leave her face. He saw something like fear shadow the gray of her eyes and he saw her catch and hold her breath. Then quickly she took the glass and left the room.

Again and again during his life, Vridar's gaze had met a woman's, as only now it had met Molly's, and he had been delivered helpless into an indefinable power. He had felt the depth, the only profound depth, of life; the only altitude beyond words; the only meaning, bright and hot at its core, in the vast reaches of thought. In these moments, it seemed to him, he had touched the one universal truth. There had been such a moment years ago when he skated on the ice with Helen; and another when, facing Neloa, he had seen beyond the surface of her life and had read her mind. But this that he felt, that shook him like a bugle, that circumferenced all his homelessness and gave it a home, answered to no name and was to be found in no books. In the great blur of consciousness, nevertheless, it was the one real thing, the one changeless truth; but it lay so deep under life and was so solitary and ancient that he could only feel its power for a moment and then lose it, as if unexpectedly he had touched the earth's heart.

When Molly came with another drink he looked at her again. There was nothing in her eyes now. What he had seen there was gone. In her eyes now were surfaces without depths, notions without intensity or outline or form. They were civilized eyes and there was no meaning in the civilized.

He felt more at ease now. He sipped his drink and watched McClintock and Joan. Joan was sitting on McClintock's lap and she was kissing him lightly—a large amorous kiss, Vridar reflected, that was paid in tiny installments—and whispering in his hair. Clearly enough she was McClintock's to do with as he pleased.

Ignoring Molly, who sat discreetly apart, Vridar stared at Forenoon. What was there in this fellow that made him so at-

tractive to women? He was handsome but there was about
him so much craft and stealth, so much insincerity in his
mouth, so much greed in his eyes. Nevertheless, the girls
adored him. . . . And next, Vridar studied Joan. Like her sister, she had brown hair and gray eyes and a clear healthy skin.
Her body was shapely enough. But Vridar found her wholly
unalluring. Her emotions like summer days were too much
alike. She was a summery girl and Molly was a summery girl:
June girls, with only a hint of spring; August girls, with only a
hint of November. They would both be midsummer wives:
growing calm and murmurous, growing plump for death. . . .

But Neloa: she had the tragic in her, and passion that could
be dark and wild. And with whiskey homesickness he thought
of her. Neloa and the Antelope Hills and all the desolate backdrop of his home were in the blur around him; until he sank
into self-pity and loneliness, with memory walling him in. His
glass was filled again and he drank. His stare during a long
hour of silence was fixed on his hands. . . .

And suddenly he rose without speaking and got his hat and
staggered out.

VI

•

HE WALKED under a clear bright sky. Looking into the
valley of stars or into the north at the mammoth shadows
of sleep, he thought of his homeland, with quiet nights full of
silence, its mountains mute with age. And he thought of Neloa.
For two weeks now she had not written, nor had he, and he
was done with her now. She could go to hell and high water
for all he cared. She could break her faithless neck or be the
mistress of all the earth's bawcocks or take to whoredom and
little he would care. . . .

But these reflections made him sniffle with grief. The mist

of his eyes was condensed to tears, and great sobs rose and
choked him. There came out of him a sudden bawling sound,
as if he had been branded with a hot iron; and then, in despair
with himself, he smote his forehead to clear his wits. He
looked back and saw the light. McClintock was there, laying
hairy hands to an amorous maid; and he was here, bubbling
with woe like a spanked child. All around him were women
but he had none of them. He thought of them with wolfish
hunger: of their breasts and thighs and lips; he peopled his
fancy with them and devoured their presence, until he was
only a male, the one male, the avid life-principle, fecundating
a voluptuous spermy mass around him. He was an organ
throwing seeds and all life, warm and supple, pressed upon
him; and in this that was meaningless was the only meaning;
in this that was beastly and shameful was the only beauty, the
only good. What he wanted, standing here now, silent and
furious and staring at the light, was an orgy of lust so that he
could deliver himself from bondage, from sterile saintliness
and fear. He wanted to thrust his emotion, sharp and piercing,
into the heart of life.

But he went on down the street, being too sober for courage,
and turned north. He had gone a block or two when he was
accosted by a negress. She was a foul hag, toothless and old.
Vridar stared at her and wondered if she was a beggar or a
lunatic; and she took him by an arm and tried to lead him
into an alley; and in a whining voice she said to him, "Only
two bits, kid. Just a quarter. Just two bits....."

Understanding but faintly, yet knowing her purpose to be
vile, Vridar jerked away from her and ran. He glanced back
and saw her watching him. For a little while they looked at
each other; and then she approached, but softly, lest she
frighten him away. And again Vridar took to his heels and he
did not pause until he came to the lighted areas of town.

Standing on a corner he pondered the matter. He still had
no good notion of what she had proposed. His mind reached
out to the Bible, with its records of degeneracy; and he
thought of words he had seen—sodomy and lesbianism and
necrophilia, nymphomania and pedophilla erotica and zoö-

erasty and satyriasis—terrible words all, black with significance, but vague and perplexing in his own mind. He thought of gonorrhea. McClintock had come home with gonorrhea and had yelped thereafter when he went to the bathroom. And that and syphilis and all these others were common, it seemed, to the human being but not to other animals; and Vridar thought with wonder of his own kind. . . .

"The son-of-a-bitch!" McClintock had howled. "I spent five bucks on that skirt and she give me this! . . . Did you know some sorority girls is plain damn whores? . . ."

And Vridar thought, too, of ancient Sybaris and its women, and of Francastoro's Syphilus, and of the gusto picaresco of Ashur-bani-pal. These and many more were bright lights, still shining in the dead acres of history. Life had touched Villon and Salome, Psyche and Proserpine and Semele, and they had burst into flame; and the ashes of the flame, somehow, were pox. . . .

But all this, it occurred to him now, was a whiskey meditation. His mind had cleared. Under the stars there was good, there was evil, and his life was dedicated to the good. And while he walked the streets, he remembered, with a little bitterness, that he was to be a great and good man. He was to be a scourger of sin, a trumpet on the narrow lane into Heaven. . . . But when he passed a lovely girl, and noted her quick glance of inquiry, his heart leapt and his resolutions fell like dust. He turned to look at her and saw that she was looking back at him. He followed her then, but discreetly; and when he saw that she was loitering, he stopped by a window and looked in. She turned and glanced back at him and smiled. Was she a harlot, he asked himself. Great God, how was he to know! Girls were an undecipherable lot. With hearts lusting, they could look as sweet and demure as a nun; and they seemed unaware that the earth was bogged in sin, crying for prophets; and that God, who had gibbeted His Son between two thieves, was full of woe. Even the best of women wore their virtue lightly. It was only a gown, diaphanous, clinging; and gracefully, without shame, they could lay it aside. . . .

McClintock would take a virgin to church on Sunday and seduce her on Sunday eve. And that showed what shameless trulls women could be! Intimacy of flesh was all right: there could hardly be life without it: but Sunday was not the time for it, and a living-room sofa was not the place. On Sunday the heart ought to lift in prayer and the soul ought to journey among the white altitudes. . . .

Such were Vridar's meditations as he stared unseeing at forty pairs of shoes. The girl who had smiled at him was gone now. He went up the street and another girl smiled—a stodgy wench with arms like a bridge beam. Vridar looked back and he saw that across her rump she was as broad as a doorway. He had no interest in her. If he were to sell himself into sin, it would be for a slender fragrant girl, for a shy and modest girl. . . . I ought to go home, he thought. But he stopped on a corner and watched girls pass, his heart lusting after them. They filled him with intolerable pain. They made him afraid of himself; for he had, again and again, an almost uncontrollable wish to go after one and crush her in his arms until she yielded and ran limp. It would be a small, an indefinable, thing that would make his blood surge: the turn of a head, the moving curve of a breast, or something in the walk.

And when he turned home at last, his starved eyes searched the streets. When he was beyond the lights, he saw no girls and he drew a deep sigh. As he climbed the stairway of his home he was set upon by a strange wish. It leaped out of nothing and sat like a devil in his mind and he despised himself for it. He strove to put it away but it grew in size until he was full of it. He hoped that McClintock caught gonorrhea tonight.

On the next morning Forenoon was derisive.

"You're a hot one," he said. "I didn't know a girl could scare your pants off." He stared in pity at Vridar and Vridar scowled. "Joan wanted to know was you impotent or bashful. I said you was impotent. I said you was just a steer."

"Go to hell!" Vridar said.

"I said you didn't have any beard. That, I said, showed you was only a steer."

"Shut it up! Say much more and you'll think I'm a steer!"

Forenoon eyed him with sardonic contempt. He rose and walked round him as if to see what sort of animal he was. And then he snickered and clapped a hand to his snickers.

"Why don't you be a monk? Then you could just read the Bible."

Vridar looked up at him, his eyes murderous. Then he gathered the clothes he had worn and hung them in a closet and while he was in the closet, Forenoon shut and locked the door.

"Let me out!" Vridar howled.

"You're in a monastery now," McClintock told him. "Women won't scare you now. . . . You want a bible?"

"I'll kill you when I get out!"

"You're a monk now. I'll buy you a rosary or something. How about some beads?"

Vridar seethed with fury and listened. He heard Forenoon dressing and in a little while he heard him gather his books and leave the house. Vridar smote the door but it was sturdy and well-secured: he was trapped here, locked up like a wayward child, as he had been at the Jew's; and in blind rage he jerked clothes down and kicked them; seized one of Forenoon's coats and tried to tear an arm off; and then in frenzy tore a silk shirt into ribbons.

For three hours he remained within this closet and during this while he plotted vengeance: evolving one scheme and another, dwelling in earnest thought on the details of each. His first plan was to bring upon Forenoon a public scandal. He would denounce him from the housetops as a thief and a wastrel and a liar; and then he perceived that this would not do, for they were both thieves, even though Vridar looked on his own pilfering as the avenging of an insult. . . . His next plan was to expose Forenoon's identity, and his unscrupulous cunning, to a dozen ravished virgins. He would write letters to them. He would say:

Dear Miss Bateman:

It may interest you to know that Jack Welland is A. M.

McClintock, that he is a liar and a fraud, and that he has three bastards in Salt Lake City; and that the number of simpletons like yourself who have trusted him is enough to fill any ordinary asylum. . . .

Or he would say:

It is the judgment of one who has seen you that you are remarkably stupid. It should have occurred to you—as quite certainly it has not—that Jack Welland is a cheap modern synonym for Don Juan. Was it Byron who said women ought to be taken and used and thrown away? It amuses me, dear lady, to observe how nicely you support that statement. . . .

But no: he would not stoop to such underground methods. He would punish aboveboard with clean powerful blows. He would tell Forenoon to stand up and then he would drive a fist into the villain's teeth; or, more romantically, he would invite him to a duel. And for a long while he was left meditating on duels and on glittering exploits with pistol or sword. He wished that dueling was in vogue now. If it were, he would get a brace of pistols and a ton of ammunition and retire to six months of practice; and then he would be, like Plummer of Alder Gulch, a dead shot and a dangerous man. At once he would challenge a score of persons to duels: snobbish fraternity men, Archibald Drake, Neloa's three lovers, and McClintock. In a gray dawn somewhere under a ceiling of oaks he would shoot all of them and calmly sheathe his pistol and walk away. Or he would open their veins with a sword. . . .

But these meditations sickened him. He thought of the smell of blood and the darkness and agony of death, and he knew that he could never kill a man. He recoiled even from the killing of mice and rats and horseflies. Nor could he strike Forenoon in his teeth, because another's pain distressed him more than his own. . . . No, his blood was whey. He was only a woman with a man's parts. And he wished with intensity that choked him that he could go forth, as the conquerors of history had gone, and raze kingdoms in the name of Jesus, invoke death in the name of God. To his greedy ambition, the Corsican runt had sacrificed armies; and Alexander had done so, and the Caesars; and these were great names in the long corridor of time. Nero and Ivan the Terrible were still held in respect.

But he—he sat in a closet, a witless zany who recoiled from murder and might; who called himself a socialist because he despised war; and who, when put upon as now, fretted in rage and then turned his other cheek. He still believed in the Nazarene. He was homeless in a Christian world. . . .

Nor did these thoughts comfort him. He threshed about again, lusting for vengeance; and when he heard Forenoon enter the room, he howled with profanity and threat.

"Hello!" said Forenoon. "You still in there? . . . I told your profs you was a monk now. You'd gone into the desert, I said, to flog yourself a while." Forenoon began to whistle. "Say, I got you a suit of camel hair. Go to Nevada. That's got a wad of desert. Wyoming, too. There's big opportunities in this country for monks. . . . Ever read about Jonah? There's a gink for you to pattern by. . . ."

In a few minutes he came over and unlocked the door. Vridar stepped out and grinned but the muscles of his face twitched. He went to the kitchen and ate.

During the evening, McClintock said he was stepping out. He shaved, he oiled his hair and powdered and rouged his face, and then he began to dress. He had a new flame, he said. Her name was Alice Hanson and she was a pretty article to look at. She didn't wear corsets or garters, and when she kissed, she gave all her skill to it.

"You better go back in your monastery," he said. "You got a bible? My God, you should have a bible. . . . How do you know what to believe without you read a bible?"

He leered at Vridar and showed him his new studs and he went to a mirror and looked at his handsome face.

"Them studs," he said, "I swiped them. You know, that jewelry shop I worked in last Saturday. And a swell opera glass. You should see it. Your eyes would stand out like the breasts of a woman."

Then he went to the closet. His amazement he vented first in a grunt and next in a howl. He was holding the silk shirt that Vridar had torn into ribbons. And suddenly he dropped it and sprang to a wardrobe and seized a shirt and ripped it in two.

"Stop that!" Vridar yelled.

Forenoon raced to the closet, seeking Vridar's garments there; he plowed inside, barking with rage; and in one leap Vridar sprang to the door and shut it and locked it.

"Let me out!" Forenoon roared. "You son-of-a-bitch, I'll beat your brains out!" He raised a great storm in the closet. He smote and howled, and he jumped on the floor until the building shook. "You'll be sorry! I'll beat you till your tongue hangs down like a steer's dewlap! You lousy stinking Antelope hick!" He was profaning wickedly now.

"Stop it!" Vridar said. "You'll break the door!"

"You're cockeyed right I'll break the door! I'll tear the God-damn house down!" He was bellowing like a fiend now. He said he would knock all Vridar's teeth down into his tonsils. "You pig-feeder! You Antelope cow-milker! I swear to Christ I'll beat your gizzard out! . . ."

At this moment the door was opened and the landlady came in, her eyes almost weird with fright and rage. The closet door was shaking and Forenoon behind it was cursing and kicking, and the woman looked at the door as if spellbound. Then she went to the door and tried to turn the key, and McClintock, meanwhile, poured at her his insulting abuse.

"You son-of-a-bitch, you better let me out! You gutter-snipe! You beardless half-witted Mormon!"

Then the key was turned and Forenoon, bounding furiously out, struck the woman and hurled her to a window; and glass fell in a shower and the woman screamed. She struggled to her feet and screamed again and Forenoon stared at her. And she looked at him and wailed like a squaw and wrung her hands.

"Let's beat it!" Forenoon said to Vridar.

Still looking at McClintock as if he were the Devil, the woman left the room and then peered in. Her teeth chattered

"No you won't."

"Why won't I? What would you do?"

"I'd call my father."

"Your father! I'd run him through a meat grinder and feed him to the cats. I'd cut his ears off."

"Yes, I'll bet."

"What color's your eyes?"

"Blue, I guess."

"I'll find out," Forenoon said. But when he started toward her, the door was softly closed. He opened it and looked out but nobody was there. He returned and looked at Vridar. "What the hell do you think about her? Is she a halfwit?"

"I don't know."

"Well, I'll be all curled up in her bed in a week."

Vridar listened to Forenoon's boasting and said nothing. He was thinking with melancholy tenderness of this girl, and of himself as her guardian, and of the noble work that he would do in life. He would be a big brother to this girl. She would be his sister and he would guide and teach her and she would be all right.

VII

ON THE next morning, Forenoon prowled in hallways, looking for the girl. He stood on a chair and peered through transoms; he tried one door and another and found them all unlocked. And in the evening of this day, when Vridar was trying to study and McClintock was pressing a suit, the girl opened the door and looked in. She stared at them gravely as if they were strangers from a far shore.

"I'll be damned!" Forenoon said. "You back again."

"Yes," the girl said.

"Come on in."

"No."

Vridar thought perhaps she would come in if he spoke. He liked to believe that her interest was in him and that she trusted him.

"Won't you come in?" he said.

"No."

His self-esteem momentarily collapsed. Well, she was only a silly thing after all: orphan asylums and poorhouses were full of her seed. She could be abducted and sold into a harem for all he cared. And he tried to ignore her.

"Let's go to a show," Forenoon said.

"When?" asked the girl.

"Right now."

"All right."

Forenoon lathered his face and began to shave, and Anna watched him; and Vridar, self-appointed guardian of innocence, hated her and wished all women were dead. No sensible girl, he assured himself, and least of all a stranger, would go anywhere with McClintock. Even a simpleton would know that he had only one purpose in mind. . . . He looked at the girl but she was unaware of his scornful eyes. She was gazing at Forenoon with rapt interest.

"Run along and get ready." She shut the door and went away. McClintock grinned. "When I get done with her she'll wear a surprised look for life."

"Balderdash!" Vridar said.

"All right. Just notice how she acts tomorrow. She won't cost me a cent. Just a show ticket, that's all."

Vridar went to the long front porch. He came out here, he would have told you, because he was sick of McClintock and his ways, of women and the world; but his real reason, unperceived by himself, was a desire to waylay Anna and admonish her. He wanted to say to her, "Take my advice and leave that man alone. He'll ruin you." And still deeper within lay the words: "I'm the kind of man you should go with. I'm the kind all women should go with. You must be awfully silly not to know that. . . ."

But though he paced, with his emotions savage, from end to

end of the porch, he saw nothing of Anna; because she, foolish wench, intolerable blockhead, was busy whitewashing her face. And Vridar was still here, striding like a mighty one, delivering his wrath into phrases, when Forenoon and Anna emerged, the first busy with feeble witticisms, the second with giggles.

"Aufwedderseen!" Forenoon called. "Odoise and Bone joor!"

Vridar scowled at him. McClintock stopped on the sidewalk and spoke again.

"Eine der Taguszeit beeten!" he called, for he had studied German. "Moot fassen!"

"Das dumme Geschwätz!" Vridar said.

"Vreed and me," he said to Anna, "we both speak a dozen languages."

"Yes, I'll bet."

"Don't we, Vreed?"

"Run along, run along!"

"What language you want me to talk in? French? Spanish? Jap? Swedish?"

"Russian," Anna said.

"Sure. Lodl-pook ig yikkum doglogoskowsky. Miggum thwab viginsky ag toag wog shikklevitch." He looked at her and grinned. "How's that?"

"Aw, go on!"

"You're ignorant," Forenoon said. "You wouldn't know Russian if you heard it."

They went down the street and Vridar watched them go. When he could no longer see them from the porch, he went out to the sidewalk, but they had disappeared. He returned to the house, walking like an old man, and went into the huge emptiness of his room. Mertyl was devoting himself to a book. What a calm and unemotional zany his brother was! He would sit for hours, poring over logarithms and equations and formulae as senseless as runes; indifferent to the vast reaches of life and love, the fragrant and devious lanes, and all the fabulous cloudland of dream. . . . But Vridar in this year, as in years past, as in many years to come, knew nothing of Mertyl and Mertyl's thoughts. He regarded him now as a pious lad, a bit innocuous, a bit sluggish: likely to become a missionary or a husband: a dull and studious fellow for whom two and two were four. And when, in a later year, he discovered all that Mertyl was, all that he, too, had suffered and buried. . . .

Vridar strove to study but books made him furious tonight. Books, he reflected, were the epidermis of experience: lovely sometimes, as hair was lovely, and living in the way that hair lived, without blood and heart. He left the room and walked in dusk. He thought of Neloa, for she had not written in a long while. Perhaps she was kissing another man now. And as he looked at the city's lights, he wished he had the strength, the courage, to debauch himself—to get drunk and find a woman and go to bed.

He returned to the porch and sat here, despising himself. In a little while McClintock and Anna came out of the night. They came in silence and entered the house and Vridar followed them in. Forenoon sat on a bed and looked very cynical and vindictive.

"Must a-been a quick show," Vridar said.

Forenoon's sneer spread to his eyes. It wrinkled his forehead and drew lines to his ears. And he stared at Vridar with infinite contempt.

"You'n have her," he said.

"Who?" Vridar asked; but he knew.

"That lousy filthy trull."

"I don't want her."

"Sure you do. You'n be a missionary with her. You'n clean her up and teach her to bathe." He wrinkled his nose as if smelling a stench. "God! You smell her?"

"Smell her! I don't go around smelling girls."

"You wouldn't have to go far to smell her. I thought first it was the house. Then we got out on the street and I thought I was smellun the street. But it was her all the time. She stinks like fury." He groaned and clutched his face. He looked up and spoke again. "I don't mind clean dirt. Country dirt. But hers is civilized dirt. . . . Mary Smith, she was never clean; but hell, she didn't stink!" He stood up and made a face.

"Didn't you take her to a show?" Vridar asked.

"Don't be funny with me. When I spend money on a woman I invest it. Like in a bank. I expect interest. . . . If I spend any money on her it'll be for soap. Dutch cleanser." He got his book of telephone numbers and turned the leaves. "I'n learn you a lot," he said, looking at Vridar. "You're just a greenhorn. One thing you got a-learn is this: some girls smell all right and some smell like fried cabbage. Always take a sniff of a girl first."

With his book of numbers he went to a drugstore. He came back and bathed and then rubbed himself with scented oil.

"Let's go to a dance," he said.

"When?"

"Tonight. Right now."

Vridar considered. "Where'd we go?"

"Bonneville. Swell dancers there. And they don't stink, either."

"I haven't any clothes."

"Wear mine."

"I'm sick of wearing yours."

"All right. But you won't find many friends let you wear their clothes. You don't appreciate that. You ever stop to think how much I do for you?"

Vridar began to tremble. He thought of all those bitter times when he went to dances in Rigby and never danced; when he stood in self-hatred and looked on until his heart broke and he wept. In memory he could hear the tragic loneliness of violins.

"Come on. You won't learn no younger."

"Let me think."

He left the house, trying to see his way clearly. Going to a corner, he stared up and down the street, and far away in the dark he could hear, or believed he could hear, a violin. It was playing a waltz and the mournful tenderness of it made him shake. And in this moment he realized long afterward, he made one of the important decisions of his life. He swung in feverish haste and ran back to the house and burst in.

"I'll go!" he said.

VII

⸻

•

THE Bonneville was the largest and most vulgar hall in the city. While a grocer's clerk, Vridar had heard of its doings and had inferred the character of persons who went there. Its patrons were shopgirls and harlots, young men from all trades, and drug peddlers and sharpers and erotic mountebanks. A few months ago, he would no more have gone to Bonneville than he would have entered a den of vice; but he had traveled far in four months. Passions long held in check, hungers that had never fed, were possessing him now. He was still pious, he was still greedy for a pure and noble life; he still clung to the unction of a mission on earth; and he despised, with a mightiness born largely of self-pity, the hypocrisy and pomp, the Edens and fleshpots of the world; but he was now driven by a hunger and a loneliness greater than his will.

And tonight, dressed in his own shabby suit, but wearing shoes and necktie belonging to another, he went with misgivings, yet with a singing heart. Young men, he reflected, often went to the dogs. The road to hell was broad and odorous, a lusty journeying from tavern to tavern, and he was on his way to a tavern now. God alone knew what would come of it. He might become a guzzling libertine, an overgorged pig, befuddling his wits and dissipating the fine lucid quality of his mind. Perhaps, once he yielded to indulgence, he would so lust after carnal things that no power could save him, so sotted would he be. And these reflections both terrified and pleased him. It was good to think of himself as a man bloated with ravishments, as a man fleeing to the devil; for he had been such a good youth and the pride of so many. For so many terrible years he had tried to do the right thing and had been paid with aconite. . . .

"Listen," Forenoon said. "I know lots of swell girls here but they like swell dancers. You'll have to just pick up some till you learn."

Vridar considered. The question in his mind was silly but he had to ask it.

"How," he said, "do you—pick them up?"

"Oh, just bow and smile and say, Can I have this dance?"

"Thanks," Vridar said.

They entered an enormous hall. It was alive with music and dancing and lovely girls. Vridar felt abashed. He tried to slink away, wishing to hide for a while, but Forenoon grasped his arm and led him, crimson and expostulating, to the flood of light. They stood by a huge rope—the floor was fenced off—and watched the crowd; and Vridar's heart sank. He wished he had not come. For out on that gleaming floor was such grace, such variety of movement, such adroit gliding and skimming and whirling, that he felt lost. He saw no one who seemed not to dance well. And besides all this, the men were so polished and insolent, the girls so splendidly haughty, that in comparison with them, he imagined himself to be the gawkiest oaf anywhere. If he tried to dance, he would be hissed, as likely as not, and perhaps thrown out like a sack of meal.

"Well," Forenoon said, "let's dance."

"No!" Vridar turned rigid with fright. "You dance. I—I'll stand here."

"Oh, come on!"

"No, I said! You dance. You dance and I'll watch how you do."

Forenoon was flattered. He went to a group of girls and a few moments later he was gliding superbly in a one-step. This involved one-step glide, attempted, Vridar observed, by only a few, was for him an amazing feat. He could never do it. If he practised a thousand years, he could never do anything like that.

He drew a deep sigh and looked about him. Standing in groups were scores of young men and young women. Some of them, he noted, were much like himself: their faces were starved and hopeless, as if they had tried to dance and had been jerked off the floor. But the idle girls tongued gum with open-mouthed relish and looked as unapproachable as the summit of Mount Everest. And next Vridar studied the men who danced. He summarized all of them as fops and carpet knights. In a college they would be fraternity brothers, raucous and empty and well-groomed. He despised them and pitied his race.

McClintock came, nimble and leering, close to the rope.

"Come on!" he said. "Get you a jane!"

Vridar stared at McClintock's girl: she was tall and queenly and scornful. She looked at Vridar, half in wonder, half in astonishment, and floated away. He turned and went outside.

For several minutes he stood in cold air and looked at the stars. His destiny lay up there. He was born, not to lope around in sexual antics, but to scourge impostors and build stairways to light. History's great men, as often as not, had been bachelors; and those who had taken women, as Byron and Napoleon had done, soon threw them away. What did Wordsworth know of dancing? or Keats or Shelley? Newton and Rabelais? Imagine Dante shimmying around a vulgar hall! . . . No, he ought to be sitting by a fireside, under a golden lamp, with the *Odyssey* on his knees. He ought to be writing sonnets or studying Wagnerian opera or reading Kant. . . .

But the music poured out upon him, frenzied, mad: a tide of sound, full of the jungle and of mating; a medley of preludes and overtures to lust. It was Belial's orchestra, playing to the fallen angels. And Vridar moved away from it, thinking he would go home; but his feet were heavy and he stopped. Why should he go to an enormous cold room and a dead book? Here was life around him, delirious with passion, and here were women, ready for the male. In his room were the ashes of Rydal Mount. Here was the raw spermy stuff of life. Here hunger beat in the tom-toms, barked through the cornets, roared in the trombone. It was life. Its furious vitality called to him and he answered, for it was his heritage and his meaning, and books were only an annotated death. And he paced around in darkness and he was racked by an awful heartache; and he knew in this moment that he would have to dance, that he would have to get into life and feel it and smell it, or go mad.

Fighting for calm, he went twice around a block and then entered the hall. He entered with a fixed, an unalterable, purpose, that gave to his face a desperate soberness and to his eyes a morbid stare. He saw a group of girls apart, and one of them, he thought, looked rather dowdy and forgotten. Perhaps she would dance with him. He went to this girl and in a voice that shook he asked:

"Will you dance with me?"

She turned and looked at him. She was shapeless of body and sour of mien. She hesitated; and then, "All right," she said and walked to the floor. Vridar followed. He gave a ticket to the man at the gate. He circled the girl's waist, hardly knowing what he did, and moved off, his emotions rocking him like savage wind. Never daring to look at her, he plodded and stumbled, his face burning, all his flesh burning, under the stares which he imagined were upon him. The dance was a fox-trot but it might as well have been an Elizabethan jig for all he knew. He kept his eyes down and fumbled with sightless courage round and round.

Then the girl stopped.

"I want a-quit," she said.

"You—you what?"

"I said I want a-quit! You heard me."

She walked away and Vridar was left here on the floor. The hall was like sheets of pale fire. In the glowing mist, he saw dancers moving round him, knew they were looking at him; and he plowed through them, going like one to his death, and found the night. He hid in shadow where none could see and tried not to remember. The girl had spurned him and walked away and memory of this was like memory of nightmare. "My God!" he groaned and began to shake. All his muscles and nerves seemed to be in violent mutiny and he jumped about and flogged himself. He called himself a fool and smote his breast. He called himself a dolt and a milksop and a block-head, a lummox and a halfwit, and said he would kill himself: the one personality, unpitying and calm, speaking in scathing derision of the other. . . . Well, he would go back and dance, and to hell with what anyone thought. "I'll go back!" he said, speaking aloud. He hopped around and shook himself. And to assure himself, he reflected—as in how many former whiles and with what fruitless results!—that these dancers were not worth his shoe-string. They were an assortment of nobodies. Not one of them would ever reach beyond his home township: they would be housewives and clerks and bond-salesmen and whores. "So why should I care!" he cried. "What difference," he thought, in utter despair, "does it make to me!"

And so he jumped around here like a crazy fellow, now abusing himself, now reasoning; and he was not vanquished yet. Once he set his heart on a thing, he was like his father: he never turned back. He could be outraged until his grief was like gall, his self-esteem like a handful of chaff; but he would rise again and fight. He would try, with what cunning he had, to restore his confidence, to clear his wits, and he would return, like a man driven by lashes, to the scene of his humiliation.

And now, as he entered the hall, he was almost white with desperation. Now he would meet scorn with scorn. And now, too, because he loathed his weakness, he resolved to force himself, as with a hot pike, to the severest ordeals: to refuse to count one girl more approachable than another; to go, in every case, to the first one he saw. . . .

"Will you dance with me?"

She looked at him with slow painstaking care. Her glance went down to his feet and came back to his eyes; and in the way she stared at him, he could see no disdain: only a well-disciplined curiousness, patient, unamazed. She did not speak. And Vridar waited; and in a moment a fellow came up and led the girl to the dance.

Sweating under the studied thoroughness of this rebuke, Vridar swung and looked around him. He went to the group of girls nearest him.

"Will you dance with me?"

She turned as if mildly astonished. She was chewing gum, and flakes of rouge patched the flesh of her lip.

"You speakun to me?"

"I asked if you'd care to dance."

She looked at the other girls and then looked at Vridar and grinned. The other girls pretended not to see him. Vridar waited for several moments.

"Will you?" he said.

"No," the girl said. Her face hardened and she turned away.

Feeling his courage sink, Vridar swallowed as if his mouth had been full and looked round him again. He chose another group and went over to it. He asked the same question. The four girls fell twittering against one another. They all looked at him as if amazed and then laughed outright. And Vridar fled to a corner to meditate. His forehead was wet and a muscle in his face twitched. He looked at the girls, hating them, praying that they all married blackguards and pimps. And while he stood here, McClintock came.

"What's a-matter? Why don't you dance?"

"They won't dance with me." He looked at Forenoon and added: "I guess they like your type."

"It's because you can't dance," Forenoon said. "I tell you: come with me and we'll butt into some."

"It wouldn't do any good."

"Sure. Come on." And as they moved through the crowds, McClintock advised him. "Don't let girls see you watchun them. They don't want a-be sized up. If some won't dance, you'n drag them on. Some women like to be knocked around. Some like to be kidded. Some like to be flattered."

With Vridar faithfully at his side, McClintock accosted three girls.

"Hello," he said. "Seems like I know you. You go to the College?"

The girl addressed was nonplussed and a little amazed, but she was also, Vridar could see, a little pleased.

"These are college girls," McClintock went on, speaking to Vridar. "Ain't you seen them on the campus?"

"I—I think so," Vridar said.

The girls looked at one another. They were flattered.

"Damn it," Forenoon said, "I know now where I seen them. I seen them at the Junior Prom. . . . Didn't I?" he asked of one of the girls. One of the girls giggled, another's face broke into a smile. "How about a dance? I bet you don't have a dance left." The girls looked wonderingly at each other and then at Forenoon.

"You go to the College?" one asked.

"Sure," McClintock said. "So do you. I've seen you there."

"You must a-been seeun ghosts," she said.

McClintock now affected a troubled earnestness. He appealed to another girl. "Honest now, aren't you a Chi Omega?"

"Heck no," the girl said. "I wish I was."

"You're the Chi Omega type," Forenoon said. And he quickly added: "Let's dance." He took her arm and led her away and Vridar was left facing the other two.

"I—uh—will you dance with me?"

"You go to the College?"

"Yes."

"You know Ann Morris?"

"Ann Morris? No, I guess not."

"She goes. She's a Delta."

There was a long silence. The two girls quite ignored him now. Vridar didn't know whether he should stand his ground or slink away. And should he ask again for a dance? He glanced at his shoes, at his hands; he drew forth a letter and tried to look at it with sober interest, and he rocked a little on his heels and toes and shrugged; but he felt unspeakably silly. Persons roundabout, he noted, were staring at him curiously. He began to sweat and he felt drenched with heat and weakness. Then he moved away, looking, meanwhile, over the crowds, as if he had thought of someone whom he must see. He even stood tiptoe and peered. And he moved from place to place as if searching and his acting was thorough. Instead of retiring and becoming lost, he kept himself in view; he went from group to group, his gaze sweeping the hall; and he returned, after a few minutes, to those who had watched him curiously, determined to convince them, beyond all doubt, that he was actually seeking someone. His face showed increasing disappointment. He scowled and looked annoyed and from time to time he glanced at a clock in the building's end. And this dramatizing of his shame and fear became so real for him that he almost believed, after a while, that he was searching. He lifted his brows, he would show sudden interest, as if he recognized the one he sought; and he would go rapidly away, looking over heads, as if to keep his quest in sight.

He was still acting his part when McClintock grasped his arm. And now, instead of being himself, Vridar clung to his pretense. He tiptoed, with a hand on Forenoon's shoulder; and he said, "I think I saw a college girl here." And in a few moments (and quite as he had intended) he had McClintock staring about, and they went together, exploring from group to group.

Vridar was satisfied. The curious, he believed, must be convinced now. Instead of regarding him as a frightened rabbit, they must suppose that he was bold and oblivious, and that none but a worldly fellow could have prowled around in such fashion. And they had forgotten, he hoped, his humiliating episode with the girls.

"Come on," McClintock said. "Let's butt into some more." Vridar went with him and presently Forenoon said, "I see two. Don't look. One in red, one in blue." They turned and came back and Vridar glanced at the girls. They went through the crowd and lost themselves and returned.

"Hello," Forenoon said. "Where you been hiding?"

"Us hidun!" one cried.

"You remember me?" Forenoon said. "I danced with you at the Odeon." He turned to Vridar and shrugged. "You see? I danced with her a month ago. Now she don't know me. If I'd been the Prince of Wales or the sultan of Whamtam. . . ." The girls were looking at him now as if trying to remember. "I danced with you twice," Forenoon declared to the lovelier girl of the two. "I asked if you ever went to Bonneville. You said yes. I said I'd see you here and you said all right. And now you pretend you don't remember!" His tone was aggrieved. He shrugged again.

"Sure," said the one in blue. "I remember. You asked would I give you my phone number and I wouldn't."

"Exactly. And I been sad ever since. I been lookun for you in cellars and attics and closets and trunks and coal bins. That's why I asked where you been hiding?"

"Wouldn't you like to know!"

"Sure would. I'd sit on your doorstep and wag my tail all night."

The girl in blue twittered. The other girl smiled. Said the one in blue:

"We don't usually dance with men without a introduction."

"That's easy," Forenoon said. He bowed with his right arm across his chest and his left arm to Vridar. "Miss Beautiful, may I present Mr. Vancouver James? Miss Lovely," he said, bowing to the other girl, "Mr. James. And now I have the honor to present myself, Mr. Jack Welland of Wasatch College." The girls looked startled but they were pleased.

"You say things in a nice way," the one in blue said. "You're sure original."

"Jack Welland," the other said. "Seems like I've heard that name." She turned to her companion. "Ain't you?"

"Seems I have. You play football?"

"I'm the left halfwit—I mean halfback. James here is the middle, I mean the center."

"I knowed I'd heard your names," the girl said. She was warming to McClintock now. Her smile had lost its ice.

"And now for that dance you promised me."

"You care to dance?" Vridar asked of the girl in red.

"Thanks. I don't care to."

Vridar looked at her. What he saw in her face filled him with sudden rage. He went to a bench and sat down. . . . And twice more during this evening, he was Forenoon's companion in accosting girls; twice more McClintock danced with strangers, once dragging an unwilling maid to the floor, and once flattering another by saying she looked like Norma Talmadge.

And twice Vridar was left, bewildered and sweating, to seek a hiding-place.

During the last hour, he sat in a far corner, bitterly reflecting on women. They capitulated to the most stupid flattery. They showed no more acumen than that of a chicken with its head under its wing. Men they judged by their clothes and by their tongues: like birds, they chose as mate the one most gaily attired, employing, in an age of reason, a biology now ancient and silly. Like frost on a pane, their emotions lay on the surface, icy and rather opaque, but melting under unctuous flummery; and showing then, like the pane, a wintery emptiness beyond.

He walked home and he felt a vast friendliness toward hermits and monks and all the other weird celibates of history. Caught up by passion not of their choosing, and shaken like a rat in a dog's mouth, they went off to scourge themselves and make themselves clean. They repudiated God's vulgar way of raising life from dust. Because men—great and worthy fellows like himself—aspired to nebular kingdoms, but were overhauled, in nine times out of ten, by a woman's arms. A woman laid her hands on a mate and the law gave to her a first mortgage on him. She got a deed for him, as she might for any other sort of property; and thereupon she staked him in her domain, to use as whim prompted, for breeding and toil. If a man escaped, he was thrown into jail like a bull into a paddock. If he fled, another woman would seize him, in course of time, and the luckless zany would find himself mortgaged again; until at last, fleeing in and out of marriage, he would yield to despair, and reserve to himself only one privilege, that of death. . . .

In an ugly mood, Vridar entered his room. He stared at Mertyl a little while and then delivered himself of furious resentment against women and life.

"I'm a fool!" he cried. "I've been to a dance! I have girls on the brain! I should a-been studying and I'm running after girls like a dog after a bitch! And God knows why! . . . Why should I fool with girls? They're a bunch of nitwits! And life, what is it but a cockeyed blunder that God made and is ashamed of! Greed, superstition, lying, whoring! A big asylum in which men chase women! A thing called marriage that legalizes lust! Lust and greed, greed and lust!" He stopped, trembling with hatred. Crossing the room, he filled a cup with water but he did not drink. He looked at the cup and set it down.

"I wish I had never been born!" he roared. "I didn't ask to be born, did I? I was put here and even God Himself couldn't tell why! To eat my heart out, I guess! To be made a fool of by women! The whole beastly world is a lie and women are the biggest lie of all! I'm sick of it! . . . Who said people are honest?" he shouted at Mertyl. "They're liars and hypocrites! . . . Mert, I think I'll kill myself."

"You're talking through your hat," Mertyl said.

"Why shouldn't I? What have I got to live for? What has anyone got? The wise person kills himself as soon as he begins to think."

"Kill yourself over a woman, I guess. That would be a joke on you."

Vridar stared at his brother for several moments.

"I'm through with women," he said. He got a volume of Pope and sat to read. He hurled Pope from him and got a volume of Pater. "Mark my words. I'm through with women," he said. In a little while he came to this line:

For the way to perfection is through a series of disgusts.

He pondered these words for almost an hour. Then he rose and took his cap and entered the night.

IX

▪

HE WAS not through with women. He could no more have lived without women than without air. Morbidly sensitive, and to be, for many years to come, incurably erotic, he saw women as the core of life, with all things swimming in centripetal convolutions to their center. They drew him irresistibly. They were the gravity of being: he was water, seeking its level. And no more could he remain on the heights, in the polar air of his negations, than water could resist seeking the sea.

Because this which he felt, that laid hold of him with awful power, was more than women: it was the enormous pulse of creation, with women moving through it as its lovely, its alluring, symbols. It was the huge body of all-that-is, and women swam in it, as fish swim in the sea, and they were the fertile life in its depth, its sensuous color and warmth. And if all women were dead, this uterine pulse would still live, would still pour like fire through the waste of the uncreated. Because, in some form, it was to be seen in every tree and flower, in every field; and where it was not, there stood the unbeautiful dead.

Even when in the classroom, even when walking the streets, Vridar felt this power, this impalpable awakening of the insensate, this reaching through midnight to the sun. In countless things, infinitely small but bright with meaning, he saw its gesture: in the way a girl turned her head, in a man's sudden lift of his eyes, and in his instructors when, pausing in their feeble and shifting patterns of thought, they reached down, for a moment, to a depth that lay asleep. And now that spring was coming, he saw all life flowering from its seed.

As a matter of fact, when golden days again stood from sky to valley, or lay dreaming on the city's hills, this thing which possessed him was like an open hunger, like a fire feeding on itself. It rose in gardens of color on the lawns; it sang in girls like music in violin strings; and it was a new mightiness, like the sea's own, in the hearts of men. And books were ignored and all life gathered to the core of April. When Vridar entered a classroom, he would see on a blackboard the pathetic symbols of the meaningless. He would see the dead empty chairs and the closed books. For life was building bowers outside, and students walked again in the sorcerous lyricism of shrub and tree.

Had Vridar been living at this time where all things were half-asleep, surfeited with breathing and effort; where, in every new day, fragrant morning did not drench his senses; and where not one but a thousand things did not harken back to his youth, recalling, from its great wilderness, all its sweetness of smell and sound, all its passionate question and heartache—then he might have sat with books on his knees. During the white half-death of winter, he had held his emotions at arm's length; but now, with earth pushing out of sleep its acres of garden, and with beauty, like an odorous horn, calling the wanderer to the far journey, he was drawn back, like a vagrant stream, to the mighty current of being and all his paths led to its flood.

Early in every morning he rose and walked the streets. Or he left the city and climbed to where the wild flowers grew; and this earth, which he had cursed, so filled him with longings, reaching to nameless ends, and with its deep wonder, printed on the hillsides, piled in its blue sky, that he shook in its glory and lay on the ground and wept.

No, he was not done with girls. His intelligence, his will, had no power to hold him now. Fear of life held him; but his hunger rose, surging, like water to a dam; rose in tides, only to fall back upon itself, to rise and to fall again; until he was caught in whirlpools of emotion and spun like seadrift. He sought in books for some strength, some anchor, but he found none. The authors of books, like himself, had been rocked under emotional storms. Like Carlyle, they had been convulsed by negations; like Swift, they had gone mad under the extravagant blundering of passion; like Swinburne, they had fled naked before the winds. There was some calm (and there was much emptiness) in their pages, but there had been none in their lives.

And so, while sitting to his study, Vridar would feel upon his books the shadow of life, as if life stood near and waited; and he would lay the books aside. Within him, beat by beat, would rise an ancient and solitary hunger. He would go to the door, having no fixed purpose, and look back into the room; and he would close the door softly and find the street. He would go into the city, and the ache within him would become feverish and far-reaching. Perhaps he would walk up and down Main Street, staring at persons, wondering how they could be so quiet; or he would stand by a cabaret and listen to its music; or he would enter the park. And again and again he went to the Bonneville hall.

He would peer in or he would walk round and round the place, and then he would go home. But at last, in an April night, he forced himself to enter, and he sat for an hour, trembling in the music; until, goaded by self-contempt, he went to a woman and asked her to dance. To his amazement she smiled at him and took his arm. She led him to the floor; and while he slipped and stumbled and burned with shame, the woman talked to him, instructing him in the steps.

"See," she said, smiling up at him. Vridar stared down through mist at her feet. "See?—like this—like this. Now you try."

He glanced wildly round him, expecting to see derisive faces.

"I—I can't," he said.

"Of course you can. Now watch—see, like this."

During the whole of this dance, she lessoned him patiently, wisely; and Vridar rebuked his clumsiness, his gawkiness, and said he could never dance. And when the dance was done, he intended to flee, but the woman clasped his arm and asked if he wanted to dance with her again.

"Again!" he cried. "Good God, I can't dance."

"I'll learn you how."

"You'll be a lifetime."

"All right. But you'n learn if you'll just try."

Vridar looked at her searchingly. She was not very young. She was not lovely but she was patient and kind.

"I—but—" he said. "Well, I mean why should you bother?"

"You want to learn, don't you? And besides I like you."

"You—like me?"

"Yes."

"I don't know why you should."

"I have reasons."

Dance after dance, during a long evening, the woman spent with him on the floor. She taught him simple movements in the one-step, in the fox-trot, in the waltz. He felt more at ease, fumbled less frequently; and came at last to be aware of her as a woman in his arms. She was plump and uncorseted. The flesh of her back was warm and alive and her full bosom pressed against his heart; and yielding, after many trials, to the rhythm that was part of him, he moved with her in a waltz, through a dream of loveliness, a rhapsody of sex. She patted his shoulder and smiled up at him. She drew him closer. And Vridar stopped, his muscles falling into their old stiffness.

"Poof!" she said. "Come on now, easy, dreamy—like this." He stumbled like a wooden dummy and shrugged.

"I guess I can't." His grin was sickly.

"Sure you can. Now—come on."

He tried again; and little by little the stiffness left him, he became languorous with the rhythm, he moved again through a dream.

When the last dance was done, he looked at the woman. She smiled at him and there was something in her smile, in her eyes, that frightened him.

"You'll be a swell dancer soon," she said.

"I hope so."

As she smiled at him now, her eyelids drooped. She patted his arm.

"Will you be coming here again?"

"I—well— Sure!" he said.

"Tomorrow night?"

"I—I guess so."

"Fine. I'll be your teacher again. And now, Mr.——?"

"Hunter."

"—Mr. Hunter, if you'd like to take your teacher home?"

He looked at her. He didn't know what to make of this. It was pretty bold, it seemed to him; pretty bold, indeed. Lord, he hoped she was not a bad woman!

"That is, if you didn't come with someone."

"No, I didn't."

"If you don't care to——"

"That isn't it. I—I'd like to."

She took his arm and led him outside. They crossed the street to wait for a car. She asked:

"Your people live in Salt Lake?"

"No."

"You here alone?"

"With my brother."

"Oh, you're going to college?"

"Yes."

Again he looked at her. He did not like her mouth. It was not a lovely mouth and he had no wish to kiss it. His gaze lingered for a moment at her breast, and he knew, when she smiled and touched his arm, that she had read his thought.

They boarded a car and Vridar dug into his pocket for fare. Then he went down the aisle, looking to right and left, but he did not see her until she smiled.

"I thought I'd lost you," he said.

"You couldn't," she said, and moved close to him.

He strove to seem at ease, but he felt as if he were only a great heart, pumping bewilderment. The woman was warm and sleepy now. Once or twice she let her head touch his shoulder, lightly, and when she bent to fasten a shoe, she rested an arm on his knee. He didn't know what to make of her. And he was a fine one (wasn't he, though!), taking a middle-aged woman home. How McClintock would snort if he could see him now!

They went up Main Street and came to the statue of Brigham Young. Vridar looked at the cold stone of the man and thought of two lines he had heard:

Oh, I think Brigham Young is a funny old crank,
With his rump to the temple and his hand to the bank!

It was quite true. He did have his rump toward the Mormon temple and an arm stretched out to the biggest bank in Zion. And there was a man, Vridar reflected, who got what he wanted. He wanted women, and he had so many wives he couldn't remember their first names; so many children he couldn't tell his own from his neighbor's; and so much money he couldn't calculate its sum. He could sleep with a different woman on every night in the week, and it was this reflection that troubled Vridar most. And when Brigham's wives began to look used up, he could hike out and take a fresh bride. . . . "The scoundrel!" Vridar thought furiously. And those old codgers in the Bible: they, too, sported among the virgins like a rooster among hens. If the old custom were in vogue now, a weakling like himself, a timid quaking fellow, would have no woman at all. The celibates among the Jews were probably weaklings. They ran in self-pity to the desert and there invoked God's wrath on kingdoms and prophesied plagues. Polygamy, he could see, was only another institution of privilege. . . .

"This is my stop," the woman said.

Vridar sprang up and went down the aisle. Well, thank heaven, he knew what a man was expected to do: hop off and assist the woman, as if her legs were broken. But upon reaching the front, he found the door closed, and the motorman scowled at him and told him to get off at the rear. Red with shame, he strode down the aisle, glaring fiercely at amused eyes that watched; and when he got off, he was shaking with rage.

"Such damn cars!" he cried. "Why don't they make them all the same!"

"Poof," said the woman. "It's all right."

"It isn't!" he said, glaring at the vanishing trolley. "Nothing in life is like it should be!"

The woman became playful, like an enormous fat kitten. She rebuked him with a finger and gave him a droll wink.

"You naughty-naughty man. Life is all right."

"It isn't! It's a bag of tricks! If I couldn't make a better world I'd jump in the sea!"

"Oh, you savage man! You scare me."

"The world is a mess!" he cried, looking furiously around him. "It's a crime to be born!"

"But not to live after you're born," she said.

They walked up a hill and Vridar wished that with one mighty blow he could raze sun and stars and send God tumbling from His throne. He was in a towering rage but he didn't know at what. He wanted to kill something but there was nothing to lay his hands on; and again he said:

"If I couldn't make a better world I'd jump in the sea!"

They came to the woman's house and stopped. She looked at him and Vridar looked at her but he couldn't tell if she expected to be kissed. He was deliberating when she spoke and her words amazed him.

"You just as well come in. My husband isn't here tonight."

"Your husband!" he gasped. "Good God, you got a husband!"

"Why not?" She shrugged. "Women usually get a husband, don't they? But they don't always get rid of the louse."

"The louse!" Vridar cried, dismayed. "You mean—you mean you don't love him?"

"Oh yes. The way I love an automobile. Except I don't have an automobile."

"I guess you mean," said Vridar, waxing sardonic, "you like to see him run. . . . Well, why don't you love him?"

"Don't be silly. I've lived with him twelve years. . . . Will you come in?" Vridar took a deep breath.

"Why—" he said. "I mean I should study, I guess."

The woman was very tactful, very wise. She did not urge him.

"Some other night," she said. "We could talk a while."

"Yes," he assented hastily, "we could. I'd like to talk."

She smiled as if she understood. She offered a hand.

"Goodnight," she said.

"Goodnight."

Vridar watched her enter the house and then went down the street. He wished now he had gone in. This deeply-breathing woman made him think of Betty Mill: voluptuous Betty who baked loaves for him, who pressed his face to her bosom and kissed his mouth. He walked round a block, wondering why this woman had asked him in and if she liked him and what she wanted him to do. He returned to the house and saw a light within. Going softly to the porch, he hesitated, and while standing here, he heard the woman singing. She seemed to be very happy and he wondered what she was happy about. He listened to the words of her song.

He returned to the walk and listened but she was not singing now. That, he reflected, was rather strange. He went to a corner to meditate but he could not think: his senses were burning and scattered like flame in a wind. The path to her door, it seemed to him, led to light and meaning, and the way homeward lay across a waste of precepts and death. But he could not be sure and he was afraid.

He turned homeward and he counted his steps, not knowing why, hardly realizing what he did. There were twenty-two hundred and ninety-eight. He thought of the number as he got into bed. He was still thinking of it when he fell asleep.

X

•

O N THE next day, the United States declared war. Vridar was neither surprised nor pleased: he felt, indeed, as if he had been walking in a noisome place and had come upon a dead thing. Because war for him was not glamorous adventure. Though a lad still in his emotions, he was a man—and in some respects an old man—in a few of his thoughts. He had reflected much on war, its causes and waste and slaughter, and he hated it. War, it seemed to him, fed on jungle instincts, on dark and primordial violence; it turned the brute out of its civilized prison and gave to hungry hands the tools of death.

And so there was not in him, as there was in his classmates and professors, a patriotic fervor that burned like rash. He did not exult or see a greater vision. He did not think with vengeful lust of his enemies; for he had no enemies, least of all in Germany, and he had no need to fight. Nor did he ever believe, with McClintock and others, that the Germans raped Belgian women or cut the hands off children or drove their captives mad. Both the news and the editorials in papers he regarded as a monstrous lie. And his instructors lied, too; or, more nearly, they and editors were the victims of a national hysteria. And when, in the classroom, Vridar heard his teacher of history fall into turgid abuse of the Germans and expatiate furiously on their militarism and greed, he stared at the man and wondered if he had spent all his years in a cloister. If an educator, a man of sixty who had been president of two universities, could be so silly, so ponderously stupid, then what was the world coming to! If his professor of English could say, as he had said, again and again, that the Germans at heart were still wild and savage Norsemen; if his professor of French could say that until Germany was crushed, with half of it slain and the rest in bondage, there could be no decency on earth; and if his professor of economics, a quiet inoffensive old gentleman, could declare that Germany's purpose was the subjugation and serfdom of the world—then what was civilization but a feverish blind pilgrimage and what was an educated man but a head-hunter lost to his tribe?

The whole campus was wild with approval. Among the men, there was only one question: When are you going to enlist? Among the girls there was a new vitality, a strange eagerness: the old dark spirit of the war-dance was in their gestures and speech. In them, and in the men, old and young, there awoke a sunken heritage of the ancient. The women heard the tom-toms; they saw the male, armed with noose and war-club, preparing for the chase; and they smelled the warm fields of blood. For these were stronger in them, deeper and more eternal, than sororities and gowns and teas.

And in this atmosphere, electric with the jungle, Vridar felt lost. There was perhaps none here more emotional than himself; none whose common days were more tumultuous and hot-headed; but when he fought, he wanted to lay his life down in a decent cause. He would have fought to slay any man who exploited his race, but not the man conscripted by the exploiter. He would have fought to slay religious bigots or drug peddlers or pimps; but he would not kill a German whom he had never seen, or enlist in a cause that would be, as nearly all wars had been, a colossal butchery in the name of God. The French Revolution was a decent struggle: he would have fought in that. But the American war for freedom, wise and generous in its origins, became a grasping political gang-fight. And the Spanish-American War was so appallingly selfish, so bullying, and it stunk so of property and gold, that it sickened him to think of it. . . .

McClintock had a different opinion.

"You're a hell of an American!" he cried. "You got a-defend your country!"

"Against what?" Vridar asked.

"The Huns! The barbarians! The rapers of women and the butchers of babes!"

"That's newspaper mush."

"It's the truth. Listen, you ought a-be stuck in jail. You ought a-be deported."

"If there was a sensible country on earth," Vridar said, "I'd go to it if I could."

"Then go! Get out! You're no decent citizen."

McClintock was in a fine patriotic rage. He swore in the name of God and the flag and the mothers of men.

"You going to enlist?" Vridar asked.

"Sure. And watch me shoot the sons-of-bitches when I get over there! I'll shove a bayonet in their guts and twist it off!"

"Why? What are you going to fight for?"

"Why—why—for justice! For the honor of women. For the right of a baby to live and breathe."

"The honor of women!" Vridar said. "You're a hot one to talk about the honor of women."

"I honor women!" McClintock cried, glaring at him. "Women are our fairest jewel. Women are the cornerstone of civilization. Without women we'd degenerate——"

"That's some more newspaper mush."

McClintock was so agitated that he paced the room. He was trying to remember something, he said.

"I'll tell you why, since you're so ignorant! I'll tell you why we have gone to war!"

"Why?"

"To make the world safe for democracy!"

Vridar grinned at him and pondered these words. And at last he said:

"That's not what you mean. You mean to make democracy unsafe for the world."

The result of all this had a strange effect on Vridar. No matter where he went, he saw patriotic zealots, lusting for blood-feuds; felt their dark atmosphere of murder and vengeance; heard their demands for guns and powder and bayonets; until at last the whole frenzied orgy seemed to him to be in⸻e. It recalled to him his adolescence and his years in high school when he fought through pitch-night, hunting for the dawn. For more than a year now, he had kept close to reality, like a man hugging the shore; and an ocean of terror, like a rolling void, had been receding, had been moving out to the black immensities of the dead. But now the tide had turned. Now he felt, as formerly, that life was an enormous seething bedlam, with civilization's outposts drifting in shipwreck. Under silence he could feel, and, feeling, could almost hear, the great unrest, the sightless questing, the vast mad heartache, of life. It was a phantasm of the uncreated; with here and there, on its surface, a few waves breaking into meaning, into light, and with a few eddies falling into calm; and out of these waves stood, for a moment, the wraiths of the civilized, and in the lap of these eddies, philosophy caught its breath and meditated; and then, far out in chaos, out in the sunless wastes of distance and time, a great virgin tide, nameless, chartless, gathered its strength and rolled in, and life rocked under its coming, and had wreaked upon itself another beginning and another void. And of all this movement, stupendous and blind, he and his life, and those about him and their lives, were a small and helpless part, controlled by a destiny of which they had no notion, shaped by a power that had violence but no will. They were adrift in a limitless body of change that was changeless; on an ocean of doing that had no purpose; on a flood of darkness that set faint lights and washed them out and set them again. And in all this, madness was the moving, the creative, spirit; for it wrought its strange figures and destroyed, heaped its aimless tides to their aimless destinies; and life was its spindrift, seeking its way to consciousness and to air and to beauty; but in an unexpected hour, when purpose began to glimmer and hands reach to anchors, then the great emotion shook in its depth and drew its enervated surface into its body and gave to it its original force. And this process of enfeeblement, men called culture, and this process of renascence, men called war.

So it seemed to Vridar. He had gone into the depths and had known their darkness and terror and he had fought his way back to the shore. He had felt intimations of abysses and heights, of the formless wonders beyond consciousness, of the blind mightiness of the all-in-all, that can never be felt by a sane man. And in war now, and in the spirit of war, he felt what he had felt years ago—with this difference, he would have said: these persons around him, like McClintock, caught only the glow, only a vitalizing warmth, of that awful body, and he had felt its heat. He had felt how its power, ravening and sightless, could build only to destroy; could become violent and could suck into the black womb of the unconscious, all its long pilgrimage toward zeniths and suns. But these men, and these women, too, felt only that it was part of their heritage, their racial knowledge, as indeed it was; and they missed its utter power of destruction.

No: war for Vridar was not an adventuring into glory. It was only a path to that darkness where he had lived. It was not a part of the civilized life; and if pursued, as it commonly was, in the name of God, it could mean only that God was the ruthless and terrible deity of the uncreated. But even so, he might have dismissed it for what it was, and he might have gone his way in peace, looking with amused eyes at the turmoil of his fellows, had not the madness around him recalled to him what he had been. If blood-lusts had not been rampant, he might have saved himself from a throwback to his danger-zone. But he could not leave this city and nowhere in this city could he find a refuge. Newspapers were its journal. Professors had its shadow on their faces and bands vented the jungle-cry and the battle-call. Men appeared in uniforms; soldiers marched with guns and with sabers agleam; and girls turned their thoughts to the flow of blood and to the healing of wounds. Peace overnight had been routed from the city and war waved its flags from the housetops.

And wondering what he could do to save himself, Vridar thought of love. He thought of Neloa; but there came from her a few hasty lines, saying she wanted to be a Red Cross nurse; saying she was thrilled to death; saying Vridar would be her soldier boy now. Furiously he answered her:

Dear Neloa:
    Your attitude toward war is too stupid and silly for words. War is madness and I've been in and out of madness and have had enough. But go on and become a nurse. Make a complete fool of yourself and be done with it. But don't talk of my being your soldier boy. Wilson is a traitor and this war is being fought for commercial reasons and those who have brought it about will sit at home and count their gain. I refuse to take part. I'll go to jail first and rot; so if you want a soldier boy, hike out and find some dumb egg who wants to give his blood in defense of Morgan. And luck to you!

VRIDAR.

But the war wrought in Vridar more than a handful of similitudes. It affected him in a deep and unpredictable way. Afraid of life hitherto, and longing for security, for a refuge, he now threw his caution overboard and entered life. He did not conquer his fear. He renounced it. Because it seemed to him that the world was headed toward ruin, and in the upheaving chaos to come, his shrinking would be futile and absurd. Perhaps in a few months he would be fighting in France. In a year or two, most likely, he would be dead.

He resolved, therefore, to leave his hermitage and to pursue pleasure. He hungered mightily for physical love. Neloa could become a nurse and worship her head-hunting mannikins; and he, meanwhile, would make passionate love to every girl he met. While time was left, in the year or two standing between him and dust, he would break hearts and ravish girls and go to the devil in his own way. And besides, when he thought of girls, he lusted for vengeance. He luxuriated in petty spite because a woman had deceived him and because life had made of him a fool. He could not forget how he had floundered, only eight months ago, like an outraged simpleton in a bog. All women, he liked to think, were cheats and frauds, and he wanted to break their hearts and send them into a nunnery, howling with grief. And beyond all this, he could see in women, in love, the only power to save him from terror.

But to do all this, he had to have clothes. A girl measured a man by the crease in his trousers and the polish on his shoes. Her interest was not amorous but economic. They were all hunting, McClintock said, for a husband; and a husband meant a fellow who would buy a nest for babies and furnish it. "If you want to stand in swell, say you've got lots of dough. Tell her you'll take your bride on a honeymoon to Italy. A girl'd rather go to Naples with a hunchback than settle down with Romeo in a one-room flat. . . ." And Vridar was wondering how to get stylish clothes when Forenoon suggested another thieving exploit. There were places where a man could buy a suit on credit. He had to pay a small sum and give references; but nothing more.

"You game?"

"Sure. I don't give a damn what I do."

"Let's go now," McClintock said.

They went to State Street.

"We need names. Let's figure that out."

They walked round a block and plotted the matter. Forenoon's name was to be Earl Tavish, Vridar's was to be Richard Jones. Their address was to be 468 K Street.

"I done this once," McClintock said. "They'll ask me questions and then they might ask you the same questions. We got a-give the same answers."

"All right," Vridar said. "My name is Richard Jones. Yours is Earl Tavish."

"And we live on 468 K Street."

"I am twenty-one and you are twenty-two."

"And we are cousins."

"All right, we're cousins."

"And we don't have any telephone. If you give a number they'll call up. If you don't, they send a messenger out."

"Your name," Vridar said, "is Earl Tavish. You're a college student."

"And your name is Henry Jones."

"You said Richard Jones."

"Yes, Richard Jones. Well, we got everything straight?"

"I have. What about you?"

"Don't worry about me. I was working this game when you were still learning to say mama."

They chose a store and entered. They climbed a stairway and looked at suits. Vridar was very calm, but McClintock, he observed, was nervous. McClintock glanced guiltily about and acted for all the world like a thief out of jail. They chose suits and went down the stairway and to a window; and the clerk said:

"These gentlemen want these suits on credit."

The man behind the window was a lean cunning fellow. He looked at Vridar and then at McClintock and McClintock began to shake. Anyone, it seemed to Vridar, could read guilt in Forenoon's eyes and he wanted to strike him and walk out.

Another man came to another window and called to Vridar. Vridar went to this window and McClintock went to the other window. "The game's up!" Vridar thought, and for a moment he was terrified. He saw himself in solitary confinement, eating stale bread.

"Your name?" the man asked.

"Richard Jones."

"And where do you live, Mr. Jones?"

"468 K Street."

"How long have you lived there?"

"Two years."

"Your mother live there?"

"No."

"Where?"

"In Wyoming."

"Oh. Where in Wyoming?"

"Jackson Hole."

"Where is that?"

"South of Yellowstone Park."

There was a pause. Vridar could hear the other man questioning McClintock. He could see sweat on McClintock's brow.

"Is the other gentleman with you?"

"Yes."

"A relative?"

"My cousin."

"Does he live with you?"

"Yes."

"Mr. Jones, how old is your cousin?"

"Twenty-two."

"I see. What is his name?"

"Earl Tavish."

"His occupation?"

"College student."

"Oh, I see. Do his parents live in Salt Lake?"

"Yes."

"Their address?"

"743 South Ninth."

Vridar's answers were still glib but he knew he was being trapped. In a moment he would be bounced out of here and thrown into jail. McClintock now looked like a man under sentence of death. The sweat was running down his cheeks and his mouth was white.

Vridar was now called to the other window. The cunning inquisitor looked at him sharply, and Vridar saw a glitter of triumph in the man's eyes.

"Your name?"

"Richard Jones."

"You know this man here?"

"Yes."

"Are you relatives?"

"Yes."

"How?"

"Cousins."

"And your cousin's name?"

"Earl Tavish."

"Do his parents live here?"

"Yes."

The man paused and looked at McClintock. He looked at Vridar.

"That's rather peculiar," he said. "Mr. Tavish says his parents are dead. And he says you two are brothers. . . ."

With the cry of an animal goaded, McClintock swung and leapt from the store and dashed like a coyote down the street; and Vridar, after a moment's hesitation, bolted out and followed him. He expected to hear furious cries or to be grasped by hands. He expected shouts of *Stop thief!* and *Catch that thief!* but there were no shouts, and he rounded a corner, close on McClintock's frantic heels, and the two of them sped eastward and disappeared. They ran for a mile and they were breathless and drenched when they stopped.

"You're a bright one!" Vridar gasped. "You're the—biggest fool—I ever saw!"

"Listen!" McClintock said. "You—think—we're safe?" He stared down the street. "Is that a man coming?"

"Who cares! Crooks like you ought to be jailed. You haven't any brains. . . . My God, how could we be brothers!"

"I forgot," McClintock said. "I thought we were brothers. And then I remembered we had different names and I said we were half-brothers. . . . But it was you!" he howled. "You said my parents were alive!"

"Good hell, how was I to know your parents were dead!"

McClintock sat under a tree and mopped his face. He looked up and down the street and listened. Vridar stared at him with pity.

"You haven't as much nerve as a rabbit."

"I got plenty nerve. I just got mixed up."

They walked north. McClintock said they would try another store.

"Unless you're afraid," he said.

"Afraid! I don't give a damn what I do. . . . But this time I'll plan it. I'm sick of your muddle-headedness."

"All right, you plan it. Let's get off somewheres and memorize the whole lingo."

They went to their room and Vridar wrote on paper all the questions he could think of, and their answers; and for two hours they diligently memorized. He included such details as their labors and where they had labored and for whom; their common acquaintances among the folk of the city; the courses they were taking in college; and the number and names of their brothers and sisters, and the names of their parents, and the ages of all these. . . .

"But the important thing," he said, "is to keep cool." He considered a little while and added: "I might become a professional crook some day. Life is nothing but a swindler's game. But I wouldn't choose a gink like you for a partner."

"Go on! I'm the slickest actor you ever saw. Watch me this time."

"All right. But if you begin to sweat I'll walk out."

They went to another store and chose suits. They were called to windows and questioned. While giving his answers, Vridar watched himself, careful lest he be too glib, lest he be too hesitant, striving for a nice balance between the two. And his manner was cool and a little weary throughout.

Then they were called to the same window and their answers were verified.

"You want to take the suits now?" the man asked.

McClintock was on the point of saying yes when Vridar kicked him.

"Well," Vridar said quietly, "it doesn't really matter. We have a date in a little while and we wanted to wear them. But if you'd rather send them out——"

The man looked at him searchingly for a long moment.

"We usually deliver them," he said. "I guess you could take them now."

Vridar was careful to show no eagerness. He turned to McClintock.

"I guess we could wear our last summer suits. Is yours cleaned?" Both the men, he knew, were watching him closely.

"Why, uh—mine," McClintock said. "Gosh, it's pretty dirty."

"But you could wear it today," Vridar said. "It's no dirtier than mine. . . . Or we could call the dates off."

One of the men spoke. It was all right, he said. They could take the suits now.

After the suits were delivered to them, Vridar walked calmly, McClintock rather hastily, to the street. When outside, Vridar stopped and gazed in a window of this store. He knew that the men inside were still watching him. McClintock stood up the street as if ready to flee and Vridar called to him. He asked him to come and look at some neckties. Then Vridar entered the store and bought a necktie and he saw that the men were no longer suspicious. He found the street and went home.

In their room, Vridar and McClintock put on their suits. McClintock swore loudly and declared he would get another suit. Vridar was very quiet. The experience had sickened him. He had outwitted two cunning men and he was proud of his skill as an actor; but he had deceived his own kind, he had betrayed confidence in his integrity; and this, it seemed to him now, and it was to seem so until he died, was the blackest and the most unpardonable of all human crimes. He told McClintock he was done with theft and that he would order no more groceries. And he took his suit off and laid it away.

XI

•

H E LAID it away but only for a little while. The zyme of madness was working in him again. Often in nights he would sit up in a cold sweat; and during daylight hours, after he had been thinking of war, deliberating it as a way to his own peace, to his own death, then he would feel again the dread of former years. Then the world was full of afreets and jinni, barghests and gnomes; and history was a record of demonology—of the weird doings of Hanuman and Mumbo Jumbo and Thoth, of Anubis and Set. And he paid for the suit, discharging the debt by letter, and he put the suit on and walked the streets.

For he could no longer spend time in his room. With a roof above him and walls around him he felt entombed. He felt as if he were again in the sunken bowl of his home, with the dead yellow sun pressing down, with the gray loneliness of mountains closing in. He had to be outside where his gaze could reach into distance and his emotions could range to the stars.

And he was driven also to seek the company of others. Mertyl was a studious youth, still fretting among the whim-whams of theology. McClintock's talk was of plunder and war. And his professors, instead of being lighthouses in a crumbling world, were busy whetting their prejudice to a rapier's edge. More and more, as days passed, their academic routine was convulsed by storm, and there jetted out of them an ancient barbarism, as hot and destructive as fire. And Vridar's teacher of German, finding himself unpopular and his classes deserted, quietly disappeared.

It was desperately, therefore, that Vridar forsook his studies and turned to the city's life. He fancied himself a reckless and headstrong fellow, eager for love, quick for a fight. He saw himself, with equal ardor, leading an insurrection or ravishing a maid; as the master mind of a pack of swindlers, or the incorruptible surgeon of a sick world. And in the conjuring of his multiple and hot-headed destinies, he was well pleased. He was ready to build or demolish civilizations; but all that he did, all that he had power to do, was to dance in six evenings of every week, as well as in two or three afternoons; and to become so nimble a dancer that he won prizes; and to become a posturer in love.

Because he went, not with zest for careless doings, but as a man venturing timidly into water, with a lifebelt under him.

Vridar's lifebelt was a body of scruples. Or, more exactly, his scruples were a cyst and he was pocketed in feeble mummery, in serio-comic clowning; and this, his defense now against experience, was later to become his inscrutable mask.

After going to three dances, and finding himself doing rather well, he resolved again to ravish girls and break their hearts. It seemed to him—so immature, so childlike, were his emotions—that he could avenge himself on women by engaging himself to a score. To every girl with whom he danced, he made love in a scared and desperate way; and as he found himself smiled upon, he became a little bolder and he wooed with virginal ardor and dramatized himself as well as he could. And of the girls in the city, he was betrothed, eight weeks later, to four.

It was at the Odeon hall that he met Laura Cunningham. She was a lovely sylphlike girl, with dusky eyes and a sweet mouth. She was humorless and earnest; she had what she dignified as high ideals; she had a mission in life. Her mission, she said, was to make some good man happy; to be mother and sister to him, as well as wife, and to inspire him and to keep him from evil and to instruct him in those tender devotions which men scorned.

"Think you could make me happy?" Vridar asked.

"I guess I could," she said, and her laugh was like a sob. "You look very unhappy."

"I am," he said. His voice almost shook with grief. He thought of himself as the most wretched, the most misunderstood, man on earth. Laura's touch on his arm was gentle, womanly.

"Vridar, why you so unhappy?"

"Oh," he said. He shrugged at a mountain of woe. "I guess I'm just built that way."

"You ever been in love?" He groaned and hesitated and admitted that he had. Laura was now all interest and compassion. "And—? Were you—? Did she—?"

"She deceived me," Vridar said. "I don't like to talk about it."

Laura squeezed his arm. She called him a poor dear. So many women, she said, were heartless vultures, feeding on the trust of good men. Her voice took on a warmer intimacy.

"Lots of men are woman-haters," she said. "But you'll learn, Vridar, there's good women and bad women. You have to know which is which."

"I guess so," he said. He considered. "Yes, I guess so."

"And some day," said Laura nobly, "you'll find a good woman. She'll make you forget."

They were now following a heavily-wooded street. The night was quite dark. Obeying an impulse, Vridar slipped an arm to Laura's waist. He expected her to protest but she did not. She yielded to his pressure and brushed his shoulder with her cheek.

And as they walked, Vridar's thoughts turned to sex. He felt a bit giddy and wanted to kiss her. But Laura's thoughts, he knew clearly, were not of sex at all. She seemed to treat him as she might a brother or an uncle; she still spoke, in a voice vibrant and sad, of bad women and of good women and of the latter's power as a healer of men. She had known two heart-broken fellows. She had gone with them but she had not loved them. She had been their sister, their angel of mercy, their inspiration and light. They were married now.

"I visit their homes," she said. "We're like brother and sister. We think a lot of each other in a pure way."

This talk bored Vridar. It annoyed him. In Laura's words, in her mission of sisterhood on earth, he smelled something unwholesome and sickly. It was Christian, he supposed, but he did not like it. And with his arm pressing her uncorseted flesh, it was hard to think about it.

When she came to her home, she smiled like a nun and said she could not ask him in. Vridar stiffened, with all his amorous longings ready for retreat, yet looking back. Could they not, he asked, step into the hallway?

"Why yes," Laura said. "For a minute."

She entered a dark hallway and he followed. She turned to him and in the light from the door he studied her face. There was no passion in it, no hunger, no loneliness. Her gaze was clear, fawnlike, and a little questioning. For several moments neither spoke. And then:

"I guess you better go now," Laura said.

But Vridar did not budge. He wanted to kiss her lovely mouth.

"You might—" he said. He looked out at the street and heard wind in the trees. "You might kiss me goodnight."

Laura rebuked him with a frown, a patient sisterly frown, that she had used before.

"No, Vridar. A good girl doesn't kiss every man she meets."

"Well, but we—" he said. "It's like—it's as if we'd known each other a long time. It seems that way to me."

"Yes," she said, and sighed. "All right." She tiptoed and offered her lips and he touched them with his own. "Now you must go."

He felt sullen, put upon. He had a furious notion to threaten: to cry, "If you send me now I'll go to the dogs!" Instead, yielding to an impulse that astonished him, and that on the next day, when he recalled it, astonished him even more, he jerked her toward him and folded her in his arms. She fought against him with tiny hammering blows. He grasped her hands and sought her mouth.

"Don't!" she cried. "Vridar, don't be a fool!"

This sobered him. He pushed her away and turned to the door. She sprang forward and clutched his arm.

"Vridar."

"What?" he said, scowling at her.

"You're not mad at me?"

"Goodnight," he said.

"Vridar!" She went with him to the porch. She grasped him and strove to make him look at her. "Vridar," she reproached him, "you expect too much. Why don't you go with a bad girl?"

"I guess I will," he said.

"Vridar, you don't mean that. Please look at me." He looked at her, his eyes dark and lonely. "Aren't you going to see me again?"

"I don't know," he said.

"Please! I want you to."

"You think I'm a lecher," he said.

"I think you're a what?"

"Oh, just an ordinary woman-chaser."

"*I do not!* I like you. I think I might learn to love you. But love doesn't grow in a moment, you know."

"Bosh," he said. He looked at her pityingly, wondering if she would ever feel love. Perhaps not. What did she know of violent passions, tempests leaping from the hour, hunger like a hot iron reaching to the core of life?

"Vridar, say you'll see me again."

"I don't know."

"Please. I want you to." She now came up and placed hands on his shoulders. He looked at her soft dusky eyes. "Vridar," she said, "if you want to kiss me again, you can."

"I don't want to. I wanted to once but not now."

"Why?"

"I just don't want to."

"Then I'll kiss you," she said. She tried to pull his stubborn head down. "All right," she cried, "I'll kiss you here!" and she quickly kissed one of his hands. Then she ran to the door. She went inside and looked out, smiling. "I bet I dream about you." And in a low soft voice she whispered, "Vridar dear, goodnight!"

It was also at the Odeon that he met Kitty Murdock. Kitty was the sort of girl who baffled him. She lured and repelled, in one moment filling him with tenderness, in the next with rage. Her moods changed like the mountain sunsets of his home: now burning with a clear golden intensity, now fading into a shadowed pool of lilac; now heaping autumn brown and loneliness, now a mist of gray. In no two hours, almost in no two moments, was she the same. Vridar felt in her something tragic and bitter but he could not summarize it. He felt in her a lyric rapture, a melody of emotion, that fed on nothing real, nothing earthly, but drew its fire from a distant nothingness.

When he first saw her, she was sitting in a corner alone. He asked her to dance and she assented with a grimace of weariness. She danced wearily twice round the hall. And then, with the suddenness of light, she changed. She drew closer to him and looked up and smiled; and she began to sing. It was a soft idyl of song, hinting of pastoral acres and of green fields and running brooks. And while she sang in a low voice she seemed dynamic with a morbid passion that was full of the sun, yet very dark.

After the dance he sat by her. He looked at her and she did not seem to mind. She was not beautiful but he liked her face: her tremulous irresolute mouth, her flushed cheeks, the strange intentness of her dark gray eyes. And unexpectedly she turned and looked at him and gave him a droll wink.

"How about it?" she said. "Do I pass muster?"

"Why——" he said.

"I know you," she said, her lips curling. "I've known you for years."

"Known me!" he cried. "Where?"

"Everywhere. In Utah, in Shanghai. In Oregon and Maine."

"I don't know what you mean," he said.

"Let's dance," Kitty said. "Then maybe you'll understand."

They danced again. During this while, Kitty looked up at him, her face very earnest, her eyes searching. Vridar became embarrassed. He tried to seem inscrutable and at ease, not knowing what sort of person he had here. She was a little mad, he knew, but her madness was indefinable, like that of the eagle or the hawk.

"Don't you understand yet?" she asked.

"I—I don't know," he said.

She snuggled close to him, her hair in his face; and they danced round and round. When the dance was finished, Kitty left him and disappeared. For a while Vridar searched for her in the crowds. He danced with other girls but his eyes were alert for Kitty. He did not see her again in this evening, and he went home, feeling very wretched.

On the next evening he went to the Odeon and looked for her but she was not there. He retired to a corner and sulked; and while he was sitting here, counting his woes, fighting against the old darkness and dread, Kitty appeared out of no-

where and sat by him. Vridar stared at her, wondering if he
saw her as an apparition out of sleep, as he had seen Bonnie
Adams. He wondered, with foolish unreason, if this might not
be Bonnie herself.

"You know me yet?" asked Kitty. He did not speak. He
looked at her and tried to understand what she meant. "It's
queer," Kitty went on, "that I should know you and you
shouldn't know me."

"I don't know what you mean," Vridar said.

"You're not stupid, are you?"

"I suppose."

"Do you know people by their names and faces?"

"I guess so. How do you know them?"

"By what they have done."

Her words startled him. He looked at her more sharply.

"You mean you know me by what I've done?"

"Let's not dance tonight," she said. "Let's walk."

They left the hall. Turning from a lighted street to a dark
one, they went south, and came at last to Liberty Park. During these two miles not a word was said. Vridar was uneasy
and perplexed. This girl was a riddle and he had no idea of
what she intended or why she was walking here. She was not,
he told himself, a harlot but she acted like one.

When they were sheltered by trees, he put an arm round
her, experimentally. She put his arm away.

"Be yourself," she said. "You're not yourself now."

He was annoyed. He deliberated walking off and leaving
her.

"I'm a normal animal," he said, speaking with fierce resentment. "Biology will be biology after we're dust."

Her response to this amazed him. She went down the walk
like a banshee, chanting a weird dirge; running her naked
arms through foliage; pirouetting to a lawn and falling there
in languishing abandon, her arms spread to the grass, her eyes
closed; and then rising and coming toward him, with her steps
heavy and dead.

"That's biology," she assured him. "That was a little allegory
all for you."

"You crazy goof!" he cried, lost in bewildered admiration.

She tiptoed and looked up at him, her eyes half-eclipsed.

"Kiss me," she said. "Kiss me and get it off your mind. Then we'n be friends."

"Go to hell," he said. He was nonplussed. He felt very silly.

"You want to. Don't lie about it."

Then something broke within him. All his inhibitions fell like a dam under dynamite and he jerked her to him. Her arms went up and around his neck. But when he stooped to kiss her, the tides of his passion rolled back and the dam stood between him and her, like a wall of concrete. He shoved her away.

Taking his hand, she led him to a flowering tree and sat on the grass. She told him to sit and he fell to the earth, his senses in chaos.

"Vridar, look at the stars. Did you ever look at the stars much?"

"I guess so," he said, and he looked at the stars.

"Did you ever wonder about them?"

"Sometimes."

"Can you—can you get any meaning out of all that? Or anything? . . . We sit here now but what do we mean?"

"Not very much, I guess."

"What does life mean? Does anyone know?"

"I don't imagine," he said.

"Vridar, doesn't it all get you here?" She pressed a hand to her heart. "Doesn't it hurt when you think about it?"

"Yes," he said.

"Doesn't it—can you—O my God!"

With a cry of anguish she threw herself to his lap. She wept, and he had never seen one so goaded by grief: none save himself in times that were gone. And he understood now. All that Kitty had said, all that she had done last night and to-night, was instantly clear. . . .

It was an hour later when he walked her home. She was weary now and a little sardonic.

"I won't ask you in," she said. "Houses are jails." She took his lapels. "Do you know me now?"

"Yes."

"How long have you known me?"

"Years and years."

"Do you think we ought to see each other again?"

"I don't know."

"It wouldn't be wise. . . . But we'll never be wise, will we? You'll always be a mad angel, trying to fly when there's nothing to fly to. I'll always be a woman who should have been a man."

"We'll never grow up, I guess."

"And we'll always be lonely. We'll always live alone."

"And some day we'll kill ourselves."

"And the world will say we were crazy. The world is stupid, isn't it? The world eats and sleeps."

"And snores."

"And builds asylums. . . . Well, kiss me goodbye."

"It isn't goodbye."

"Well, don't kiss me, then. Kisses do things to us."

She entered a house and Vridar went to a corner and sat under a tree. For a long while he thought of Kitty and looked at the stars.

It was at a Mormon dance that he met Martha Grant. She was a little stout, a little fat, and quite unlike, in both appearance and character, either Laura or Kitty. She was indolent and voluptuous, full-bodied and womanly and warm. Her gestures were sensuous and lazy. Her plump bosom and her ripe mouth—everything about her was hungry female, natural and unashamed.

And Vridar knew she was the kind of girl he should be with. Laura was bogged in her scruples. Kitty was morbid and volatile. But Martha was as sane and healthy as a cow. Freud and the new psychology, neuroses and phobias and distempers, these meant nothing, these had no power to mean anything, to her. She was a hundred and forty pounds of appetite and coquetry and allurement.

After dancing five times with her, Vridar took her home. On her porch was a swinging seat and they sat here a long while.

She asked Vridar to talk. He was a college man, she said, and he ought to know a lot of interesting stuff.

"Tell me something interesting," she said.

He hardly knew what to talk about. He turned over in his mind the subjects he had been studying: English literature, French history, German, psychology. . . .

"My teacher of German is a German. He beat it the other day."

"Oh, he did? Why?"

"Because he's a German."

"But isn't he an American, too?"

"Yes, but he was a German first. Professors don't like Germans now. It's the war."

"Don't talk about the war. All the good-lookun men will be shot. They'll just leave the old married ones and the cripples. . . . Talk about something else."

Vridar considered again.

"The French Revolution, you're not interested in that?"

"Gosh no. I think I studied it in high school."

"Well, you don't like poetry, I guess."

"Not much. Oh, once in a while I do. I like love-poems."

"Do you like Wordsworth's poems?"

"Wordsworth? I guess I studied him once. You mean Henry Wordsworth Longfellow?"

"No. William Wordsworth."

"Did he write love-poems?"

"Well—not exactly."

"I wouldn't like him then."

For a third time Vridar considered.

"Well," he said, "there's psychology. It's interesting. My professor of psychology hates Freud. He says Freud is a fool. An erotic fool, he says.

"What does erotic mean?"

"Oh, it means—well, too much interest in sex."

"It does! I guess I'm erotic." And with a warm amorous laugh she fell to his shoulder and brushed his face with her hair. She sat up and tried to look dignified and curious. "What does this Freud believe?"

"Oh, he thinks babies can be sexually stimulated. He thinks men fall in love with their mothers and girls with their fathers. And that human beings are repressed. . . . Lord, he preaches a lot of piffle!"

"What would he say about me? I've been in love a hundred times." Vridar stared at her. "I guess he'd say I was a case." She laughed happily, flattered by her thoughts. She looked at him earnestly. "Tell me: is a woman erotic if she likes to be kissed? I mean if she likes to be kissed a lot, hours at a time."

Vridar's heart leapt. He moved to draw her to him and then groaned and sank his face to his hands. Then he looked at her.

"Why?" he said. "Do you?" His voice shook.

"I'm afraid so." She drew a long breath, as if annoyed by her folly, as if pleased by it, too.

Vridar was confused. The old conflict rose and stormed within him. One of his emotional convictions, denied, and even ridiculed, by his intelligence, was that kissing, and especially ardent kissing, was sinful. McClintock had told him of soul-kissing: of the sucking of tongues, and of mouth-to-mouth caresses that endured, in passionate exploration, for a long while. And Vridar had been sickened and enraged by what McClintock said.

But he wanted to kiss Martha now. He wanted to spend himself in an orgy of rapture, but he knew he could never kiss her in the way she wanted to be kissed. He had kissed Neloa many times, but always chastely, always a little guiltily. And now he stared at his hands, pretending to be lost in meditation.

"I don't know what Freud would say," he declared at last. "He'd probably say you had a compulsion."

"O Lord!" she cried. "What is that?"

"An unreasonable wish to do something."

"Unreasonable! It isn't unreasonable."

"I know," he said, perjuring himself. "But—well, that is what Freud would say."

"Then he *is* a fool." She now looked at Vridar with genuine interest. "Where does this Freud fellow live? Isn't he locked up?"

"He lives in Europe."

"That explains it. They don't have any beautiful women over there. . . ."

But Vridar barely heard. He was absorbed by the fight going on within. He prayed that something would snap and set him free, so that he could take this girl, so that he could rise to manhood and claim his right. But he was only a fool, terrified by the hunger of a woman's mouth. When a girl offered herself, he quaked and ran cold, as if his veins were filled, not with blood but with embalming fluid. . . .

"I guess I'd better be going," he said. He stood up. He made excuses about study and early morning work. Would he come and see her again, Martha asked. Yes, indeed. When he was not so busy. When his mind was not fretted by a thousand and one odds and ends of duty.

Martha now rose and offered her hand. Vridar took her hand and looked at her, his mind haunted and guilty, his eyes dark.

"Well, goodnight," he said.

"Goodnight. And call me soon."

"I will."

Never in his life—not even during his high school years—had his self-loathing been more furious than now. Hatred of himself blinded him and he stumbled homeward, wishing some power would strike him dead.

XII

APRIL 9—Tonight I danced until I melted my collar. Forenoon had a girl for me but this lad demands a girl with a characteristic. I took home a Miss Alice Hunter. No relative, though. And what an amorous little Mormon she turned out to be! Forenoon says the Mormon girls are much more loving than the Baptists and whatnot. I fooled around with Alice so long I missed my car and had to walk three miles home. I am writing this at three in the morning. The whole experience seems tasteless now.

April 10—Got a note from Neloa. I think there are two girls down here who love me more than she does. In disgust, after reading the note, I went to a dance. I took a girl home named Gertrude Ivins. She wouldn't kiss tonight but said she would next time. On my way home I weighed. I have lost ten pounds in ten days. That shows what kissing and dancing do to a man. . . . Lord, what a glorious spring day! I can't understand spring when I think of war. I can't understand war when I think of spring.

April 11—Last fall I think I loved McClintock but I hate him now. I hate his ribald tongue and his ruthless way with women. I hate his cowardice and his petty thieving and his ungenerous heart. I'd take pleasure in knocking him as cold as zero and burying him. . . . A poem of mine appeared in the school journal. A blank verse effort called Learn to Live. Several congratulated me, but one of them, a professor of English, thinks Amy Lowell's bombast is poetry. I'd like to know just how worthless my truck is. When I write it, it seems good, but when I read it days later, it seems awful. . . . Went to a dance at the Le Grande hall. A pretty bunch of girls. I got two telephone numbers and went home.

April 12—Wrote a letter to the girl who jestingly signs herself my sweetheart. She seems to be an impossible daughter of the lewd. After writing the letter, I called three girls and made three dates.

This is the letter Vridar wrote to Neloa:

Dear Neloa:

It seems useless for us to pretend any more. You're a born flirt and you have an incurable interest in other men. I am now going out with girls. I suggest you turn your vagrant heart loose and step out with all the men in Rigby. As for myself, I expect soon to go to France and let them shoot me. That will solve one problem for both of us.

VRIDAR.

April 13—During the afternoon, I spent two hours hugging this pretty daughter of our landlady. She smells clean now and she looks clean. She is a modest girl, and yet, like most girls, she sees no harm in hugging and kissing. But she is very different from the average type of hugging girl. [Vridar spent only fifteen minutes with her in a hallway and kissed her only once.] . . . Went to a dance tonight with Laura. She let me hold her in my arms quite a while tonight. She surprised me by saying, "I guess I'm in love with you." "All right," I said, "let's get engaged." So now I'm engaged to two girls and don't imagine I'll marry either.

April 14—I took Anna Mullen to a dance tonight. She's a pretty girl and she kisses like fury but I'll stake my head on her virtue. She is not bashful but she is sweet and modest. She lets me kiss her but she won't let me touch her breasts. Damn, she's sweet! After we came home I sat in her living-room and hugged her until I was dizzy. Then I went to bed and I felt the sanest I've felt in two weeks.

April 15—Received a letter from Neloa. Maybe I'll give her another chance. She's awfully stupid. She can understand that two and two make four but she could never understand what made a fool of John Calvin. I can't see my years ahead without her; and with her, they look dark. God help me out of this mess! God help any man who falls in love with a woman!

This is the letter he received from Neloa:

Sweetheart:- I'm going to ask you for another chance. Are you ready to let me try again? If I fail I will do something worse than go to France and get shot. You are very wrong, dear, when you think your death would mean nothing to me. If you go, I will go to England as a missionary. You are certainly more to me than all the ordinary "dear boys" on this old earth. You are dearer to me than any other person I ever saw. O sweetheart, you are not the only person suffering this winter!

You said in one of your letters that I've seen Harvey. I have not. In fact, I haven't seen him since a year ago. You ask me if I want to give you up, if I love another man, if I don't think our love will lead to tragedy. And I answer all three questions with an emphatic NO.

Sweetheart, I have asked for one more chance. I want more than *your* friendship. I want to give you more than friendship. Let me have one more chance and let me sign myself

Your sweetheart,
NELOA.

April 16—I had a date last night but I ditched it. I couldn't go. I couldn't eat or sleep. I could only think of my past and of my love for Neloa. I fool around with other girls here and I think I'm falling in love; but I know better. Just the same, I'm afraid to go back to Neloa. I'm afraid of the years ahead. I don't know why but I am. And if I could break away from her now and forget her, that would be wisest and best. But, God I don't know, I don't know! I feel the old craziness tonight.

April 17—We moved today. Forenoon threw a skillet through a window and Mrs. Mullen kicked us out. We're up on the hill now. In the afternoon Mullen found out where we were and called up and Forenoon answered him. Mullen wanted pay for the window. Forenoon talked to him something like this:

You weasel-faced hog-eared dog-tooth son-of-a-bitch! What do you mean bothering me? I'll come down there and run you through a meat-grinder! What? . . . Listen, you half-witted Mexican! I'll be down there in ten minutes! I'll knock you clear over the Mormon temple! I'll seduce your daughter and give her triplets! How's that? . . . Try it! You hunchback! Go on and have me arrested! I'll fill your belly with powder and stick a fuse through your navel and blow you all over China! . . ."

I guess I'll pay for the window. I'm tired of paying for what this fool breaks up.

Took Martha to a dance tonight and then tried to make love to her on her porch. But I couldn't. I kissed her but I couldn't make love. Something sticks in my heart. Something makes everything dark and desolate and I have to go home. I can't forget Neloa. When I kiss another girl I see Neloa's face. And then everything around me is queer and I begin to shake.

April 18—Received a letter from Neloa. It made me furious. She says Arnold Hess is an educated man. She gave as a reason his ability to dance. Good God, no man worth his salt can dance! And as further proof she sent me a letter which Hess wrote to her.

This is the letter, copied by Vridar with painstaking exactness:

Manchester, England
3/29/17

Dear Friend:—

Just a line to answer your most kind & welcome letter I received and was glad to hear you was enjoying your Self as it leaves me doing about the same thing only I am most to fat to do enything but laugh and look wise now and again. The change hasn't hurt me physicaly for I weigh 173 lbs so you can fancy me being so short. I feel like the Story of the pillican whos bill can hold more than his bellycan he can carry enough in his beak to last him a week but I don't see how the hell he can. I've had more than one nose stuck in my mouth for the citys are in darkness & sometimes so fogy you cant see a light 3 feet away and some people have more than 3 ft of a nose especially if they want to stick it in Some one's elses business and I wish they had of sent my dog out here. There is joy in serving the Lord & trying to keep his commandments for I know the Gospel is true and tho the world hate us but we have the truth and some day they will find it out. The world dont want no religion that interferes with their pleasures for never in my life have I seen people so pleasure mad as now. Let us not forget the Lord for after all is he who gives us all even life its Self. I do wish all people would look at life as they should we are hear to prepair our Selfs for the next life & if we dont do nothing we cant expect eny reward and may the Lord bless you with his Spirit to guid you through the path of life and lead you back into his presents is the wish of your Bro in the Gospel

ARNOLD HESS

Vridar read this letter with a sinking heart; not for its wretched illiteracy, but for its smugness, its unctuous dullness.

He himself had almost gone on a mission. He now shuddered at the thought. And in his journal he added this comment:

> There is something vicious in trying to convert another person to your religious belief. The motive is unclean and it stinks. I don't know what the uncleanness is, but before I die I'll figure it out.

> April 19—Got my story back from *Saturday Evening Post.* If I ever become a great writer I'll have to climb bigger mountains than any I've seen yet. Anyway, I ought to be kicked for sending anything to the *Post.* It is a journal for those who do all their thinking with their emotions and who buy what is advertised. . . . Went to a dance given by the L. D. S. nurses. These Mormon nurses know what they want and they sail right after it. I took one home and she piled on to my lap and I thought I was in for what Forenoon calls a good workout. But I'm a virgin yet and that's the rub. I was born to be a monk.

> April 20—After a dance tonight I asked Anna to marry me. She said yes. Good God, what a beast I am! I despise myself. I'm now engaged to three girls and I'm not worth any of them. I wish I'd have an accident and be killed. I'm half-crazed all the time. I can't get hold of anything that means much. In a month or so I have to go home and I'd rather die than go. . . . Today the freshmen shaved Forenoon's head. To see him without any hair is as pleasant a sight as I can remember.

> April 21—I sat for hours today as if in a trance. When I can't get out and run wild I'm lost. Sunday is a day of death for me.

> April 22—Tonight Martha said she would marry me. Laura wants to marry me in June. Kitty says she will marry me in a couple of years. Anna says she will marry me as soon as her dad will let her. And I wish I had the courage to marry one of them. I hardly know which one. Laura, I guess. Kitty is too morbid. Martha would be faithless. Anna is too unschooled. She says ain't and I'm feelun swell and It's a pippin.

> April 23—Tonight I took Anna to a dance. In her parlor I asked her to let me go the limit. She wept and then con-

sented. And I backed down. I couldn't do it. I have a silly notion that I should be honest with women. I don't expect ever to see Anna again. . . . Mert went home yesterday, sick of school.

April 24—Went to a dance tonight and got dead drunk. [Vridar drank two glasses of wine and strove to believe he was drunk.] Forenoon and I were kicked out today and moved to the Plandome hotel. Forenoon called our landlord a cockeyed swindler and we were given thirty minutes to get out. Called on Kitty tonight and she was so drunk she didn't know me from St. John.

April 25—Liquored up and went to a dance. Took home a girl named Susie Austin. She came into my arms as if she belonged there and clung like a cat to a skirt. When I got home, I found Forenoon in bed with a tall naked blond. He hired a room for me and I slept there. I dreamed of Susie all night.

April 26—Took Martha to a dance. Asked her to marry me tomorrow and she said she would. I can't understand girls at all. Any woman who would marry me is a simpleton. I'll never make any woman happy. I'll never be anything but the fool I am. And I don't think any of these girls are in love with me. They're in love with love. Isn't it true that nearly all women fall in love with love and merely use a man as a springboard for the leap? . . . I feel queer tonight. I'm going with one of my classes to the asylum at Provo. I want to see the crazy. I can't understand why.

April 27—Spent the evening with Martha. We drank a little wine and she sat on my lap. She said we loved and that love needs no legal sanction and asked me to be intimate. I said all right and I tried to but I couldn't. The whole past rose like delirium. I went home and I shook all night. Pretty soon I must go back to Idaho or enlist or something else. God knows. God help me to decide!

April 28—Spent the day with Laura in Liberty Park. I like her but I don't love her. Thought of intimacy with her sickens me. She seems too right, too good and splendid, for that sort of thing. Sexual passion seems as alien to her as to violets. I wish I had a sister like her.

April 29—Today I went to Provo and through the asylum. I am sitting now in my room and I feel awfully queer and lost. I saw dozens of imbeciles and lunatics today. I felt as if I belonged there. It's the way I felt two years ago. I talked with an insane man and he told me how it was with him: he can't rest or sleep, an evil thing is always on his track. And I knew what he meant. I understood. . . . All life is slipping away from me tonight. God, I wish I could die. I'm going for a walk.

April 30—I walked all night. I can't get rid of the thing. I look at my eyes and I'm terrified and I must do something, today, now. Great God, I wish I'd been born dead!

XIII

•

S UCH was Vridar's record during those weeks when his life was drawing to another crisis. Years later he often looked back upon this time and he saw it as one of the three most crucial periods of his life. He saw with what ironic chance, by what casual and aimless doings, his journey was again laid downward into the valley of shadows. And still, no other way, it seemed to him in reflection, might have been more fruitful of sanity and peace. For these are the other roads which, by another spin of the wheel, he could easily have taken:

He could have been caught pilfering and sent to jail. In a jail he would, beyond all doubt, have gone mad. He would have been removed to an asylum and he would have threshed through delirium to his death.

Or he could have married Anna Mullen, as, in one hour, he almost did. His life with her would have been all tragic waste. Because Anna had the soul of a prostitute; and when he saw her again, two years later, she was a harlot, walking the streets.

Or he could have enlisted and gone to war. He might have been killed—and that, he reflected, would have ended his melodramatic epic of nonsense; or he might have been crippled or gassed or shell-shocked and left to suffer the ingratitude of his country. In any case he would have seen—as every soldier who went to France saw—an hour of glory turn to wormwood.

Or he might have become a wanderer and gone south: to spend his years in vagabondage, his dreams in derision. He might have joined the human driftwood and gone from eddy to eddy, unsocial and homeless and lost. . . .

He could have been driven to any of these. He deliberated all of them, even the first, regarding it in all hours as imminent. In one day he would ponder marriage, trying to choose Anna or Martha, Laura or Kitty as his bride; and in the next day he would yearn to the open road and blue hills, with a blue horizon at their far end. In one day he went with McClintock to enlist; and he did answer questions, undress and submit to measurements, before seizing a chance and ducking out.

And as May approached June, he was feverish with inner conflict and on the brink of collapse. He slept little and ate little. Most of the hours he spent on the streets. He withdrew from the College, detesting its shallows and hysterias, seeing in them more and more clearly the patterns of the uncivilized. Again and again he strove to debauch himself, but upon the road to pleasure stood the invincible fortress of his scruples. With all his strength he tried to be reckless and devilish, an unconscionable person without care; but his gestures toward paganism, toward the voluptuous charnel houses, left him shaking with fear and shame.

And in these wretched ways he spent his sanity and his time. It is impossible to say what he would have done, where he might have gone, if he had been left to his own whims. For there was imposed upon his pride a stinging experience. He was humiliated to the dust; he was driven again to furious hatred of himself. And out of his shame was forged for him a new decision and again his road was clear.

He went on a Sunday evening to see Laura. After a day of doubt and struggle he had resolved to marry her, choosing her because she seemed more chaste and dependable. Unlike Anna, unlike Martha, she did not excite in him a feverish lusting. No: she appealed, it seemed to him, to the nobler instincts of men. She would be a steady anchor, calm and incorruptible, and with wise foresight she would lead him to health and peace.

All these thoughts when he entered the door were in his earnest humorless face. He greeted her with grave decorum. He crossed the room, soberly rubbing his hands, as if he fancied himself at his own fireside in his own house. Tremendous seriousness looked out of his eyes. The weight of destinies lay in the fixed purpose round his mouth.

Before speaking again, nevertheless, he looked at his bride with critical interest. He thought her eyes, her manner, were a little chilly tonight. Well, no doubt; he had not seen her for eight days. She resented his silence now. "Hello, Laura," he had said, and he had said no more.

But she was lovely, no doubt of that. Her eyes were of a most unusual color. They were sad eyes and they haunted him. Her mouth was as sweet as a girl's mouth could be, and her body was slender, girlish, without the ecstatic opulence of Martha's, without Kitty's suppressed fire. Besides all this, she was a senior in high school, and after they were married, they would go to a university together. Some day they would teach together. Or perhaps she would teach, he would write; and when he was famous, with men hunting him down for his autograph, they would tour the earth, passing in serene fulfillment from shore to shore.

Yes, he reflected, she would do. She aroused in him no devastating hunger. Unlike Neloa. . . . The intrusion of Neloa gave him pause. He glanced round him, as if lost, and went over to a chair and sat down. Color rose to his face, a hot flush of betrayal. Neloa! Neloa! The name was ringing in his mind. He rose and looked round him again.

"I wonder if—if I could have a drink."

Laura stared at him a moment. She went into another room

and returned with a drink. She gave it to him and did not speak.

"I been thinking," he ventured and looked at her. He drank again and gazed at her over the glass.

"So have I," she said.

He did not like her tone. It was too formal and cold. He set the glass down and went over to her but she waved him aside.

"What do you mean?" he asked.

"Don't kiss me," she said. "I don't want you to."

"Oh, you don't!" Her words amazed him. He said, "Why not?"

"Because I don't," she said. Her stare was level and searching.

"We're engaged, aren't we?"

"I don't know as we are. You've never given me any ring." These words made him furious. He hated jewelry.

"No ring! What the hell difference does a ring make?"

"Vridar, don't shout at me."

"I'm not shouting!" he roared. "A ring! So it's a ring you're in love with!" He stared at her, his scorn withering. "My God!" he said.

"Listen, Vridar, sit down."

"To hell with sitting down!"

"Well, lower your voice or I won't talk with you."

"All right. If you want me to go, say so."

"I want to talk with you."

"Go ahead."

"Vridar, I like you a lot. You know that."

"Like me! You said you loved me."

"I don't."

"What!" he cried.

"But I like you an awful not. I like you the way I like a brother."

Vridar was amazed again. He had been no surer of sunrise than of this girl's love.

"You're trying to be funny," he said. "I'm in no mood for jokes."

"Tell me," said Laura. "Why did you come over tonight?"

"What a hell of a question! To see you, of course." He hesitated a moment and then blurted his secret: "I came to ask when we'll be married."

Laura now smiled. It was a weary smile, a little pitying.

"Never," she said. "I'm not going to marry you."

"Oh, you're not!" Vridar faced her, choked by his emotions. He felt goaded to outrage.

"Sit down," said Laura calmly. "I want to tell you why."

If Vridar had been less vain, less morbidly sensitive, he would have taken his cap and walked out. But he had no power to admit defeat. That this girl should not love him, he found plausible enough; but that she had the effrontery to tell him so to his face, this he could not believe. Utterly baffled, he sank to a chair.

"Go on," he said.

"Vridar, you know you're a very thoughtless person? You're not like other men."

"I know it," he said, scowling at her. "And thank God for it."

Laura's mouth curled a little. He saw the scorn and hated her.

"No woman," she said, "will ever be happy with you."

"No? . . . NO?"

"No," she said.

He stared at her with murderous spite.

"Why not?"

"Because you're too selfish."

"Me selfish!" he howled.

"Don't shout that way." Her tone was sharp. "You're the most selfish man I've ever met."

"Thanks," he said.

"Shall I tell you how?"

"Suit yourself." He loathed himself now. He wished he had the strength to curse her and go.

"How long have we been going together?"

"I don't know," he said. "I don't give a damn."

"Six weeks," Laura said.

"Oh, six weeks."

"And in all that time you've never given me a single thing. You've never given me a single box of candy or a single bunch of flowers." She was speaking with some vehemence now. She was speaking as one who had been grievously done by.

And Vridar sat in amazement under her charge. Not for his life could he have spoken, so deep and mighty was his astonishment.

"Other men," Laura was saying now, "give me things. When it's my birthday they give me a present. You never even asked when my birthday was. And when they call to see me, they bring flowers or candy or something else. . . . But you—you've been here fourteen times and you've never brought a single thing. . . . Nothing but yourself. And that's why I say you're the most selfish man I ever saw."

She stopped, as if her indictment was finished. Vridar stared at her in helpless bewilderment. A long silence fell. And then:

"And so," Laura went on, "you just as well not come to see me any more. If you want to we'n be good friends. I still like you a lot but not in the way I did. . . . We'n be brother and sister," she said. And she added with a strange little smile: "But even brothers, they give to their sisters sometimes."

Vridar's wits were clearing now. There had gathered within him a scorn that was dark and blind, and up through it now, pushing toward utterance, came his thoughts. He rose to his feet and looked down at her. His eyes were so morbidly bright with contempt, with the excoriating nihilism of his mood, that she shrank under his stare.

"So that's it," he said. "It's all clear now."

"Vridar, don't look at me that way!"

"You want a man who totes flowers. You want a man who sweetens his kisses with candy. You think candy and flowers mean love." He paused, feeling that his words lacked edge and vigor. They did not express at all the overwhelming scorn that convulsed him. He grinned now and Laura trembled and backed away.

"All right," he said, holding her terrified gaze. "Flowers and candy do have their meaning. I have a friend who uses them.

Each seduction costs him a box of chocolates, a handful of roses, and two bunches of sweet peas." He went over to his cap. He swung and faced her, feeling he had not driven his rapier home.

"Very well, Miss Cunningham, you have done me a favor. Most girls trade their bodies for candy and flowers but I did not know you were one of them. My mistake. Accept my apology." He stared at her for a long moment. "Marry one of these carpet knights who call with an armful of violets. In a few years, you'll have a houseful of kids. I'll be a famous man then and you'll be reading my books." He stopped again, feeling rather mean and silly. He got his cap and hesitated and then turned. His grin was a leer of bitterness and hurt pride.

"Some day," he said, his voice shaking, "some day you'll remember tonight. Goodbye." And he swung the door wide open and was gone.

He walked to his room in a cold sweat. His humiliation was so galling that he did not look at passersby, but went, like a whipped thing, until he was alone. In self-abasement he sank to a chair and bowed his head and the sweat ran off his face and down his hands and the sickness in his soul was like aconite. His thoughts and his emotions gathered their chaos to the same void.

And when midnight came, he still sat here. He was sitting here when the clock struck two, when it struck four, and when daybreak filled the room. Then he rose and packed his few belongings. He called a railway station and asked when the next train went north.

He had two hours to wait. He rummaged among his things and then sat again on the chair, his face bowed to his hands. A photograph of Neloa Doole lay on his knees.

PART FOUR

JUNE 17, 1923

Today in Black's Green Pastures and Piccadilly *I came across this:*

But I will tell you my belief, that all the battles and wars that ever were in the world have not caused the fifteenth part of the misery and tragic suffering that have been caused by this very thing you are laughing at—those false ideals formed before marriage.

I

○

THE ROAD lay clear ahead, and over it, the train thundered into the north. But Vridar, sitting by a window, looking out at a carpet of farms, sweeping by endlessly, found his misgivings multiplied with the miles. Laura's crushing dismissal, without which his life might have been shaped to a different end, had sent him homeward; but now, as he thought of the Antelope Hills and of the girl who waited there, he felt, with conviction as intolerable as certainty, that he should turn back. He could not tell out of what this conviction had come. He knew only that he seemed to be journeying into dusk and his life into a rigid plot. For his journey—and this much he saw clearly—was a symbol of his defeat, or his serfdom in love; it meant that he had been conquered, and that nothing in life, nothing in his dreams or in his books, held him so powerfully as this girl whom he had tried to spurn.

But this solemn conviction of folly was not the only thing in his mind now. He looked back at the Salt Lake Valley, wishing he could have been held there in chains; he looked upon his journey as that of a vanquished weakling; but his heart sang, nevertheless, and his emotions raced ahead to the meeting. His reason, with its handful of portents, each marking a reef ahead, was like a full moon in the sky when the sun shines. And the sun and the moon, as he journeyed north, became a parable of his conflict. The moon steadily became more spectral like a nimbus of fog and the sun rose in golden flush, until the whole sky was luminous and warm, with no memory of the night. The moon had retired but it would rise again. He could spend a few weeks or a few months in sunglow, but somewhere, sometime, he would stand in moonrise to count his loss.

And it may seem strange that Vridar, looking so unerringly into years ahead, did not pause now. In later years, indeed, it seemed very strange to him. But his love for Neloa was so wildly unreasoning, so much a part of his life and his loneliness, and so completely a pattern of his vanity and his pride, that he had no power to renounce it. When far from her, he could mark the danger-zones. Then he could feel, however obscurely, that her interests were not his and could never be; that his hunger for achievement was not a part of her life; and that they would live as strangers in the same house. But when with her, or after thinking of her for a long while, she became for him, not the woman who had loved freely, but the shy lass on the Annis butte, the girl who had stood with him in the school contest, the terribly sweet thing, the symbol, the ideal, that had been the core of his worship, the beat of his heart. To have forgotten her, or to have made her seem to him what she actually was, he would have had to sever memory from ten years of his life.

Nor can words picture his longing when he stepped at last from the train and gazed at the Antelope Hills. He saw nobody and was conscious of nobody around him. He moved in dark bewilderment, yet swiftly, with his whole being fixed on one end. Setting his luggage on a corner, he waited for the mail. And so lost was he in the heartache and wonder of his homecoming that he left his things on the street, unaware that he had deserted them, and began to walk. He went out of the city and found a country lane. He began to weep. For so much in him that was bitter and desolate, so much that was sweet, choked and blinded him that he wanted to scream and rend the nightmare apart. But he could only run as he had run years ago and wish the world would break.

His heartache, not of pain only, nor in any clear way of joy, was more than he could stand. He could not run away from it or cry it out of him. And out here, where birds and flowers were so deep in memory, and where field and lane recalled so much that he wished not to remember and could never forget, he became terrified. He rushed back to the city and stared through mist at his shabby things. He had forgotten them and he knew now that they were his. Gathering them, he went up the road; and once out of the city, he was like a man pursued, covering lane after lane before the mail overtook him. Refusing to sit with the driver, he entered the truck-body where he could be alone.

While traveling through Poplar, he stared at landmarks of his haunted youth. Against that ramshackle schoolhouse, he had been driven to frenzy by Ollie Bitt; and on that canal, he had skated in delirious hours with Helen; and there, close to the great Anderson barn, he had whaled the daylights out of Alvin Kress. Yonder was the dark cold shack where he had lived. . . .

And then Poplar fell behind and the journey climbed to the hills. A few miles to go and then. . . . He would meet her with a cry, with all his life ringing in her name. And she would come to him swiftly and they would be one together, never to part again. . . . She would cry his name, too, and they would meet in the inevitable way of rivers, of fire, and of all the other things that met and belonged to each other in meeting. His life would flow into hers, her life into his, in the way of river waters. . . . Or in the way of mountain streams they would meet, surging under the impact, the infusion; and they would flow away serenely, their two lives inseparable in the common life. . . .

Only two miles to go. There was no moon now. There was the night, somewhere far under, throwing its great shadow upon the deep; but here was a golden day, misty with blueness, hushed as early dawn. She would be standing in the dooryard, looking westward for him: her eyes shaded to the sun, her heart full of the unspoken. She would be wearing a simple gown of pale blue. And she would look very queenly and splendid; and when she saw him coming, she would run down the road to meet him, her hair flowing on the wind. . . . "Neloa!" he said, whispering her name. Fleeing from loneliness, she would come to him and he would hold her very close; and he would say, "Neloa! Darling Neloa!" and then: "Neloa, you darling, you dear!" And then he would look at her and he would see that her eyes were wet. . . .

He was so shaken when he left the truck that he could hardly stand. After paying the driver he gathered his things; and then, through a blur of shimmering fields and of mountains banked like purple fog, he went up the road to Neloa's house. He rubbed at his eyes and he gazed at his trembling hands. It was all so unreal, so heartbreaking, this coming to her again. It was an awful dream, full of sweetness and terror. He wished he could seek a shelter and weep; because if he went on like this, he would break at her touch or the sound of her voice and cry like a child.

He was at the gate now. He could see nobody nor any sign of life. For a little while he stood by the gate and looked at the house. Then he went up the road, but very slowly; and when close to the house he stopped again. He thought of going back; not to Utah, but away somewhere: alone with the awful meaning of this hour. He thought of going to the door and knocking but he could not move. And while he was lost in wonder, with disappointment building large in his heart, the door opened and Neloa appeared.

For a long moment they looked at one another. He could not cry her name, he could not move. He could only look at her; and while he looked, all the strangeness of life crowded into the moment. . . . Then Neloa left the door and came toward him. She came uncertainly, as if not sure what he would do; and Vridar, no longer trembling, stood like a man of stone. The passionate cry was dead in his throat. His intolerable heartache moved back and waited.

She came up and faced him and their gaze met. His stare was now searching and ruthless. If she had come to him running, if she had shown half the eagerness that was his, he would have been frenzied in his love and forgiveness; but her eyes questioned him, her tongue was mute. Her fear he mistook for indifference. His mouth broke into a cynical smile.

"I guess I've made a mistake," he said.

She opened her eyes wide as if astonished, as, indeed, she was.

"Vridar," she said.

He shrugged and turned away and drew a long breath.

"I guess I shouldn't have come."

Much in this girl Vridar was never to understand until it was too late: the troubled darkenings in her eyes; a way of lifting her brows, as if in amazement; and a quick faint smile which, for an instant, left her face cold. It was the smile that he observed now. It infuriated him. Gathering his bags, he turned away.

"Vridar!"

She sprang to him but she did not touch him. When he turned to her, his face haggard with despair, her face, her whole body, interrogated him, as if she did not understand. And she did not understand. His morbid zest for dramatizing moments, for lifting every experience to its highest emotional pitch, was alien to her. He wanted their reunion to be piercingly dramatic. He wanted it to be intense and deep beyond the power of words. And to have it—this meeting, this hour, that should have been perfect—made a commonplace, shot to pieces with questions and doubts and fumblings—this he could not endure. Rather than this dull prose, he wanted nothing at all. Instead of it, he preferred the monastic sterility of heartache, the lone integrity of pain.

And so he deliberated for several moments, wondering what he should do. If he went away, dismissing her in this silence, he could never come back; and if he remained here, where other eyes perhaps watched, the whole experience would become so silly, so cheap and theatrical, that it would be an ominous portent of days to come.

He looked at her and he saw that she still waited, her face puckered with questions. But she understood nothing at all. Love for her, as for her relatives and friends, was a casual mating and a birth. It was not a bright and pulsing wonder. It was not impetuous and moon-struck and unutterable. . . .

"Let's take a walk," he said.

He turned down the road and she went with him, obedient as a slave. For a mile they did not speak. They went over hills to mountainside and river lands where, in another summer, they had spent so many hours; and when Vridar stood on the brink, looking down, he was haunted by old trysting-places, by memory of what had been said and done. He felt very desolate. If there had been in Neloa the power to take his hand and to say with him, "Down there we loved. We've been down there: hours and hours we have spent down there, together, alone. Each hour was a lovely and a perfect thing. We were close together then and the world was shut away and forgotten, and such hours we shall never see again. We are older and wiser and we suffer now. . . . But darling, let us remember those days and cherish them, for we were children, and we knew, as we shall never again know, the meaning of life. . . ."

But these were not her thoughts. They were Vridar's, and they filled him with such sadness that he felt rent apart. Taking her hand, he led her to a fir, and he looked round him like a man who has been away for a long time and has come home. He turned to her and for a moment she met his eyes.

"Look at me," he said. She met his searching gaze but for a moment only. And he was annoyed now, as in times past, by her refusal to look at him. "Turn round here," he said.

Neloa flushed. She, too, was annoyed. Her resentment gave him a strange savage pleasure. It was ruthless and spiteful, born out of hurt vanity and hurt pride.

She gazed far away at mountains and her eyes darkened and Vridar stared at her for a long while. And then, with unconscious cunning, with remorseless purpose, he set about to break her will. In this hour, as in countless hours to come, he forced her to tears.

He never understood until years later why he did this, and he perceived then, in reflection, that his reasons had been three. Of least importance now—but to become steadily of more importance as time passed—was the fact that her tears, and his own tears in answer, stirred his sexual hunger and gave to it softness and glamour and a deeper intensity than he felt in other whiles. The second reason—powerful now but steadily to diminish in power—was his notion that tears purged her; because when she wept, her eyes lost their stealth and memory and became luminous with love. And his third reason—both now and later the most important of all—was the artist in him: a starved wish to dramatize all things relating to himself. Each lovely experience had to run through a soft prelude; had to deepen in power and intensity, building to a crisis; and had, upon completion, to be stamped with the inevitable finality of a thing that had wrought for itself a perfect destiny.

But making Neloa weep was not an easy task, as he had already learned. There was no hysteria in her. Her emotions had no need of catharsis, and only by abuse, only by reproaches and threats, could he break her resistance and bow her head. . . . .

"You don't love me," he declared. "Why pretend you do?" She glanced at him as if alarmed. She did not speak. He resumed. "I came today to tell you we're through. What you want is an ordinary man. You want a glutton for sexual lust, a liar, a cheat, a fraud. You have no sense of decency. Right and wrong mean no more to you than Sakti and Nirvana. You sin, and you sin again, and it means nothing to you. You have no shame, no regret. You have no understanding, no pity, no conscience. You tell me a story of wrong and you think I ought to like it. You think I ought to forgive and forget. Most men would have spurned you. They would have kicked you out of their lives. But I—simpleton that I am, fool that I am —I send you to school. I say I'll try to forget. I say in time it will not matter. And you take all that for granted. You think that forgiveness like gastric juice is secreted by a gland."

He looked at her and considered. Her eyes still gazed at the far hills, her mouth was still hard. And now Vridar spoke with savage bitterness.

"I have gone through hell for you! I've suffered more than you'll ever know about suffering! And what does it mean to you? Nothing! I could break my heart for you and that would mean nothing. I could go mad and be locked up and what would you do? Marry another man. Forget me in a month. . . . No: you haven't any heart! You have only a blood-pump!"

He was shaking now. He rose to his feet.

"Do you think I'll marry you? Do you think I have a life to throw away? Not on a girl like you! Go marry one of your lovers! I have work to do and I'm going on and I won't spend my years with a person—" He broke off, choking. "Listen!" he roared at her. "After you told me what you did last summer I decided to run wild! And did I? God no! I tried to! Only God Himself knows how hard I tried to! . . . Well," he said, speaking more quietly, "I went with girls. I could have slept with girls. I tried to be a drunkard and a whore-chaser but I couldn't be anything but a simple fool. And why? I don't know. I can't do what you did. I can't be a dog and look upon every woman as a bitch. It takes your kind to do that. And besides—" He stopped again. "And besides——"

His eyes were wet now. He looked at her but he could barely see.

"Well, I have ideals. I have an ideal of love, of marriage. I believe in being honest with the woman I love. I believe in loyalty. And I couldn't go to the dogs, that's all. . . . Great God, I couldn't!"

He sank to earth and bowed his head and wept. In a few moments he felt a hand on his arm. A hand gently cupped his chin and tried to lift his head.

"Don't!" he cried; and his agony now, in spite of all its self-pity, was as genuine as agony can be.

"Vridar," she said.

He flung away from her and threw himself to earth. Then all his anguish burst from him in a terrible cry and he leapt to his feet.

"I hate you!" he shouted. "Haven't you made me suffer enough! Go on away! My God, go on away!"

He turned up the mountain, hardly knowing what he did; and Neloa came after him, crying his name. She overtook him and grasped his arm and strove to hold him.

"Don't!" he said.

But Neloa was aroused now. She was weeping, too, but her grief, unlike his, was deep and soundless. Save for her eyes, nobody would have known she wept.

"Vridar!" she said.

He tried to fight away from her but she clung desperately. With both arms round his neck she dragged him down and he sank weakly, all his resistance, all his fury gone. She drew him to her and held his head to her breast; and her tears fell to his cheeks but she made no sound of grief. She held him for many minutes and did not say a word. Like a mother she rocked him, and what she might have said, she had no power to say. And Vridar became aware, little by little, that he lay in her arms against her heart, and joy filled him and memory for a little while was far and dark. He could realize only his tragic, his overwhelming, love for this girl; and the days they had spent together in bewilderment and dream; and his idolizing of her for ten years; and the sweet nearness of her now. . . .

"Neloa," he said, "I worship—you—still."

"Yes," she said.

"I can't give you up."

"I can't give *you* up," she said.

"And Neloa, promise you'll be what I want. Promise you won't let me go mad."

"I promise," she said.

"Neloa——"

He sat up, shuddering. He threw himself to her lap and reached round her with terrified arms.

"Neloa, don't leave me! Promise you'll never leave me! . . . Say you'll help me to—to not go mad: . . . Neloa, speak!"

Neloa drew him close to her and laid her wet cheek to his. She clasped one of his hands but she did not speak.

II

┃┃┃

•

JUNE 1—Last night I told Neloa all about my disgraceful
winter in Salt Lake. She forgave me and now we are
sweethearts as long as there is life. My only prayer is that
she will love me as I love her; that we are making no mistake; and that our understanding of one another will
deepen with the years.

June 2—But I can't forget. How I hate this place, hate it,
hate it! Here where I have suffered so much, everything
recalls to me the dark and lonely hours and what she told
me and all the enormous emptiness of life. I feel I am going
insane here. I walk from spot to spot, remembering. Not
an inch of ground here, not a tree, not a stone, but is full
of memory. Not a badger hole, not a bird cry, not a single
foot of the horizon: it is all haunted. It is all full of meaning and yet is meaningless. *I wish I had not come back!*

June 3—I hate this place. God, how I hate it! I wish this
whole Antelope country would sink into hell. It pushes in
on me and I can't eat, can't sleep. I can only walk around
and remember what once I did here, what I did there. . . .
Neloa, you don't know what suffering is. You couldn't understand. You have never known the awful agony of the lost
and dark.

June 4—My fourth day here and I seem to be hatred and
nothing else. I not only hate this country with all the
strength of my heart, I hate those men. I hate Harvey
Kress, the Mormon hypocrite; and if I ever meet him I'll
kill him. And this is no boast. I know, something deeper
than reason tells me, that if we ever meet one of us will die.
. . . I should go away from here. I should have gone to war.
But I know as certainly as I know anything that I can never
give Neloa up. In some hours I despise her. In some hours

my contempt for her chokes me. But I can never give her up. . . . Dock was over today. All his nonsense related to Neloa; vague hints of her doings with men, rumors, gossip. The whole country, he says, is talking about her and what she has done; and of the fool she has made of me. And I said it was all a lie but I knew it was not a lie. Why in the name of God do I have to suffer all this shame!

June 5—I walked out to the Dooles. I registered according to Wilson's proclamation that every able-bodied man must get ready for the Christian slaughter. . . . Neloa did not seem eager to see me today. I don't know why. As I approached, I saw a man leaving, but I could not tell who he was. And I was too proud to ask. Note: I am not too proud to fight. . . . We went on the river and spent the day and there was in her a strange aloofness. I spent the night at the Doole home, reflecting that love makes fools of wise men and bigger fools of fools. I guess I'm about as simple a zany as you could find in Idaho. When I'm with her I seem to be only a child. My emotions are childlike and trusting until something—usually a change in her eyes—puts me on guard. Then I go crazy and abuse her and we both weep and everything seems to be all right. But I know in my heart of hearts that everything is not all right and I am afraid.

June 6—Mater and dad say I may as well marry this fall. God, I am only a kid yet! In some ways I seem to be too simple and stupid for words. In some ways I am an old man. And besides I must be sure of Neloa. I'll never marry her until I am convinced that she understands and regrets what she has done. I won't live with a woman whose memory turns slyly back to old loves. In her comparison of me with other men I won't be the positive degree. Thus:

Positive:	dear Vridar
Comparative:	dearer Dave
Superlative:	dearest Harvey

Or:

Vridar loves good
Dave loved better
Harvey loved best

And I feel intimations of just that sort of thing.

June 7—Yesterday I went off alone and worked. When alone I have plenty of time for thought and God knows I have plenty to think about. But all my thinking brings me to the same dead end. I love her and need her, and all thought comes finally to rest there.

June 8—Unable to stand the loneliness, I went with dad hunting elk. We saw no elk the first day but I chased a bear and her cubs over two mountains. I thought of killing them but I hate to kill things. We slept by a fire under a pine that night and on the next day we followed three elk for seven miles. I was glad they got away. I'm always glad when the game gets away from me. . . . On my return there was a letter from Martha. I returned it unopened.

June 9—Tomorrow is Sunday!

June 10—A downpour of rain. All day it rained floods; and at last, unable to stand it, I set out and arrived soaked to the skin. After drying by a fire I sat with Neloa and cursed the weather. All I know is that I'm the happiest when with her, most wretched when away; and that I must be with her always. Even when she makes me suffer I'd rather be with her than anywhere else. . . . Told her tonight I want to get a Ph.D., but a Ph.D., I could tell, meant nothing to her. In the world of education her thoughts have never risen above conjugating verbs and drawing maps. And what a fool I am to think of marrying her!

June 12—While working today I saw Dock. He is still whispering tales. It seems that men are telling stories of their intimacy with Neloa—and some of the stories are lies! *(And some, God knows, are true!)* While listening to Dock I tried to seem indifferent; but everything he said burned like acid, and at last I had to go away and be alone. I went to the river and hid. It was midnight when I came to the house.

June 13—I had to see Neloa today. I went out to curse her but I could not. When she came to me, smiling, her eyes glad, all my words were chaff. My love for her becomes more hopeless with each day. When I touch her, when I feel her hand on my arm or hear her voice, all the darkness leaves me and I stand back and I am lost. So it will be, I know now, until we are both dead.

June 17—Today we went to the river and were together for sixteen hours. The sixteen hours passed like sixteen minutes in fairyland. I thought of death while looking at her and the river; and I said, "Neloa, let's die now while we're happy. Let's not go on as most married persons do and learn to hate each other. In this moment our love is perfect and in death we could keep it so." She looked at me in a strange way and said all right.

"Do you mean it?" I asked. "Will you die with me—now?"

"Yes," she said.

I thought she was not in earnest. To test her I led her to the bank and I said we would both jump in. And I knew when I looked at her that she would have jumped. She has contempt for death. I can't understand it.

"You must love me," I said, "if you'll die with me."

"You big silly," she said. "Of course I love you."

"But not that much. Not enough to die for me."

"Enough for anything," she said.

I could not believe this. And yet I did believe it for a little while and I was happier today than I have been since Sept. 6. But such happiness cannot last. I know that something lies ahead.

June 19—I was unable to sleep last night and today I had to ride out to see Neloa. I wish I had jumped in the river with her. Because today I found her alone in the kitchen with another man, and second to one other, I hate him most deeply. And how did she act when I walked in? How was she behaving toward Dave Wolf who once lay with her? How indeed! Was her manner toward him aloof? Is the sun made of frost! Do fish live in syrup! She was smiling at him and talking, and when I walked in she looked guilty and the man acted as if she was his wife. The son-of-a-bitch! He thinks I know nothing about what he did. It's a secret—do you see?—between them. And for one awful moment I felt murder. I know now how the murderer feels when he strikes; for everything went black around me and I could feel something awful in my hands. It was hunger to strangle and tear. . . . And then this terrible feeling left me and I began to shake. I did not speak. I watched them all the while they talked and she smiled at him and he grinned at her; and they seemed to have a secret in common, as, to be sure, they once had. And then I felt the awful lust returning and I couldn't see very well and I went outside without speaking and got on my horse and rode away. I did not even know which way I was riding. I hardly knew I was riding or what had happened to me and all I wanted was to get out of sight and hide. . . . I'm afraid of what I'll do. Not for myself: I'd as soon die as live. With Neloa or without her, I can see no happiness in life for me. I want to murder in the way a starved wolf wants to eat. But I cannot bring disgrace on my parents. . . . And Neloa, does she help me? Good God, she's an awful fool! I wish I could hate her. I wish I had the strength to kill her and myself and so be done!

June 24—All week I tried to work and forget. I have lost fifteen pounds since coming home. And today I did not intend to go out but I weakened when noon came and I jumped on a horse and rode out like a crazy fellow. And was she watching for me? Did she come to the road to meet me? No, dear sir, she was in the house and Wolf was there. She was cooking dinner and he was sitting by the table and you would have thought for all God's kingdom they were husband and wife. And did she come to kiss me? Was she glad to see me? . . . Lord, God, what a fool I am! If she suffered as I suffer, I'd try to understand and love her and make her forget. But she. . . . I can't understand what she means. It seemed to me that she felt a little triumphant and that she wanted to make me jealous, as if I had not been fool enough. But I'm not sure. I want to be fair to her because I love her. And I do know that she almost ignored me and did not speak to me, though she glanced at me and smiled. She is either awfully cunning or indescribably stupid. And I—who ever heard of a bigger fool, a more incurable nitwit!—I actually sat around and stayed for dinner and said never a word. And when I could endure no more of it I rode away. . . . One thing I do know: next time I find Wolf there I'll settle matters with him. Dock says Wolf is telling that he was intimate with her. God brand me as a liar if I don't make him eat his words!

June 25—I am going mad. The only thing saving me is work and I work until I can hardly stand. Every day I box with Mert. I like his hardest punches. I wish he would knock me cold, dead. I want to be punished, beaten, torn into raw meat. I want something to arouse in me all the savage lust of ancient man; for I have things to do. I am going out to find trouble and I'm going to fight with fists and if I get licked, I am going to fight with guns.

June 27—I do nothing but box with Mert and work. The rumors are spreading in the valley. A high school classmate dropped in today and told of stories in the valley. As he put it, "Shard Higgins says you'n marry her but he beat you to it." I asked who Shard Higgins is. Am told that he is the terror of Ririe and that when he gets through with a man, there's nothing but hide and blood left.

June 29—I went to the valley today. The stories about Shard Higgins seem to be true. He is telling right and left of his doings with Neloa. All right, Mr. Higgins, you're a lying son-of-a-bitch and before long I'll tell you so to your face!

July 1—Good God, everyone is talking about Neloa. Heard today that Alvin Kress—cousin of Harvey, that missionary dog—says he has been there, too. He's another liar. I gave him a beating once and next time I'll finish him. . . . I'll see Neloa tomorrow. I'll learn if she has heard these stories and what she thinks and feels. And then—then I'm going to knock these stories down the throats of the men who told them. If I can't, I'll use a gun. God help me, I will!

III

•

ON THE next day, it was a grimly earnest young man who rode to the Doole farm. Abnormally proud and sensitive, he saw in the gossip about Neloa a challenge to his manhood: she was his woman, and no matter what she had done or how thoughtless she had been, he would have to defend her against insult. It never occurred to Vridar that, inasmuch as the stories were founded in truth, he could most wisely have done nothing at all. His code of honor at this time of life had little of wisdom in it. It declared simply that if Neloa's honor was accused, he would have to fight the accuser; for he missed the bitter irony of the circumstances and saw only the blow at his pride.

It was, indeed, the whispering of his own name that galled him most. What sort of man, folk were asking, could this Vridar be?—that he should love a girl, that he should plan to marry a girl, whose reputation smelled of guilty hours. They must look upon him as a strange simpleton. It would be said of him—as, in matter of fact, one report had already declared —that his only interest in her was lustful and that he was her present lover and that he did not intend to marry her at all.

What he must do, then, and all that he could do, it seemed to him, was to call every story a lie and to punish the one who told it. Down the throats of everyone in Antelope, save only two men who knew otherwise, he would force belief in Neloa's innocence. He would make it appear that these tales were told by unsuccessful wooers; because in this Antelope country, at least a dozen men would have married her, and three, it was said, would have died for her. . . .

But if in his foolhardy undertaking, Vridar missed the irony, he was not unaware of his own ridiculous part. His humiliation in years before had never been so bitter, nor was it ever to be again. He wanted to flee this country and this disgrace; but he had no power to go, no will to renounce this girl. He was caught in a trap and he had to fight his way out. And resigning himself to the worst, and hoping that, in the days to come, he would find death, he turned grimly to the fight.

When he walked into the Doole house, his face was so strangely white that nobody spoke. Neloa's parents looked at him: Mrs. Doole with her sad and tragic eyes, Tim Doole with his dark stealthy ones.

"Where's Neloa?" Vridar asked.

"Why, she's up to the sheep-camp," said Mrs. Doole. "She's cookun for the sheep-shearers."

"Sheep-camp!" Vridar cried. "Where?"

"The head of Birch Creek."

Vridar sank to a bed. He looked at Mrs. Doole and then at Tim. He loved Mrs. Doole, for she was gentle and patient and kind; but in this moment he hated her. He hated the sly and crafty Tim. This father and this mother heard stories of Neloa but they refused to believe or they did not care. Tim himself had put her in the way of temptation. . . . Great God, what blind idiots parents could be!

Vridar rose and went outside. He mounted and turned homeward and he said he was done with Neloa and that she could go to hell in her own time and way. And for a little while he rode furiously over the hills. But at last he drew rein and considered and he looked into the south where Birch Creek lay and he reflected that Neloa was up there in the company of lewd men. Her sister Connie was with her but Connie was only twelve. And wasn't it all a pretty picture! It showed—thank God if it didn't!—how stupid she was and how little she cared. And for another mile he dashed furiously toward home.

But he stopped again and this time he swung and rode south. He was not going to see her, he assured himself, but he knew he lied. He would ride around a while. He would ride around to clear his wits and Neloa could go to hell and brimstone and be damned. But he lied and he knew he was going to Birch Creek. . . .

On the flats of Antelope he met Curt Obbing. Curt in the stories about him was the most lecherous man in Antelope and he acted the part. He had been on a mission and he had preached brotherhood and gospel in a far land and he went to church now and sang pompous hymns and prayed; but his heart was black. Three nameless children in Antelope could have called him father. . . .

"Hello!" Curt said. "Why in so big of a hurry?"

Vridar stopped and looked at the man. Curt came over, his manner fawning, his blue eyes mirthfully insincere.

"Where you off to?" he said. "Hell, I know where you're hot-footun it to. You're off to Birch Creek to see your girl."

"How'd you know she's on Birch Creek?"

"Oh me, I know a lot of things. I ain't been around the world for nothun." The smile left his face. He tapped Vridar's leg with a patronizing hand. "I'm oldern you," he said. "I should ought to advise you, I think."

"Oh, the hell you should! About what?"

"Now don't get your rump up. I mean well. Like a Christian. Like one to another in the brotherhood of men."

"To hell with the brotherhood of men. What's your advice?"

"This," Curt said. He rolled a cigarette and studied Vridar's face. "You aim to marry Neloa, don't you?"

"That's my business."

"There you go now! Flyun off of the handle like a kid. This-here I want a-say is for your own best good."

"All right! Let's have it."

"Neloa's a fine girl. I like her dandy. But there's lots a stories told about her. I think you should know."

"What stories?" asked Vridar, turning pale.

"All kinds. They ain't nice stories, that's a sure thing. And I thought you ought a-know. . . . If I was to marry a girl, I wouldn't want people a-tellun such things. By God, I'd see they didn't, that's all."

"Who's telling stories?"

"Well now, that's a horse of another color. I don't spill any beans, you know. But you, I guess you could find out if you tried."

"You mean Dave Wolf for one."

"I ain't a-tellun. It might be and it might not be."

"How can I do anything?" Vridar roared. "Who tells these stories!" He reached down and grasped Curt and shook him. "You!" he cried. "I suppose you've been lying about her, too!"

"Me?" said Curt, alarmed. "God no. Me, I never talk about women. . . ."

Vridar smote his pony and galloped away. He climbed a long mountain to its top and on all sides of him he could see small valleys and dwarfed peaks. Presently he came upon a ewe. She was standing alone in a glen and in her right side was a panful of maggots, swarming in an awful white sickliness, like things boiling in their own grease. This ewe like many others had been cut in shearing and had come off here to die. Her eyes were already dead and Vridar knew she would stand here until she dropped. The maggots would breed in the wound and slowly push into her, and her intestines would become a rolling mass of worms. He looked into the sky and saw three vultures sailing round and round.

Then he went on, and he thought now, as he had thought so many times as a child, of man's ruthless ways and of the helplessness of all things that were brought under his hands. A little way farther he saw another ewe, also abandoned to death; and he was sickened and enraged; and when he rode into camp, he was trembling with fury and pain.

Around a long table in the sun nine men were eating. Neloa stood close by, serving from a hot stove. And Vridar's swift glance told him three things: that the men resented his intrusion, that they were bantering Neloa, and that she was pleased by the banter. He sprang from his horse and went over to her. His unreasoning desperation is shown by what he did.

He grasped Neloa's arm and told her in a savage whisper to come with him; and when she resisted, astonished by his face and his way, he clutched her arm with fingers of murder and jerked her toward him. He led her thirty yards away and swung her to face him.

"What you here for!" he cried, speaking in a voice that she did not know. "You're leaving right now!"

She strove to jerk free. She stared with alarm at his convulsed face and then glanced at the men who were feeding and watching.

"Don't," she said.

"I'll kill you!" Vridar cried. "You idiot! You fool! What did you come here for?"

"Let me go," she said.

"You're leaving this place! You hear me?"

"I won't. I'm the cook here."

If men had not been watching, it is hard to tell what Vridar would have done. He would have hurled her to earth, and if she had looked at him with contempt, as she sometimes had, he might have killed her. But nine men were watching him; and he knew in spite of his frenzy that he was being absurd.

"Are you coming?" he asked.

"No."

"All right. Give me the ring. We're through."

"Vridar."

"Don't Vridar me! Give me the ring!"

"I won't."

"Go to hell, then!"

He started off but she clung to him; and Vridar, humiliated by the eyes that watched, admonished her to have reason.

"You can't go," she said, and her face now was quite as desperate as his. "When supper's over, then we'n talk."

He considered a moment.

"I'll be down in the trees," he said. He went to his horse and mounted and rode away.

He had not been in the trees long when he heard running feet. Neloa came on a path through the aspens and never before in her manner had Vridar seen so much distress. He knew she had doubted finding him here. And when she saw him, her face lost most of its anxiety; and Vridar, watching her like a hawk, saw her relief, saw her shrug, saw the old scorn; and what he saw aroused his slumbering wrath.

"Now tell me," he said, "why you're here. Speak fast. I've no time to waste."

"You know," she said, her eyes reproachful and a little terrified.

"Why? Be quick!"

"To cook. You know why."

"You mean you come off here to cook for a gang of lewd vulgar men. You mean——"

"They're not vulgar," she said.

"You're a liar! I know what their interest in you is. And I know what your interest is in them."

"Vridar!"

He grasped her arms. His aching fingers closed in like steel. "You fool!" he cried.

"You're hurting me. Please don't."

For a long moment he searched her eyes and face.

"What have you been doing here?"

"Vridar! You can't insult me that way!"

"Insult you?" he said, and he grinned. "Is it possible?"

"I'll go," she declared, trying to shake his hands off. "I didn't come here to be insulted."

His mood changed. He crushed her to earth and shook her as she fell.

"Don't talk to me about going!" he cried. "I'll kill you in a minute! I'll——"

"All right, kill me. I wish you would."

"I will damned quick!"

She looked at him. Her voice in this moment was steady and calm.

"Do it," she said. "I'd rather die than live this way."

"Live this way! Well, whose doings is it? Is it my fault if everyone is talking about you! Is it my fault if you run off with a bunch of men! I'd talk, by God! You're a complete fool! You don't know anything and you won't learn and I don't know why the hell I keep coming to see you!"

"I don't know either," she said.

"One of these days," he roared, "I won't come! There's a limit! I won't stand everything!"

"And one of these days," she said quietly, "I'll kill myself."

This statement made him pause. He looked at her with sudden interest.

"That's a cheap threat," he said. "Cowards kill themselves. People worth anything fight until they die."

"I'm tired of fighting," she said. "I can't do anything to please you."

"Yes, great God, what do you do! I suppose you did this to please me! I suppose you did those other things to please me!"

She struggled and rose to her feet. She looked round her and her eyes were haunted.

"I'm sick of life," she said. Her voice trembled. "I can't stand much more of this."

"All right, lady. You don't have to. Give me the ring."

"I won't."

"Why?"

"Just because."

"You don't want to leave me and you don't want to shoot square with me. What the hell do you want?"

"I do shoot square with you."

"Yes, indeed, indeed! When I step out of the house, in pops Dave Wolf. You spend the day with him. You act as if a part of you belonged to him and you were glad. You——"

"I'm just friendly."

Vridar stared at her. He was so overcome, for the moment, with astonishment and rage that he could not speak.

"Friendly!" he cried at last. "Friendly? You fool! You hopeless fool! . . . Why should you be friendly with him? Do you love the low-down skunk?"

"He's not a low-down skunk."

"You lie again! You love him and why the Christ don't you admit it!"

"I don't love him. I never did."

"But you like to have him around! You like his cheap nasty nonsense, his vulgar dirty mind! Vanity! You're all vanity! And my feelings, what the hell do you care about them?"

Again his rage leapt. Again he grasped her so savagely that she cried with pain. He hurled her from him and then ran and seized her and broke her to earth; and he went down on his knees before her, murderous, with fury blinding his sight.

"Listen! You know the stories told about you? You know what Shard Higgins says? What Dave Wolf says? What Alvin Kress says? . . . Answer me! Do you know?"

"Alvin Kress?" she said.

"Yes, that freckled dog! You know what he says?"

"No. What?"

"That's he's been intimate with you!"

"He? . . . He lies."

"Oh, he lies, does he! Maybe not." Vridar forced her to look at him and he studied her eyes for guilt. "You ever go with him? . . . Answer me!"

"Yes."

"Oh," he said as if she had struck him. His thoughts went like a storm of fire into the past: to his days in Poplar, to Helen's birthday party, to the fight by the barn. "You mean—you went with *him?*" he asked, doubting that he had heard.

"Yes."

"When?"

"Oh—a year ago last spring."

"How many times?"

"I don't know. Not many."

"And were you—intimate with—him?"

"Vridar!"

"Answer me!"

"No."

"No? Then why should he talk?"

"You'll have to ask him."

"What did you do with him?"

"Nothing. Just went to a dance."

"How?"

"How what?"

"How did you go!"

"In a buggy, I guess."

"And he kissed you?"

"I don't remember."

"You liar! . . . Did he?"

"I guess so."

"What else?"

"Nothing."

"Look at me. . . . I said look at me!" Neloa turned and for a moment her gaze met his. Then her gaze fell and the color deepened in her cheeks. "Why can't you look at me? . . . Why?"

"I can."

"All right, do it."

"I don't want to."

"Oh, you don't want to! Your heart is too damned guilty! . . .

Answer me: what else did you do with that son-of-a-bitch?"

"Nothing."

He sprang forward and shook her until her teeth clicked.

"I'll kill you!" he howled. "I've had enough of your lies! Answer me or I'll choke your heart out!"

"I—I wish you would."

"Answer me!"

He released her and for a moment she bowed her head and shook. When she looked up her eyes were bright and wild. There was a strangeness in her face that he had never seen there.

"Answer what?" she said.

"What else did you do?"

"Oh—" She bowed her head and moaned. Vridar stood up.

"I'll give you five seconds to answer," he said.

She looked up at him.

"And if I don't will you—kill me?"

"No." He was appalled by the hope in her voice. "I'll leave you. All right. . . . One—two—three—four——"

"Wait! He—he put his hands here."

"Here? Where?"

"Here." She laid a hand on her breast.

"Oh!" said Vridar, and his laugh was strange. "He put his little hand there, did he? And what did the little hand do? Answer. One—two—three——"

"He just tickled."

"Fine!" Vridar cried, goaded almost beyond control. "Dandy, by God!" His mad laugh rang again. "Just put his hand in and tickled, did he? Fine, fine!" He walked out into the sun, trembling with the old sickness. He fought for control and came back and looked at her. "What else did he do?"

"Oh, let me think!"

"You don't have to. That's the only sort of thing you ever remember."

"Well, he—tickled my hand."

"Oh, your hand. By God, that's swell! Where on your hand?"

"Here." She indicated her open palm.

Again Vridar's thought leapt to his dark past. In Annis, in Poplar, among grammar school pupils, the tickling of a girl's palm had been looked upon as the lewdest of all gestures. It meant a wish to embrace. And Vridar was remembering this as he looked at her now.

"What else did he do?"

"Nothing."

"Swear to it."

"Nothing, so help me God."

Vridar drew a long breath and sat down.

"And what did Shard Higgins do?"

"I don't even know him."

"That's a lie!"

"It's not. I've never seen him."

Vridar knew she spoke the truth and for several moments he looked at her. "Neloa," he said. His rage had melted to tears. It had been destroyed by the sickness that had filled him. In spite of himself, he could feel only tenderness now; because he was so abject, so lonely, and his love for her was so deep.

"Neloa, do you love me?"

"Yes."

"Then why do you do these things?—come off here, I mean. The whole country is talking about you. The whole country says I'm a fool. Don't you care how I feel?"

"I had to come. Daddy sent me."

"Oh, your dad! It was your dad who got you in the first scrape! He ought to be hanged." His rage died and he looked at her. "Neloa, come here." She came to his arms and he talked to her through his grief. "Won't you ever see my side of the thing? You're to be my wife. And everywhere I hear stories of men who have lain with you. . . . Don't you think I have any heart, any pride? If you were in my place, I'd move heaven and earth to make things easier for you. I'd die if necessary to help you believe again. . . . I'd be very careful not to do anything, say anything, to make you remember. Neloa, why don't you help me?"

"I want to," she said.

"Do you think I can listen to these stories and do nothing? I can't. I love you. And I'm going to every man and make him eat his words. . . . Will you stand by me?"

"Yes," she said.

Vridar looked at her and the words that he intended to say died in his throat. He wanted more than simple affirmations. He wanted some statement, some gesture, that would convince him past all doubt that she did care, and that she, too, was humiliated by gossip, and that she desired to go with him to another life and forget. But nothing in her words or manner spoke deeply of these things.

He pushed her from him and went into a ravine and hid. For an hour he lay on the ground and wept. And when he came back it was dark and Neloa had gone. He went quietly through the trees and looked at the camp and he saw the men talking, and he saw Neloa in firelight, smiling at their words. Feeling haggard and whipped, he got his pony and rode home.

IV

━━━━━━━━━━━━━━━━━━━━━━━━━━━━━━━━━━━━━━

•

THE NEXT six weeks, Vridar decided, when looking back from a later time, were the stupidest weeks of his life. It was during this while that he set about, with inexorable purpose, to wipe the stain from Neloa's honor, and he went from one violent extreme to another, feeling, in quieter moments, that he was an absurd fool, yet driven by pride, by humiliation, to strike again and again. And because he wanted to die, he struck with savage courage.

After the meeting on Birch Creek, Neloa went as a hired girl to Swan Valley lying east; and Vridar, after four wretched days, followed her and sought work as a farm-hand. He labored across the road from her and in every evening after labor was done he crossed the road and spent the time with her until midnight. They would walk down a fragrant canal bank or across fields smelling of hay; or they would stand in the darkness of a huge barn. And all these evenings—there were six of them—were the same. They ran from reproach into violence, and from violence into tears; and Vridar would feel better then, hoping he had touched at last that sleeping part of her which he had never reached. But he would realize on the next evening that his effort had been futile and with desperate earnestness he would try again. He wanted to strike into the depth of her and bring her womanhood to life. He wanted to arouse her to such fury, to such purging grief, that all her vanity, all her insincerity, would be sloughed away. But he could only make the girl weep, only stir the adolescent surface; because the woman in Neloa lay beyond his scorn.

On a Saturday night they went to a dance. Vridar's reasons were two. He had never been to a dance with her. He had heard stories of how she danced. . . . "Vreed, you ought a-see her," Dock Hunter had said. "She hugs a man up liken she was growed to him. By God, she presses her bubbies agin him so tight she nigh shuts his wind off! . . ."

But of far greater importance than his wish to dance with her or to watch her dance was his other reason. He had been told that Harvey Kress often came to this valley and went to these dances. He was a gay dog, legend said, and women ran after him with hearts breaking. After hearing this, Vridar spent an afternoon, while mowing round and round a field, thinking of this man. This man it was who had sneaked into Neloa's room in Idaho Falls; who had precipitated those events which led to Vridar's anguish; and who, beyond doubt, was still ravishing simple girls and leaving them to the fury of husbands. And in this afternoon, Vridar resolved to murder Harvey Kress.

If he found Kress at the dance he would kill him and of this he had no doubt. Of how he would kill him, he did not pause to think. There would be a way. And then he would be tried and hanged for it but he did not care. . . .

"We're going to a dance," he said to Neloa. He cunningly watched her and he saw that she was pleased.

"Goody!" she said.

"It'll be a grand evening," he said. "Things will happen to-night."

She looked at him, troubled by his voice.

"What things?"

"Oh, just happy things. We'll dance together. We've never danced together, you know." He still watched her shrewdly. "We'll just dance with each other. Is that how you want it?"

"Yes."

"You won't dance with any man but me. You mean that?"

"Yes."

"All right. Run and get ready. I'll go in overalls."

She ran to the house. Vridar watched her go and his smile was cynical. Thought of a dance, he reflected, gave her more joy than he had ever given her. She was only a child. . . .

They rode to the dance with Vridar's cousin, a big hard-fisted youth; they came to the small ugly town of Irwin with its four buildings: a store, a poolhall, a dancehall, and a schoolhouse; and when they drew up at the hall, Vridar could hear music and dancing feet. They entered the hall and he saw a typical scene of the American outpost: big rough men in overalls and denim shirts, with a few, here and there, gro-tesquely set off by gaudy shirts and cheap colorful ties; and old women by the walls, with small children playing over their laps; and bashful youths cluttering the entrance and looking on with starved eyes; and a floor alive with the fierce jigging and hugging of the dance.

Vridar led Neloa to a bench. Before dancing, he wanted to learn if Kress was here, so that he could watch the man and await his chance; and he said to Neloa, "Wait just a minute and I'll be back."

He sought his cousin and said:

"Tell me if you see Harvey Kress. I've got some business with him."

Then he returned to dance with Neloa but she was gone. He stared round him, searching for her in the idle crowd, never supposing she would dance first with another; and his amazement was beyond words when he saw her in the arms of

a stranger. For a little while he could not believe his senses.
He brushed at his eyes and looked away and then looked at
Neloa again.

He swung and went outside into night air and looked at the
stars, trying to realize the meaning of what she did. He saw
men out here and he went among them, wishing he knew
Kress by sight. His cousin Luke came to him and asked him
to step aside.

"Is Kress here?" Vridar asked.

"I ain't seen him."

"If you see him, let me know at once."

"All right. . . . Listen, Vreed, you want some drink?"

"Drink. You mean whiskey?"

"Yes."

"Sure I want some drink!" He gave five dollars to Luke.
"Get me all that'll buy. I want stuff that kicks."

"All right," Luke said, and grinned.

Luke went out of sight into the dark. Vridar listened and
could hear no music and he knew the dance had stopped. Entering the hall, he shouldered his way from group to group,
looking for Neloa; and before he saw her, the music struck
again. And when he saw her he would have been no more
startled if a man had knifed him. She was in the arms of Mike
Andern, one of Vridar's boyhood enemies, and Mike looked
over at him and grinned. Vridar went to a dim corner and
watched.

She danced very close to Mike, with her head on his heart;
and Mike's arm was far around her and Vridar thought his
hand was on her breast. But he could not be sure. He was so
frenzied that he could barely see. In a few moments, Mike
danced close to Vridar and looked down at him and grinned
again; and he patted Neloa's shoulder and Neloa looked at
Vridar and smiled. They danced close together in the manner
of sweethearts and Vridar saw that her face was radiant, her
eyes shining, her whole body electric with music and the man's
arm. . . .

Vridar swung again and left the hall.

He found Luke waiting for him with a quart of whiskey.

They went into shadow and Vridar drank almost a fourth of the quart without taking the bottle from his lips. The stuff went down into him like a stream of fire. It made a pool of flame of his stomach and burning filaments of his nerves.

"You seen Kress yet?"

"No."

"Keep your eyes open for him."

Luke drank and Vridar drank again. He went with Luke to a hiding-place and for a little while he stood here, surprised by the change going on within. He felt very queer and he wanted to laugh. He did laugh and Luke asked:

"Hey! what's the matter you?"

"Nothing, I guess. Why?"

"What you laughun about? You sound cockeyed."

"I—I am cockeyed."

Vridar walked twice around the hall, and then, crazed with whiskey, he strode in. He saw Neloa dancing with a third man and he pushed toward them and struck the man a blow in his ribs. The man sank back, his face distorted by pain, and then moved away. Vridar faced Neloa and his eyes were terrible to look at. He jerked her toward him and tried to dance but he only staggered, with the hall swimming in darkness. And into her ear he poured such abuse and threat as she had never heard before.

Now in this valley there was a dangerous fighter whose name was Brig Flammer. Vridar had heard of him. It was told in legends that had gone far how Brig trounced every stranger who came to the Irwin dances. Most of his victims, it was said, he sent to hospitals to meditate on their folly. . . . And while Vridar was staggering about the hall with Neloa, Brig Flammer very dramatically entered his life.

Vridar was dancing at the moment—or trying to, really, because he was so drunk he could hardly stand—when a blow spun him like a top. He released Neloa and glared at a mist of faces. He sprang forward and struck the man nearest him and sent him and his partner to the floor. Then he looked round him and he heard a voice speak. Desperate and ready, with fists clenched, he looked through whiskey-fog, trying to see this man; and he did see him, after a little, and he could tell that the man's grin was evil.

"I hit you!" the man said. "I'm the one who done it!"

With murder in his heart Vridar stared at the man.

"All right!" he shouted. "Come outside!"

"No. We'll fight right here."

"To hell with you! Come on!"

Vridar started for the door and the crowd came after him. Of what happened from this moment, when he headed for the door, until the next morning, when he came to his senses, he remembered very little. He remembered that when he left the door he fell off a high step and sprawled. He remembered that men held his arms and that other men stood off and measured blows at his face; that he fought desperately to be free; and that in one moment of freedom, he struck a man in his teeth. . . . He remembered voices that said, "It's my turn to hit him now"; and that he was knocked down and set on his feet and knocked down again. . . .

Of events after that, he knew only what he was told. An officer stopped the brawl and Vridar was dumped into his cousin's Ford and driven home and put to bed in a haymow. When he came to, he was bruised and bloody from his head to his feet.

V

•

HE WENT to the canal and washed himself and then found a clear pool and looked at his face in the pool. It was an unsightly face of cuts and bumps. The flesh round his eyes was black and one cheek was torn and his nose looked like pulp. Despising himself, he crossed the road and got his wages and went home. . . .

His parents stared at him and were amazed. Had he been

run down by a truck or kicked by a mule or had he walked off a cliff? Over Vridar's distorted face spread a sickly grin.

"I been in a fight," he said.

"He's been to war," Diana said. "The German army run over him."

"Looks to me," Joe said, "like someone hit him with a axe."

"Son," said Prudence, "you gettun to be a common hoodlum? What fight you been in?"

"Oh, just a fight," he said.

He applied poultices to his eyes and liniments to his nose and cheek. Well, he was damned glad no teeth had been knocked out. And he reflected while looking at his face that the beating had probably done him some good. His wits seemed to be clearer now, as if a lot of nonsense had been threshed out of him.

While riding home, he resolved not to see Neloa again. She had made a fool of him, a drunken simpleton, and he had been thoroughly trounced. But he was like a drunkard still and Neloa was his whiskey. He renounced her and for six days he shrugged whenever he thought of her; but hunger rose again within him and loneliness drew him to the road. Mounting his pony, he assured himself he would go somewhere, and he went on old trails over the hills and followed them to blind ends. He came at last to the highway and he followed it until the Doole house was in sight and he stopped and looked at the house. "To hell with her!" he said. He went on and he would have ridden to the house if he had not seen three men in the yard. Who they were, he did not know, but their presence settled the matter. Going down the road, he passed out of sight, but in every little while he would stop and try to think; and then he would ride on. And he kept riding until his journey became a symbol. He was leaving her, it seemed to him, though he could not be sure. One part of him led the other part and the latter wondered what was going to be done.

He came to Poplar and still pushed into the west. He came to Ririe. Stopping here, he considered: not knowing whether to return or to disappear. It would be interesting to ride out of her life on this Sunday afternoon and leave her to grow old in astonishment. . . . "I'll never come back," he thought. "She'll never see me again." And he stood here in Ririe with his gaze fixed on the ground. "I should be going now," he thought. "I should be riding on and on. . . ."

For an hour he stood here. One hand rested on his pony and his eyes saw nothing at his feet. Now and then he would draw a deep breath and look up. Now and then he would dig at the earth with the toe of one shoe. . . . The sun had set now. He stood here in fixed bewilderment, in a deep and quiet indecision, with no power to move. "I should be going," he thought. "I'll be going soon. . . ."

Then Jim Terris, a high school classmate, spoke to him. It was Jim who had told him of Shard Higgins.

"Why you old son-of-a-gun!" said Jim. "What you standun here for?"

"Hello," Vridar said.

"You poor fish," said Jim. "Shake hands." Vridar shook hands. "I know, you're lookun for a job. By heck, you want a job."

"What job?" Vridar said.

"Pitchun hay. . . . Darn it, Vreed, what's the matter you? You act funny to me."

"I guess so," Vridar said.

"You in a trance? Here, man, shake my paw again. Congratulate me."

"What for?"

"I'm married."

"I'm sorry. I thought you had more sense."

Jim took Vridar's hand and shook it again. He was very happy, he said.

"Come on, let's go."

"Where?"

"To dad's. Arlee, she's dyun to see you." Arlee was Jim's sister.

"Don't," Vridar said. He looked at Jim. "Where's this Shard Higgins live?"

"Miles from here, man. Why?"

"You know why."

"He's still tellun the same story. Everyone's heard it now."

"Tell me where he lives."

"Darn it, you can't go now. It's dark. . . . I'll tell you: we'll go to a dance next Saturday night. You'n see him then."

Jim went to his horse and mounted and told Vridar to come with him and Vridar did so and they rode away. They went to the Terris farm and ate. Across from Vridar sat Arlee and she watched him closely and Vridar was annoyed. She was not unlovely but she was short and plump and serene. He wanted to hurl his plate in her face. He felt, indeed, an impulse to slay this whole family because they talked to him and he did not wish to talk. It was impossible to understand what they said. They asked him about college and about God knows what and he answered in monosyllables. . . .

"He must be in love," Arlee said. "He acts like a man in love."

"What?" said Vridar, looking at her.

"I said you must be in love."

"Oh," he said.

He slept outside on a stack of hay. The sky above him gleamed like a jeweler's trinkets and the night was very still. He looked at the stars and thought of his pony, feeding below; and he said within, "I should be going. I should be riding on and on. . . ."

For almost a week he pitched hay and ate his meals and said little. He was like a man who had become a stranger to himself. His hours, his doings, were very unreal. While eating or while at work, he listened to Jim's banter and he knew that Jim was trying to arouse him; but all that Jim said or did, and all that Vridar himself did, seemed to be meaningless now. When he crawled into bed he sank at once into deep slumber, and when he awoke, he could remember no dreams. He marveled at himself and strove to understand.

On his fifth day here he received a letter from Neloa. It said:

Dear Boy, why didn't you come to see me last Sunday?

I waited all day for you. I waited Monday and Tuesday and Wednesday. Then I heard you are working at the Terris place and I don't know if this letter will reach you but if it does, write to me. I'm so lonesome and I watch the road all day long.

Your sweetheart,
NELOA.

Vridar read the letter and went out to the fields. He sat on a dyke. He read the letter again. It stirred something within him and for a moment the old passion awoke; but he shook it off and sank again into calm. He knew that if he read the letter many times, he would rise and go to Neloa; and he did not want to go; and he tore the letter into strips and watched them float away on a stream. Then he grasped his fork and set to work.

"Tonight's the dance," Jim declared on the next afternoon. "We better quit early and slick ourselves up."

"What dance?" Vridar said.

"The Ririe dance. Tonight Shard Higgins will peel your hide off."

"Oh, he will!"

They went to the house. If Vridar wanted his head washed, Arlee said she would wash it. And perhaps he could wear one of Jim's suits.

"Thanks, I'll go this way."

He lathered his face and shaved with Jim's razor. Jim's wife —a quiet plump girl who looked like a nun—was digging wax out of Jim's ears.

"We got some wine," Jim said. "You want some?"

"I guess so."

"Arlee, get him a bottle. Darn his skin, he needs something. I never seen him like this."

"He's in love," Arlee said.

Looking in the mirror, Vridar could see Arlee. She sat behind him and was watching him. Vridar saw that her ankles were thick, that her bosom was like two loaves of bread. But she had lovely eyes and a lovely throat. . . .

"Get him some wine!" Jim howled.

Arlee went into another room and returned with a pitcher of wine. She poured wine into a glass and Vridar drank it and she asked if he wanted more.

"I guess so," he said.

After shaving and washing, he sat on a wooden tub outside. Jim appeared from time to time and stared at him. Arlee framed herself in the doorway and stared at him, too, but Vridar never looked up, though he knew that Arlee was watching him. He wished she would go off and break her neck.

Vridar rode his pony to Ririe but he did not know why. So divorced, during this while, were two personalities within him that the one hardly knew what the other did. The one was sunk in weariness but the other still plotted. And the plotting one, summarizing the likelihoods of the next hours, knew what the pony would be used for. . . .

He danced with Arlee and with Jim's wife, both of whom bored him to tears. They were awkward and they murmured with apologies; and Arlee emphasized her humility by patting his back.

"You're a swell dancer," she said.

"Thanks," Vridar said.

"You dance a lot in Salt Lake?"

"I guess so."

"Vridar, what you thinking about?" He did not answer. His eyes searched the throng for Shard. "Shame on you!" He looked down at her.

"What did you say?"

When the dance was finished he went to Jim.

"Is he here?"

"Yes."

"Point him out to me."

"Across the hall. . . . You see Quirl Avery? Second man to the right."

Vridar looked at Shard. He was a big raw-boned fellow with lean jaws and reddish hair. Vridar took a deep breath. He said:

"All right. You going with me?"

He crossed the hall with Jim at his side. He faced Shard Higgins and for a long moment he looked at him.

"Is your name Shard Higgins?"

"I guess it is. That's what folks call me."

"My name is Vridar Hunter."

"The hell you say. Well, what's on your mind?"

Vridar closed his hands. He put his left foot a little forward, his right a little back: he was ready to strike a blow.

"You know Neloa Doole?"

"Neloa Doole? . . . What business is that of yourn?"

"Neloa is the girl I intend to marry."

Other men were listening now. Other men had closed in.

"The hell you say! Well, you want me to congratulate you, I guess."

"I've been told," Vridar went on in a voice that shook, "that you've been telling stories about her. Dirty rotten stories, I mean."

Shard lifted yellow brows in astonishment.

"Me?" he said. Then he tried to laugh. "Well, what if I did?"

"Did you?"

"That's my business. Mebbe I did, mebbe I didn't."

Vridar clenched his right hand and drew his arm back.

"If you did," he said, "you're a God-damned liar!"

There was no mistake about Shard's astonishment now. It was genuine. He drew himself to his full height and the evil grin left his face.

"Listen," he said, narrowing his eyes, "you know who you're talkun to?"

"I don't give a damn! I'm going to marry Neloa! No son-of-a-bitch can talk about her! If I hear any more stories out of you I'll beat your brains out and if I can't beat them out I'll blow them out with a gun! You understand what I mean?"

Shard's laugh was a whinny of derision. He looked at the men standing around. And Vridar, sensing his advantage, knowing that this man had faltered, was quick with his next words.

"I don't know if you told the stories or not. If you did, I'll be waiting for you outside." And he turned and left the hall.

Stuttering with amazement, Jim came up to him.

"God blast my skin!" he cried. "Vreed, you got him bluffed! That's the first time I ever seen him bluffed!"

"Go back," Vridar said, "and see if he's coming."

Jim went to the door and looked in. He came back.

"He's still in there. I don't think he'll come out."

"I'll wait a few minutes," Vridar said.

He waited almost a half-hour and then went to his pony. He mounted and rode south and stopped at a crossroad. Should he ride east or west? If he turned westward, there could be no coming back. For almost an hour he sat here and considered. Then at a furious gallop he rode into the east.

It was a beautiful night. From fields to the north of him came the smell of hay and orchards, and from the fields to the south came the smell of ripening grain. He went up a hill and in a current of warmer air he caught the smell of fruit. The sky was a low-hanging realm of clouds and the clouds moved like shutters in confusion and lights appeared and vanished above the swimming dusk.

When he came to Poplar he drew the horse to a walk. He could feel under him the heat of the beast and he got off and walked, but the pony pranced behind him and he mounted and rode again. As the miles fell into distance, a part of his apathy fell with the miles. He had ridden out to the margin of life and now he was galloping back to its terrible depth, and he began to sing as he rode up into the hills and the sky.

When he came to Antelope he stopped and looked at the Doole farm. The buildings were only shadows, deeper than the shadows they cast. In daylight they were ugly things, with no secrets at all; but now they were strange with the meaning of darkness. Even the ramshackle barn, made of poles and straw, was a sorcerous thing. It took witchcraft from the clouds and stars and its straw sides were like glimmering veils, and its poles, thrusting up from the roof, were faintly luminous spires.

Vridar entered the gate and hitched his pony in the barn and walked across the yard to the door. The lower panes of the window were bright but the upper panes were almost black. He stood by the door and listened. Neloa would be asleep in this room with Connie, and across the room, in a bed on the floor, would be her brothers, Robin and Luther and John. He tried the door and found it unlocked, as he knew it would be; and gently he opened it and looked in. The smell of breath came to him but no sound. He closed the door and sat on the step.

He wanted to write a letter to Neloa—something in the mood of this hour—but he had nothing to write with. Searching the yard for paper, he went at last to the privy, but only a mail-order catalog was here; and then he took his shoes off and opened the door and stepped inside. He found paper and a pencil. He looked over at Neloa's bed but he could not see her face. Then he left the house and softly closed the door and sat in starglow to write.

> Now is the moment when, if we could take
> Enchantment by the arm and find the trails
> Leading to temples and the holy grails,
> Our love could flee the wrong and fear and ache
> And loss of one irrevocable mistake;
>
> And, kept too long within its petty jails,
> Nighthawking in the dark, could set its sails,
> Daringly like pilgrims, and come wide awake!
>
> Victorious we could be now; but you,
> Retired to dreams, have missed the road ahead.
> In future years, tonight may always be
> Declaring what might have been for you and me;
> And what we could have done but did not do,
> Restoring to silence what was never said!

Opening the door, he dropped the paper inside and then went to the barn. He intended to ride home but now, changing his mind, he resolved to sleep here. After watering and feeding his pony, he spread hay by a wall and lay down but he did not go to sleep. He was too happy in being here, so close to her, after his pilgrimage of the last week; and he strove only to realize that she was a bare hundred yards away and that he would see her in a little while. The sky was clear now and he could see the stars and by their position he could guess the time. He left his bed and looked at the house, wishing that Neloa would find the paper and read it and come to him. . . .

When the east paled, he walked up the road, leading his pony. He went to a hill and hid there and watched the house. As soon as smoke rose from the chimney, he came over the hill and galloped up to the door.

VI

᎐

HE KNOCKED on the door and entered and he found Tim filling a kettle and Mrs. Doole combing her hair. The room smelled of sleep and smoke.

"Is Neloa up?" Vridar asked.

"Why, I don't know," said Mrs. Doole. "Neloa, Vridar is here." She looked at Vridar and gave him a tired wrinkled smile. "I guess she'll be out in a minute."

Vridar left the house and walked in the yard. In a few moments the younger children came out. Impatiently Vridar waited for Neloa but she did not come and he went to the door of her room.

"You up?" he called.

"Yes," said a sleepy voice, "I'm up."

He went in. He saw his poem on the floor. Neloa smiled at him and brushed her long hair.

"You're sure early," she said.

Vridar looked at her sisters, Connie and Blanche, and wished they would get out of the room. Connie looked at him with mocking eyes as if she knew all about love and its tyranny; and she said:

"You must be in a awful big hurry to see someone."

Connie then swept the room and Vridar's romantic verses were gathered to a pile of dust. With annoyance waxing to rage, he recovered them and left the house. His day was spoiled now. No matter how he tried, he could not make of his love a glamorous thing. It deferred to chores and brooms and cooking and the brushing of hair. Its parable was swept like a dead wing into a dustpan and would have been thrown into a stove. Its moments of beauty were lost in the smell of frying pig and in a babble of nonsense about breakfast and in all the dull prose of filling stomachs and scouring dishes and making beds. Never had he come here, full of poetic light, aglow with preludes to great and perfect moments, without having his lyrics flattened out like dough under a rolling-pin. . . .

Nor was he able in such hours as this, after his pride had been struck, to hide his scornful dismay. It was recorded in the self-pitying darkness of his eyes. It was in his scowl, in his mouth, in the way he moved. And he reflected now, while standing by the barn, that he had debased himself again. He had spent two hours writing a sonnet and he had decided that it was a pretty fine sonnet, too. He had left his job in the valley and had flung a challenge at Shard Higgins and had ridden twelve miles; and what had he got for it? . . .

"Breakfast!"

Why had he come? Why did he persist in being such a fool? If love was no more than a smile and a clattering of pans and the noisy relish of eating, then it was not worth the bother. Love, in the great and fragrant legends, had been infinitely more than that. For Daphnis and Chloe, for Aucassin and Nicolette, for Orpheus and Eurydice, it had been much more. . . .

"Vridar, breakfast!"

He turned and looked at Connie.

"All right," he said.

He wondered whether to go in or to ride home. What was the sense of going in? He would sit at a table and eat, as if life were chiefly a matter of filling stomachs; and he would sit back, as he had done before, and watch Neloa rinse and dry dishes, knead a pompous vulgar mass of dough, make beds, carry wheat to chickens, swill to pigs; and love, all the while, would have to await its time. . . . In these reflections, to be sure, Vridar was aware of his unreasoning selfishness. It was this awareness that made him furious and that urged him to go home. Bread had to be mixed. But was love to be only a gawky intruder among household tasks! Dishes had to be washed. But must love always wait on soap suds and the feeding of pigs! And if it must. . . .

"Vridar, you in a trance?"

It was Connie again. She came toward him and her eyes were amused.

"What you want?" he asked.

"I been callun breakfast an hour. Why don't you come?"

"I'm not hungry."

"You liar. You're always hungry. . . . You mad at Neloa?"

"Hell no. Why should I be?"

"I bet you are. . . . Well, come and eat and you'll feel better."

"I feel all right."

"You don't look all right. You look mad."

He gave her a feeble grin. He protested.

"But I'm not hungry. I don't want a-eat."

Connie took his arms and led him to the house and when Vridar entered he strove to look calm and dignified. He went to a basin and washed and he kept his face out of sight. But his effort was useless. He could feel sullen wrath in his heart and its shadow on his face. He ate a little breakfast but he did not look at Neloa; and he was aware, all the while, that Neloa was gay and light-headed, and he despised her for pretending that everything was all right. His unhappiness seemed not to matter at all. He had written a sonnet to her but he might as well have twiddled his thumbs or made a face at the moon.

When breakfast was done, he crossed to a window and sat on a chunk of wood. Tim talked to him and Vridar answered but his voice sulked. It was murder that he felt; a vengeful spite that fixed on no object; but under the spite he was soft with pity and tears. Again and again he glanced at Neloa and he knew that she was working swiftly and that when her tasks were done she would go with him anywhere to spend the day. This thought chastened him a little. He began to feel mean and unworthy and to wish that everyone would hate him. And in this moment, when he was castigating himself and feeling shame, Dave Wolf entered the room.

The man came in, grinning and jovial, as if he belonged here. He spoke to the parents and said hello to Neloa and cupped Blanche's chin and winked at her; and he nodded in friendly greeting to the sons. But he did not speak to Vridar. He glanced at him and turned away. And Vridar, with rage leaping to possess him, got to his feet and looked at Neloa; and when, after a long moment of waiting, she did not meet his gaze, he left the house.

He went to the barn and he intended to ride away if she did not come; and he was not at all sure that she would come. He led the pony out; and then, to give her time, he tinkered with the bridle, examined the throatlatch and bit and reins, and he watched the house. In a few moments Neloa came to the door and looked at him. Vridar now affected to be unaware of her. He drew the reins and mounted, and when he started for the gate, Neloa came running to him. She grasped the reins and stared at him.

"Look out," he said. He reached down to unclasp her fingers.

"Vridar!"

"Let me go," he said; but he hoped, of course, that she would not.

"Why?" Neloa asked.

"Don't ask silly questions. Take your hands away."

"I won't."

He looked round him as if helpless, as if defeated; and he knew that again he was being absurd. The Dooles were watching him from a window, and they were thinking, most likely, that he was a childish simpleton. But what did they know of his reasons! What did they know of that philandering hypocrite in their house!

"Let me go!" he said sharply. "Go back to your Davy boy."

"Vridar!"

He tried to release her fingers but they were like steel. He grinned at her and his grin was twisted and cynical.

"All right. Am I to sit here all day?"

"No. Please get off."

"Why should I?"

"Vridar, please!"

"Why?" he shouted.

"Because I want you to."

"That's a lie. Go on back to your pimp."

"I don't want to!"

"Oh, you don't want to. You've been with him all week and now you want a change."

"You're unfair!" Neloa cried, and her eyes flashed.

"Didn't he come over to see you last Sunday?"

"No."

"You mean he wasn't here?"

"He didn't come to see me."

"No?" Vridar snorted. "I guess he came to see your mother!"

"I don't know why he comes."

"Oh, you don't! Isn't that splendid! By God, isn't that a pretty piece of ignorance!"

"Vridar, please don't go."

"He comes to see you!" Vridar cried furiously. "Why lie about it? He knows you're engaged to me! And he keeps coming! Why?"

"I don't know why."

"You do!"

"I tell you I don't."

"Because you encourage him! Do you think he'd come if you told him to get out? Would he come if you didn't sit around and simper at him as if he were still your lover? Good God, you idiot! The male doesn't snoop around when the female doesn't call!"

"I don't call. He means nothing to me."

"You liar! He flatters you. You like to think that men are dying for you. He wants to marry you and you like to play with him like a cat with a mouse. Except you want to sleep with him instead of eat him."

"That's a lie!" Her eyes blazed with hurt and fury.

"Yes?"

"Yes!"

His grin was scornful.

"Well, it's queer—isn't it?—that this man can talk about you, telling what you did, and that you should smile at him and invite him back."

"I don't invite him. Stop saying that."

"No, you don't invite him!" Vridar shouted. "Then what the hell do you call it? He keeps coming! He looks at me as if I were a fool! And he's making a damned silly feeble-minded knothead out of you! . . . And I suppose you think I'm going to stand it all my life! You think I'm going to sit around like a bag of sawdust and watch you grin at old lovers, do you? You—" He stopped, choked with fury. "Take your hands off!"

"I won't. If you go I'll go with you."

For several moments he looked at her. She did not look at him but her hands on the bridle were so rigid with purpose that the knuckles were white. Vridar spoke again and his voice was quieter now. It was ominous.

"Will you tell me just what you expect? Am I to go on forever in humiliation? Do you think I have no heart, no pride? . . . What sort of a fool do you think I am?" Neloa did not speak. She was looking westward over the hills. "Does it mean nothing to you if another man grins at me as if to say, Take her, brother, but I beat you to it? If men everywhere are talking about you as if you were a whore? And if I'm looked upon as a simple fathead who is being taken in. . . . Well, I suppose it doesn't mean anything to you."

"It does."

"Oh, it does, does it? What the hell do you do about it?"

"What can I do?"

"Tell that son-of-a-bitch to get out of your sight and stay out! . . . Listen. . . . Well, never mind. I'm going now."

"No!"

"What shall I do?"

"Stay with me."

"Oh, go in the house and let that homely bastard grin at me! Is that it?"

"No. We'n go off somewhere."

"Run away from him? No, thank you. . . . I'll tell you what I'm going to do. I'm going to make him eat his words."

Vridar sprang off the horse and led the horse into the barn. He came back and looked at Neloa.

"Well, what do you say?" Her gaze turned to him in swift bewilderment. "Are you with me or him?"

"With you."

Vridar started for the house. Midway he stopped.

"You go to the barn," he said. "I'll call him out." Neloa went to the barn and Vridar went to Luther Doole who was playing in the yard. "Go in the house," he said, "and tell Dave I want to see him. Say I'm out by the barn."

He returned to Neloa. From a pocket he took a watch—a gift from his mother—and told her to hold it. He searched his pockets for other things that might be destroyed in a fight. His hands shook; his whole body shook from head to feet. A door was slammed shut but he did not look up. Feet sounded in the yard and drew nearer, and a moment later Dave Wolf was looking at him. Neloa stood by the barn. Her face was white. Vridar's gaze met Dave's and the two men stared at each other; and in Dave's eyes was cunning derision, but in Vridar's eyes was remorseless hate. And then Vridar spoke.

"I've been told," he said, "that you've been talking about Neloa. I suppose you know I'm to marry her."

"I've heard something the sort," Dave said.

Vridar drew a long breath and closed his hands.

"Is it true you've been talking about her?"

"How you mean?"

"You know how I mean!" Fury blinded Vridar and shook him with its courage. He advanced a step and his eyes were paralyzing in their wild wrath. "You've told you were intimate with Neloa! I know all about that, you dirty son-of-a-bitch, and for a cent I'd cut your heart out!" He advanced and Dave retreated. "You're a lousy stinking dog!" He shot

He placed her half in shadow, half in light; he measured his distance; he told her to look steadily at the lens.

"In this picture," he said, talking to her in an impersonal way, "I want the vampire in you. I want the harlot. So think of your past and its pleasures and let your eyes be full of them. Think of that evening in the hotel and those nights at Nevel's and that evening on the bed by the wall. Think of nothing but them."

She came toward him, her face dark with protest.

"Stay there!" he cried. "Just be yourself! . . . Back a little. . . . You say you didn't love those fellows and you wouldn't have married them. All right. So look as hard and ruthless as you can." He considered a moment, wondering how to persuade her. "You're a swell actor," he went on. "You can look like an angel or a devil. I've seen both in you. And now I want the devil. . . . "

And Neloa, annoyed by his persistence, yielded to his wish; and over her face came such hardness and cunning as he had never before seen there. For a little while he was so amazed that he could only stare at her.

"Well, hurry!" she said, and her voice was like her eyes.

"More," he said quietly. "Can't you look any more devilish? Let's see all the cruelty and cunning that a woman's supposed to have. You can act the part. You ought to be an actress. You should be a Lady Macbeth. . . . There. Hold it."

He closed the shutter. Neloa came over and looked at him, and again he was lost in wonder at what he saw in her face.

"Now," he said, still looking at her curiously, "I want the other side of you."

He drew her to a lovely spot. He stood her against a fragrant autumn thicket and he unfastened her hair and spread it in a mantle down her back and over her shoulders and across her breast. And then, to decoy her into tremulous wonderment, into tears, he began to abuse her. He spoke in derision and reproach, fury and threat; he went over to her and shook her; he mocked her with a cynical grin and with bitter words; and then, changing suddenly, he looked at her with

all the earnest devotion of his heart and chided her gently.
And in a little while tears filled her eyes and she looked at
him through a mist of tears. There was no cunning in her face
now.

"You're looking into the future," Vridar said. "Soon we'll
be husband and wife, hand in hand. We'll live together
twenty, thirty, forty years. We'll trust each other, building
my life in yours, your life in mine. . . . Neloa, look down the
years to what you can see."

With her head raised and with her body tense as if for
flight, she looked with wet eyes at blue mountains beyond.
And Vridar closed the shutter again.

He led her to the bank and they sat here and for a long
while he talked. Of both sides of her, he said, he had a picture
now. The one girl he hated and the other girl he loved, and
for both he had names. He had read a Russian story in which
the heroine was called Mifanwy and she was simple and sweet
and unaffected like the part of Neloa he loved. The other part
of her he would name Moll.

"Moll," he said, "is an old word for prostitute." Neloa
glanced at him, and Vridar resumed, watching her all the
while. "Moll and Mifanwy you are to me. You are two persons. But you can't be two persons and live with me. The
Moll in you must die. . . . Neloa, do you understand?"

"Yes," she said.

"All right." For a few moments he was silent. "I doubt,"
he said at last, "we should marry at all. I've told you that.
But you won't listen. . . . In the first place, I don't love you."

"That's a lie," she said.

"It's not. I did love you but not now. And are you still
willing to marry me, knowing that?"

"Yes," she said.

"Nonsense! Why should you marry a man who doesn't love
you?"

"You do love me."

"I tell you I don't. And I don't respect you. I have contempt for you. I don't trust you. And I don't think you love
me and I don't think you'll ever be anything but what you

are." She started to speak but checked herself. "And are you still willing to marry me?"

"Yes."

"You're a fool. How much do you want to marry me?"

"A lot."

"How much is a lot?"

"Oh—deep as life."

"But don't you realize you can never live with me? I'm a violent person. I'm a half-mad person. And I can't help it. I may kill you some day. You know that?"

"No you won't," she said.

He considered again. In a full and generous moment he said this:

"Neloa, I'll never make you happy. I can make no woman happy. I am too selfish and ruthless and ambitious. Darling, you'll never be happy with me. . . . And I do love you. I love you more than life. But I love with a love that is awful and tragic. And I think you ought to marry someone else and find happiness with him. . . . Don't you?"

"No."

"Are you willing to be unhappy with me?"

"We won't be unhappy."

"Yes we will. Please don't expect what we can never get."

Neloa looked at him and then at the blue hills. For a long moment she was silent. And when she spoke, her words amazed him.

"I'd rather be unhappy with you," she said, "than happy with anyone else."

In this statement she had said more, and had said it with greater earnestness, than he had ever heard her say before. He drew her to his arms and kissed her mouth and laid his cheek to her cheek.

"Neloa, dear, do you love me that much?"

"Yes."

"And you're willing to suffer with me?"

"Yes."

"And you won't ever regret it?"

"Never!"

"No matter how unhappy I make you? No matter what I say or do?"

"I'll never regret it."

"And you'll be the kind of wife I want?"

"I'll try."

"Then tell me this: why have you acted so the past week? You used to come and kiss me but you don't any more."

"I—I didn't know you wanted me to."

"Wanted you to! Don't you know I love you more than life?"

"Sometimes. Just sometimes."

"All the time. Even when I'm abusing you, I love you no less."

"It—it seems like you do."

"And Neloa, remember this: no matter what I do, no matter what happens in the future, I'll always love you with all my heart. I'll love you that way until I die."

Her fingers tightened on his arm.

"And I'll love you that way, too. No matter how you treat me, I'll love you as long as I live."

"And nothing, nothing will ever shake our love."

"Nothing."

"We promise that, don't we? No matter what comes, no matter if death comes, we'll still love."

"Yes," she said.

He laid her head to his breast and he could see her head move under the beating of his heart.

And in this evening he set in his journal these words:

> I had a talk with Neloa and we are to be married in three days. I still tell myself I should not marry her but I'm helpless. When I'm away from her I seem to know what I should do but when I'm with her I realize I can never do it. I can't live without her! Everything goes crazy and dark when I try to think of life without her! And if I marry her, I'm afraid of what will come. . . .
>
> May God help me!

VIII

•

THREE days later, Vridar and Neloa were married. Deferring to her wish, he sent invitations to relatives, and sixty persons came to the wedding. His home overflowed with cousins and uncles and aunts and inlaws. There was a great feast. There was lewd talk about brides and bridegrooms, and vulgar excited interest, touched with malice, in nuptial nights. Rose O'Rourke came, and his Aunt Agnes and his Aunt Villette; and their tongues wagged in ribald anecdote. There was absurd clowning in the front yard. Mertyl took photographs of one and another in ridiculous postures: of Agnes with a crescent of watermelon from ear to ear; of a cousin grinning like an idiot; and of Rose, arms outstretched to heaven, face theatrically sober, as if she exhorted God.

And Vridar reflected on the old pagan festivals and on the lusty primitive interest in mating and birth. He looked at the amorous eyes of the women, the envious eyes of the men. There was in all of them the spirit of the tribal dance. But it was not his spirit. He was a very sober young man, and it was said of him, by one and another, that he seemed to look upon his wedding as a funeral. To these remarks he offered a faint grin of pity. For he had with him two photographs: one of Mifanwy and one of Moll; and he stole away, again and again, to look at each. The one of Mifanwy showed a radiant girl in tears, with gorgeous hair like a cloak about her; and the one of Moll showed a creature of the streets. He was marrying one of them but he did not know which one. . . .

After the guests had left, Prudence took her son with her into the fields and she told him of a dream. It was a dream she had the night before. It troubled her and she could not get it off her mind.

"It haunts me," she said. "Son, how do you interpret it?"

Vridar tried to shrug the matter away. Most dreams, he said, were nonsense. They were the meaningless delirium of sleep. . . . But he was troubled, nevertheless, by this dream. It fell like a darkness over this hour.

"She looked so pale and homeless," Prudence said. "Son, I'll never forget it. It—it haunts me."

"Fiddlesticks. It doesn't mean anything."

"It does. It means something, I know." She began to weep and Vridar took her in his arms. "Son, I want you to be so happy! I'd give my life to make you happy. But I'm—I'm afraid! . . . It was awful! Oh, it was awful and I can't forget it!"

Vridar went off alone and thought of this dream. It was foolishness, he told himself. It was too silly for words. But it was with him in enormous meaning and the meaning of it filled the earth; became fixed and intolerable in the landscape, in his mind, in the way he moved and thought; and he went to Neloa and asked her to walk with him. But he did not mention the dream at once.

"You're my wife now," he said. "It—it seems funny. For years I've—and now you're my wife. . . . Does it seem real to you?"

"Yes," she said.

"Isn't it funny to think of me as—as your husband?"

"No."

He held two photographs to her gaze.

"I've married a girl," he said. "Tell me which one."

"This," she said, and she pointed to Mifanwy.

"But the other, where is she?"

"Oh, she's dead." And before Vridar could protest, Neloa seized the photograph of Moll and tore it in two.

They walked again and Vridar thought of the dream.

"I want to tell you about it," he said. "It's awfully silly, but—well, I guess I should tell you. . . . Do you want me to?"

"Yes."

"The time was five or ten years in the future and the place was a big city. On the streets of this city, Mater saw you as a harlot. She saw you go from street to street. She says you were very thin and lonely and you seemed to be looking for someone. . . . Then you came to a big house. I lived in this house and it was of stone and had a great fence around it and a huge gate. You came to the big door and knocked timidly and I opened the door. Then you went down on your knees and begged me for forgiveness and mercy. She says I looked at you a long while. Then I spurned you. I kicked you from the door. You went away. . . . What do you think of such a dream?"

"I don't know."

"And a little later she saw you again. You went off alone and you looked all around you. She says she knew you were thinking of death. You seemed to be hunting a way to kill yourself. . . . Well, it's silly, isn't it?"

"I don't know," she said.

He stopped and faced her. He looked at her eyes and they were strange and bright, and there was something in them that he could never have found words for. It was something that made him tremble and look away. It was something that made him look at her again.

"Neloa."

"What?"

"Why do you look at me that way?"

"What way?" she smiled, and her smile, too, was strange.

"You looked—Neloa, what are you thinking of?"

"Nothing."

"Tell me. . . . Neloa, please."

"Oh—nothing."

"Please!"

She did not speak. She gazed beyond him at mountains, and he studied her face, trying to understand the smile there.

"I was just thinking," she said.

"Neloa, you're not going to listen to a silly dream! Are you?"

"I wasn't thinking of the dream."

He looked at her eyes and her smile and he felt the blood leaving his cheeks. In this moment, in this silence between them, he felt something awful—a deep and dark bewilderment that was the morning of their future, and its sunset and its sky. He searched her eyes and the faint contempt around her mouth. He tried to draw her to him but she put his hands away. She looked at him and shrugged. She laughed; and in her laugh, as in her shrug and her smile, there was something that chilled him. There was the terrible depth of this girl, the sleeping part of her, looking at him now. . . .

"Neloa!"

Then he turned away. He looked into the future and he saw there only loneliness and the dark.

Just in case you haven't read them, here is a selection of best-selling genuine Pocket Books and Cardinal Editions. If your newsdealer doesn't have a complete assortment, you may order titles direct from POCKET BOOKS, INC., Rockefeller Center, New York 20, N. Y. Enclose the retail price as noted for each book, plus 5c per copy for handling and postage. A complete list of titles in print will be sent to you, free, upon request.

C-3 IN TRAGIC LIFE

by Vardis Fisher. A moving and sensitive revelation of an imaginative boy's first 15 years. Vridar Hunter feared the wild country in which he lived. Savage beasts, venomous snakes, fierce storms, and the harsh winter cold filled him with terror. The brutality of nature haunted him. He fought against the sense of sin that threatened his manhood.—A Cardinal Edition (35c)

GC-1 THE CARDINAL

by Henry Morton Robinson. This frank but reverent story of a young American priest has created more excitement than any other novel of its kind published in recent years. His rise in the Church, his personal and spiritual problems, and his ultimate elevation to the high office of Cardinal . . . all of these make for inspiring and enriching reading. For some people, it will be simply a wonderful story, filled with color and pageantry. But for all, it will remain the one great modern novel that gives a clear and fascinating picture of the inner workings of the Catholic Church.—The first of a distinguished new line of "Cardinal Giants" (50c)

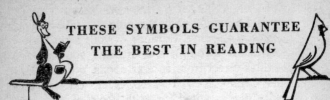